The main street was narrow and crooked, only one file of troopers was between Raj and the attack. Horace spun beneath him with a roaring growl, and his hand swept out saber and pistol. A grid of green lines clamped down over his vision, and the outlines of the Colonial troopers glowed. One strobed; the one with his carbine in his hands. Still a hundred paces away, a long pistol-shot but not impossible for a skilled man on dogback to make with a shoulder-weapon.

Raj moved his wrist. A red dot settled on the Colonial's midriff. His finger squeezed the trigger. *Crack.* The carbineer flipped over the cantle of his saddle. *Crack.* Another down. Place the dot and the bullet went where Center indicated it would. *Crack— crack—crack.* The revolver was empty, and the Colonials were through.

A clang of steel on steel as a scimitar met his saber. He flexed his wrist to let the sharply curved blade hiss by, then cut backhand across the Arab's face. A second was barreling in with his blade upraised. Horace lunged with open mouth for the Bazenji's throat. Raj stabbed, and the point of his weapon went in below the breastbone. He ripped it free with desperate strength, wheeling. Raj rose in the stirrups and chopped downward; there was a jar like the blade hitting seasoned oak, and a splitting sound. It nearly wrenched from his hand, sunk to brow-level in the Colonial's skull, but the weight of the falling body pulled the metal free.

In the background rifles barked as the troopers put down the dogs of the dead Arabs where they stood snarling over their masters' bodies.

"Damn, that was too close," he said. "Anyone wounded?"

The sergeant of the color-party was looking at him wide-eyed.

"Spirit, ser," he blurted. "Five dead wit' five shots!"

Raj felt a flush of embarrassment. He wasn't actually a first-rate pistol-shot; the sword was his personal weapon of choice, and with that he was very good. With Center's eerie trick, you didn't *have* to be good. He didn't much like the experience. It was too much like being a weapon yourself, in another's hand.

Whatever works, he thought.

precisely, said the unhuman voice in his head.

THE GENERAL SERIES

The Forge
The Hammer
The Anvil
The Steel
The Sword

THE SWORD

Book V of THE GENERAL

S.M. STIRLING

DAVID DRAKE

BAEN

THE GENERAL, BOOK V: THE SWORD

Copyright © 1995 by S.M. Stirling & David Drake

A Baen Books Original

Baen Publishing Enterprises
P.O. Box 1403
Riverdale, NY 10471

ISBN: 0-671-87647-3

Cover art by Paul Alexander

First printing, March 1995

Distributed by Simon & Schuster
1230 Avenue of the Americas
New York, NY 10020

Printed in the United States of America

Dedication: To Jan.

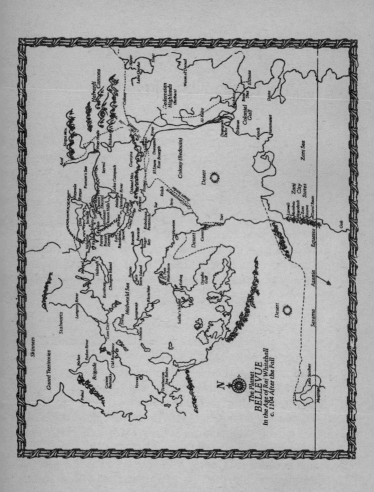

The Planet
BELLEVUE
In the Age of Raj Whitehall
c. 1184 After the Fall

CHAPTER ONE

"Raj?" Thom Poplanich muttered.

Then, slowly: "Raj, how old are you?"

Raj Whitehall managed a smile. "Thirty," he said.

The perfect mirrored sphere of Sector Command and Control Unit AZ12-b14-c000 Mk. XIV's central . . . being . . . showed an image which seemed to give the lie to that. Raj was tall, 190 centimeters, broad-shouldered and long-limbed, with wrists that would have been thick on a much larger man. His eyes were gray; there were wrinkles beside them now, and deep grooves running from beak nose to the corners of his mouth; gray frosted the bowl-cut black hair at the temples. It wasn't the gray hairs or the scars on the backs of his hands that made him seem at least forty, or ageless.

It was the eyes.

Thom looked at his own image. Nothing at all had changed since that moment when he'd frozen into immobility, five years ago. Not the unhealed shaving nick on his thin olive cheek, or the tear in his floppy tweed trousers from a revolver bullet. Raj had tried to shoot their way out when they'd been trapped here, far below the Governor's Palace, in labyrinths unvisited since the fall of galactic civilization. It hadn't worked. There was no escaping from some things.

life is change, Center said. The voice of the ancient computer was like their own thoughts, but with a vibrato overtone that somehow carried a sense of immense weight

1

like a pressure against the film of consciousness. **even
i change.**

Raj and Thom looked up, startled. "Center? You're
alive?" Thom asked.

No words whispered in their skull. Thom looked at his
friend. *Raj looks like an old man.* For five years he'd fought
the battles of the Civil Government, under the orders of
Barholm Clerett, current occupant of the Chair . . . and
with the ancient battle-computer whispering at the back
of his mind. Five years of that could change a man.

*I haven't changed a hair, outwardly . . . but that's
the least of it.* Five years of mental communion with
the machine that held all Mankind's accumulated
knowledge. Five years, or eternity. He thought of
his life before that day, and it was . . . unimaginable.
Less real than the scenarios Center could spin from
webs of data and stochastic analysis. He'd been as
carefree as a young man could be, whose grandfather
had been Governor until the Cleretts usurped the
Chair. Free enough to strike up an unlikely friendship
with a young professional soldier, to share an interest
in the relics of pre-Fall Federation civilization hidden
down here.

The two men gripped forearms, then exchanged the
embrahzo of close friends. Thom could smell coal-smoke
and gun-oil on the wool of his friend's uniform jacket,
that and riding dogs and Suzette Whitehall's sambuca
jasmine perfume.

The scents cut through the icy certainties Center's
teaching had implanted in his mind. Unshed tears
prickled at his eyes as he held the bigger man at arm's
length.

"It's good to see you again, my friend," he said
quietly. "Back from another campaign?"

"Back from the Western Territories, nearly a year,"
Raj said. "It went . . . successfully. On the whole."

observe. The cool voice of the unliving mind spoke in their brains:

A trumpet sounded, flat blatting notes under the lowering rainclouds, echoing back from the narrow shoulders of the cutting heading down to the river. The platoon columns of Civil Government troops halted and the giant riding dogs crouched. Men stepped free and double-timed forward, spreading out like the wings of a stooping hawk. Thom could see the advancing enemy columns halt; they were barbarians in the black-and-gray uniforms of the Brigade, the rulers of the Western Territories for the past five centuries. Their banners held the double-lightning flash, white on red and black.

Before the enemy a few hundred meters ahead had time to do more than begin to recoil and mill, the order rang out:

"Company—"

"Platoon—"

"Front rank, volley fire, *fwego.*"

BAM. Two hundred men in a single shot, the red muzzle-flashes spearing out into the rain like a horizontal comb.

The rear rank walked through the first. Before the echoes of the initial shout of *fire* had died, the next rank fired—by half-platoons, eighteen men at a time, in a rapid stuttering crash.

BAM. BAM. BAM. BAM.

Center's viewpoint was Raj, looking out through his eyes. The field guns came up between the units.

"If they break—" the officer beside Raj said. Thom recognized him as Ehwardo Poplanich, his cousin.

The troopers advanced and fired, advanced and fired. The commanders followed them, leading their own dogs.

"If," Raj replied.

The guns fired case-shot, the loads spreading to

maximum effect in the confined space. Merciful smoke
hid the result for an instant, and then the rain drummed
it out of the air. For fifty meters back from the head of
the column the Brigaderos and their dogs were a carpet
of flesh that heaved and screamed. A man with no face
staggered toward the Civil Government line, ululating
in a wordless trill of agony. The next volley smashed
him backward to rest in the tangled pink-gray intestines
of a dog. The animal still whimpered and twitched.

Only the smell was missing. Thom swallowed dryly,
past a tight throat.

The advancing force had gotten far enough downslope
that the reserve platoon and the second battery of guns
could fire over their heads. Shock-waves from the shells
passing overhead slapped at the back of their helmets
like pillows of displaced air. Most of the head of the
Brigaderos column was *trying* to run away, but the
railroad right-of-way was too narrow and the press behind
them too massive. Men spilled upslope toward the
forested hills where the Civil Government's nomad
auxiliaries waited.

Just then the mercenaries themselves—Skinners from
the northeastern steppes—opened up with their two-meter
sauroid-killing rifles. Driving downhill on a level slope,
their 15mm bullets went through three or four men at a
time. A huge sound came from the locked crowd of enemy
troops, half wail and half roar. Some were getting out
their rifles and trying to return fire, standing or taking
cover behind mounds of dead. Lead slugs went by
overhead, and not two paces from him a trooper went
unh! as if belly-punched, then to his knees and then flat.

The rest of his unit walked past, reloading. Spent brass
tinkled down around the body lying on the railroad tracks,
bouncing from the black iron strapping on the wooden
rails.

"Fwego!"

✧   ✧   ✧

Raj shook his head slightly; his hands were making unconscious grasping motions.

"Yes, that's . . . well, I came to say goodbye."

"Goodbye?" Thom asked sharply.

"That's right," Raj said, turning slightly away. His eyes moved across the perfect mirrored surface of the sphere, that impossibly reflected without distorting. "Things . . . well, Cabot Clerett, the Governor's nephew" —and heir, they both knew— "was along on the campaign. There were a number of difficulties, and he, ah, was killed."

observe:

Cabot's snarl turned to a smile of triumph as he leveled the revolver at Raj; he was a stocky dark young man, much like his uncle. His finger tightened on the trigger—

—and the carbine barked. The bullet was fired from less than a meter away, close enough that the muzzle-blast pocked the skin behind his right ear with grains of black powder. The entry-wound was a small round hole, but the bullet was hollowpoint and it blasted a fist-sized opening in his forehead, the fid of hot brain and bone-splinters missing Raj to spatter across his desk. Clerett's eyes bulged with the hydrostatic shock transmitted through his brain tissue, and his lips parted in a single rubbery grimace. Then he fell face down, to lie in a spreading pool of blood.

Strong shoulders crashed into the door. Raj moved with blurring speed, snatching the carbine out of his wife Suzette's hands so swiftly that the friction-burns brought an involuntary cry of pain. He pivoted back towards the outer doorway.

Raj's officers crowded through. Among them was a short plump man in the knee-breeches and long coat and lace sabot that were civilian dress in East Residence. His eyes bulged too, as they settled on Cabot Clerett.

Raj spoke, his voice loud and careful. "There's been a terrible accident," he said. "Colonel Clerett was examining the weapon, and he was unfamiliar with the mechanism. I accept full responsibility for this tragic mishap."

Silence fell in the room, amid the smell of powdersmoke and the stink of blood and wastes voided at death. Everyone stared at the back of the dead man's head, and the neat puncture behind his ear.

"Fetch a priest," Raj went on. "Greetings, Illustrious Chivrez. My deepest apologies that you come among us at such an unhappy time."

Chivrez's shock was short-lived; he hadn't survived a generation of politics in the Civil Government by cowardice, or squeamishness. Now he had to fight to restrain his smile. Raj Whitehall was standing over the body of the Governor's heir and literally holding a smoking gun.

"Spirit of Man of the *Stars*," Thom blurted. "You came back to East Residence after *that*? Barholm was suspicious of you anyway."

Raj gave a small crooked smile and shrugged. "I didn't reconquer the Southern and Western Territories for the Civil Government just to set myself up as a warlord," he said. "Center said that would be worse for civilization than if I'd never lived at all."

an oversimplification but accurate to within 93%, ±2, Center added remorselessly. Over the years their minds had learned subtlety in interpreting that voice; there was a tinge of . . . not pity, but perhaps compassion to it now. **the long-term prospects for restoration of the federation, here on bellevue and eventually elsewhere in the human-settled galaxy, required raj whitehall's submission to the civil authorities. too many generals have seized the chair by force.**

Thom nodded. The process had started long before Bellevue was isolated by the destruction of its Tanaki Spatial Displacement net. The Federation had been slagging down in civil wars for a generation before that, biting out its own guts like a brain-shot sauroid. The process had continued here in the thousand-odd years since, and according to Center everywhere else in the human-settled galaxy as well.

"Couldn't Lady Anne do something?" he asked. Barholm's consort was a close friend of Raj's wife Suzette, had been since Anne was merely the . . . entertainer was the polite phrase . . . that young Barholm had unaccountably married despite being the Governor's nephew. The other court ladies had turned a cold shoulder back before Barholm assumed the Chair; Suzette hadn't.

"She died four months ago," Raj said. "Cancer."

A brief flash of vision: a canopied bed, with the incense of the Star priests around it and the drone of their prayers. A woman lying motionless, flesh fallen in on the strong handsome bones of her face, hair a white cloud on the pillow with only a few streaks of its mahogany red left. Suzette Whitehall sat at the bedside, one hand gripping the ivory colored claw-hand of her dying friend. Her face was an expressionless mask, but slow tears ran from the slanted green eyes and dripped down on the priceless snowy torofib of the sheets.

"Damn," Thom said. "I know she wanted every Poplanich dead, but . . . well, Anne had twice Barholm's guts, and she was loyal to her friends, at least."

Raj nodded. "It was right after that that I was suspended from my last posting—Inspector-General—and my properties confiscated. Chancellor Tzetzas handled it personally."

"That . . . that . . . he gives graft a bad name," Thom spat.

Raj smiled wanly. "Yes, if the Chancellor didn't hate me, I'd wonder what I was doing wrong."

A flash from Center; a tall thin man in a bureaucrat's court robe sitting at a desk. The room was quietly elegant, dark, silent; a cigarette in a holder of carved sauroid ivory rested in one slim-fingered hand. He signed a heavy parchment, dusted the ink with fine sand, and smiled. A secretary sprang forward to melt wax for the seal . . .

Raj nodded. "I expect to be arrested at the levee this afternoon. Barholm's worried—"

worried at the probability of events which *would* occur were raj whitehall any other man. observe:

—and troops in the blue-and-maroon uniforms of the Civil Government's army cantered across the brick-paved plaza before the Governor's Palace. It was late, the gaslights flaring along the streets of East Residence, but the hurrying throngs of civilians crowded aside to the sound of the bugle and the iron clamor of field guns on the cobblestones. Light sheened on metal, the dull enamel of helmets, brass saber-hilts, the wet fangs of the giant riding dogs.

The troops reined in before the gates and deployed in line, stepping off the saddles of their crouching dogs and working the actions of their rifles, click-*clack* a thousand times repeated. The field guns swung about, teams unhitched, trails falling to the ground with heavy thumps as the gunners lifted them off the limbers. The breechblocks clanged as 75mm rounds were pushed home.

An officer strode up to the gates. "Open!" he barked.

"In whose name?" the watchstander replied, turning gray about the lips. Only a platoon was deployed across the gilded ironwork of the main gate. "By what authority?"

"Fix—" the first officer said.

"*Fix—*" a hundred voices repeated it.

"—*bayonets*."

A long repeated rattle and clank as the long blades snicked onto the rifles. A uniform flash of gaslight on steel as they came to present.

"In the name of the Sovereign Mighty Lord, Governor Raj Whitehall," the officer went on, grinning. He waved back to the riflemen and guns. "And there's my authority."

The watchstander nodded stiffly. "Open the gates."

—and Raj walked through congealing pools of blood in the Audience Hall. The bodies of the Life Guards sprawled across it, where they'd tried to make a stand behind barricades of ornate gilded furniture. Barholm Clerett sagged on the Chair itself, the pistol that had blown out the top of his skull still clenched in one hand.

Raj hooked the body out of the high seat with his toe and turned. A howl arose from the soldiers who crowded the great chamber, a howl that died into a steady chant:

"*Raj! Raj! Raj!*"

Thom laid a hand on Raj's shoulder. The muscle under the wool jacket was like india rubber. It quivered with tension.

"You *should* make yourself Governor, Raj," he said quietly. "Spirit knows, you couldn't be *worse* than Barholm and his cronies."

Raj smiled, but he shook his head. "Thanks, Thom— but if I have a gift for command, it's *only* for soldiers. Civilians . . . I couldn't get three of them to follow me into a whorehouse with an offer of free drinks and pussy. Not unless I had a squad behind them with bayonets; and you *can't* govern that way, not for long. I'd smash the machinery trying to make it work. Barholm is a son-of-a-bitch, but he's a *smart* one. He knows how to stroke the bureaucracy and keep the nobility satisfied, and he really is binding the Civil Government together with his railroads and law reforms . . . granted a lot of his hangers-on are getting rich in the process, but it's working. I couldn't do it. Not so's it'd last past my lifetime."

observe:

—and they saw Raj Whitehall on a throne of gold and diamond, and men of races they'd never heard of knelt before him with tribute and gifts . . .

. . . and he lay ancient and white-haired in a vast silken bed. Muffled chanting came from outside the window, and a priest prayed quietly. A few elderly officers wept, but the younger ones eyed each other with undisguised hunger, waiting for the old king to die.

One bent and spoke in his ear. "Who?" he said. "Who do you leave the keyboard and the power to?"

The ancient Raj's lips moved. The officer turned and spoke loudly, drowning out the whisper: "He says, *to the strongest*."

Armies clashed, in identical green uniforms and carrying Raj Whitehall's banner. Cities burned. At last there was a peaceful green mound that only the outline of the land showed had once been the Gubernatorial Palace in East Residence. Two men worked in companionable silence by a campfire, clad only in loincloths of tanned hide. One was chipping a spearpoint from a piece of an ancient window, the shaft and binding thongs ready to hand. His fingers moved with sure skill, using a bone anvil and striker to spall long flakes from the green glass. His comrade worked with equal artistry, butchering a carcass with a heavy hammerstone and slivers of flint. It took a moment to realize that the body had once been human.

Raj shivered. *That* was the logical endpoint of the cycle of collapse here on Bellevue, and throughout what had once been the Federation; if it wasn't prevented, there would be savagery for fifteen thousand years before a new civilization arose. The image had haunted him since Center first showed it. It felt *true*.

"Spirit knows, I don't *want* Barholm's job," he went on. "I like to do what I do well, and that isn't my area of expertise. The problem is getting Barholm to understand that."

barholm's data gives him substantial reason for apprehension, Center pointed out. **not only does raj whitehall have the prestige of constant victory, but more than sixteen battalions of the civil government's cavalry are now comprised of ex-prisoners from the former military governments.**

Squadrones and Brigaderos; Namerique-speaking barbarians, descendants of Federation troops gone savage up in the desolate Base Area of the far northwest. They'd swept down and taken over huge chunks of the Civil Government, imposing their rule and their heretical Spirit of Man of This Earth cult on the population. Nobody had been able to do anything about it . . . until Barholm sent Raj Whitehall to reconquer the barbarian realms of the Military Governments.

Governor Barholm had officially proclaimed Raj the Sword of the Spirit of Man. The prisoners who'd volunteered to serve the Civil Government had seen him in operation from both sides. They *believed* that title.

"Then stay here!" Thom said. "Center can hold you in stasis, like me—hold you until Barholm's dust and bones. You've done all you can, you've done your duty, now you *deserve* something for yourself. It won't further the reunification of Bellevue for you to commit suicide!"

probability of furthering the restoration of the federation is slightly increased if raj whitehall attends the levee, Center said.

"I must go. I *must*. I—"

Raj turned back, and Thom recoiled a half step. The other man's teeth were showing, and a muscle twitched on one cheek. "I . . . there's been so much dying . . . I *can't* . . . so many dead, so many, how can I save myself?"

"They were enemies," Thom said softly.

"No! Not *them*. My own men! I used men like bullets! There aren't one in three of the 5th Descott Guards remaining, of the ones who rode out with me against the Colony five years ago. Poplanich's Own—raised from your family estates, Thom—had a hundred and fifty casualties in one battle, and *I* was leading them."

Thom opened his mouth, then closed it again. Center cut in on them, an iron impatience in its non-voice:

leading is the operative word, raj whitehall. you were leading them. observe:

"Back one step and volley!" Raj shouted, hoarse with smoke and dust.

Around him the shattered ranks firmed. Colonial dragoons in crimson djellabas rode forward, reins in their teeth as they worked the levers of their repeating carbines. The muzzles of their dogs snaked forward, then recoiled from the line of bayonets.

BAM. Ragged, but the men were firing in unison.

"Back one step and volley!" Raj shouted again.

He fired his revolver between two of the troopers, into the face of a Colonial officer who yipped and waved his yataghan behind the line of dragoons. The carbines snapped, and the man beside Raj stumbled back, moaning and pawing at the shattered jaw that dangled on his breast.

"Hold hard, 5th Descott! *Back one step and volley*."

observe:

The men's hobnailed boots clattered on the surface of the pipe; the sound was dulled, as if they were walking on soft wood, but the iron left no scratches on the plastic of the Ancients. The surface beneath the fingers of his left hand might have been polished marble, except for the slight trace of greasy slickness. There was old dirt and silt in the very bottom of the circular tube, and it stank of decay; floodwater must run down from the gutters of Lion City and through this pipe when the floods were very high.

Behind him the rustle and clank of equipment sounded, panting breath, an occasional low-voiced curse in Namerique. Earth Spirit cultists didn't have the same myth of a plastic-lined tube to Hell; the center of the earth—This Earth—was their paradise. This particular tunnel was intimidating as Hell to *anyone*, though. Particularly to men reared in the open air—there was a touch of the claustrophobe in most dog-and-gun men. There certainly was in *him*, because every breath seemed more difficult than the last, an iron hoop tightening around his chest.

this is not an illusion, Center said helpfully. **the oxygen content of the air is dropping because airflow is inadequate in the presence of over six hundred men. this will not be a serious problem unless the force is halted for a prolonged period.**

Oh, thank *you,* Raj thought.

Even then, he felt a grim satisfaction at what Army discipline had made of last year's barbarian horde. *Vicious children,* he thought. Vicious grown-up children whose ancestors had shattered civilization over half a continent—not so much in malice as out of simple inability to imagine doing anything different. Throwing the pretty baubles into the air and clapping their hands to see them smash, heedless of the generations of labor and effort that went into their making. *Thirteen-year-olds with adults' bodies . . . but they can learn. They can learn.*

The roof knocked on the top of his helmet. "*Halto,*"

he called quietly. The column rustled to a halt behind him.

A quick flick of the lens-lid on his bull's-eye lantern showed the first change in the perfect regularity of the tunnel. Ahead of him the roof bent down and the sides out, precisely like a drinking straw pinched between a man's fingers.

you are under the outer edge of the town wall on the north side, Center said. **.63 of a kilometer from the entrance.**

M'lewis had come this far on his scout; he'd checked that the tunnel opened out again beyond this point, and then returned. Raj had made the decision to proceed, since maximum priority was to avoid giving the entrance away. And the little Scout had been right, air *was* flowing toward him; he could feel the slightly cooler touch on his sweating face.

Of course, the air might be coming through a hole the size of a man's fist.

"Crawl through," he said to the man behind him, clicking off the light. "Turn on your backs and crawl through. There's another pinch in the tunnel beyond. Pass it down."

He dropped to the slimy mud in the bottom of the tunnel and began working his way farther in. The plastic dipped down toward his face, touched the brim of his helmet. Still smooth, still untorn. The weight of the city wall was on it here, had been for five hundred years. Mud squished beneath his shoulder blades, running easily on the low-friction surface of the pipe. The weight of a wall fifteen meters high and ten thick at the base, two courses of three-by-three meter stones on either side, flanking a rubble-concrete core.

Do not *tell me how much it weighs*, he thought/said to Center.

Now he was past the lowest point, and suddenly

conscious of his own panting. Something bumped his boots: the head of the man behind him. One man following, at least. Two or three more, from the noise behind. No way of telling what was farther back, how many were still coming, whether the last five hundred or five hundred fifty had turned and trampled Ludwig in a terror-filled rush out of this deathtrap, this anteroom to hell. The plastic drank sound, leaving even his breath muffled. Sweat dripped down his forehead, running into his eyes as he came to hands and knees. He clicked the bull's-eye open for a look when the surface began to twist beneath his feet. Another ten meters of normal pipe, and then—

Spirit, he thought. What could have produced *this?*

the pipe crosses under the wall at an angle of forty degrees from the perpendicular. this section is under the edge of a tower, Center said with dispassionate accuracy.

The towers were much heavier than the walls. The sideways thrust of one tower's foundations had shoved the pipe a little sideways . . . and squeezed it down so that only a triangular hole in the lower right-hand corner remained. This time the fabric *had* ruptured, a long narrow split to the upper left. Dirt had come through, hard lumpy yellow clay, and someone recent had dug it out with hands and knife and spread it backwards.

Raj waited until the man following him came up behind. "No problem," he said, while the eyes in the bearded face were still blinking at the *impossible* hole. "Come through one at a time; take off your rifle, helmet and webbing belt, then have the man behind you hand them through. Pass it on."

He kept moving, because if he didn't, he might not start again. One man panicking here and the whole column would be stalled all night.

He took off the helmet and his sword belt, snapped

the strap down over the butt of his revolver, and dropped the bundle to the floor.

"Keep the lantern on," he said to the soldier behind him.

Right arm forward. Turn sideways. Down and forward, the sides gripping him like the clamps of a grab used to lift heavy shells. Light vanishing beyond his feet; they kicked without purchase, and then the broad hands of the trooper were under them, giving him something to push against. Bronze jacket buttons digging into his ribs hard enough to leave bruises. Breathe in, *push*. Buried in hell, buried in hell . . .

His right hand came free. It groped about, finding little leverage on the smooth, flaring sides of the pipe, but his shoulders came out, and that was the broadest part of him.

For an instant he lay panting, then turned. "Through," he called softly. "Pass my gear, soldier." A fading echo down the pipe, as the man turned and murmured the news to the one behind *him*.

It had only been a little more than his body length. Difficult, but not as difficult as concrete would have been, or cast iron, anything that gripped at skin and clothing. The light cast a glow around the slightly curved path of the narrow passage.

Again he waited until the first man had followed, grabbing his jacket between the shoulder blades and hauling him free.

"Second birth," he said.

The Squadrone trooper shook his head. "The first was tighter, lord," he said. His face was corpse-pallid in the faint light, but he managed a grin. Then he turned and called softly down the narrow way:

"Min gonne, Herman."

Not much further, Raj thought, looking ahead. Darkness lay on his eyes like thick velvet.

.21 kilometers.

observe:

"Quick," Raj said to the man with the charges.

The door opening right into the rooms above the arch of the gateway was barred. Raj thrust his pistol into the eyeslot and pulled the trigger; there was a scream, and somebody slammed an iron plate across it. The cloth bundles of gunpowder tumbled at his feet.

"Good man," Raj said. "Now, pack them along the foot of the door, in between the stone sill and the door. Cut them with your knife and stick the matchcord—right." He raised his voice; more men were crowding up the stairs, some to take the ladder and others filling the space about him. *"Everyone down the corridor, around the corner here. Now!"*

The quick-witted trooper and Raj and a lieutenant—Wate Samzon, a Squadrone himself—paid out the cord and plastered themselves to the wall just around from the door. The matchcord sputtered as it took the flame. Raj put his hand before his eyes.

White noise, too loud for sound. He tensed to drive back around to the door—

—and strong arms seized him, body and legs and arms.

"Ni, ni," a deep rumbling voice said in his ear. "You are our lord, by steel and salt. Our blood for yours."

Lieutenant Samzon led the charge. A second later he was flung back, hands clapped to the bleeding ruin of his face; he stumbled into the wall, and fell flat. The men who followed him fired into the ruins of the door and thrust after the bullets, bayonets against swords, as their comrades reloaded and fired past their bodies close enough for the blasts to scorch their uniforms. When they forced through the shattered planks, the men holding Raj released him and followed them, with only their broad backs to hold him behind them.

❖   ❖   ❖

Raj blinked back to an awareness of the polished sphere that was Center's physical being. That had been too vivid: not just the holographic image that the ancient computer projected on his retina; he could still *smell* the gunpowder and blood.

if you had not struck swiftly and hard, the wars would have dragged on for years. deaths would have been a whole order of magnitude greater, among soldiers of both sides and among the civilians. as well, entire provinces would be so devastated as to be unable to sustain civilized life.

Images flitted through their minds: bones resting in a ditch, hair still fluttering from the skulls of a mother and child; skeletal corpses slithering over each other as men threw them on a plague-cart and dragged it away down the empty streets of a besieged city; a room of hollow-eyed soldiers resting on straw pallets slimed with the liquid feces of cholera.

"That's true enough for a computer," Raj said.

Even then, Thom noted the irony. He was East Residence born, a city patrician, and back when they both believed *computer* meant *angel* he'd doubted their very existence. That had shocked Raj's pious country-squire soul; Raj never doubted the Personal Computer that watched over every faithful soul, and the great Mainframes that sat in glory around the Spirit of Man of the Stars. Now they were both agents of such a being.

Raj's voice grew loud for a moment. "That's true enough for the Spirit of Man of the Stars made manifest, true enough for *God.* I'm not God, I'm just a man—and I've done the Spirit's work without flinching. But I'd be *less* than a man if I didn't think I deserve death for it." Silence fell.

"They ought to hate me," he whispered, his eyes still seeing visions without need of Center's holographs. "I've left the bones of my men all the way from the Drangosh to Carson Barracks, across half a world . . . they ought to hate my *guts*."

they do not, Center said. **instead—**

A group of men swaggered into an East Residence bar, down the stairs from the street and under the iron brackets of the lights, into air thick with tobacco and sweat and the fumes of cheap wine and *tekkila*. Like most of those inside, they wore cavalry-trooper uniforms—it was not a dive where a civilian would have had a long life expectancy—but most of theirs carried the shoulder-flashes of the 5th Descott Guards, and they wore the red-and-white checked neckerchiefs that were an unofficial blazon in that unit. They were dark close-coupled stocky-muscular men, like most Descotters; with them were troopers from half a dozen other units, some of them blond giants with long hair knotted on the sides of their heads.

There was a general slither of chairs on floors as the newcomers took over the best seats. One Life Guard trooper who was slow about vacating his chair was dumped unceremoniously on the sanded floor; half a dozen sets of eyes tracked him like gun turrets turning as he came up cursing and reaching for the knife in his boot. The Life Guardsman looked over his shoulder, calculated odds, and pushed out of the room. The hard-eyed girl who'd been with him hung over the shoulder of the chair's new occupant. The men hung their sword belts on the backs of their chairs and called for service.

"T'Messer Raj," one said, raising a glass. "While 'e's been a-leadin' us, nivver a one's been shot runnin' away!"

— they do not hate you. they *fear* you, for they know you will expend them without hesitation if necessary. but they know raj whitehall will lead

from the front, and that with him they have conquered the world.

"Then they're fools," Raj said flatly.

"They're men," Thom said. "All men die, whether they go for soldiers or not. But maybe you've given them something that makes the life worth it, just as you have Center's Plan to rebuild civilization throughout the universe."

They exchanged the *embrahzo* again. Thom stepped back and froze, his body once again in Center's timeless stasis.

Raj turned and took a deep breath. "Can't die deader than dead," he murmured to himself.

CHAPTER TWO

The great corridor outside the Audience Hall shone with the delicate colored marble and semiprecious stone that made up the intaglio work of the floor. The walls were arched windows on the outer side, and religious murals on the inner—icons of the Saints, lives of the martyrs, stars, starships, Computers calling forth Order from Primeval Chaos. Though the day was overcast, hidden gaslights threw a bright radiance through mirrors.

Soldiers in the black uniforms and black breastplates of the Life Guards stood along the walls every few paces, rifles at port; officers had their swords drawn and the points resting at their boots. The uniforms were Capital-crisp, but the faces under the plumed helmets were closed and watchful—square beak-nosed faces, dark and hard, on men slightly bowlegged from riding as soon as they could walk. The Life Guards were recruited from the Barholm family estates back in Descott county, from vakaros and yeoman-tenant *rancheros*. When Descotters ate a man's salt they took the responsibilities seriously, in the main.

Suzette adjusted Raj's cravat, beneath the high wing collar of the dress-uniform jacket. There was a fixed, intent look on her face. Raj recognized it; it was the look you got when the overall situation was completely out of control, so you focused on the immediate skill you *could* master. Suzette had been brought up in East Residence, and her family had been patrician for fourteen

21

generations. Court etiquette—and the intricate currents of court intrigue—were as much her heritage as the saddle of a war-dog or the hilt of a saber were to him.

He'd seen the same look on a Brigade trooper's face, adjusting the grip on his sword and the angle of the blade—as he rode into the muzzle of a cannon loaded with grapeshot.

Three of his Companions were standing around, with similar expressions. *They* were looking at the Life Guards, and figuring the odds on a firefight if an order came through to arrest Raj on the spot. *Not good*, he thought.

"Relax," he said quietly. "There isn't going to be any trouble here today."

The party around Raj Whitehall stood in a bubble of social space, lower-ranking courtiers and messengers either avoiding their eyes or staring fascinated at the famous General Whitehall; for the last time, if rumor was correct. Many of them were probably thinking how lucky they were never to have risen so high. The stalk that stood out above the others was the first to be lopped off.

Which is why the Civil Government doesn't rule the whole Earth, as it should, Raj thought with an old, cold anger.

correct, Center replied. Then it added pedantically: **bellevue. earth will come later.**

The crowd parted as a man came through. He wasn't particularly imposing; no more than twenty-one or so, and slimly handsome. His left arm ended at a leather cup and steel hook where the hand should have been. His uniform was standard issue for Civil Government cavalry, blue swallowtail coat and loose maroon breeches, crimson sash under the Sam Browne belt; all tailored with foppish care, but travel-worn and stained with sea salt in places. He carried his round bowl helmet with the chainmail neck-guard and twin captain's stars tucked under his left arm. The right fist snapped to his chest as he saluted, then bowed to Suzette.

"Messer Raj," he said. "My lady Whitehall." A smile as he glanced past them to the other Companions. "Dog-brothers."

"Spirit," Raj said mildly, shaken out of his strait preoccupation with what would probably happen in the next half-hour. "I thought you were back in the Western Territories with the 5th, Barton."

Not to mention with Colonel Gerrin Staenbridge; Barton Foley had gotten into the 5th as Gerrin's protégé-cum-boyfriend. He was far more than that now, of course.

"Administrator Historiomo decided," the young officer said, voice carefully neutral, "that since the Brigade survivors in the Western Territories were cooperating fully, a number of units were surplus to garrison needs."

"Which units?" Raj said.

Barton cleared his throat. "The 5th Descott Guards," he said.

Raj's Own, as they liked to call themselves.

"The 7th Descott Rangers, 1st Rogor Slashers, Poplanich's Own, and the 18th Komar Borderers," he went on.

The cavalry units most closely associated with Raj, and the ones commanded by the men who'd become his Companions, the elite group of close comrades he relied on most.

"In addition, the 17th Kenden County Foot, and the 24th Valentia," he continued.

Jorg Menyez commanded the 17th: a Companion, and the Civil Government's best infantry specialist, able to turn the despised foot soldiers into fighting men of sorts. The 24th . . . *Ferdihando Felasquez.* Good man . . .

"And last but not least, the 1st and 2nd Mounted Cruisers."

Recruited from the defeated barbarians of the

Squadron, after Raj crushed them in a single month's campaign back in the Southern Territories, three years ago. They'd always been warriors; under civilized instruction, they'd also become quite capable soldiers. The commander of the 1st Cruisers, Ludwig Bellamy, had made the same transition; but as a Squadrone nobleman he also regarded himself as Raj's personal liegeman. Tejan M'Brust, the Descotter Companion who'd taken over the 2nd Cruisers, probably thought the same way—although he wasn't supposed to, being a civilized man.

"They're all," Barton went on, with a slight smile, bowing over Suzette's hand, "on their way back. Together with the field artillery. I came ahead on one of the steam rams, but everyone should be here in a day or three, if the weather stays fine."

Beside Raj, Colonel Dinnalsyn pricked up his ears. The artillery specialist had hated being separated from his beloved weapons. He'd trained those crews himself.

Joy, Raj thought. It just *happened* to look like Raj's own personal army was heading back to the East Residence at flank speed.

Antin M'lewis cracked his fingers. "What happen t'Chivrez?"

The Honorable Fedherko Chivrez had been sent out to take command of the Western Territories after Raj conquered them—and had arrived to find the Governor's promising young heir Cabot Clerett dead at Raj's feet, with a smoking carbine in Raj's hand.

Suzette gave him a single cool violet look from her slanted eyes and then turned them away, her face the unreadable mask of an East Residence aristocrat.

Raj remembered Cabot's eyes bulging, as Suzette shot him neatly behind the ear, in the instant before his trigger finger would have punched an 11mm pistol round through Raj's body. Chivrez had seen; Chivrez had been

Director of Supply in Komar back five years ago, and had tried to withhold supplies from Raj's men. Two Companions named Evrard and Kaltin Gruder had run him out a closed window headfirst, then held him while Antin M'lewis started to flay him from the feet up. Raj had gotten the supplies and won the campaign.

The trouble with that sort of method was the long-term problems. On the other hand, if Raj *hadn't* gotten those supplies, his troops would have been wiped out by the Colonials in the desert fighting. You paced yourself to the task, and if the task got done you worried about secondary consequences later.

"Ah." Barton Foley considered the tip of his hook. "Well, Messer Chivrez seems to have betrayed the Governor's trust and absconded with some of the Brigade's treasures."

observe, Center said.

A bedroom in the palace of the Generals of the Brigade, in the Western Territories. Chivrez thrashing, his arms and legs held down by four strong men, another pressing a pillow over his face. The stubby limbs thrashed against the bedclothes. After a few minutes they grew still; Ludwig Bellamy wrapped the body in the sheets and hoisted it. Even masked, Raj recognized Gerrin Staenbridge as the one holding open the door.

The scene shifted, to the swamps outside Carson Barracks. The same men tipped a burlap-wrapped bundle off the deck of a small boat. It vanished with scarcely a splash, weighed down with lengths of chain and a cast-iron roundshot weighing forty kilos. Gerrin raised a meter-diameter blazon of the Brigade's sunburst banner, crafted in silver and gold with the double lightning flash across it picked out in diamond.

"Pity," he murmured. "Not bad work in a garish sort of barbarian way, and it would buy a good many opera tickets and dinners at the Centoyard back home. Ah, well—authenticity."

He tossed the disk after the bureaucrat's body. It sank with a popping bubble of marsh gas. Somewhere off in the swamps a hadrosauroid bellowed.

Antin M'lewis grinned uneasily as the Companions exchanged glances. They knew, of course . . . but he wasn't quite sure if Messer Raj knew. They were all of the Messer class by birth themselves; he'd levered himself up into it by hitching his star to Messer Raj's wagon. *Ye takes t'risk a' fallin', too,* he thought.

M'lewis had started off as a Bufford Parish bandit, a sheep stealer by hereditary profession, and made even that most lawless part of not-very-lawful Descott County too hot for him. Enlistment had been the alternative to a rope—or a less formal appointment with a knife. He'd met Raj over a little matter of a peasant's pig gone missing despite a no-foraging order. One look had told him this was a man who had to be either served or killed, and he'd made *his* decision. It had led him near enough to death more times than he could count, and also to advancement beyond his dreams.

On the other hand, one of the things that surprised him about gentlemen born was how bad they were at making use of their advantages. There were good points to a rough upbringing. One of them was being able to say the unsayable.

"Ah, ser," he suggested, leaning forward and whispering, "what wit' t' lads comin' in s'soon, mebbe we'uns ud better dip out loik—come back wit' better company inna day er two?"

Raj spoke in a clear, conversational tone, without looking around: "I'm attending this levee as ordered by the Sovereign Mighty Lord, Captain M'lewis. You may do as you please."

M'lewis spat on the intaglio floor. *Spirit. Mebbe I should a' stayed in sheep-stealin'.*

He followed nonetheless; he might have been born a thief, but he'd eaten this man's bread and salt.

A metal-shod staff thumped the floor, and the tall bronze panels of the Audience Hall swung open. The gorgeously robed figure of the Janitor—the Court Usher—bowed and held out his staff, topped by the Star symbol of the Civil Government.

Suzette took Raj's arm. The Companions fell in behind him, unconsciously forming a column of twos. A Life Guard officer stepped forward.

"Your weapons, Messers," he said, his face expressionless.

Raj made a chopping gesture with his free hand, and the forward rustle of the Companions died. He handed over ceremonial revolver and court sword. This time it was Barton Foley who whispered in his ear:

"A company of the 5th arrived *with* me, sir. If you're arrested . . ."

"Captain Foley, the Sovereign Mighty Lord's orders will be *obeyed* by all troops under my command—is that clear?"

observe, Center whispered in his mind. Raj, in a cell, darkness and the flickering light of lanterns. Rifle-fire from the halls outside, flat slapping echoes off the stone, and the turnkey's shotgun pointed through the bars at Raj's face, the hammer falling as he jerked the trigger . . .

"I've served my Governor and the Spirit of Man to the best of my ability," Raj added. "I chose to assume that the Governor, upon whom be the blessings of the Spirit always, will see it the same way."

The functionary's voice boomed out with trained precision through the gold-and-niello speaking trumpet:

"General the Honorable Messer Raj Ammenda Halgern da Luis Whitehall, Whitehall of Hillchapel, Hereditary Supervisor of Smythe Parish, Descott County!

His Lady, Suzette Emmaenelle—" *None of his other titles,*
Raj noted. He'd been officially hailed *Sword of the Spirit
of Man* and *Savior of the State* in this room.

He ignored the noise, ignored the brilliantly decked
crowds who waited on either side of the carpeted central
aisle, the smells of polished metal, sweet incense, and
sweat. The Audience Hall was two hundred meters long
and fifty high, its arched ceiling a mosaic showing the
wheeling galaxy with the Spirit of Man rising head and
shoulders behind it. The huge dark eyes were full of
stars themselves, staring down into your soul.

Along the walls were automatons, dressed in the tight
uniforms worn by Terran Federation soldiers twelve
hundred years before. They whirred and clanked to
attention, powered by hidden compressed-air conduits,
bringing their archaic and quite non-functional battle lasers
to salute. The Guard troopers along the aisle brought their
entirely functional rifles up in the same gesture.

The far end of the audience chamber was a hemisphere
plated with burnished gold, lit via mirrors from hidden
arcs. It glowed with a blinding aura, strobing slightly.
The Chair itself stood four meters in the air on a pillar
of fretted silver, the focus of light and mirrors and every
eye in the giant room. The man enChaired upon it sat
with hieratic stiffness, light breaking in metallized
splendor from his robes, the bejeweled Keyboard and
Stylus in his hands. A tribal delegation was milling about
before it, still speaking through its hired interpreter.

The linguist's face was professionally bland, but
occasionally a look of horror would cross his features
as he moved his lips, working out Sponglish equivalents
of the mountaineers' singsong native tongue:

"Hjburni-burni-burni—"

"Humbly we beseech you, O Sovereign Mighty One,
Sole Autocrat, our poverty prevents other than our
traditional border auxiliary duties—"

Center broke in: **more accurately rendered: back off, stonehouse-chief, or we'll see what terms the colony offers its border auxiliaries—we're closer to al kebir than east residence.**

"Hjurni-burni-burni, burjimi murjimi urgimi—"

"In our humble huts in the mountains, we seek only to till our poor fields in peace—"

we're your allies and *you* pay *us* for guarding the passes;

"—kuljurni ablurni hjurni-burni Halvaardi burri murri—"

"—and surely there are closer, richer lands which need the attention of your talented administrators—"

—so the next tax collector who asks for "earth and water" from the halvaardi gets thrown down a well to find plenty of both.

Barholm made a slight gesture with one hand, and the tribesfolk were ushered out, protesting, amid a ripe stink from the butter they used to grease their braids. One of the wooden clocks they carried on their belts gave its mechanical *kuku, kuku* as the pillar that supported the Chair sank toward the white marble steps; at the rear of the enclosure two full-scale statues of gorgosauroids rose to their three-meter height and roared as the seat of the Governor of the Civil Government sank home with a slight sigh of hydraulics. A faint whine sounded, and the arc lights blazed brighter. At the center of the mirrors' focus Barholm blazed like a shape of white fire.

Raj took three paces forward and went down in the ceremonial prostration—the full prostration, since his former titles were stripped from him. He rose and knelt the prescribed three times; by his side there was a quiet rustle of silks and lace as Suzette sank down with an infinite gracefulness.

"What punishment," Barholm boomed, his voice amplified by the superb acoustics of the Audience Hall,

"is fit for him who was foremost in Our trust? Yea, what baseness is more base, what vileness more vile, than one into whose hand the Sword of the State has been entrusted—when that most wretched of men turns the Sword against the very root and foundation, the Coax Cable of the Spirit—"

In East Residence, rhetoric was the most admired of the arts—far ahead of, for instance, military or administrative skill; infinitely more so than engineering. A speech like this could go on for hours, when the entire content could be boiled down to "kill him."

The semicircle of high ministers stirred behind their desks. The tall slender form of Chancellor Tzetzas turned sharply to hiss General Gharzia, Commander of Eastern Forces, into silence; the elderly soldier was listening to a messenger—a courier in tight leathers, not a court usher or an aide. From the floor, Raj watched Gharzia's face congeal like cooling lard. He didn't have to pay attention to what Barholm said, he knew how that would end . . .

Gharzia rose and circled to Tzetzas' side. The Chancellor tried to shake off the hand that plucked at his sleeve, then turned to listen with a tight, controlled fury that would have frightened Raj if he'd been in Gharzia's shoes. People who seriously annoyed the Chancellor tended to have accidents, or develop severe stomach problems, or be killed in duels.

Raj had never seen Tzetzas frightened before. It was a far less pleasant experience than he would have thought; whatever his other vices, nobody had ever even accused the Chancellor of cowardice. To make him interrupt the ceremony of triumph over his most hated rival, it had to be something massive.

"And—" Barholm noticed the movement to his right and broke off, flipping up the smoked-glass eyeshield. "Tzetzas! *What* do you think you're doing?"

The raw fury in his voice made Tzetzas check half a step. The Governor was the Spirit's Viceregent on Earth; if he ordered the Guards to cut the Chancellor to pieces on the steps of the Chair, they would obey without hesitation. That had happened in past reigns, more than once. Wise Governors remembered that those reigns had been short . . . but Barholm Clerett had been growing more and more unstable since his wife died.

"Sovereign Mighty Lord," Tzetzas said, his voice a cool precision instrument, handled with faultless skill. "I deserve your anger for my boorishness. Yet concern drives your servant. The Colony has invaded our territories; news has arrived by heliograph."

There was a chain of stations between the frontiers and East Residence; high-priority messages could be relayed in hours, where couriers would take days or weeks. Only the Colony and the Civil Government possessed such means, on Bellevue.

"You interrupt me for a *raid*?"

The Bedouin and the Civil Government's Borderers had been stealing girls and sheep and cutting each other up over waterholes since time immemorial. It was a peaceful week that passed without a minor skirmish, and there were several *razziah* a year from either side. It usually didn't even cause a ripple in the profitable trade carried on between the more civilized urban element on both sides of the frontier.

Tzetzas threw himself down on his knees. "Not a raid, Sovereign Mighty Lord. Invasion. The Settler of the Colony himself, Ali—and his one-eyed brother and general, Tewfik. They have taken Gurnyca."

A low moan swept through the Audience Hall. That was the largest city on the lower Drangosh river and the closest major settlement to the eastern frontier.

The mad anger disappeared from Barholm's face, as cleanly as if cut with a knife. A minute later, so did the eye-hurting brilliance of the arc lights. By contrast, the Audience Hall seemed black.

"The levee is closed," Barholm said, in a flat carrying voice.

There were yelps of protest from petitioners. The officer of the Life Guards barked an order, and hands rattled on stocks as the rifles came to present-arms.

"An immediate meeting of the State Council will be held in the Negrin Room," Barholm said into the sudden stillness. "All others are dismissed."

Raj rose to one knee. "Sovereign Mighty Lord," he said calmly. "Does the Sole Autocrat wish my presence?"

Barholm paused, looking over his shoulder. "Of course," he said. A snarl broke through the mask of his face. "Of course!"

"*Sayyida*," the man said, bowing with hand to brows, lips and heart; his dress was the knee breeches and jacket of an East Residence bourgeois, but his tongue was the pure Syrian Arabic of Al Kebir, capital of the Colony. "Peace be with you."

"And upon you peace, Abdullah al'Aziz," Suzette Whitehall replied in the same language, the rolling gutturals falling easily from her tongue.

Her maids had replaced the split skirt, leggings, and blond wig of court formality with a noblewoman's day-robe; she wrote as she spoke, glancing up only occasionally. The steel nib of the pen skritched steadily on the paper.

"Are you ready?" she said.

"For the Great Game?" the Arab replied, smiling whitely in his neatly trimmed black beard. "Always, my lady."

"Good. Here are papers, and a sight-draft on Muzzaf Kerpatik."

The Whitehalls' chief steward, among other things. A Borderer from the southern city of Komar, and no friend of any Arab, but also not likely to let personal feelings interfere with his work.

"My instructions, *sayyida*?"

"Proceed at once to Sandoral on the Drangosh. Military intelligence for my lord, if it presents itself; for myself I wish full information on the higher officers of the garrison and the local nobles: loves, hates, histories, feuds, alliances. Also any information from the Colony."

He took the papers and repeated the bow, using the documents for added flourish. "I obey like those multiplex of wing and eye who served Sulieman bin'-Daud, my lady," he said cheerfully. "That city I know of old." He'd done similar work for her the last time Raj commanded in the East, four years before.

"See that nobody stuffs you into a bottle," she added dryly, dropping back into Sponglish.

"I shall be most careful," he replied in the Civil Government's tongue, faultless down to the capital-city middle-class crispness of his vowels. "There is yet much to be done to repay my debt to you, my lady. And," he added with a cold glint in his dark eyes, "to those Sunni sons of pigs in Al Kebir, also."

Druze were few on Bellevue; less, since the Settlers had decided to purify the House of Islam a generation ago. Those sniffed out by the mullahs could count themselves lucky to be sold as slaves to the sulfur mines of Gederosia. The path from there to Suzette Whitehall's household and manumission had been long and complex . . .

"Your family are provided for?" Abdullah nodded. "Go, then, thou Slave of God," Suzette said, once more in Arabic, playing on the literal meaning of the man's name. "Thy God and mine be with thee."

"And the Merciful, the Lovingkind with thee and thy lord, *sayyida*," he replied, and left.

"Fatima," Suzette went on.

"Messa?"

"Take this to the Renunciate Sister Conzwela Dihego; she's second administrative assistant for medical affairs to the Arch-Sysup of East Residence. It's an authorization to mobilize priest-doctors and medical nuns, with the necessary supplies and transport for immediate dispatch to Sandoral."

"Wasn't she with us in the Western Territories?" the Arab girl asked.

"Yes; and Anne got her that job on my say-so when we got back." Suzette sighed; she missed Anne. "Quickly. And send in Muzzaf."

The Companion sidled through the door as Fatima left; the opening showed a controlled chaos of packing. He was a short slight man, with the dark complexion of a Borderer and a singsong Komarite accent. He was dressed in jacket and breeches of white linen, the little peaked fore-and-aft cap of his region, and a sash which nearly concealed the pepperpot pistol and pearl-handled gravity knife he preferred. He bowed deeply, a gesture much like Abdullah's.

Nearly a thousand years of conflict had left the Borderers much resembling their enemies of the Colony, though it was a killing matter to suggest it aloud.

"Messa Whitehall," he said, showing white teeth against his spiked black chin-beard. Like everyone else in the household, he was reacting to the news of Raj's reinstatement with almost giddy relief. "We campaign again?"

"Yes," Suzette said.

She pushed a document across the table with a finger. "One of your relatives is contractor for the East Residence municipal coal yards, isn't he?"

Muzzaf nodded; men from Komar and the other Border cities were prominent in trade all over the Civil Government, and in the new joint-risk companies.

"Subcontractor, Messa. The primary contract is farmed

to an . . . associate of Chancellor Tzetzas." He took up the paper and whistled silently. "That is a great *deal* of coal."

"Subcontractor is good enough. Have him release that amount to the Central Rail; and drop a suggestion with their dispatching agent that they begin to accumulate rolling stock *immediately*. Sweeten the suggestion if you have to."

"Immediately."

They exchanged a smile; Chancellor Tzetzas had confiscated all Raj's wealth . . . all that he had been able to find, at any rate. Neither the Chancellor nor Raj knew exactly how much the Whitehalls had had; Raj left such things to Muzzaf and Suzette . . . and they had anticipated the evil day long before. Raj knew how to handle guns and men, and even politics after a fashion, but money could also be a useful tool.

Silence fell as the steward left, broken only by the scritching of the pen and the faint thumps and scraping of the packing in the outer chambers. On the bed behind her were Raj's campaigning gear: plain issue swallowtail jacket of blue serge, maroon pants, boots, helmet, saber, pistol, map case, binoculars. Beside it was her linen riding costume and a captured Colonial repeating carbine, her own personal weapon . . . and the one, she reflected, that had disposed of the Clerett's heir.

A pity, she thought absently, tapping her lips with the tip of the pen before dipping the nib in the inkwell again. *A very pleasant young man.*

And easy to manipulate. Which had been crucial; like his uncle, he'd been mad with suspicion against Raj. With envy, too, in young Cabot's case: of Raj's reputation, his victories, his hold over his soldiers, and his wife.

A pity she'd had to kill him. Particularly just then. Shooting people was a crude emergency measure . . .

Which reminded her. She crossed to her jewel table

and reached beneath for a small rosewood box. A tiny combination lock closed it, and she probed at that with a pin from a brooch.

Yes, the crystal vials of various liquids and powders within were all full and fresh—there was a slip of paper with a recent date inside to remind her, one of Abdullah's many talents.

You never knew what sort of help Raj would need . . . whether he knew it or not.

"You *will* triumph, my knight," she whispered to herself, closing the box with a click. "If I have anything to do with the matter."

CHAPTER THREE

Governor Barholm stood while the servants stripped off the heavy robes; apart from Raj, they were the only people in the chamber who didn't look terrified . . . and they didn't have to watch the Governor's face. A sicklefoot had that sort of expression, just before it pivoted and slashed open its prey's belly with the four-inch dewclaw on one hind foot.

The Negrin Room was three centuries old. Walls were pale stone, traced over with delicate murals of reeds and flying dactosauroids and waterfowl; there was only one small Star, a token obeisance to religion as had been common in that impious age. The heads of the Ministries were there: Chancellor Tzetzas, of course; General Fiydel Klostermann, Master of Soldiers; Bernardinho Rivadavia, the Minister of Barbarians; Mihwel Berg of the Administrative Service; Gharzia, Commander of Eastern Forces. The courier from the east as well.

It was strange not to see Lady Anne Clerett, the Governor's wife. Barholm didn't have anyone he really trusted now that she was dead, and it was affecting his judgment.

"Heldeyz," Barholm snapped. "*Give* us the report, man."

Ministerial couriers were men of some rank themselves, but it was still strange how unintimidated Heldeyz looked, even facing the stark fury in Barholm Clerett's eyes. His

own were fixed and distant, in a face still seamed by
trail dust.

Barholm went on fretfully: "I *don't* know why Ali has
done this. The treaty after the last war was generous to
a fault—particularly since we *won* the war. The gifts of
friendship . . ."

observe:

Sweating slaves heaved at bundles of iron bars, heaping
them on the flatbed rail-cars and lashing them down. One
slipped and fell to the paving stones of East Residence's
main station. A bar snapped across; as a clerk bustled
over a guard rolled the broken end beneath his boot.

"Spirit," he said in a tone of mild curiosity. The interior
of the fracture showed a gray texture. "That's not wrought
iron, it's *cast.*"

Cast iron came straight from the smelting furnace; it
was hard, brittle and full of impurities. Only after
treatment in a puddling mill did it become the ductile,
easily worked material so valuable for machinery and
tools.

The clerk cleared his throat. "I think you'll find," he
said significantly, "that the Chancellor has inspected the
manifests quite carefully."

The guard grinned; he was a thin man with a long
nose and a pockmarked face, an East Residencer by birth
with all the ingrained respect for a good swindle that
marked that breed. He brushed his thumb over the first
three fingers of his right hand. The clerk smiled back.

"Sovereign Mighty Lord," Raj said. "I think you'll find
that quality, quantity, and delivery dates on our tribute—
pardon, our gifts of friendship—to the Colony have been
below the Treaty terms."

Figures scrolled before his eyes, and he read them
in an emotionless monotone worthy of Center.

Barholm blinked. He turned his eyes on Tzetzas, and a fine beading of sweat broke out on the Chancellor's olive face. "Sole Autocrat," the minister said, spreading his hands. "When contracts are handed out, something always sticks—so many layers of oversight, so many hands—you know—"

The Governor's fist struck the table. Gold-rimmed *kave* cups bounced and clattered in their saucers.

"I know who's responsible for seeing that the payments were met!" he roared; suddenly there was the slightest trace of Descott County rasp in his Sponglish. "You *fool*, I don't expect you to work for your salary alone, but I *did* expect you to know enough not to piss in our own well! D'you have any idea what this war is going to cost in lost taxes and off-budget funding?"

He paused, and when he continued his voice was calm. "You'd better have some idea, because you're going to pay the overage—personally."

"Sovereign Mighty Lord," Raj said. "Right now, I think we'd better concern ourselves with the state of the garrisons on the Drangosh frontier."

Barholm snapped his fingers. "Gurnyca had a garrison of—"

"Ten thousand men, Sole Autocrat," Mihwel Berg said helpfully. "At least, ten thousand on the paybooks."

Chancellor Tzetzas busied himself with his papers. When Barholm spoke, it was to General Gharzia.

"General," he said, his voice soft and even, "tell me— and if you lie, it would be better for you if you had never been born—how many troops were *actually* on the strength of the Gurnyca garrison? In what condition?"

Gharzia licked his lips, going gray under the tanned olive of his skin. "Two thousand, Sovereign Mighty Lord. In . . . ah, poor condition."

Somebody had been collecting the pay of the missing eight thousand. All eyes turned to the Chancellor.

The ruler turned back to the courier from the east. "Now, Messer Heldeyz," he said evenly. "Your report, please."

"Yes, Sole Autocrat."

Heldeyz stared at his hands. "I met the Colonials fifty klicks south of Gurnyca," he began. "They—"

observe, Center said:

Terrible as an army with banners. Barton Foley had quoted that to Raj, once; it was a fragment of Old Namerique, from the codices that survived the Fall.

There were plenty of banners in the forefront of the Colonial host that crossed the Drangosh. The green flag of Islam, marked with the crescent, or with the house blazons of regiments and noble *amirs*. The peacock-tail of the Settlers; that meant Ali was present in person. And a black pennant marked with the Seal of Solomon in red. *Tewfik.* Ali's brother, disqualified from the Settler's throne because of the eye he'd lost in the Zanj Wars, but the Colony's right arm nonetheless.

Raj recognized the terrain instantly; he'd campaigned out east himself, five years ago. Generations of the Civil Government's soldiers had taken their blooding in that ghastly lunar landscape of eroded silt, and all too many left their bones there. Just north of the border and the river forts, by the look of it, in one of the locations where the right—the western—bank was too high for irrigation. In consequence nothing grew there, except for a few bluish-green native shrubs.

The oily-looking greenish-gray waters of the Drangosh were a kilometer and a half across. A bridge of boats had been built across it, big river-barges of the type used for trade up and down the river from Sandoral to Al Kebir and the far-off Colonial Gulf. *Good engineering,* Raj thought; as good as the Civil Government's army, or a little better. The barges were lashed together with huge sisal cables as thick as a man's waist; then timbers and planks were laid across to make a deck, and pounded clay half a meter thick on top of that to give the men and animals a firm surface. There were even straw balustrades on either side, chest high, to keep the beasts from spooking at the water curling up around the blunt prows of the barges.

Men flowed across in a steady stream: Colonial dragoon *tabors*, battalions, riding in column of fours, mainly. Mounted on slender Bazenjis and greyhounds, lever-action repeating carbines in scabbards by their right knees, scimitars or yataghans at their belts, bandoliers over the chests of their faded scarlet djellabas. The sun glittered on the polished spikes of their conical helmets, and the pugarees wound about them fluttered in the breeze. Between the blocks of cavalry came guns: light pompoms, quick-firers throwing a two-kilo shell from a clip magazine; field guns, much like the Civil Government's 75mm's; and heavier pieces drawn by oxen. Those were cast-steel muzzle-loading rifles, heavy pieces up to 150mm, siege guns. And there was transport, light dog-drawn two-wheel carts, heavy wagons pulled by sixteen pair of oxen.

Officers directed the traffic with flourishes of their nine-tailed ceremonial whips, each thong tipped with a piece of jagged steel.

Where— Raj thought. Center's viewpoint shifted to the western bank.

In the Colony's army, as in the Civil Government's, infantry were usually second-line troops, good enough to hold forts and lines of communication. Ali—Tewfik, probably—had sent his over first, and they were hard at work. Swarms of men stripped to their loincloths or pantaloons, burned from their natural light brown to an almost black color, swinging picks and shoveling dirt into the baskets others hauled. They moved over the land like disciplined ants, and a pentagonal earthwork fortress was rising around the western end of the pontoon bridge. A fairly formidable one, too; deep ditch, ten-meter walls, ravelins and bastions at the corners with deep V-notches for the muzzles of the guns. The Colony's green flag and the Settler's peacock already flapped around a huge pavilion-tent in its center. Within, ditched roadways had been laid out, and neat rows of pup tents, heaps of stores, and picket-lines for the dogs were rising.

Enough for—

"Sixty thousand men," Raj said. "Fifty thousand cavalry, ten thousand infantry or a little more to hold the bridgehead."

Heldeyz stopped, flustered. "Yes, *heneralissimo*," he said; evidently the news of Raj's demotion hadn't reached the eastern marches yet. "That's my estimate. How did you know?"

"Logistics. If Ali's planning on moving as far north as Sandoral, that's the maximum number he can supply overland from the bridgehead. Our forts at the border can hold out for six months or more, even if the Colony put in a full attack—which they won't or they couldn't put that large a field army into action. They'll have blockforces around the frontier strongpoints, but they can't use river transport to supply Ali. So they moved north and crossed upstream of the forts."

Both the Colony and the Civil Government had put generations of effort into those defenses. The giant cast-steel rifles in the forts would smash anything that tried to steam past them on the river. That ruled out supply by riverboat.

"Ali—Tewfik—must have built a railroad line to the east bank," Raj said. "But on the western shore, it'll be animal transport. Even with what they can forage, no more than fifty thousand men and riding dogs. They wouldn't bring less, not for a full-scale invasion, and they couldn't feed more."

Barholm shot Raj a considering look. "Go on," he said to Heldeyz.

The courier nodded. "I met—"

observe, Center whispered in Raj's mind:

Heldeyz knelt before a throne. It was lightly built, of cast bronze fretwork, but inlaid with gold and gems in a pattern that flared out behind the seat like a peacock's tail. A man in shimmering cloth-of-gold sat on it. Throne and man glittered when stray beams of light penetrated the lacework canopy that slaves held above it; a spray of peacock feathers sprang from the great ruby in the clasp at the front of his turban. Around the Settler stood generals and noblemen, a few Bedouin chiefs in goathair robes and ha'ik, mullahs in black, servants with flasks of iced sherbert, crouching clerks and accountants with paper and pen and abacus. None of them came within the ring of guardsmen, black slave-mamluks with great curved swords naked in their hands, or bell-mouthed riot guns at the ready.

"Your master, the *kaphar* king, has offended me grievously," Ali said, speaking fair Sponglish. "He has violated the terms of our treaty . . . and my father's blood cries out for vengeance. No duty is more sacred. Yet Allah, the Merciful, the Lovingkind, enjoins us to peaceful deeds."

Ali's face was heavy-featured but regular, the curved beak of the nose dominating, offset by full red lips and a forked beard. His eyes were large and brown, luminous and somehow disturbing. Apart from an occasional twitching tic of his right cheek, the expression was one of mild reason.

An officer approached, going down on both knees and bowing until the point of his helmet-spike touched the glowing Al Kebir carpets that covered the ground before the Settler's pavilion and campaign-throne.

"*Amir el Mumineen*, Commander of the Faithful, the infidel emissaries from the city of Gurnyca crave the honor of your presence."

Ali's eyebrows rose slightly. He leaned back in the portable throne, and servants stepped forward to spray rosewater from crystal ewers through rubber bulbs. He sipped sherbert from a glass globe through a silver straw and waited.

"By all means, let them enter," he said gently.

The delegates ignored Heldeyz, prone on the carpet before the Settler. There were half a dozen of them, mostly in the dress of wealthy merchants, one in Civil Government uniform. They threw themselves prostrate; a gesture that only the ruler of the *Gubernio Civil* was legally due. In fact, it was forbidden to any other on penalty of death, but the Governor was in East Residence, and Ali was very much present before their gates with fifty thousand men.

"Sovereign lord," the head of the delegation mumbled into the carpet; he was an elderly man, sweating in the heat, the wattles under his chin sliding down into the expensive but dust-stained silver lace of his cravat. "Spare us."

Well, thought Raj. *That's straightforward enough.*

"Surely," the *alcalle* of Gurnyca said, "we may make amends to Your Supremacy for any offense we have unwittingly given. We are but poor merchants, not the lords of State. We have no knowledge of high matters. Yet if wrong has been done you, we are willing to pay. Surely there can be peace—who would benefit from war?"

Ali smiled. "There may be peace, if God wills. There is but one God, and all things are accomplished according to the will of God." He nodded, and added in his own tongue: "*Salaam, insh'allah.*"

One ringed hand stroked his beard, and he flicked a finger at a clerk. "You spoke of payment. The tribute from you *kaphar* ingrates is in arrears to the extent of—"

"—twenty-one hundred thousand gold *dinars*, O Lion of Islam," the clerk said. "That is not counting interest on late payments at—"

"Silence," Ali purred, a lethal amusement in his voice. "Am I a merchant, to haggle? By all means, if this is made good, let there be peace."

Even under the Colonial guns, that brought a wail of protest. "Lord, Lord," the alcalle said. "We are but one city! There is not that much gold in all Gurnyca, not if we stripped the dome of the cathedron and the fillings from our teeth."

"Both of which," Ali pointed out genially, "will be done if the city is put to the sack." He raised a hand. "It is the time of prayer. Surely, we may speak again of this later; and you shall return to your city with an escort and safe passage. In the morning, I shall give my final decision."

The scene shifted, the sun dropping toward the horizon and both moons high, looking like translucent glass against the bright stars. Date palms and orange groves stood in darkening shadow as the Gurnyca elders and Heldeyz rode their dogs through the belt of irrigated land surrounding the city. Water chuckled in the canals that bordered the fields, oxen lowed, but there was no sight or sound of human beings, no smoke from the whitewashed huts of the peasantry. Fields lay empty, scattered with tossed-aside hoes and pruning hooks; a manor stood ghostly among its gardens, with only the raucous sound of a peacock strutting along the tiled portico.

Frontier reflexes, Raj thought grimly. *They know when to make a bolt for the walls.*

There were no buildings or trees within a half-kilometer

of the fortifications, only pasture and field crops; and the city defenses were first-rate. Raj remembered them well from the archives, which he'd memorized long before Center entered his life. Modernized a century ago, and then again in his father's time. A clear field of fire, good moat, new-style walls sunk behind it, low and massive. Ravelins and bastions at frequent intervals, giving murderous enfilade fire all along the circuit, with a strong central citadel near the water. The guns were cast-iron muzzle-loaders like most fortress artillery, but formidable and numerous; there were some very up-to-date rifled pieces among them.

Resolutely held by a strong garrison, the city could have held for months against the Colonial army—and it would be impossible to bypass. Taking it by siege would require full-scale entrenchments, pushing artillery positions forward inch by bloody inch, escalade trenches, until enough heavy howitzers were close to the wall and you could pound it flat. Even then, storming it would be brutally expensive. By that time, the Civil Government would have had time to mobilize its field armies in the East and march to the city's relief. It was a strategy that had worked a dozen times in the endless eastern wars.

If the garrison was up to strength and competently led.

Center's viewpoint switched to the escort, a full half-battalion of them, two hundred and fifty men. They didn't look particularly impressive at first sight, dark bearded men, many with the tails of their pugarees drawn across their faces like veils. Raj looked for telltale signs: their hands, the wear on the hilts of scimitars and carbines, the way they sat their dogs, how often they had to check or spur to keep their dressing.

These lads have been to school. Their commander was a stocky man, one of the ones with the tail-end of his turban drawn across his face. Scars seamed the backs of his hands, and another gouged down from forehead to nose . . .

. . . and his eye was unmoving on that side. *Tewfik*. Raj cursed to himself. With a glass eye for once, rather than his trademark patch. He'd met the Colonial commander once, in a parley before the Battle of Sandoral, four years ago. *What's he doing there?* It was a job for a minor emir, not the commander-in-chief.

An image flickered through Raj's consciousness, tinged somehow with irony: himself, leading the 2nd Cruisers through the tunnel under Lion City's walls.

Point taken, Raj noted dryly.

The white dust of the road shone ruddy with the setting sun, streaked with the long shadow of the tall cypresses planted by its side. They came to the outer gatehouse of the city's defenses, where the highway crossed the moat on stone arches. Civil Government troops opened the iron portals: infantrymen, slovenly-looking even for footsoldiers. Raj ground his teeth at the rust on one man's rifle barrel. They eyed the Colonial troops with the prickly nervousness of a cat watching a pack of large dogs through a window. Heldeyz saluted their officer and opened his mouth to speak.

Tewfik drew his revolver and shot the man in the face.

A red spearhead seemed to connect the Arab's hand and the guard officer's nose for an instant, and then the footsoldier jerked backward as if kicked in the face by an ox. His helmet rang against the stone of the gatehouse, the last fraction of the *clank* lost in the snapping bark of carbines as the Colonials cut loose with their repeaters. They boiled forward, screaming in a wild falsetto screech. One of the Civil Government soldiers managed to get a round off, the deeper boom of his single-shot rifle painful in the confined space. Then he went down under a Colonial officer's yataghan, still stabbing upward with his bayonet.

The fight in the gateway lasted bare seconds, leaving

Heldeyz and the city fathers sitting their dogs and gaping at the litter of bodies. Puffs of off-white smoke drifted by; the Colonials were wasting no time. Dozens of them stuck their carbines through gunslits in the doors and fired blind, as fast as they could work the levers, sending a lethal hail of the light bullets to ricochet off the stone walls within. Hand-bombs and axes pounded the doors open. The rest of the Colonial force formed a dense four-deep firing line at the inner gate, thumbing reloads from their bandoliers into the loading gates of their weapons. Heldeyz's head whipped around at the high shrill scream of a Colonial bugle.

Mounted men were pouring out of the orchards that ringed the city, spurring their dogs. The animals bounded forward at a dead run, covering the ground in huge soaring leaps as they galloped with heads down and hindlegs coming up nearly to their ears on every jump. Rough hands threw the courier aside as the column poured into the strait confines of the gatehouse and broke out into the cleared ground beyond; a battery of pompoms followed, their long barrels jerking wildly as the gunners lashed their dogs. Iron wheels sparked on the paving stones, and behind them the roadway was red with crimson djellabas . . .

Barholm's fist hit the table as the courier's words stumbled into silence. He didn't have Center's holographic visions to flesh them out, but there was nothing wrong with his wits.

"They *knew* the wogs were there in force and they didn't keep a better guard than that?" he said.

"Sole Autocrat, the garrison was under-strength and badly trained," Raj said quietly. "In any case, they paid for their folly."

"Yes," Heldeyz said, his eyes remote. "They paid."

observe, Center said.

✧   ✧   ✧

The scimitar flashed in the sun. A heavy *thack* sounded, with the harsher wet popping of fresh bone underneath. The *alcalle*'s head rolled free; his body collapsed from its kneeling position, heavy jets of arterial blood splashing into the reddish mud that stained the ground. Clouds of flies lifted, then settled again. The executioner flourished his heavy two-handed curved sword ritually.

The smoke from the burning buildings covered the smell, even from the pyramid of heads the Settler's mamluks were building beside the outer gate. Few of the chained coffles of Gurnycians marching out paid much attention to it; their faces were mostly blank, eyes to the ground. Mounted Colonial guards urged them on with snaps of the *kourbash*, the long sauroid-hide whip. They were the lucky ones: pretty women, strong young men, craftsmen, and children old enough to survive the trip south to the markets of Al Kebir.

Ali pointed. "No, cut that one's throat," he said, indicating a Star priest with a thin white beard. The executioner lowered his sword.

The old man's eyes were closed; he was praying quietly as the black-robed mamluk stepped up behind him and drew the curved dagger. Ali giggled when the body toppled thrashing to the ground.

"The *halall*," he said, sputtering laughter. The ritual throat-cutting that made meat clean for Muslims to eat. "Is it not fitting, for these beasts?"

Raj noted a mullah's lips tightening at the blasphemy. Nobody spoke.

The good humor on Ali's face turned gelid as he gripped Heldeyz's face in his hand and turned it to the heaps of severed heads.

"Do you *see*, infidel?" he screamed. "Do you *see*?"

A portly man in a green turban shoved his way through the crowd. A string of prisoners followed him, mostly girls in their early teens, with a few younger boys. He prostrated himself.

"Oh guardian of the sacred ka'ba, you wished—" he began in a falsetto voice.

Ali released the Civil Government courier. "Yes, yes," he said impatiently. His hand flicked to a girl and a boy. "Those two, and don't bother me again before the evening meal." He jerked his head at his guards. "Come. Bring the pig-eating *kaphar*."

Wagons took up most of the roadway, oxen lowing under the load. Inside, in the cleared space within the walls that Civil Government law commanded, were huge heaps of spoils; officers were directing the troopers as they piled it in neatly classified heaps. Cloth, metalware, tools, coin, precious vessels from the Star churches and temples . . . Beyond, only a few buildings still stood. As Heldeyz watched, a merchant's townhouse collapsed inward about the burning rafters, the thick adobe walls crumbling like mud. A ground-shaking thump, and the great dome of the Star temple followed; Raj recognized the sound of blasting charges.

"See, unbeliever," Ali went on. "The pig and son of pigs Barholm—it was not enough that he cheated me of the blood-price of my father's death, he expected me—*me*—Ali ibn'Jamal, to sit among the women and do nothing while he conquered all the world. Conquered all the world, then turned on me! Turned on the Faithful! No, *kaphar*, Ali ibn'Jamal, Guardian of Sinar, Settler of the House of Islam, is not such a fool as that.

"Tell Barholm I am coming for him." Ali's mouth was jerking, and his voice rose to a shrill scream. "Tell him I have something for him!"

Colonial soldiers were setting a sharpened stake in the ground. They dragged out the Arch-Sysup Hierarch of the Diocese of Gurnyca. He was a portly man, flabby in middle age, stripped to his silk underdrawers. The black giants holding his arms scarcely lost a step when he collapsed at the sight of the waiting impaling stake . . .

Silence fell around the table. At last, General Klosterman cleared his throat.

"Well, I don't think there's much doubt as to Ali's intentions," he said.

Barholm nodded abstractedly. "General Klosterman, how long would it take to mobilize all available field forces and meet the Colonists in strength?"

Klosterman paled. Master of Soldiers was an administrative post, but it did give the elderly officeholder a good grasp of the state of the Civil Government's defenses.

"Lord, Ali has fifty thousand of his first-line troops with him. If we summoned *all* available cavalry, we couldn't field half that in time to meet him south of Sandoral, or even south of the Oxhead Mountains . . . and forgive me, Sovereign Mighty Lord, but the troops we could summon would not be in good heart."

observe, said Center.

This time Center's projections started with a map. Raj recognized it, a terrain rendering of the Civil Government's eastern provinces. The Oxhead Mountains ran east-west, then hooked up northward; north of it was the sparsely settled central plateau, and to the south and east was the upper valley of the Drangosh and its tributary. That was densely settled in part, where irrigation was possible; elsewhere arid grazing country, with scattered villages around springs in the foothills.

Colored blocks moved, arrows showing their lines of advance. He nodded to himself; so and so many days to muster, supplies, roadways, the few railroad lines. Twenty thousand men maximum, perhaps thirty thousand if you counted the ordinary infantry garrisons called up from their land grants. And . . .

Men in blue and maroon uniforms fled, beating at their dogs with the flats of their sabers or with riding whips. A ragged square stood on a hill, with the Star banner at its center. Black puffballs of smoke burst over the tattered ranks, shellbursts, and Colonial field guns hammered giant shotgun blasts of canister in at pointblank range. Men *splashed* away from the shot in wedges. A line of mounted dragoons drew their scimitars in unison, flashing in the bright southern sun. *Five battalions*, Raj estimated with an expert eye. *Twenty-five hundred men.* Trumpets shrilled, and the scimitars rested on the riders' shoulders. Walk-march. Trot. The blades came down. Gallop. Charge. A single long volley blew gaps in their line, and they were over the thin Civil Government square. The Star banner went down. . . .

"Lord," Klosterman went on, "with humility, my advice is that we throw as many men into Sandoral and the eastern cities as we can. Ali cannot take them quickly."

Tzetzas spoke for the first time. "But he *could* bypass them," he said.

Raj nodded silently, conscious of eyes glancing at him sidelong.

observe, said Center.

From horizon to horizon, the land burned; ripe wheat flared like tinder under the summer sun, sending clouds of red-shot black into the sky. Denser columns marked the sites of villages and manor-houses. In an orchard, peasants worked under Colonial guns, ringbarking the trees and piling burning bundles of straw against their roots.

A flicker, and he was outside a city: Melaga, from the look of the olive-covered hills around it. Raw red earth marked the siegeworks about it, a circumvallation with a high wall topped by a palisade. Zigzag works wormed inward from there, each ending in a redoubt protected by earth-filled wicker baskets. Swarms of men hauled cannon forward and dug at the earth. Guns boomed from the city walls, and men died in the siegeworks, but more took their places. Howitzers lobbed their shells into the sky, the fuses drawing trails of smoke and fire until they burst within the walls . . .

"No, that would be far too uncertain," Tzetzas went on. "Instead, well, the treasury is unusually full. We could offer Ali twice, three *times* the previous tribute."

Barholm snorted. "After we shorted him on the last agreement? I can just *see* him quietly going back to Al Kebir, demobilizing his army and waiting for the gold to arrive."

"Sovereign Mighty Lord," Heldeyz said, "he's not here for gold. He's here for blood. He's . . . he's not going to be bought off. You have to see him—"

ali would agree to the increased tribute, but remain on civil government soil, probability 97%, ±2. observe, said Center.

"Filth!" Ali screamed. He strode through the pavilions, kicking over platters filled with whole roast lambs, rice pillaus, fruits, and ices. "You call this a feast of welcome! Filth!"

The syndics of the town shrank backward, looking around with the instinctive gesture of men in a trap with no exit.

"That pig Barholm, that two-dinar Descotter hill chief who calls himself a conqueror, it isn't enough he makes me wait for my tribute, but he insults me too."

Ali stopped, smiled, relaxed. The expression was far more frightening than the bloodthirsty madness of a minute before.

"Well then, we'll have to show the *kaphar* what it means to insult the Commander of the Faithful, won't we?" he went on.

He eyed the assembled syndics with much the same expression that a farmwife would have, standing in the yard and fingering her knife as she selected a stewing pullet.

observe:

A younger Ali knelt behind a girl. Gardens bloomed around them, thick with flowers and softly murmurous with bees; the stars shone above, the only light on the rippling water of the fountain save for a few discreet lanterns. Ali had a hand on the girl's neck, pushing her face below the surface of the water as he thrust into her. He let her rise for an instant, long enough to take one breath and scream.

It bubbled out as he pushed her down again. Her hands beat against the marble of the pool's rim, leaving bloody streaks on the carved stone.

observe:

Ali sat at a chessboard, across from a grave white-bearded man. The pieces were carved from sauroid ivory and black jadeite; they played seated on cushions of cloth-of-gold, beneath a fretted bronze pergola that served as support for a huge vine of sambuca jasmine. A slender girl naked except for the filmy veil that hid half her face poured cut-crystal goblets full of iced sherbert. Droplets of condensation stood out on the silver ewer.

"Checkmate, Prince of the Faithful," the older man said. "Congratulations. This is your best game yet."

Ali looked down at the chessboard, his lips moving as he traced out the possible movements. When he moved, it was so swiftly that the serving girl had time for only the beginning of a scream.

His hand grasped the *cadi*'s white beard, and the dagger slashed it across. He threw the tuft of hair in the older man's face.

"Sauroid-lover," he screamed. "You dare to insult me?"

The old man drew himself up. "You forget yourself, Ali," he said. "I am appointed by the Settler to guide your footsteps. You must learn restraint—"

Ali moved again, very quickly. The curved dagger in his hand was hilted with silver and pearls, but the blade was layer-forged Sinnar steel, sharp enough to part a drifting silk thread. It sliced more than halfway through the *cadi's* throat. The old man turned, his blood arching out in a spraying stream of red across the priceless silk of the cushions and the white body of the girl. Ali stood silent, panting, watching the body tumble down the alabaster steps of the gazebo. Then he turned toward the servant, smiling. Blood ran down his mustaches, and speckled his lips.

observe:

Ali sat on the Peacock Throne of the Settlers, in a vaulted room whose ceiling was an intertwining mass of calligraphy picked out in gold, the thousand and one names of Allah, the Merciful, the Lovingkind. From a glass bull's-eye at the apex, light streamed down, mellow and gold, to the tessellated marble floor. Guards stood motionless around the walls of the great circular chamber. Others dragged a man forward; he was stripped to his baggy pantaloons, a hard-muscled man in his thirties with a close-cropped beard and a great beak of a nose.

"Greetings, Akbar my brother," Ali called jovially. "How good, how very good to see your face again!"

The Settler's brother drew himself up and spat on the marbled floor. "You have won, Ali," he said disdainfully. "Yours is the Peacock Throne. Bring out the irons and have done."

"Irons?" Ali said.

That was the traditional punishment for the losers, when a dead Settler's brothers fought for the throne. Only a man complete in his limbs and organs could be

Commander of the Faithful; Tewfik was disqualified because he had lost an eye in battle. A red-hot iron fulfilled the same purpose.

"Irons?" Ali said again. "Oh, may Allah requite me if I should put out the eyes of one born of the same seed, of Jamal our father."

Eunuchs brought out a stout iron framework, like a high bedstead with manacles at each corner. Akbar began to bellow and thrash; the guards held him down with remorseless strength while the plump, smooth-faced eunuchs snapped the steel cuffs around wrist and ankle.

"Shaitan will gnaw your soul in hell if you shed a brother's blood!" Akbar yelled.

Ali stood and made a gesture. The guards saluted with fist to brow, and marched out of the great chamber.

"I? Shed your blood? Never, my brother."

Ali stood by the iron rack, stroking his beard. He pulled a handkerchief from one sleeve of his pearl-sewn robe and made as if to wipe his brother's face; when the other man opened his mouth to shout a curse Ali deftly stuffed the length of silk into it.

"There. It is unmannerly to interrupt the Settler. Do you not remember, brother, how you boasted to your captains during our brief, unfortunate civil strife—how you boasted to them that I should be sent into exile on an island in the Zanj Sea with only a mute crone to attend me? That a . . . how did you phrase it? A perverted bastard son of a diseased sheep like me did not deserve the delights of the hareem, and that the pearl-breasted beauties who served me would be shared among your *amirs*."

He clapped his hands. A line of women filed into the throne room, the long robes of their *chadors* brushing the floor and the sleeves hiding their hands.

Ali turned. "Zufika, Aisha," he said. "All of you—hide not the light of your faces."

Obediently, they dropped the filmy black cloaks to the floor. Several of them were carrying long slim knives; two bore a charcoal brazier between them, holding the metal frame with iron tongs. Others set a stool by the iron frame. Ali sank down with a satisfied sigh.

"No, I shall not shed a drop of your blood," he said. "But you surprise me, with this unseemly conduct. Don't you know it is unfitting for an entire male to look on the faces of the Settler's women?"

Zufika came forward, the knife in her hand. "Attend to it, my sweet one."

Through the gag, Akbar began to scream.

"Sovereign Mighty Lord," Raj said quietly.

Silence fell; even Barholm checked himself, dropping the finger he'd been wagging under Chancellor Tzetzas' nose.

"With your permission, lord, I'll take command in the East. Superseding the Commander of Eastern Forces and the garrison commandants."

There were nods all around the table, even from Gharzia. Right now the high command in the east was the sort of honor you took with you to an unmarked grave.

"And I'll take seven thousand cavalry *to* the border."

"Ridiculous—"

"That'll strip the garrisons of—"

"D'you want Ali to march right into East Residence—"

Raj raised his hand. "Sovereign Mighty Lord, the troops are on their way to East Residence as we speak. Most of the garrison of the Western Territories. Veteran fighters, the cream of our armies."

Barholm looked at him narrow-eyed. *And the soldiers most loyal to you.* The thought needed no words.

"That's forty-five hundred men, perhaps a little more. I'll take another two thousand of the Brigaderos prisoners who've been reequipped and organized along Civil Government lines, and some of the battalions who were with me in the Southern Territories campaign and are now attached to the Residence Area command."

Gharzia was scribbling on his pad. *"Heneralissimo—"* he began, giving Raj the title he'd been formally stripped of *"—that'll* still leave you well below Ali's numbers, discounting his infantry and line-of-communications troops. Shouldn't we pull back more of the Southern and Western Territories garrisons?"

Raj spread his hands. They were brown with sun, battered and nicked and callused from swords and reins, as out of place in this quiet elegant room as the man himself.

"That would take too long. Messers, Sole Autocrat, we don't have the *time.* Please understand, no matter what I do, the border area is going to get the worst working-over it's had in a century or more."

observe, Center said.

—and Colonial dragoons rode through a Borderer hamlet, tossing torches through the windows. Fire belched back, red flames and sooty smoke turning the whitewash black above the openings. Here and there a limestone lintel burned with white-hot fire as it sublimed.

—the last of a line of Arabs picked himself up off a woman and adjusted his robe. She lay motionless in the dust of the street, eyes empty, spittle running down from the corner of her mouth. The Colonial kicked her in the ribs, then called an order to the others. He had the crossed lines of a *naik*, a corporal, on the sleeve of his djellaba. Two of the troopers picked the woman up by the ankles and wrists, grunting at the limp dead weight. The naik jerked a thumb, and they dumped their semi-conscious victim head-first down the well.

—bursting charges spouted plumes of smoke and rock

and pulverized dirt across the massive sloping front of the dam. It stretched two hundred meters across a U-shaped valley amid dry rocky hills, a stone-paved road on its top and stone and iron gates at one side where the tumbling water of the flume was channeled into a canal. For long moments nothing seemed to happen, and then water sprouted from the surface where the explosives had been laid. It gouted like erupting geysers, turning to rainbow splendor at the edges under the bright noon light. The sappers whooped and danced as the rushing torrent eroded the earthwork of the dam like a lump of sugar under a spout of hot tea. Then the earth shuddered as the dam collapsed in earnest, and the lake headed downstream in a roaring wall of brown silt and tumbling rocks.

"Yes, yes," Barholm said. The other advisors were silent as the two Descotters met each other's eyes.

"I think I can retrieve the situation," Raj said calmly. "Provided, of course, I have my Governor's full confidence. *Do* I have your confidence, my lord?"

Barholm's lips tightened. "Yes, yes," he said again. He snapped his fingers for a parchment, wrote, signed, extended his hand for the Gubernatorial seal. It thwacked into the purple wax with an angry sound.

He pushed it across the polished flamegrain wood of the table. Raj picked it up. It was a delegation of viceregal power, requiring all officers and officials of the Civil Government to tender him full cooperation—rare for a commander sent out into the *barbaricum*, unheard-of within the borders.

If I smash the Colonials, Raj thought—unlikely as that seemed right now—*that'll be the last strong opponent the Civil Government faces*. He'd reconquered the Southern and Western Territories; the Base Area was far away, and the Zanj states of the Southern Continent even farther. Once the Colony had been beaten back, Barholm Clerett's position would be safer than any Governor's in the past five hundred years. Safe enough that he would certainly no longer need a *heneralissimo supremo*.

"Yes," Barholm repeated. "Who could doubt that you have my *full* confidence?"

Raj stood, bowing and tucking the Gubernatorial Rescript into the sleeve-pocket of his uniform jacket.

"Then if you'll forgive me, Sovereign Mighty Lord, Messers."

His face held an abstracted frown as he left the room, ignoring the murmur behind him. Landing five thousand men and thirty guns, with all their dogs and stores, wasn't easy at the best of times. Getting them straight off the ships and headed east fast without a monumental foul-up would be real work.

disembarkation would be most efficiently achieved as follows, Center began.

CHAPTER FOUR

Corporal Minatili clattered down the steep wooden steps into the hold of the freighter, his hobnail boots biting into the pinewood. The ship was pitching less now that the sails were furled and the steam tug was bringing it into port.

Minatili shook his head, still a little bewildered at the sight. He'd grown up in Old Residence, in the Western Territories, and he was familiar enough with fine building. But Old Residence had shrunk steadily since the Brigade conquered it, with forest and groves and nobles' country-seats spreading over the old suburbs. These days it was just a big city.

East Residence was a *world*. It sprawled over the seven hills on all sides of its deep U-shaped harbor: houses and factories, up to the heights where gardens and marble marked the patricians' quarter and the Gubernatorial palaces. A haze of coal-smoke hung over it, a forest of masts and smokestacks darkened the water; squadrons of low-slung steam rams with their paddles churning the water, big-bellied merchantmen with grain from the Diva country of the far north, or ornamental stone and wine from Kelden, whole fleets of barges down from the Hemmar River. And all over the hills, the tracery of gaslight like fairy lights, still bright in the predawn hours.

He hoped he'd have time to see the great Star Temple that Governor Barholm had built. It was supposed to make the one in Old Residence look like a hut—and now, that seemed possible.

Minatili's feet and body took him through the crowded hold of the troopship without more than an occasional jostle; after the cleaner air on deck, the stink of it hit him again. His eight-man section was waiting by their gear.

"What's t'word, corp?"

"We're heading east," Minatili said.

His own Sponglish was fluent now, but it still carried the accent of the Spanjol more common in the Western Territories. He'd been recruited into the 24th Valencia when Messer Raj came to make war against the Brigade; before that his local priest in Old Residence had taught him his letters and numbers, which was one reason he'd made watch-stander and then corporal so fast. Most of the Civil Government's infantry were of peon stock, and almost all illiterate.

He made a quick check of the gear laid out on each of the straw pallets. Waterproof blanket, blanket, long sword-bayonet, cartridge pouches with seventy-five rounds, another fifty in a cardboard box, entrenching spade or short pick, mess tin, canteen, haversack, spare clothing if any, bandage packet, blessed chlorine powder for purifying water, three days' hardtack . . .

The corporal picked up one of the Armory rifles and stuck his thumb into the loop of the lever before the handgrip. A push and the block went *snick*, snapping down at the front so the grooved ramp on top led to the chamber. He peered down the barrel, raising it to the light. *No rust, not too much oil.* He snapped the lever back: *clack*. A pull on the trigger brought a sharp *click* as the pin fell on the empty space where a cartridge would lie in combat.

"Not too bad, Saynchez," Minatili said. "Awright, git the kit on."

A chorus of grumbles. "Yor all gone soft," he said relentlessly. "Be off yor backsides soon."

He swung his own on. Webbing belt, pouches, shoulder-straps, haversack and bayonet went on like a coat; all you had to do was snap the buckle on the belt. Everything else went into the blanket roll; you rolled that up into a sausage, strapped the roll shut with leather thongs, then bent it into a U-shape and slung it over your left shoulder with the tied-together ends at your right hip. He grunted a little as it settled down, shrugging until it rode properly; you could wear blisters the size of a cup if you didn't adjust it just right.

An officer and bugler came down the main hatchway. The brassy notes of *Full Kit* and *Ready to Move Out* sounded, loud through the dim crowded spaces. The troops erupted in cursing, crowding movement, all but the most experienced veterans—*they'd* gotten ready beforehand. Minatili grinned at his squad.

"Happy now?"

It was a lot easier to put your gear on when a couple of hundred others weren't trying to do the same, and that in a hold packed with temporary pinewood bunks.

Saynchez snorted. He was a grizzled man in his thirties, one of two in the squad who'd been out east with the 24th the last time. He'd also been up and down the ladder of rank to sergeant and back to private at least twice; it was drink, mostly.

"We goin' east fer garrison, er t'fight?" he asked.

"Messer Raj didn't tell me, t'last time he had me over fer afternoon *kave* n' cakes," Minatili said dryly.

He wouldn't be looking forward to garrison duty, himself. Some preferred it; in between active campaigns Civil Government infantry were assigned farms from the State's domains, with tenant families to work them. You had to find your own keep from the proceeds, minus stoppages for equipment. Provided your officers were

honest—which Major Felasquez was, thank the Spirit—
the total came to about the same as active-service cash
pay. About what a laborer made, with more security and
less work. But it sounded *dull*, especially to a city boy
like him, and he hadn't joined up to be bored.

Mind you, some of the fighting in the Western
Territories had been more interesting than he really liked.
He remembered the long teeth of the Brigade curaissiers'
dogs, the lanceheads rippling down, sweat stinging his
eyes, and the sun-hot metal of the rifle as he brought it
up to aim.

"Word is," he went on, relenting, "that t'wogboys is
over the frontier. Messer Raj's bein' set out to put 'em
back."

Saynchez shaped a silent whistle. Minatili looked at
him hopefully; the far eastern frontier with the Colony
was only a rumor to him. Saynchez had been with the
24th when Messer Raj whipped the ragheads and killed
their king.

"Them's serious business," the older private said.
"Them wogs is na no joke."

"Messer Raj done whup 'em before," one of the other
soldiers said.

"Serious," Saynchez said softly. "Real serious."

Minatili slung his rifle. The bugle sounded again: *Fall
in*.

A locomotive let out a high shrill scream from its steam
whistle. Its two man-high driving wheels spun, throwing
twin streams of sparks from the strap-iron rails beneath.
The long funnel with its bulbous crown belched steam
and black smoke, thick and smelling of burnt tar. Behind
it eight iron-and-wood cars lurched against the chain
fastenings that bound them together. They were heaped
with coal, and heavy. It took more wheel-spinning and
lurching halts before the train finally gathered way and

rocked southward through the city towards the Hemmar Valley and the long journey east.

Raj's hound Horace snarled slightly at the train. He ran a soothing hand down the beast's neck, clamping his legs slightly around its barrel. Other riders were having more trouble with their animals. Hounds tended to have good nerves; it was one of their strong points. They also tended to do exactly as they pleased whenever they felt like it, but everything was tradeoffs. Horace moved forward at a swinging walk, stepping high over the rails, his plate-sized paws crunching on the cinder and crushed rock of the roadbeds.

More coal trains pulled out, building up the reserves at the stations farther east along the Central Rail; barges lay beside the dock, heaped with the dusty black product of the Coast Range mines. Other trains were making up, of slat-sided boxcars with *40 hombes/8 dawg* freshly stenciled on their sides; forty men, or eight riding dogs. The railyards sprawled along a good part of East Residence's harbor. Barholm Clerett had built more kilometers of line than the previous ten Governors combined; whatever you said of him, he was a builder. Temples, forts, railways—the great Central Line from the capital to Sandoral completed at last—dams, canals. Much of it financed with the plunder from Raj's campaigns, and dug by captives from them.

It was a mild early-summer day, the sky blue except for a few puffs of high cloud, both moons up—Maxiluna was three-quarters full, Miniluna a narrow crescent. Like the one on the Colony's green banner, the crescent of Islam.

Raj shook his head at the thought. Beyond the moons were the Stars, and the Spirit of Man of the Stars.

Today there were more soldiers than railway men in the marshaling yard. Men heaved rectangular crates onto the bed of a railcar. Each had the Star of the Civil

Government stenciled on its side, and *11mm 1000 rnds*.
A group of artillerymen—they were stripped to their
baggy maroon pants, but those had a crimson stripe down
the outside of the leg—was manhandling a field gun
onto the flatcar behind, heaving it up a ramp of planks
and lashing the tall iron-shod wheels down to eyebolts
on the deck. Oilcloth covers were strapped over the
muzzle and breech, to keep dust and moisture out of
the mechanism. Near-naked slaves with iron collars
embossed with *Central Rail* were pulling in handcarts
loaded with rations: hardtack, raisins, blocks of goat
cheese, sacks of dried meat, barrels of salt fish. A farrier-
sergeant of the 5th Descott came by leading a string of
riding-dogs on a chain lead snapped to their bridles;
they surged away in wuffling alarm as a locomotive
hooted, and the man clung until his feet were nearly
off the ground.

"Pochita! Fequez! Ye bitches brood, quiet a'down, er
I'll—*sorry, Messer Raj*—"

"Carry on, sergeant."

"—I'll skin yer lousy hides, *quiet* there."

The giant carnivores calmed, but their ears stayed back,
and lips curled away from teeth as long as a man's finger.
Few of the beasts had ever seen a steam engine before,
much less ridden in a train. For that matter, few of the
troopers had either, even the natives of the *Gubernio
Civil*; most of them were countrymen, the cavalry from
border areas or backwaters like Descott County. What
the half-savage westerners he'd brought into the service
thought of it, the Spirit only knew.

A platoon of infantry passed him, rifles at their right
shoulders and blanket rolls over the left. He read their
shoulder-flashes, and gave the officer a salute.

"Glad to have you with me again, 24th Valencia," he
said. "That was good work you did at the siege of East
Residence, and the pursuit."

The lieutenant at their head snapped out his sword and returned the salute with a flourish. The men raised a deep shout of *Raj! Raj!* Some others picked it up, until he waved them to silence. In the relative quiet that followed, he heard a noncom cursing at a fatigue-party:

"Didn't hear t' General tell ye t'stop workin', did ye? Move yer butts! Put yer *backs* inta it."

What with one thing and another, it's probably for the best there's no time to address the men, he thought mordantly.

A speech from the commander was customary before taking the field, but the last thing he needed right now was the inevitable spies—in East Residence they were even thicker than fleas and almost as common as bureaucrats—giving a lurid description of his troops crying him hail. Far too many Governors had started out as popular generals; bought popularity more often than not, but winning battles would do as well. It made any occupant of the Chair suspicious, and usually more comfortable with mediocrities holding the high military ranks.

He looked around at the bustling yard: chaotic, but things were getting done.

"Good work, Muzzaf," he said to the man riding at his side.

The little Komarite looked up from his clipboard; there were dark circles under his eyes. "A matter of times and distances, *solamnti*," he said. "No different from calculating tonnages or profit margins." He grinned. "A pleasure working for a man who understands numbers, at that, my lord. Too few military nobles do."

Few nobles have Center advising them, Raj thought. Aloud: "I say again, good work."

It was that: a formidable bit of organization. Railways had been around for a long time now, but there had never been enough of them, or enough uninterrupted kilometers of line, to move large forces. He'd had enough to do managing the men; Muzzaf had been invaluable once Raj explained the basic idea. This was going to change warfare forever. Not that the railways were that much faster than dogback yet, but they were untiring—and more importantly, they could carry heavy supplies long distances at the same speed as light cavalry, without draft beasts eating up their loads or dying.

And it never hurt to acknowledge when a man did something right, either. Another thing too many nobles did was simply snap their fingers and expect things to fall into place. It was the engineers and administrators that made the Civil Government more than another feudal pigsty.

Muzzaf grinned. "Half of it was your lady's labors," he said. "Without her keeping the patricians off my back . . ." He shrugged meaningfully.

Raj nodded. Suzette Whitehall had been born in East Residence, to fifteen generations of city nobility. Nobody knew how to work the system better. It was one of her manifold talents. *The wonder is she picked a hill-squireen like me*, he thought with a smile. He'd been nothing in particular then, just another land-poor Descotter nobleman making his way in the professionals like his fathers before him.

And where—

"My lady," he said.

She stood with the command group, but she turned quickly at the sound of his voice. Her smile was slight, but it warmed the slanted gray eyes; Horace crouched, and Raj stepped free of the stirrups and bent over her hand. She was in Court walking-out dress, lace skirt split at the front and pinned back to show embroidered leggings, mantilla, the works. It surprised him; he'd expected her traveling gear. Fatima was beside her, carrying a tray with a bottle of Kelden Sparkler and several long-stemmed glasses, each with half a strawberry on its ice-cooled rim.

He reached out a hand—not for the wine, it was too early for him—but for the fruit. She touched his fingers with her folded fan.

"That's ammunition, my knight," she said.

A party of officials was picking their way through the shouting chaos of soldiers and guns and dogs, heading his way. He recognized the Municipal Prefect of East Residence—the Governors didn't allow the city an *alcalle* of its own, knowing the fickleness of an East Residence mob—and he looked deeply unhappy. Raj braced himself.

"*More* time lost," he growled deep in his throat.

Suzette touched him on the arm. "A minute, darling," she said. "I expected this. That's Rahol Himentez, and he had a mob stone his townhouse when the coal ran out one winter. He's had a bee in his breeches about it ever since."

She swept off towards the dignitaries.

"—winter reserves," Raj could hear the Prefect bleating. "And the enemy's on the *Lower* Drangosh, not the Upper—"

But he stopped, and his flunkies with him, milling around as Suzette's soothing voice cut through the plaintive whine.

Beside him, Gerrin Staenbridge chuckled with admiration. "Cut off by the flying squadron, by the Spirit," he said. "Commandeered my mistress to do it, too."

One of the other officers laughed. "Small loss to you," he said. Staenbridge had an eye for handsome youths.

"Well, she *is* the mother of my heir," he pointed out, and cocked an eye toward the civil servants Suzette had intercepted. They were beginning to move back towards the headquarters building, in a sort of Brownian motion gently shepherded by the women.

Raj nodded curtly. "Right, gentlemen," he said to the

circle of battalion commanders; most of them his Companions, all of them veterans. "Now, you've all got your maps?"

They did, although some of the ex-barbarians, Squadrones and Brigaderos, were looking at them a little dubiously. The Civil Government's cartographic service was one of a number of advantages it had had over the Military Governments. Unfortunately, the Colony's mapmakers were just as skillful.

"This campaign," he went on, meeting their eyes, "is what we've been training for these past five years."

"Conquering half the world was a *training exercise*?" Ludwig Bellamy blurted.

Raj nodded, with an expression a stranger might have mistaken for a smile. "No offense, Messers, but we're not fighting barbarians this time. If we hold out a sausage grinder, they're not going to scratch their heads, mutter and then obligingly ram their dicks into it while we turn the crank.

"These are disciplined troops with first-rate equipment, operating closer to their base of supplies than we will be. And they have a first-rate commander; Tewfik ibn'Jamal is nobody's fool. I've fought him twice; lost one, won one—and the time I won, Tewfik had his father Jamal looking over his shoulder and jogging his elbow. Jamal was no commander."

Gerrin nodded. "This time he's got Ali along," he pointed out. His square, handsome face was dark olive, more typical of Descott than Raj's, who had a grandmother from Kelden County in the northwest. "Ali's not only no commander, by all accounts he's a raving bloody lunatic."

"That's our only advantage, and we'll need it. Messers, no mistakes this time. We move fast, and we hit like a hammer. Gerrin, detail two hundred of the 5th to me, and I'll take them ahead on the first train. You'll be rearguard here and come in on the last with the remainder of the battalion."

He held up a hand when the other man began to protest. "I need someone here I can trust to see the plan carried out, Colonel."

"We also serve who only stay and chivvy bureaucrats," Staenbridge said.

"Ludwig," Raj went on. "We're short of rolling stock. I'm giving you the 1st and 2nd Mounted Cruisers" —the former Squadron troops— "and the 3/591, 4/591 and 5/591" —all Brigaderos from the Western Territories— "and you'll follow on dogback. Entrain your baggage, commandeer what remounts you need from the Residence Area pens, and keep to the line of rail. You can pick up supplies at the railstops; nothing on the men but their weapons and personal gear. Understood?"

Ludwig Bellamy slapped one gauntleted fist into the other. "*Si, mi heneral*," he said, his Sponglish as pure as a native Civil Government officer; it even had a hint of a Descott Country rasp.

Nobody would mistake him for an Easterner, though. He stood a finger over Raj's 190 centimeters, and the hair cut in an Army bowl crop was yellow-blond. He'd been the son of a Squadron noble, one who surrendered to Raj to keep his lands. Ludwig had been part of the deal, a hostage for his father's good behavior. He was far more than that now. The man beside him was like enough to be his brother, and was his cousin-in-law; Teodore Welf, former second-in-command of the Brigade.

He tapped his fingers on his sword-hilt; unlike his kinsman by marriage, he kept the shoulder-length hair of a Military Government officer, and wore the basket-hilted longsword of the Brigade rather than an Easterner's saber.

"Good thinking, *mi heneral*," he said. "Some of the men . . ." He shrugged at the shrieking locomotives around them. "Well, they're not used to these modern refinements."

"True, Major Welf," Raj said. *Meaning,* he thought, *that steam engines scare them spitless.* They probably thought they were captive demons. "It'll toughen them up, too. See that they get in some drill with their Armory rifles, Ludwig."

Bellamy tossed his chin upward slightly in affirmation; with a slight start, Raj recognized the gesture as one of his own. *How times change.*

"The Brigaderos can use some hard marching," Ludwig Bellamy said judiciously. Welf shrugged unwilling agreement. "They're good shots and good riders, but a bit soft in the arse."

For that matter, there were plenty of officers in the Civil Government's armies who wouldn't dream of campaigning without half a dozen servants and a wagonload of luxuries.

Not the ones who went to war with Raj Whitehall, though.

"So." Raj turned to the other commanders. "Jorg, you and Ferdihando will bring the 17th Kelden Foot and the 24th Valencia on the next series of trains, right after me and my detachment of the 5th."

Jorg Menyez was a slender balding man, with receding brownish hair and mild blue eyes, red-rimmed as usual. He was violently allergic to dogs, the reason he'd gone into the low-prestige infantry service.

"Infantry first?" he said in mild surprise. He'd shown what foot soldiers could do if properly trained and led, but it was still odd.

"I need reliable men in Sandoral right away," Raj said. "Osterville's in charge there. Dogs aren't the most urgent priority, where dealing with Osterville's the problem."

There were a few snickers. Osterville had been sent to take over in the Southern Territories after the reconquest, when Raj was recalled in not-quite-disgrace. The command of the Fortress and District of Sandoral was quite a comedown. None of the officers who'd been with Raj had supported Osterville, for all that he was one of Barholm's Guards; that was one reason he'd lost the political struggle with Mihwel Berg of the Administrative Service. None of it was likely to make him kindly-disposed toward the *Heneralissimo Supremo*.

Menyez sneezed thoughtfully into a handkerchief. "He's supposed to have twenty thousand men there," he said. "I doubt there's half that fit for duty." Osterville would be drawing the pay of the vacant ranks; it was a common enough scam, if not on quite that scale.

"Five thousand if we're lucky, but that's more than enough to make trouble if Osterville's a mind to," Raj said. *Insane to make trouble with the Colonials over the border*, he thought absently—but he'd seen what jealousy could do to a man's mind. "Which is why I want your riflemen in place."

"*Si, mi heneral.*" Menyez frowned. "How *did* Berg manage to get Osterville canned from that post? Berg's not a bad sort, for a pen-pusher, but Osterville was one of Barholm's Guards, after all."

Raj shrugged. "He's pretty sure I did it," he said. "Spirit knows why. In any case, we'll cross Messer Osterville when we come to him. Movement: after Colonel Menyez, the remainder of the cavalry," he went on, listing the battalions. "Any questions?"

Kaltin Gruder, the commander of the 7th Descott Rangers, shrugged his heavy shoulders. Pale scars stood out against the olive tan of his face.

"*No problemo, mi heneral,*" he said. "Thrashing the

wogboys has its attractions; the looting's good and I like the smell of harem girls."

Raj clenched his teeth for a moment. There were times when the task of restoring civilization on Bellevue was like pushing a boulder up a greased slope. Gruder was a professional; he wasn't supposed to be thinking like a MilGov barbarian noble or an enlisted man . . . then he caught the grin and answered it.

I talk to Center too much, he thought. *Angels have no sense of humor, it seems.*

The cool irony that touched the back of his mind was wordless, but it communicated none the less.

"Colonel Dinnalsyn, you'll space the guns out between the battalions. One last thing: we've a new issue of splatguns." There were exclamations of delight; the rapid-fire multibarreled guns were the first new weapon the Civil Government had adopted in a hundred twenty years. Raj had had them run up in the Kolobassian armories on his own authority—to Center's designs.

"Four per battalion. Remember they're infantry weapons, not guns; push them forward, and we'll give the Colonials some of the grief their repeaters and pom-poms do to us. If that's all, then, we'll get under way."

The Companions slapped fists in a pyramid of arms. "Hell or plunder, dog-brothers."

Gerrin Staenbridge watched the tall figure of the General ride away. "As I remember it, wasn't Lady Anne Clerett the one who dropped a word about Osterville in our Sovereign Mighty Lord's ear? I wonder who talked to *her*?"

They all looked in Suzette's direction. Staenbridge grinned. "Behind every great man . . ." he quoted.

"You know, Messers," he went on, drawing on his gauntlets, "I was with Messer Raj back when he took command of the 5th in the El Djem business, south of Komar. Only five years . . . and that one man has changed the world—and changed himself."

"Haven't we all," Kaltin Gruder said, touching the long scars on his face. The Colonist shrapnel that had carved those furrows had killed his younger brother, on Raj Whitehall's first independent campaign. "Haven't we all."

CHAPTER FIVE

"Damned hot," Tejan M'Brust said, using an end of his neckerchief to wipe his face.

"No shit," Ludwig Bellamy replied.

He reined aside to the verge of the road, his dog stepping wearily over the ditch and hanging its head, panting, under the shade of a plane tree.

The troopers' dogs were panting too, a massed sound like hundreds of wheezing bellows as they rode by in column of fours. A knee-high fog of dust rose from the crushed rock surface of the road; he sneezed and hawked and spat to one side. The Descotter followed suit and offered him a canteen, water with vinegar. It cut the gummy saliva and dust nicely. Bellamy drank and watched the 1st and 2nd Mounted Cruisers go by, the dogs at a fast ambling walk. Both units were under strength—they'd paid a substantial butcher's bill in the Western Territories and hadn't had time to recruit back to full roster yet—but they shaped well, to his critical eye. A few were even talking or joking as they rode, though most slumped a little, reins in one hand and eyes fixed on the rump of the dog ahead. The unit dressing was crisp, though.

"They're shaping better than the Brigaderos," M'Brust said, echoing his thought. "I don't think there's a regular cavalry unit better, my oath I don't. Not even the 5th Descott."

Ludwig nodded, grinning tiredly. His people, the

Squadron, were accounted wilder than the Brigade; they'd come down from the Base Area later, and the Southern Territories they'd conquered had been a backwater. But these battalions had been longer under Messer Raj's discipline and were first-rate material to begin with, once they had childish notions about charging with cold steel knocked out of them.

For a moment the skin between his shoulders crawled, as he remembered the Squadron host advancing into volley-fire and massed artillery. The chanting, the waving banners, the sun bright on a hundred thousand swords . . . and Raj Whitehall waiting, his men a thin blue line looking as fragile and ordered as a snowflake by comparison. Waiting, then raising his sword and chopping it downward. . . .

He shook it off, removed his helmet and let the air dry his sweat-damp hair. To their left the land rose in rocky hills, dry and shimmering with heat in the summer sun. To the right were gentle slopes, citrus orchards, and then open grain-fields with peons bending over their sickles as they reaped. The dusty yellow of the wheat was like flashes of gold through the glossy green leaves of the fruit trees. More to the point, between road and orchards passed a rock-lined irrigation channel, and a slow current of water. It was dry and intensely hot here in the southern foothills of the Oxheads—the land was sloping down toward the sand deserts of the borderlands—and the sight and sound of the water was intoxicating. He squinted at the sun, then remembered to take out his watch and click open the cover; in the Southern Territories, even wealthy nobles hadn't carried them. There was no point; nobody needed to know the time that precisely, and they were impossible to keep repaired, anyway.

Civilization. "Benter," he said to the younger brother who was his aide. "Twenty minutes. Water the dogs."

He turned and heeled his dog westwards down the line of march; behind him the cool brassy notes of the trumpet sounded, and the signalers of each company passed it back. When it reached the rear of the column the last unit halted first—you had to do it that way, or the whole mass would collide with each other, like a drunken centipede. His lips quirked at the memory of his father trying to halt a mass of Squadron warriors on the move, back when he was a boy. *That* had taken the better part of an hour, even with the paid, full-time fighters of the household guard.

The three Cruiser battalions of ex-Brigaderos were full strength . . . except for their stragglers. Teodore Welf rode up, red in the face from the heat and from embarrassment.

"Major Bellamy," he said, saluting.

"Major Welf," Ludwig replied, glancing past him.

They spoke Sponglish, although the Squadron and Brigade dialects of Namerique were fairly close: regulations, and it was best to stay in the habit, since more than half the officers in their units were seconded Civil Government natives like M'Brust.

Men and dogs had collapsed in the road. Others were leading their animals from the wayside to the ditch, walking slowly with their legs straddled. A few had trotted over despite their saddle sores and lay with their heads and shoulders buried in the life-giving coolness. Ludwig frowned and jerked his head toward them.

Teodore cursed and drew his sword, spurring to the ditch. "Up and out of there, you slugs!" he shouted. The flat of the weapon whacked down on shoulders. "Purify it first, damn your arse! You can't fight with the runs!"

The soldiers stood, dripping. Officers rode up, as dust-caked as their men, and the troopers formed lines. Some led the dogs downstream; others scooped their canteens full and added the blessed purifying chlorine powder; it was a rite shared by the Spirit of Man of This Earth cult they followed and the Star Church of the Civil

Government, but not all commanders were equally pious. Messer Raj insisted on the full canonical treatment— water for human drinking to be purified by powder or by ten minutes at a hard rolling boil, with no exceptions.

The Spirit favored him for it, too. It wasn't uncommon for armies in the field to lose five men to dysentery for every one killed in combat. That didn't happen to troops under Raj's command.

Welf trotted back. "Sorry, Ludwig," he said. "The Western Territories aren't this hot."

Ludwig nodded. The Western Territories were damned cold and rainy, to his way of thinking—his own ancestors had plowed through them on their way to the southern side of the Midworld Sea, and he was glad of it. Of course, even the Western Territories were warm and dry compared to the Base Area, which explained why the Brigade had stopped there; they'd been the first of the Military Governments to pull up stakes and move south.

"And your fine gentlemen aren't used to sweating this hard," he replied, smiling to take the sting out of it.

"True enough," Welf said. He flexed the arm that had been broken by a Civil Government bullet outside Old Residence, nearly two years ago. "I'd never have dared drive them this hard, back . . . well, back then."

Ludwig nodded. Even the troopers had been nobles of a sort back home, with a few hundred hectares and peons to do the work. Of course, that had its compensations: plenty of leisure to practice and hunt. So they were fine riders, and mostly good shots. The Brigade had armed its men with muzzle loaders, but rifled percussion muskets, not the flintlock smoothbores that had been the best his people could make or maintain.

"How's my fair cousin?" Teodore went on.

"Marie? Still pregnant, according to the last letter," Ludwig said. "Thank the Spirit. Otherwise she'd be trying to outdo Messa Whitehall and riding with us."

Teodore shuddered elaborately. He turned to watch a dog-cart creak up, loaded with sunstruck Cruisers, their dogs on leading-ropes behind. "Throw some water on those!" he ordered.

Ludwig put his helmet back on. The leather-backed chainmail of the pentail thumped on his neck, and sweat from the sponge-and-cork lining ran into his hair and down his cheeks, greasy and stale.

"I'm beginning to wish we'd taken the train," he said.

"Getting there's half the fun," Teodore replied, blinking red-rimmed blue eyes.

A trainload of artillery began to pull out of the East Residence station, guns and men riding on flatcars, the draft dogs in boxcars farther back from the engine. As soon as it cleared the switchpoint, the remainder of the 5th Descott jogged forward, breaking into platoons as they swarmed into the last two trains.

"Alo sinstra, waymanos!" *By the left, forward march.* Ten minutes, and the final platoon was loaded into its boxcar.

Gerrin Staenbridge looked around. "The last?" he said.

Muzzaf Kerpatik looked just as exhausted as he did. "The very last, *mi colonel*," he said.

Staenbridge ran a hand over his chin, the sword-calluses rasping against the blueblack stubble. "Hard to believe." *Sleep. Razors. Food.* He didn't believe in those anymore, either.

Some sort of Palace flunky-in-uniform was wading toward him over the tracks and the litter of the three-day emergency. They'd been operating in battle mode: throw anything that breaks or isn't needed out of the way and think about cleaning up later. That included a fair bit of broken-down rolling stock, as well as dead dogs, dead draft oxen, about fifty tons of coal that had spilled in odd spots and wasn't worth the time and effort of collecting, and spare gear. Central Rail stevedore-slaves, dockworkers, and press-ganged clerks lay about in various stages of collapse.

But no soldiers. Every man, dog, gun, and round of ammunition was on its way east. *Spirit of man, I could sleep for a week.*

If that flunky meant what he thought it did—another message from some hysterical fool in the Palace who wanted his hand held—he'd be *talking* for a week. The people up on the First Hill hadn't grown any less terrified of Ali over the last couple of days, and they were still given to brainstorms, most of which started and ended with keeping more troops around to protect their own precious personal fundaments. If he'd wanted to listen to bleating, he would have stayed at home on the family estate and herded sheep.

"See you in Sandoral," he said to the little Komarite, and ran for the second train.

It was moving as he clamped his saber hand on an iron bracket and swung up onto the rear platform. This car had been tacked on at the last minute; it was the type used to carry railroad company guards through bandit country, with bunks and a cookstove inside. He'd found it parked on a siding, and be damned if he wasn't going to keep it all to himself; that way he'd stand some chance of getting a little sleep in the fifty hours or so it would take to get to Sandoral. There was some hardtack and dried sausage in his duffel—

The smell of curry startled him as he opened the rear door of the guardcar; his stomach growled a reminder of how long it had been since he ate. Fatima cor Staenbridge—the *cor* meant freedwoman—glanced around from the little stove.

"Ready in a minute, Gerrin," she said.

He opened his mouth to roar, thought better of it, and sat down, sighing and unbuckling his sword belt.

My own damned fault. He'd rescued the girl during the sack of El Djem more or less on impulse; rather, she'd picked Barton Foley to rescue her from a gang of Descotter troopers bent on gang rape, and he'd helped out. He'd *kept* her on impulse, too; Barton had needed some experience with women—a nobleman had to marry and carry on his line eventually, whatever his personal tastes. She'd managed to keep up in the nightmare retreat through the desert, after Tewfik mousetrapped them, which demanded some respect; she'd also gotten pregnant—whether by him or Barton was a moot point and no matter—which was more than the wife he visited once a year for duty's sake had managed to do.

"Imp," he said.

She stuck out her tongue at him and handed him the plate. *Spirit, she's still only twenty.* He'd freed her, of course, and acknowledged the child—two, now—his wife hadn't objected at all, since by Civil Government law he could divorce her for not giving him an heir. The children had to stay with her back on the estate most of the time after they were weaned, of course, as was fitting.

He began shoveling down the fiery curry, washing it down with water and a surprisingly drinkable red. Drinkable compared to ration issue, that was. *And to think I was accounted a gourmet once,* he thought. Polo, hunting, balls, theater, fine uniforms and parades and good restaurants, handsome youths, witty conversation . . . surprising how little he'd missed them, in the five years since Raj Whitehall had been given command of the 5th Descott and sent out to teach the wogs not to raid the Civil Government borders.

I resented him then, he mused. Gerrin had been senior . . . but he'd needed a commander to bring out his best. A furious perfection of willpower possessed Raj; Gerrin could recognize it without in the least desiring to have it himself. *And it's never been boring.* Back then, he'd been so bored he'd fiddled the battalion accounts out of sheer ennui.

He finished the plate. Fatima was sitting on the edge of the bunk, eyes demurely cast down; a good imitation of humility. *What an actress. The stage lost something when she was born Colonial.* Natural talent, he supposed, plus being hand-in-glove with Suzette Whitehall in her impressionable years.

Gerrin sighed again. As far as he was concerned, sex with women was like eating plain boiled rice without butter or salt—possible, but . . . *On the other hand.* A soldier learned to make do with what was at hand; when all you had was boiled rice, that was what you ate.

The mournful sound of the locomotive whistle echoed through the night. It was evening, and twilight was falling over the rolling hills of the Upper Hemmar River. To their right the last sunlight glittered on the surface of the river below, like a ribbon of hammered silver tracing its way through the darkening fields. The same light caught the three-meter wings of a pterosauroid as it soared over the water, gilding the naked skin and the short plush white fur of its body. Higher, the hills were dusty-green with olive trees, or carpeted with vines in their summer lushness. Terraced fields of barley were brown-gold on the lower slopes; cypresses and eucalyptus lined the dusty white streaks of roadway and surrounded the whitewashed adobe of villas.

Raj looked up from the maps. Center could provide better, holographic projections with all the information you needed, but he'd been raised with paper and it still had something the visions lacked. His father had taught him to read maps, going around Hillchapel—the Whitehall family estate, back in Smythe Parish, Descott County—with compass and the Ordinance Survey, until he learned to see the ground and the markings as one.

"*Sentahvo* for your thoughts, my heart," Suzette said.

She had her *gittar* in her lap, gently plucking at the strings.

"Thinking about Descott, and Hillchapel," Raj said. "Damn, but it's been a long time since we've seen it."

Suzette nodded. She'd fitted in surprisingly well; if she considered it a bleak stone barn in the middle of a wilderness, she'd never said so. Well, compared to East Residence, that was what it was; a kerosene lamp was a luxury, in Descott. Most of the County was upland volcanic wilderness, thin forest and thinner stony pasture where you needed ten hectares to feed a sheep. Bandit country too, and bad for killer sauroids.

He missed it.

"This is as domestic as we get, I'm afraid," Suzette said lightly.

Raj glanced around the railroad car. It had been fitted with table and chairs; there was a commode behind a blanket screen, a couple of skins of wine-and-water hanging from the wall, a lantern overhead, and a box of field rations—Suzette's version, and a vast improvement on Army issue. One of his aides was snoring on the floor.

In a car behind, the troopers were singing—they probably thought of it as singing, at least—in a roaring chorus:

> *"We're marchin' on relief over burnin' desert sands*
> *Six hundred fightin' Descotters, t' Colonel, an' t'band*
> *Ho! Git awa', ye bullock-man—ye've heard t'bugle blowed*
> *The Fightin' Fifth is comin', down the Drangosh Road—"*

"We're luckier than they are," Suzette said, lifting her head and looking off into the gathering night. "We're together, at least. . . . Their women have to sit and wonder. And every time someone rides up to the farmhouse door

it might be a messenger with a bundled rifle and saber
that's all they'll see of a lost husband, or a son."

"It's not much of a married life I've given you," Raj
said.

Suzette smiled at him. "I wouldn't exchange it for any
other," she replied. "I don't think you're one of those
who're allowed to have a normal life, anyway."

"Not yet, at least," Raj said. *Never*, went unspoken
between them.

It wasn't as if Barholm would give Raj an honored
retirement, even, as a reward for victory.

i have found it unwise to use the term never,
Center said.

Suzette's fingers strummed the *gittar* again. Raj pulled
the greatcoat around his shoulders and let his head fall
back. *Just a moment*, he thought. *A moment's rest.*

"*Git* yer arses out offen t'floor," the sergeant barked.
"We'll be there anytimes."

Corporal Robbi M'Telgez blinked awake.

"Jist when I waz gittin' t'hang a sleepin' on these things,"
he said mournfully, picking straw out of his hair and
yawning in the hot close darkness of the boxcar, thick
with the smell of sweat.

The train was slowing, swaying more from side to side.
All around was the flat irrigated plain of the Upper
Drangosh. M'Telgez put his eye to the slats in the boxcar;
it was good-looking country, dry but fit to sprout shoelaces
where there was water. The wheat and barley were in,
the fields being plowed for a summer crop of corn or
millet; cotton and sugarcane and indigo were all well
up, and there were orchards in plenty as well, mostly
dates and citrus.

Good land fer the gentry, hell on farmers, he thought
idly. Rich land meant poor men to work it; they'd all be
peons around here. *Hotter n' blazes, too.*

They passed through a belt of country places, retreats for rich cityfolk built in an open, airy style that looked indecent somehow compared with the foursquare solidity of the houses he was accustomed to—but then, Descott was a long way north of this, and highland country too. He didn't suppose it got cold here even in winter. Then there were shanties on both sides of the rail line, crude booths of straw and reeds. He swore softly when he saw who was in them, besides refugee peasants from the countryside. Among them were men in Civil Government uniforms, only infantry, but still . . . they looked *hungry*.

"Ain't they supposed to pay 'em when they calls 'em in from t'farms?" he said.

The troop sergeant laughed sourly. "Wuz ye born yesstiday, M'Telgez?"

Trooper Smeet put his eye to a crack. "Good's a place t' croak as any," he said mournfully. "We'll a' git kilt, ye know. I hadda dream—"

The rest of the platoon threw bits of hardtack and cold bacon-rind and anything else handy.

"Ye keep sayin' thayt long 'nuff, it'll happen, yer bastid," M'Telgez said disgustedly.

Smeet grinned; he was missing his two front teeth, and his face was a brown wrinkled map of twenty years' service. "Ye knows a way 't live ferever, loik?"

Just inside the city walls the train screeched to a stop; he braced himself against the planking and shaded his eyes as the doors were thrown open.

"*Come* on," the sergeant yelled again.

The boxcars emptied rapidly, the men stretching, the dogs barking with hysterical relief. It was just as hot outside, with the dry baking heat that he remembered from the first campaign down here five years ago, but at least you could breathe in the open. M'Telgez unsnapped the lead-chain of his mount and spent a moment soothing her.

"Sooo, quiet now, Pochita, ye bitch," he said. A tongue the size of a washcloth and rough as industrial abrasive lapped at his face. "Quiet—down, girl."

Out of the corner of his eye he could see Messer Raj and the company commander and the captain in charge of the Scouts—M'lewis and his Forty Thieves were along, best to double-strap your pouch—talking earnestly. He worked faster, sliding his rifle into the scabbard at the right front of his saddle, tightening the girth and breast-straps, checking the neck-bandolier and the fastening on the saber hanging from the other side. He slid the blade free a handspan and tested the edge, then checked the loads on the revolver he had tucked into one boot-top.

Messer Raj would have a job of work for them to do, and no mistake. He'd been in the 5th Descott for five years now, and that was one thing you could rely on.

"Nice to be loved," Barton Foley said.

"Not when they get in the way," Raj replied.

They rode at the head of the column, slowly. Cheering civilians packed the sidewalks, hysteria in their voices. Rose petals and rice showered down on the troops, as if they were a party of groomsmen bringing a bride home from her father's house. Individuals darted out to offer bottles of wine to the soldiers or, even more dangerous, food to the dogs. *What do they think's going to happen when they stick a roast in a war-dog's face?* Raj thought, turning in the saddle to see one of the crowd reeling back and clutching a gashed-open forearm. The crowd-stink was as palpable as the blurring waves of heat that radiated back from the whitewashed adobe of the buildings and soaked the uniform coat beneath his armpits.

The noise was spooking *all* the dogs, a solid roar between the whitewashed, blank-walled, flat-roofed houses.

"Trumpeter!" Raj snarled. "Sound *Draw.*"

The sharp notes cut through the white-noise background of the crowd, as they were designed to cut through the clamor of battle. Two hundred hands slapped down on the saber hilts slung to the offside of their saddles; two hundred blades came free in a single slithering rasp, then flashed as they were brought back to rest over the shoulder. The dogs knew the calls as well as the men, and they snarled in unison, a chilling bass rumble. Long wet fangs glistened, each backed by half a ton of carnivore. War-dogs were bred for aggressiveness and trained to kill, and the bristling snake-headed posture of these indicated they were perfectly ready to do just that.

The crowd screamed and surged away; there would be deaths in the trampling . . . but not nearly as many as there would be if Ali sacked the city, which was what was going to happen if they kept getting in his way. Overhead, doors slammed shut as the wrought-iron balconies emptied. Raj heeled Horace into a trot; the bugler signaled again, and the whole column rocked into motion behind him. The iron wheels of the splatgun battery clattered behind them.

"Well, that'll make us less popular, *mi heneral*," Baron said.

"Popularity be damned," Raj replied, feeling some of the tension drain out of his shoulders.

They broke into the *Plaza Real*, the square that formed the center of all Civil Government cities. The usual buildings fronted it: the Star Temple with its gilded dome, the arcaded Government House, the townhouses of wealthy landowners and merchants . . . and the cavalry barracks, conveniently to hand in case of trouble. Highly unusual were the tents and shanties that had gone up all over the square, crowding right up to the ornamental fountain and gardens in its center; the sour smoke of their cooking fires lingered, and the stink of an overloaded sewer system.

"Refugees," Raj said grimly. "Must be fifty or sixty thousand of them inside the walls."

"Sandoral has fifty thousand people in normal times," Suzette said. "With that many more . . ."

Raj nodded. "We'll definitely have to do something about that."

They drew rein before the barracks, a series of two-story buildings connected by walls and iron-grille gates, enclosing a central parade ground. They smelled even worse than the rest of the city, not just the inevitable aroma of dogshit that was inescapable where cavalry were stationed, but the fetid stink of overcrowding and neglect. They *looked* neglected—gates awry, stucco flaking in damp patches from the walls. But with the units as under strength as his intelligence had it, they shouldn't be crowded—and washing was hanging from the windows, women and children too numerous for camp followers leaning out and pointing, or lounging in the doorways.

"Captain Foley," Raj said. "Dismount the men, rifles, and a watchstander and troop here. Then accompany me, if you please."

The bugle sang. The men sheathed their sabers and pulled the Armory rifles out of the scabbards. Another call, and the dogs sank to a crouch; the men stepped free of the stirrups and bent to loop their reins over the hitching rail and watering trough that lined the plaza side of the garrison buildings. A long clicking sounded as they loaded their weapons; the 5th Descott didn't carry guns for show, and when they made a threat they meant it.

An officer came out of the main gate, fastening his sword belt. Raj ran an eye over him: thirty or so, but with an older man's belly straining against the sash and belt, unshaven, the blue uniform coat stained under the armpits. He didn't expect soldiers to waste time trying to look strack in the field, but in garrison keeping neat reminded them that they *were* soldiers; it was a sign of self-respect. They had running water here, for the Spirit's sake! And every eight-man section of cavalry troopers was allowed one soldier's servant to handle routine fatigues.

Also an officer should set an example.

Just about what I expected, in short, Raj thought, a cold anger tightening its hand under his breastbone. He returned the stranger's salute.

"Captain Hamelio Pinochet, 47th Santanner Dragoons," the man said.

"*Heneralissimo* Raj Whitehall," Raj replied. "I'm here to take command, Captain."

The unfortunate officer swallowed, attempting to brace to attention. "Ah, *mi heneral*, you'll understand, with the emergency and the refugees—"

"I understand perfectly, Captain." With housing at a premium, somebody had seen the profit potential in renting out the military's spare space. "Lead on."

Milling civilians looked at them curiously as they walked through the long barracks halls; each had space for a hundred men's cots, with rooms for the lieutenants and a suite for the company commander, plus a ready room and mess. Right now they were crowded with twice that number or more of refugees; from their clothes, well enough off to be making a fortune for whoever was running this scam. A swelling murmur ran through them as Raj passed. By the time they reached the buildings still in military use, it had preceded them a little; enough for protesting feminine squeals to be fading as women were hustled out of the barracks, and for the soldiers to have made emergency repairs. Not *much* in the way of repairs. Gear was piled in heaps all over the floors, few of the men were in full uniform, and there were still cards and dice lying in some corners. The troopers stood braced at the foot of their cots, visibly willing their vital functions to cease.

Raj ignored them for a moment. Instead he stripped a rifle out of the rack by the locker at the head of a cot and worked the action. "No rust here, at least," he said mildly. Then:

"Captain Pinochet, how many men are on muster here? You're rated at four battalions." Twenty-four hundred men or so, in theory.

"Ah . . . about one thousand, sir. Most of the officers aren't, ah . . ."

"Present at the moment, yes," Raj said. "Fall the men in, if you please, Captain."

Raj crossed his arms and waited while the bugles rang. It took a very long time for the garrison troops to sort out their equipment. *Starless Dark knows what shape the infantry's in,* he thought with a mental wince. This was the elite cavalry.

"Ten'*hut.*"

The noncom's bark brought the men to a ragged attention as Raj strode out; the banner of the 5th Descott was at his back, and his personal blazon. The two companies of the 5th tramped out at the double, and fell in at his back with the smooth economy of endless practice, the uniform crash of their hobnails sounding across the drillground and echoing back from the barracks and stables that ringed it.

Raj waited for a minute. "Men," he said at last, "I'm going to keep this short and sweet."

He pointed over his shoulder. "There's a bloody great wog army coming up the Drangosh; they're about five days' march that way. I've got troops coming in from the west, but we're going to need every man who can ride and shoot. That means *you.* Every soldier, that is. I'll be back in a few hours, and I expect to see you looking and acting like soldiers by then." He paused again.

"Captain Pinochet, please send runners to the remaining

battalion officers of this command. You may inform them that any man holding the Governor's commission not present when I return may consider himself dismissed from the service." He turned his head to the bugler. "Sound *dismissed to quarters.*"

The garrison left much more quickly than they'd assembled. Raj nodded once, tapping a thumb against his chin. "I think they're getting the message," he said. "Now for Osterville."

Antin M'lewis was muttering under his breath. Raj knew the song without needing to hear words or tunes: it was an old Army ditty whose chorus went *Lovely loot/ That's the thing makes the boys git up an' shoot!*

Commandant Osterville's house was a looter's dream. The outer gates were gilded wrought iron, the inner Zanj ebony studded with miniature silver sauroid heads. A chandelier of Kolobassian crystal hung overhead, to light the three-story atrium. Floor and sweeping staircases were of marble; the walls held gilt-framed mirrors and paintings; man-high alabaster urns held trailing bougainvillea . . . Punkahs swayed, moving air cooled by fountains playing over fretted stone and scented by orange-blossom.

The majordomo bowed himself out of the way—a plump eunuch with a Colonial accent. *Poor bastard can't help it,* Raj thought; but they always put his teeth on edge. Osterville had put on weight and lost a lot of hair since Raj had seen him last. He'd always been ambitious, and Capital-smooth; now he had a sour pinch to his mouth and lines between there and his nostrils. Which were turned up as if at a bad smell. There was a crowd of hangers-on by him, aides and flunkies and the battalion commanders of the garrison.

"Whitehall," Osterville said frigidly. "What the devil do you think you're doing, coming in here and giving orders outside the chain of command?"

There was a murmur of indignation from the flunkies; but the battalion commanders stayed stony-silent, with a slight unconscious withdrawal, as if Osterville had something contagious. Raj gave them a swift glance. None of them had been living on their pay here—not with Osterville's example before them, not if Abdullah's reports were true—but they didn't love the Commandant for it. Especially not now that their careers and lives were on the line.

Raj reached into his jacket. "Commandant Osterville. By Gubernatorial Rescript, I have been given command of all Civil Government troops in this area. I hereby notify you that I am assuming control."

Osterville read through the note. "I acknowledge your overall authority," he said after a moment.

Raj could see the wheels turning behind the narrow black eyes. *Whitehall's in disfavor. Even if he wins, he'll be removed.*

"But this document does *not* give you authority to interfere in the internal command structure of the units under my authority as district commandant. You may give your orders to me, and I will carry them out as I see fit."

Divided command . . . Behind Raj, the Scout Troop—the Forty Thieves—tensed; they hadn't followed the exchange, not really, but they could read the hostility in the air well enough.

M'lewis had recruited the Scouts himself. None of them were men likely to hesitate if ordered to arrest the Commandant . . . or to take him and the others out back and shoot them, if it came to that. Osterville looked past Raj and his complexion turned a muddy gray.

Disaster, Raj knew. A good chance of a firefight right here in the city, or at least wholesale passive resistance by the garrison troops. This mission balanced on a knife edge as it was . . .

. . . and Osterville wouldn't back down. Not openly; whatever else the man was, he wasn't that type of coward.

Suzette moved forward. "Hernan, Hernan," she said, tapping him on the arm with her fan. "Last time I was in Sandoral there were more interesting things than a lot of smelly soldiers." She wrinkled her nose. "Don't tell me you've become a *complete* provincial out here, my dear. And you were such a gay blade back in the City." When someone in the Civil Government put a capital on it that way, only one city could be meant.

Osterville bowed over her hand.

"*I've* been trapped on a troop train for three days. Couldn't you find a decent meal for a poor, benighted gentlewoman so far from home? And fill me in on what passes for society out here? *And* find me a decent bath and somewhere to change out of these *impossible* clothes?"

Osterville was giving a good impression of a man who had just been struck between the eyes with a bag full of wet sand, but he rallied; after all, he *had* been at Court for the better part of a decade.

"Enchanted, Messa," he said suavely. "Business, however . . ."

Suzette made a dismissive gesture. "Oh, Raj just wants some help unloading trains." She tucked her hand under his arm. "Please?"

Osterville snapped his fingers at an aide. "Luiz, draw that up; here, I'll sign it. Certainly, certainly, my dear Messa Suzette . . . trains, you say? Logistics, clerks' work."

Raj stood silently as they strolled away across the intaglio floor. His head moved back to the officers who'd been attending Osterville, with the smooth tracking motion of a track-mounted fortress gun.

"Messers," he said flatly. "I remind you that you'll be needed with your units later this afternoon in the main

cavalry barracks. Good day to you. Captain M'lewis, if
you please."

He turned on his heel. Faintly, he could hear:

". . . quite acceptable dessert wines, but far too sweet
for table. But I've found a mountain vintage from this
village in the Oxheads . . ."

CHAPTER SIX

The City Offices of Sandoral were nearly as crowded as the barracks, although they smelled of musty paper and lamp-soot and ink rather than sewage and dogshit. Clerks in knee breeches and dirty ruffled shirts were running in all directions, waving papers in the air; abacuses clicked; wheeled carts full of folders of documents rumbled over the tiled floors of the corridors. There were petitioners in plenty about, too. The clamor died as Raj shouldered through; the forty troopers of the 5th tramping behind him with their rifles at port, bayonets fixed, were a stark reminder of why Sandoral was in an emergency in the first place.

Raj strongly suspected that most of the bureaucrats would continue to think of it as a tiresome interruption of routine right up until the Settler's troops came over the wall.

Civilization, he thought sourly, watching one man blink at him through thick lenses, fingers pausing on the counting stones. *The sacred trust I defend. The reason I obey purblind idiots.*

They clattered up a broad stairway; the upper corridor was considerably less crowded, a condition enforced by several slope-browed men with cudgels. All of whom sensibly faded into doorways at the sight of the naked steel and harsh uniform clatter of hobnails.

"You can't go in there! That's Chief Commissioner Kirmedez's—"

"Siddown," M'lewis snarled at the functionary. The man sat.

Kirmedez looked up from his desk as Raj entered. He was a thin dark man with receding hair, dressed plainly with a simple cravat. His eyes widened slightly as he took in Raj and the soldiers behind him; he rose and bowed.

"*Heneralissimo,*" he said politely. "How may I serve you?"

Raj took the measure of the man. *Honest,* he thought, *for a wonder.*

oversimplification, Center said, **but a valid approximation.** A grid snapped onto the administrator's face, with mottled patterns showing heat and the dilation of his pupils. **proceed.**

It was impossible to lie to Raj Whitehall . . . with an angel looking out through his eyes. He didn't like it, but it was useful, and he'd use any tool to get the job done.

Anything at all.

"Messer Kirmedez," Raj said, "Sandoral will be under siege by the Colonials within two weeks maximum. Possibly less."

Kirmedez sat and tapped the piles of documents on his desk. "*Heneralissimo,* this city cannot stand siege. We're grossly overcrowded, and the grain reserves are low."

Raj nodded. By law, a fortified border town like this was supposed to keep a year's reserve of basic foodstuffs, in return for remission of some taxes. He didn't need to ask what had happened to it.

"Exactly, Messer. I'm therefore evacuating all civilians to East Residence."

Kirmedez's hard thin face went fluid with shock for an instant. "That's impossible."

Raj allowed himself a flat smile. "On the contrary.

Anyone who leaves on their own feet—or on dogback or in a carriage or by ox wagon—can take whatever they wish to carry. But whenever a troop train gets in, and I expect them at four-hour intervals, the garrison is going to sweep up enough people to fill it for the return trip. There will be absolutely no exceptions. Messer Commissioner, you'd also better inform the citizens immediately, because the first twelve hundred will be leaving in about two hours on the train that brought me. Is that understood?"

Kirmedez closed his mouth. He stared at Raj for a full thirty seconds, then looked at the feral faces of the Descotter gunmen behind him.

"You mean it," he said softly.

"I'm not in the habit of making empty threats, Messer," Raj said, equally quiet.

Kirmedez nodded.

The door was open, and the word had spread swiftly. A roar sounded through the offices, shading up into a hysterical wail. Kirmedez rose and reached for a brass bell on his desk, but Raj put out one hand.

"Captain," he said to M'lewis.

The Scout commander turned and barked an order. The column in the corridor outside turned and brought their rifles up in a single smooth jerk.

"Fwego!"

BAM. The volley slammed into the lath and plaster of the ceiling. Chunks and dust rained down on the faces of those who'd come out of their offices, and down the open stairwell onto the crowd below.

"Reload!"

Silence fell amid the *ping* of spent brass landing on the tiles and the metallic clatter of rounds being thumbed home and levers worked. Gray-white gunsmoke drifted down the hall and carried the stink of burnt sulfur.

Silence fell. Kirmedez's bell sounded through it. "Back

to work, if you please," he called. "Messer Hantonio, step in here. We have a great deal to do."

He nodded thanks to Raj. "And they'll take it seriously, too. Good day to you, *Heneralissimo*."

Raj raised an eyebrow; it wasn't often you met an administrator with that firm a grip on reality.

"*Bwenya Dai*," he replied politely.

And the bureaucrat was right. There was a great deal to do, fortunately. You could forget a lot, when you had work on hand.

Chief Commissioner Kirmedez snapped his fingers impatiently. "Stop babbling, man!" His assistant fell silent.

"It doesn't *matter* if it's impossible; it has to be done anyway. Now, send out the criers. But first, send runners to all the following households."

He handed over a list. The assistant whistled. "My apologies, *patron*," he said. "I should have thought of that."

Kirmedez nodded. "Hantonio, when this war is over, I will still be Chief Commissioner of Sandoral and District, whoever is Commandant. Those men will still be wealthy and powerful. And they will remember who gave them advanced warning to gather their personal possessions and their households for evacuation."

The assistant smiled with genuine admiration.

Kirmedez smiled back. "Favors are the grease that let the civil service wheels turn, Hantonio. Never forget it."

And Heneralissimo Supremo Whitehall has done me a favor, he thought, pausing briefly. *I wonder if he realizes it?*

"Jorg!" Raj called, pleasure in his voice.

Jorg Menyez pulled up his riding steer. It lowed, then swung a long brass-tipped horn down in Horace's face. The hound whuffled and reconsidered the grab it had been thinking of making at the long-legged riding animal's shank.

"Just in," the infantry commander said.

Behind him a column of footsoldiers poured down the street, shouldering the milling civilians aside; this time they were trying their best to get out of the way, not blocking the road with their welcome. The furled colors of the 17th Kelden Foot went by, to the steady *thrip . . . thrip* of the drum.

"The heliograph says Gerrin just boarded the last train out of East Residence, and Bellamy and his trained barbs are making good time, should be here in three days maximum."

"Spirit," Raj said, mildly surprised. "It's actually working."

Both men spat to their left and made the sign of the horns with their sword-hands; Raj touched his amulet, a circuit board blessed by Saint Wu herself a century before.

"You've seen where the infantry are kenneled?" Jorg said, anger flushing his fair-skinned face.

Raj nodded. "Think they'll be fit for anything?"

"Nothing complex, but we may be able to put some backbone into them," Jorg said. "They ought to enjoy the first part of the plan, anyway. Any trouble with Osterville?"

"No," Raj said.

Menyez hesitated, then let the bitten-off syllable stand.

The barracks-yard was far more crowded this time; all the cavalry, the ragged ill-kept lines of the infantry units, the two hundred of the 5th Descott beside Raj, and the neat formations of the 17th Kelden and 24th Valencia to either side. The sun was sinking behind the western edge of the barracks; Raj narrowed his eyes against it, seeing only the black silhouettes of the troops.

"Fellow soldiers," Raj said.

Of a sort. It wasn't these men's fault that they'd been badly commanded, but he didn't intend to let the consequences keep him from carrying out the mission. A lot of them were going to pay with their lives for their officers' slackness, before this was over.

"We've very little time. The 33rd Drangosh, the 12th Pardizia" —he listed the infantry battalions, about half the two thousand available— "will turn to and begin construction of the necessary boats and gear for a pontoon bridge to cross the Drangosh and carry our invasion force. This task will be performed under the direction of Colonel Dinnalsyn of the Artillery Corps."

A long murmur swept through the packed garrison formations. Raj stood like an iron idol, hands clasped behind his back, while the shouts of *Silence in the ranks!* controlled it. None of his veterans had moved; probably because none of them were surprised at what he intended.

"The cavalry formations based in Sandoral will immediately assume control of the gates. Only military personnel will be allowed to enter the city or approach on the main roads.

"The remainder of the infantry will begin clearing Sandoral and evacuating the civilian population to the railroad station, commencing immediately. No resistance is to be tolerated. All units will be accompanied by parties of the 5th Descott, the 17th Kelden, or the 24th Valencia.

"I'm aware that you men of the district infantry battalions have been seriously neglected. Effective immediately, all arrears of equipment, rations, and pay will be made up from the stocks in the city's treasury and arsenals. For the duration, you will be quartered inside the walls—to be precise, in the housing of the evacuated civilians."

Stunned silence sank over the parade ground. The formations rippled slightly as men turned to one another, then back to the figure standing on the stone dais. A helmet went up on a rifle among the infantry, and a voice cried out:

"Spirit bless Messer Raj!"

"Raj!"

"*Raj!*"

"*RAJ! RAJ!*"

He let it continue and build for a moment, judging, waiting until they were about to break ranks and crowd around him. A raised hand brought the sound back down from its white-noise roar, like receding surf on a beach.

"Cheer after we've beaten the wogs back to their kennels," he said. "Until then, we've a man's job of work to do. See to it."

"*RAJ! RAJ! RAJ! RAJ!*"

Corporal Minatili turned back down the street. "*What's* the problem now?" he barked.

"Theynz warn't open up," the garrison soldier said timidly in a thick yokel burr. "They wouldn' give us no food either, when we wuz hongry. Turned us'n away frum d'doors."

Minatili sighed. *Raggedy-ass excuse for a soldier*, he thought disgustedly. Literally; the man's buttocks were hanging out a great rent in his trousers, and the blue of his jacket was faded to sauroid's-egg color. He had a beard, too, like a barb or a wog.

"*Here's* how ye do it, dickhead. Y'ain't askin' 'em to dance, see?"

He stepped to one side and put the muzzle of his rifle against the lock. *Bam*, and bits of lead and metal pinged and whistled across the street. The ragged soldier yelped as one scored a line of red across the side of his face. Minatili slammed the sole of his boot into the door beside the lock, and the wood boomed open against the hallway.

"What's the meaning of this?" shouted the man inside. "It's impossible—you peon scum, where's your officer? I'll have you flogged, *flogged*—"

Smack. The side of Minatili's rifle-butt punched into the man's face. Blood spattered down the lace sabot of his shirt. The soldier chopped the butt up under the man's short ribs, and he folded over without a sound. Minatili grabbed him by the collar and threw him out into the street.

"Anyone what ain't out in ten, gits shot!" he shouted to the crowd of family and servants. "Out, out, *out*. Twogs is comin'!"

A torrent of civilians poured out of the townhouse door. Minatili grinned to himself; a couple of them trampled on the head of the household before two with more presence of mind or family affection picked him up and carried him out into the crowded darkness of the street. The gas lamps were on, but the reddish light only made the milling crowd seem less human, a gleam of eyes and teeth and wailing voices in the hot night. Both sides of the street were lined with troopers, their fixed bayonets a bright line containing the shapeless movements of the crowd. Occasionally one would jab at someone who crowded too close, and a scream of pain would rise above the hubbub of confusion, fear and anger.

Minatili's grin grew broader. Back in Old Residence, he'd been a stonecutter like his father and grandfather before him. They'd have sent him around to the servants' entrance if he so much as called on a house like this. Now he got to buttstroke one of the breed of stuck-up *riche hombes* bastards. Military service definitely had its good points.

The garrison soldier gaped at him for a slow twenty seconds. Then his crooked brown teeth showed in an answering smile. The glitter in his eyes was alarming.

"Sor!" he said, saluting smartly. Then, to his squadmates: "C'mon, boyos!"

Their boots and rifle-butts thundered on the next door down. Minatili reloaded, slung his rifle and turned to Saynchez.

"How many, d'ye think?"

"Mebbe six, seven hundert," the older private said. "No different n'countin' sheep, a-back on me da's place. Me da ran sheep fer the squire."

"*Banged* the sheep, more like," one of their squad said, sotto voce.

"Wouldn't mind bangin' this one," another added. A feminine squeal came from the darkness.

"No fuckin' around!" Minatili said sharply. "That's enough—move this bunch down to t'train station. *Hadelande!*"

"Tight! Get those boards *tight* before you nail them to the stringers!" Grammeck Dinnalsyn said, for the four hundredth time.

The infantryman gaped at him, then obligingly whacked at the edge of the board with his mallet. The dry wood splintered. Dinnalsyn winced, then skipped aside to let a dozen men go by with a beam. One of his officers followed, drawing lines on the timber with a piece of chalk and consulting a crumpled piece of paper in the other. A noncom stumbled after him, holding up a hurricane lantern. Both moons were up, luckily, and there were bonfires of scrap lumber scattered along the broad stretch of riverside as well. Wagons rumbled in with more wood; wheelbarrels went by loaded with mallets, nails, rope, and saws.

"Cut here, here and *here*," the young lieutenant said, giving a final slash with the chalk. Crews sprang to work with two-man drag saws.

The first pontoon was already ready to launch down

by the river's edge, a simple breast-high wooden box of planks on rough-cut stringers, eight meters by twelve. The stink of hot asphalt surrounded it, as sweating near-naked soldiers slathered liquid black tar from pots onto the boards.

Dinnalsyn pulled out his slide rule. *Si. Now, the river's nine hundred meters; make it eight meters per barge, allow a reserve of ten percent, and—*

A dog pulled up beside him with a spurt of gravel. He looked up and pulled himself erect. "*Mi heneral,*" he said.

Raj nodded, his eyes light gray in the shadows under his helmet brim. "How's it coming, Grammeck?"

"On schedule, more or less."

"Will they float?"

"After a fashion, if we use enough tar and the wood swells tight. I'm going to float them as we finish them, that'll give the timber some time to soak."

"Good man," Raj said. "While you're at it, have your people run up steering oars and paddles. We'll put some of the garrison infantry to practicing maneuvering, that'll be important later. Here in the Drangosh valley, quite a few of them were probably riverboatmen before the press gang came through."

"*Si, mi heneral.* The Forty Thieves aren't with you?"

Raj was riding alone, save for his personal bannermen, buglers, and galloper-messengers. He nodded.

"Too much temptation in the city, under the circumstances. They're out living up to their *official* designation. M'lewis will get it done; he's a soldier, in his fashion." Raj turned in the saddle to watch the first pontoon boat being manhandled into the water. It splashed into the Drangosh and bobbed, riding unevenly. "They'll be enough?"

"*Mi heneral*, consider it done. I can finish the rest in time, if I get enough of the raw materials."

Raj's teeth showed slightly. "Oh, that ought not to be a problem. Poplanich's Own just detrained, they're out helping the 5th get the timber in, and we're moving quickly."

He paused. "One more thing; send out some of your people, use the garrison if you must, and confiscate every boat you can find; every fishing smack, barge, canoe, whatever. Not just here, in the suburbs and every section of the valley we can still reach."

"And *back*, ye bitches' brood."

The civilians still crowding the street wailed and stampeded; which was just fine as far as Robbi M'Telgez was concerned. Handling a lariat and a dog was second nature—his family were *rancheros*, yeoman tenants who herded on shares back in Descott—but this was tricky. One end of the braided leather rope was snubbed to the second-story end of a roof beam; the other was wrapped three times around the pommel of his saddle. Pochita sank down on her haunches and backed one tiny step at a time, and he could feel the thousand-pound body arching like a bow between his thighs. The rest of his platoon were doing likewise, one or two dogs to every rafter. The animals were used to working in unison, and they snarled beneath their panting as they hauled.

The adobe wall smoked dust for an instant and then collapsed towards them. Released from the pull, Pochita skipped back nimbly until her hindquarters touched the house on the other side of the irregular little plaza. M'Telgez coughed though the checked bandanna over his face; his dog sneezed massively and shook her head, the cheek-levers of the bridle rattling. *Got t'check 'em,* he thought. *They should be snug, not loose.*

Foot soldiers waded forward into the dust, rummaging for the planks and beams. They'd done the same thing here in Sandoral for material to build earthwork forts, in the last campaign against the wogs a few years ago; now they were tearing down rebuilt houses to make boats.

Always something new with Messer Raj.

Antin M'lewis sank closer to the earth, hugging it for shelter and trying to *think* dark like the moonless night. It was homelike, in an unpleasant sort of way; as a rustler by hereditary profession, he'd spent enough time like this back home working his way in past the *vakaros* pulling night guard on some unsuspecting squire's herds. Darkness, the dogs belly-down too in a gully a few hundred meters back, his face blacked with lamp soot or burnt cork. The wind moving into his face, so no scent went to the target or his dogs—infantry ahead here, but why take a chance, and there might be a mounted officer. Just like home.

Descott was rarely this hot, though. And most Descotter *vakaros* would be more alert than the wog ahead of him.

He eeled forward on his belly, moving every time the Colonial sentry's pacing turned him back toward this angle of approach. Useless sentry, the bugger was smoking a pipe and M'lewis could see the ember light with every draw, even smell the strong tobacco. Backlit by a watchfire too, which must be playing hell with his night-vision.

Mother. The wog had stopped, and his spiked helmet was turning as he looked outward. He hesitated, almost taking the carbine from over his shoulder, then resumed his steady pacing. *Mother. Spirit.*

Forward another five meters. The dust was trying to make him sneeze, but Goodwife M'lewis hadn't raised any of her sons to be suicides. Now he was behind a head-high clump of alluvial clay, right where the toweltop would pass on his next circuit.

Come on, he thought. *Git yer wog arse over here. Come t'pappa.* His weight came up on his knees and one hand. The other went to the wooden toggle in his waist, callused fingers around satin-smooth pearwood. Ready. Ready. One knee bent under him, bare toes gripping the dirt.

The Colonial muttered something in Arabic and stopped. He bent, raising one foot and knocking the dottle out of his pipe on the heel of his curl-toed boot.

Thank you, Spirit, M'lewis thought, and moved very quickly. Straighten the knee, rising, right hand whipping forward and to the left in a hard sideways flick. Following the toggle and the wire it dragged, as if they were pulling him out of the dirt. Perfect soft weight on the hand, as the wire struck the left side of the wog's neck and whipped around, slapping the other toggle into his reaching left hand—practiced ten thousand times since he was a lad, and it *worked* when you had to. Wrists crossed, jam the knee into the wog's back, *heave.*

The sudden coppery smell of blood filled the night. M'lewis went down with the Colonial, abandoning the garrote that had sawn halfway through to his backbone and grabbing his equipment to muffle the clatter. Figures had started upright at the campfire; one of them seemed to be dancing a jig for an instant. The sounds were slight but definite. A meaty *thock*, the sound of a steel-shod rifle butt in the side of a head. The wetter, duller sound of steel in flesh. And once the unmistakable crackle of a breaking neck, like a thick green branch being popped. Then silence.

M'lewis jerked the garrote free and wiped it clean on the dead Arab's pugaree. The campfire was quiet when he came up, his men finishing rifling the pockets of the dead—he could have forbidden that, and he could tell a pig not to shit in the woods, too—and sitting calmly in the same positions with wog helmets on their heads. The Scout commander nodded to them as he passed, walking out into the dark and to the edge of the little cliff. There was a gully beyond it, then low eroded clay hills, and then flat farmland. Dim enough normally at two hours past midnight, except for the hundreds of neatly spaced campfires. More lights crossed the river, over to the western bank where the smoking ruins of Gurnyca lay.

He settled in with his sketchpad and pulled out his binoculars. Railroad to the riverbank; he checked, and saw fatigue parties still working on it. *Laid on t'dirt*, he noted on his pad as he sketched. No embankment or crushed-rock bedding for the ties. Emergency line, low capacity, but still enough to carry supplies. Mounds of supplies throughout the basecamp, within the normal earthworks and ditch. Ammunition boxes, shells, sacks with dogmash and dried fish and jerked meat, skins of vegetable oil, all the hundred-and-one items that an army on the march needed. Convoys were moving across the pontoon bridge even at night: wagons drawn by skinny long-legged oxen, and long guns with the distinctive soda-bottle shapes of built-up siege weapons, battering pieces. 130mm and 160mm, he decided. Rifled guns, good artillery, but bitches to move.

Rail to the river, but oxcarts over it. No grazing, except from the farms; if Ali was moving north, he'd be foraging to support his men, but once he stopped, the convoys would have to come in every day. About ten kay of troops holding the bridgehead and pontoons, sappers and line-of-communication infantry. It all looked very professional, as good as anything the Civil Government's army could do. Not at *all* like fighting the barbs out west. The MilGov barbs were full of fight, but dim as a yard up a hog's ass, most of the time. These wogs used their heads for something besides holding their turbans up.

M'lewis finished his estimate and duplicated the numbers and sketch-map. "Cut-nose, Talker," he whispered, as he eeled backward.

Cut-nose was a ratty little man, his cousin on his mother's side. They might have been brothers for looks—

it was quite possible they *were* brothers, Old Man M'lewis had got around a fair bit before they hanged him—except for the missing organ. Then again, maybe they weren't close relations; no M'lewis would try to sell a dyed dog back to the man he'd stolen it from. Talker was a hulking brute from the mountains on the eastern fringe of Descott. They both had rawhide guards shrunk onto the forestocks of their rifles, and Talker had a couple of fresh severed ears on a loop of thong around his neck.

"Tak this t'Messer Raj," he said. "Swing east. Month's pay bonus iffn ye gits there afore me."

"Ser!" Cut-nose said, smiling yellow-brown with delight. Talker grunted.

M'lewis came to a crouch and headed back toward the gully and the dogs, the rest of the Scouts falling in behind him. He took the time to stamp his feet back into his boots before he straddled the crouching dog. He usually didn't bother with socks; a dollop of tallow in the boot served as well, if you didn't mind the smell.

"Ride," he said.

Messer Raj would have his news. It was bad news, as far as Antin M'lewis could see, but—thank the Spirit!—it wasn't his job to figure out what to do about it.

They swung into the saddle and followed the gully north, riding with muffled harness. Every kilometer or so he paused and headed for high ground; the eastern bank was generally a little above the level on the west, and there were few dwellers close to the main stream, if you avoided the raghead semaphore towers. Every stop showed Colonial watchfires on the other side; Ali's convoy guards, picketed all the way down his line of march northward towards Sandoral.

The third time showed something a little different. He closed his eyes for a minute before putting them to the glasses. There was a fair-sized Civil Government town on the other side of the river, and as he watched, the first of the buildings went up in a gout of flame. That gave enough light to watch the Settler's troops systematically stripping the warehouses and granaries before they put them to the torch; Ali'd be living off the land as much as he could, to spare the transport.

There was a migratory insect on Bellevue about the length of a man's thumb. Every century or so swarms of them would hatch north on the Skinner steppe and fly south, eating the land bare until they reached the empty deserts to spawn and die. Where they passed, famine followed.

Ali's men were more localized, but just about as thorough.

Barton Foley sat in the shade of the palm tree and tapped his lips thoughtfully with the end of his pencil. *Now, would* virile *go well with* while *in that stanza, or not?* he thought.

"Heads up!"

He sighed and tucked the volume back into the saddlebag. Someday he'd have the time to really write. *Someday I'll be dead*, he added sourly to himself— *although hopefully not soon*; twenty-one was a bit early even in this trade. *Maybe I'm not cut out to be a poet or a playwright.* History, now, that might be more interesting. He'd certainly got a close-up on some of it.

"More refugees?" a lieutenant asked.

"I don't think so," the young captain said thoughtfully, raising his glasses.

The picket of the 5th was two kilometers out from Sandoral: the roads were thick with refugees, heading into the city and then being routed out. It was better to intercept them a ways from the gates, to avoid crowding the roadways nearer the city. Two troops and a splatgun were enough to discourage even the most hysterical from bolting to the shelter of the walls. By now, most of them had gotten the message. There was a continuous traffic out of town too, hopeful magnates with their valuables in wagons, realistic ones with the hard cash on pack-dogs and the family in a fast well-sprung carriage.

It was easy duty, a way to rest the troops; a nice little date grove for shade, a good well for water. Some resourceful soul had a fire going and a couple of chickens roasting over it; the peons would never miss them. The smell was a pleasant overlay to the usual odors of dog and sweat-soaked wool uniforms and gun oil.

Foley wiped his face with his red-and-black checked neckcloth. *Ironic,* he thought. The 5th Descott had looted a warehouse full of them back in El Djem, the Colonial border town southwest of here. They'd just barely made it back alive from that one, after Tewfik mousetrapped them, but the scarves had become a unit trademark; it was as much as a soldier's life was worth to wear one, if he wasn't in the 5th.

The column of dust was heading in from the northwest, just now down into the flat irrigated land around Sandoral. Suspiciously regular dust, columns of it, with a thinner, wider film in front. Very much what a couple of battalions of Civil Government cavalry would make, riding hard in column with their scout-screens out ahead, all regulation and by the book. He waited until the first of the vedettes came into view, checked the silhouette and the breed of dog.

"Message to the *Heneralissimo,*" he said. "The Cruisers and Welf's Brigaderos are here."

Very good time, too. No more than five days from the time they left East Residence just ahead of the first trains. Even with the railroad to supply them, it was a creditable performance, particularly if the dogs were still fit for action.

He was a little surprised. Those fair MilGov complexions were extremely pretty, but he'd doubted they could take the Eastern sun.

❖   ❖   ❖

"Good timing," Raj said.

Ludwig Bellamy and Teodore Welf looked more like twins than ever, down to the thick coating of gray-white dust on their faces and the dark streaks of sweat through it.

"Rail convoys on schedule?" Bellamy asked.

They moved forward under the awning and collected bowls of soup and a bannock each; the line parted to let them through, but it was the same food as the troopers were waiting for. The medical staff—priest-doctors and nuns—was manning the pots, since there weren't any wounded to care for so far. Suzette dashed by, stopping long enough to thrust a cup of watered wine into Raj's hand. The others were dipping water out of a bucket; Ludwig waited politely until the others had drunk, then dumped the remainder over his head.

"I *needed* that," he said; the grin made you realize he wasn't yet thirty.

Neither am I, Raj remembered with slight surprise. He felt older, though.

Aloud, he went on: "I'll give Barholm Clerett that, he does get the trains running on time. We're expecting the last in at any moment. How are your men?"

"They'll be ready to fight after a night's sleep; and the dogs are mostly sound-footed. We took your advice and commandeered a big pack of remounts from the East Residence reserve before we left." Bellamy looked around. "You haven't been wasting time here."

There were few civilians left on the streets of Sandoral. Instead they swarmed with soldiers and dogs, wagons and carts, and an ordered chaos of movement under the harsh southern sun. The garrison infantry were doing most of the hauling and pushing, but they looked better fed, and far better dressed. A thud and plume of smoke and dust marked another house being demolished for building materials; off in the distance sounded the *heep . . . heep* of troops being drilled and a crackle of musketry practice. The artillery park filled most of the square, guns nose-to-trail with their limbers waiting behind, and Dinnalsyn's gunners giving them a last going-over.

"Speak of the devil," Barton Foley said, smiling fondly.

A bugle sounded, and the color party of the 5th Descott came trotting into the square, the battalion banner floating beside the blue and silver Starburst of Holy Federation. Gerrin Staenbridge heeled his mount over to the clump of officers and saluted with an ironic flourish.

"*Mi heneral*, the remainder of your force, reporting as ordered." He looked around in his turn. "I see you've started the party without me."

"Just laying in the drinks and rehearsing the band, Gerrin," Raj said. "No problem getting under way?"

"No, but there might have been if I'd lingered. Our good Chancellor Tzetzas isn't happy about having the field army so far from home, at all, at all. If I hadn't taken the last of the trains, I suspect the bureaucrats would have followed me all the way here to argue with you about it."

Raj laughed harshly. "Not with Ali so close," he said. "Although our good Commandant Osterville is almost as much of a pest, in his way. And he *is* here."

"Speak of the devil," Foley said again, his voice flat as gunmetal this time.

He took Staenbridge's arm and began whispering rapidly, gesturing with the hook on his left arm. Raj caught his own name and *Suzette* once or twice.

The Commandant of Sandoral and District was pushing his way through the thronging mass in the square; not looking very happy, and unhappier by the minute at the lack of deference, from Raj's veterans and from what were supposedly his own troops.

"Whitehall," he said. "General Whitehall," he amended; Raj's face was politely blank, but several of the Companions had dropped their hands to pistol-butts or the hilts of their sabers.

"Where the Starless Dark have you been?"

Raj straightened, finished the wine, and dipped his bannock into the stew. "Well, Commandant, I've been rather busy—getting ready for the war, you see."

Somebody chuckled, and Osterville turned a mottled color. "I'll thank you to accompany me to my headquarters," he said. "We've got several things to discuss."

"If you want to talk, *Colonel*, you'll talk here and now. Because as I mentioned, there is a war impending."

Words burst from the smaller man. "You're *destroying* my city!" he barked. "I've received petitions from every man of rank in the district—"

Raj raised an eyebrow. "I don't doubt you have," he said. "Let them petition Ali. That's the alternative, and I think they'd like his methods even less than mine. In any case, as you've made clear, you're the supreme civil authority in this area; relations with the local nobility are your responsibility."

The Commandant opened his mouth and closed it again. He snapped his fingers, and an aide put a sheaf of documents in his hand.

"Perhaps you've been too *busy*," he said, "to read these dispatches from the Capital? They've been coming over the semaphore by the dozens."

Raj mopped his bowl with the heel of the bannock and plucked the papers out of the smaller man's hand. He glanced through them, chewed, swallowed.

"Oh, I've been reading them," he said.

He ripped the thick sheaf through with casual strength, tossing the fragments into the dry hot wind. They fluttered off like gulls, and one of the newly arrived dogs of the 5th snapped inquiringly at a piece as it went by.

"I have the *Governor's* authority, signed by the Sovereign Mighty Lord himself. I received it in person, from his own hands. What are a few waggling flags to *that*?"

He tossed the last of the papers to the cobbles. "And now, Colonel Osterville, if you don't have any more problems . . ."

"But I do have *this*," Osterville said. The document he produced was thick parchment, impressively sealed with lead and ribbons.

Raj raised an eyebrow. "You have a decree from the Chair, a Vermilion Order, swaying the wide earth?" he asked, using the formal terminology.

"Not exactly," Osterville said. "But you will note it's from Chancellor Tzetzas, in the Governor's name, requiring you to cease and desist from interfering with private properties and instead attend to your assigned mission."

"From the Chancellor?" Raj said, examining the parchment. He crumpled it experimentally. It was first-quality sheepskin parchment, soft and supple. "By courier, I suppose?"

Osterville nodded toward a man in his entourage. Raj looked at him, and then around.

"M'lewis. Deal with this as it deserves," he said.

"Where are the jakes?" the Scout Captain said, putting down his bowl and unfastening his sword belt.

Like most Civil Government cities, Sandoral had public lavatories, simple brick boxes connected to storm-flushed sewers. M'lewis strode over to the nearest, and back a minute later. He was holding the now brown-streaked and stinking parchment by one corner between thumb and finger. Shocked silence gripped the Commandant's party as he walked over to the courier, unfastened the flap of his message pouch, and dropped the soiled parchment inside.

"Just so the Chancellor understands exactly what weight

I attach to his attempts to interfere with my mission and the Governor's authority," Raj said.

"You're mad," Osterville said softly. "Mad. Nobody— Tzetzas will eat your *heart*."

Raj's smile sent Osterville back a step. "Perhaps I am mad, Colonel. Perhaps I'm the Sword of the Spirit of Man. In either case, I'm in charge here." He produced a document of his own. "And this is your own confirmation, directing your troops to cooperate in the transport of the civilians."

He held it up, and one of the Companions leaned over to read it with interest.

"That! That was that witch, she—" On the edge of ruin, Osterville pulled himself back. He'd been about to say something that would be a public provocation to a challenge. He ran a hand through his hair. "Where is *she*? I haven't seen her since . . ."

Raj laughed, an iron sound. "Colonel Osterville, I've answered your official inquiries. You can scarcely expect me to stretch business to the point of giving you an itinerary for my wife. Now, if you'll pardon me—"

He turned, and the officers followed him. Gerrin Staenbridge paused, holding his gauntlets in one hand and tapping them into the palm of the other. For a moment Osterville feared he would slap them across his face in challenge, but the hard dark features were relaxed in a smile. He held the order Osterville had signed—the order that Suzette Whitehall had somehow charmed out of him. He read it, pursing his lips, then looked up at Osterville with an expression of feline malice before he spoke one word.

"Sucker."

CHAPTER SEVEN

It was the hour before dawn, a little chilly even in summer in the clear dry southern air. The massed ranks of the army knelt as the Sysup-Suffragen of Sandoral paced by, with acolytes swinging censers that spread aromatic blue smoke across the men. He reached out his Star-headed staff in blessing as he passed the colors of each unit, and the men extended both hands out, palms down, in the gesture of reverence. Behind the hierarch came four priests bearing a litter on which rested a cube of something clearer than crystal and taller than a man. Light swirled in it, growing and flaring until the watchers bowed their heads and closed their eyes in awe. It shone through the closed lids, through hands flung up before faces, then died away amid a murmur of awe.

Raj touched his amulet as he rose. "The Spirit is with us," he said. *Or at least Center is. What a cynic I've become.*

realist, Center corrected.

Is there a difference?

He turned to the command group. Which included, from necessity, Colonel Osterville.

"Gentlemen, my congratulations. You've managed a very complex operation in record time and with surprisingly little confusion; my particular thanks to Colonels Menyez and Dinnalsyn. Now it's time to show the wogs that two can play the invasion game. Colonel Osterville, I presume you'll wish to accompany the field force rather than remain in Sandoral?"

"I certainly will. Furthermore, I insist that the cavalry battalions of the Sandoral garrison be under my command."

Raj nodded. "By all means, Colonel. By all means."

Osterville shot him a suspicious glance, and found his face blandly unrevealing. He tugged at his mustachio thoughtfully.

colonel osterville is attempting to intuit the reason for your ready agreement, Center pointed out. **probability of success 12%±3.**

"Colonel Menyez, you will command the city garrison. I'm leaving you the 17th, the 24th, the garrison infantry, and three batteries of field guns. You'll also have the guns of the fixed defenses, of course."

Dinnalsyn looked up. "I've tested the militia artillery crews who volunteered to stay," he said. "Not bad at all, and the ammunition's plentiful."

Jorg Menyez nodded thoughtfully. "Any cavalry? The garrison units can stand behind a parapet and shoot, and the 17th and 24th can do anything cavalry can except ride and charge with the saber, but I could use a mobile reserve."

"I'll leave you three companies of the 5th Descott," Raj said. "That'll have to do. The field force will comprise three columns.

"The remainder of the 5th, the 1st and 2nd Mounted Cruisers, the 3/591, 4/591, and 5/591, and the main artillery reserve of thirty guns will go with me. Colonel Osterville, you'll command your garrison cavalry and two batteries. Major Gruder, you'll have the 7th Descott Rangers, the 1st Rogor Slashers, the Maximilliano Dragoons, and Poplanich's Own. Major Zahpata, you'll take your 18th Komar Borderers, the City of Delrio, and the Novy Haifa Dragoons. Plus two batteries of field guns each.

"We'll be advancing fast, close enough for mutual

support; no wheeled transport except for the guns and the ammunition reserve. Spread out, live off the land; spare lives when you can, but burn and destroy everything else, so long as you can do it quickly. Let the semaphore posts stand long enough to get off messages. Portable plunder will be transferred to the central group, and from there back here to Sandoral for eventual division; do *not* allow the men to weigh themselves down with choice bits. When Tewfik comes looking for us, we're going to need every bit of mobility we can get.

"The purpose of this exercise is to create enough havoc that Ali will be forced to divert at least part of his army from the west bank of the Drangosh. We lay waste the nobles' estates; the nobles scream for protection. He can give any particular noble the chop, but he can't ignore too many of them—hopefully, he's not so much of a bloody lunatic as to forget that, at least not yet. We can't face the entire Colonial army in the field, but we may be able to give part of it a bloody nose. Move fast, and create the maximum amount of panic and alarm; that's more important than actual damage.

"Any questions?"

A few of the officers looked at each other, but none spoke. Raj slapped on his gloves. "Then to your men, Messers, and the work of the day."

Raj mounted Horace and turned the dog and his personal bannermen down the front of the assembled force. He halted before the ranks of the infantry.

"Fellow soldiers," he said, raising a hand. "I'm off to teach the wogs the price of invading the Civil Government of Holy Federation."

Silence reigned. "I can only do that if Sandoral is strongly held behind me." He pointed south. "Ali is coming, and more wogs than you can count are coming with him. If you hold these walls, we can win this war; otherwise, we all die. I'm riding out confident in the

aid of the Spirit of Man of the Stars—and in your courage
and discipline. Which is why, when the plunder is divided,
all the infantry here will receive a full share, just as the
cavalry troopers do. Are you lads ready to do a man's
work today?"

The 17th began the cheering, and it spread down the
line as Raj rode past, his personal flag dipping in salute
as he passed each battalion's banner. The cavalry were
massed on the other side of the square; you had to use
a different manner with them.

He grinned as he reined in, facing the long rows of
helmeted riders and the panting tongues of the dogs;
they knew something was up as well, and their pricked-
forward ears were mirrors of the men's excitement.

"To Hell or plunder, dog-brothers," Raj roared.

The men gave back a single exultant bark, and the
dogs howled, thousands of them in antiphonal chorus,
a sound that slammed back from the buildings around
the plaza and made the hair crawl along the spine.

"Walk-march . . . trot."

"I might have known," Raj said, reining in on the little
hillock beside the east-bank end of the bridge.

Suzette pulled up Harbie, her riding palfrey, beside
Horace. The smaller dog wagged its tail and sniffed
Horace's muzzle; after a moment Horace gave a snuffle
in reply and turned his head away in lordly indifference.

"You do have a medical element along," Suzette said,
her eyes bright with friendly mockery. She touched the
first-aid kit slung from the saddlebow. "There's no reason
I shouldn't join them."

The boards of the pontoon bridge rumbled as a
splatgun battery crossed. Cavalry followed in columns
of fours, the plate-sized paws thudding on the wooden
pavement. Some of the dogs had their ears back at the
unfamiliar slight swaying of the surface beneath their

feet; others looked upstream or down. The men were singing, an old Descotter folktune:

> *"Goin' t'Black Mountain wit me saber an' me gun;*
> *Cut ye if yer stand, shoot ye if yer run—"*

"I can command thousands of armed men and not a single woman," Raj grumbled. *One armed woman*, he corrected himself. Suzette had her Colonial repeating carbine in a scabbard tucked under the saddle flaps before her left knee.

"Well, you did *marry* me, not *enlist* me, darling," Suzette said.

Raj snorted and returned his attention to the map. Below, the raiding force poured across the Drangosh, dogs and guns. *Twenty-five, thirty-five klicks a day*, he thought, tracing it with his finger. South and east—there was nothing close to the river to raid, but the Ghor Canal ran a little farther east, and there was a thick belt of cultivation along it. *Three or four days should bring us to* . . . A city, called Ain el-Hilwa, about halfway between here and the Colonial bridgehead opposite Gurnyca.

By that time the wogs should be well and truly terrorized.

"Scramento!" Robbi M'Telgez swore.

The carbine bullet pecked dirt from the adobe wall into his eyes. He crouched and duckwalked along it, rising slightly to peer through the branches of a flowering bush a few meters farther on. There wasn't much shooting elsewhere in the hamlet, but this was the best house; therefore the one most likely to be defended.

"Ye, Smeet, Cunarlez, M'tennin," he said. "Cover us. Five rounds rapid. T'rest fix yer stickers. We'll tak Rosalie t'breakfast."

"We'll a' git kilt," Smeet muttered. "Hunnert meters,

dog-brothers. I gits t'winda on 't lef." He blew on the round he loaded into the chamber.

M'Telgez drew the bayonet—nicknamed Rosalie from time immemorial—from the left side of his belt beneath the haversack and clipped it beneath the muzzle of his rifle. There was a multiple rattle and click as the other men of his squad followed suit.

The house ahead was bigger than most in the sprawling settlement along the irrigation ditch; probably the local headman's. It was about a hundred meters upstream from the burning wreckage of the *noria*, the water-powered millwheel that filled the distributory network of irrigation ditches. A small square house of two stories, blank whitewashed adobe below, a few narrow windows above, and most of it was courtyard enclosed by a wall. It hadn't been constructed as a fortress; it had been a long time since Civil Government troops came this far, and none of the local villages even had a defensive perimeter. From what he knew of raghead custom, the wogs built this way to keep neighbors from seeing their women. But it *functioned* perfectly well as a minor strongpoint.

"Hadelande!" he shouted, and vaulted the wall.

The three men he'd designated cut loose, firing as rapidly as they could work the levers and reload. The heavy bullets knocked dust-spouting holes in the mud brick around the windows, or went through—most of them went through, it was only fifty meters and everyone in the 5th ought to be able to hit a running man in the head at that range—beating down the enemy fire. A light bullet still pecked at the dust between his feet. He suppressed his impulse to leap and yell, concentrating on running.

The six Descotters flattened themselves by the doorway. No sense waiting there; it would just give someone upstairs time to think about dropping something unpleasant on them. He was suddenly conscious of his dry gummy mouth, the sweat trickling down from neck and armpits under his uniform jacket, the sound of a chicken clucking unconcerned out in the dusty yard. M'Telgez held out three fingers, two, one.

He and the next trooper stepped out and fired at the lock. They were lucky; nothing hit them when the crude wooden mechanism splintered. The other four fired a round each through the datewood planks while he and his partner stuck their bayonets through the gaps between and lifted the bar out of its brackets. The door burst inward, and they were through.

It was an open space of packed earth with a well in the center and rooms about it. An open staircase came down from the second story opposite him, and men were leaping down it. One pointed a long-barreled flintlock *jezail*.

It boomed, throwing a plume of smoke. Someone behind him yelled—yelled rather than screamed, so that couldn't be too serious. Armory rifles banged, and the other man with a firearm toppled from the stairs; he had a repeating carbine, which showed that this squad had a proper sense of target priorities. Then a wog was rushing at him, swinging a long scimitar.

Clang. M'Telgez caught the sword on his bayonet, and it skirled down the forearm-length of steel until it caught in the brass cross-guard. He let the inertia of the heavy sword push both weapons downward, and punched across with the butt of his rifle. It smacked into the Arab's bearded face with a crackle of breaking bone, a crunching he could feel through his hands. The Colonial pitched sideways, spinning and fouling the man behind who was trying to pull a double-barreled pistol out of the sash around his ample belly. His mouth opened in an "O" of surprise as M'Telgez spun his rifle around and lunged, driving his bayonet through the Arab's stomach and a handspan out his back.

There was a soft, heavy resistance, a feeling of things crunching and popping inside. He twisted sharply and withdrew, a few shards of white fat clinging to nicks in the blade of the bayonet. Blood spattered out; the wounded man's eyes rolled up in his head and he collapsed backward.

The men of the 5th waited an instant, taking cover behind the mudbrick columns that supported the second story of the house. M'Telgez reloaded his rifle and raised three fingers, then jerked them towards the stairs. Three men ran up them and through the open arched door at the top. A shadow moved at the corner of his eye. He whirled, just in time to see it was a veiled and robed woman with a big earthenware pot raised over her head in both hands. M'Telgez raised the muzzle of his rifle as his finger curled on the trigger, and the bullet smashed the vase into shards, leaving her standing with her hands spread and eyes wide.

He pivoted the rifle and jabbed the butt into her stomach. Air whooped out of her and she collapsed to the ground. The Descotter put a boot in the small of her back and pinned her to the dusty earth.

"Anythin' up thar?" he called sharply.

"Nothin'," a voice answered him. "Jist sommat wog kids."

"Bring 'em down," he called. "Rest a yer dog-brothers, search it. Look unner t'roof tiles, t'hearthstone, shove yer baynit inna any chink ye see. Nuthin' heavy, jist coin an' sich."

Which was a pity; cloth and tools and livestock would all fetch a good price back in the *Gubernio Civil* if they had time to send them back, not to mention the wogs themselves. A good stout wog would bring six or seven silver FedCreds sold to the slavers who usually followed the armies, a quarter the price of a riding dog. He'd picked up some coin that way in the Southern Territories.

M'Telgez banked half his pay and most of his plunder with the battalion savings account; he had an eye on a little place back in the County when he'd done his twenty-five years. There were two schools of thought on that—some held that you had about one chance in four of living that long in the Army, so it made more sense to spend it on booze and whores as it came.

Robbi M'Telgez had noticed that troopers who thought that way tended to be careless, and to make up a large share of the discouraging statistics. Besides, his family could use the money too, if it came to that.

The three men he'd sent up came down again, one holding a small wooden box. "Found 'er in t'rafters, loik," he said, grinning broadly. "Coin, by t'Spirit."

Looking on the bright side, the wogs hadn't had time to really hide much.

Another herded a group of children, the oldest leading or carrying the younger. They set up a wail at the sight of the bodies in the courtyard, then surged back again when one of the troopers scowled and flourished his bayonet. Thumping and crashing sounds came from the ground floor, as the rest of the squad searched.

"Git t'kiddies out an' a-down by t'church, t'mosque, whatever." Orders were to spare noncombatants and the unresisting. "Yer!" He shouted through the ground-floor door. "Whin yer finished, set t'cookin' oil around."

That would start the fire nicely. He took a deep breath and exhaled, letting the tight belly-clamping tension of action fade a little. A pissant little skirmish, but he'd been in the Army seven years now, since he turned eighteen, and he knew you could die just as dead that way as in a major battle.

"And Smeet, plug that."

Trooper Smeet had a tear in the side of his jacket, and it was sodden and dripping. " 'Tis nuttin'," he said. "We'll a' git kilt anyways—"

"Did I *asks* yer?" M'Telgez said, scowling. "Did I?"

"Co'pral half a year and already drunk wit' power," Smeet said, grinning with an expression that was half wince. He was coming down off the combat-high too; often you didn't really feel a minor wound until you had time to think about it. He leaned his rifle against a wall and shrugged out of his webbing gear and jacket. "I bin co'pral six, seven times—t' feelin' don't last nohows, dog-brother."

There was an ugly flesh wound along his ribs, only beginning to crust. One of his comrades washed it from his canteen, then applied the blessed powder and sealed, the priest-made bandage they all carried in a pouch on their belts. Smeet yelped and swore; the stuff stung badly, and many of the less pious men wouldn't use it on a cut unless you stood over them. M'Telgez wasn't much of a Church-going man, but Messer Raj insisted on following Church canons in such things, which was good enough for him.

The attending trooper used his bayonet to cut off one of the tails of Smeet's jacket, ripping it in half and using it to bind the padding over his ribs.

"An' git t'priest at it, soon as, or ye'll feel me boot up yer arse," M'Telgez warned. Smeet was a good enough fighting man, but he tended to be slack about kit and such.

M'Telgez looked down at the woman and smiled.

Pillars of black smoke stood out against the northern horizon. The smell drifted down with the wind, full of the unpleasant smells of things that should not burn. White-hot, the noon sun burned most color out of the land, turning the reaped grainfields to a pale yellow dust. Blocks of alfalfa and *berseem*-clover were almost eye-hurtingly vivid, and the odd patch of fruit trees or olives cast shade dense and black and sharp-edged. Where the

7th Descott Rangers waited beside their dogs, there was welcome shade from rows of eucalyptus on either side of the road, but the air was still and very hot. Insects shrilled in the dust, and a few tiny pterosauroids swooped after them, their long triangle-tipped tails flickering as they scooped cicadas into their needle-toothed little jaws.

The men squatted patiently beside their mounts, the gun teams lying down in their traces, satisfied after their drink in the roadside canal. The beasts looked glossy-coated and strong despite the heat and hard work; the all-meat diet of plundered Colonial stock agreed with them, after the usual mash of grain and beans eked out with bones and offal. Kaltin Gruder stood, eating grapes from the bunches in the helmet he held reversed in his left hand, waiting with the same stolidity as his troopers.

He ate more grapes and smiled. He'd soldiered against the Military Governments in the west without passion, and as much occasional mercy as advisable. He was a noble of the Civil Government, a Descotter, and a professional; war was his trade, the only trade unless he wanted the Church or to go home to the County and chase rustlers. The Colonials, though . . . his younger brother had died from a Colonial shellburst, in the El Djem campaign. He rubbed one thumb down the deep parallel scars that seamed the left side of his face.

This was personal.

The sound of paws came from the north, and the whistle of the pickets in their ambush positions passing them through. The scouts trotted up to him, sitting easily with their rifles across their thighs. The lieutenant who led them saluted.

"*Seyhor*," he said. "Sir. About two thousand of them; many carriages and dogs, and a substantial number of armed men."

"Regulars?"

"*Ferramenti, danad, seyhor*," the young officer replied.

"I'd swear, nothing, sir. Household guards, no twenty in the same livery."

That was the advantage of counter-attacking. Most of the military nobles, the *amirs*, and their *ghazis* would be over on the west bank, with Ali—all the ones who had any desire to fight and die for Islam, at least. Ali had gotten overconfident.

Still, it wouldn't do to emulate his mistake. Fighting for their homes and families could make even rabble desperate.

"Company commanders," he said.

Back along the road men shifted as the word passed down, fastening their webbing, here a man checking his rifle or tightening the girth on a dog. The mounts took their cues from their masters, keeping a well-drilled silence, but they bristled. The unit commanders gathered around Gruder's banner.

"The objective," he said, crouching and drawing in the dirt with a twig, "is a column of refugees about half a klick north. They're coming at fair speed for civilians, but we've gotten ahead of them. We'll debouch, deploy—so—and put in an attack. Captain Morinez, bring your guns along at the trot, if you please.

"The general order is to kill anyone who resists; let the rest run, as long as they do it on foot. We'll take provisions, spare dogs—I want to put the ammunition reserve in pack-saddles—and any high-value loot." He dumped the grapes out of his helmet and buckled it on. "Burn or smash whatever we don't take. Oh, and we're not taking any hundred-pound bundles of loot, either, so wooers be swift—or refrain."

There was a harsh chuckle, and nods. This was a military picnic so far; it wouldn't stay that way, but there was no reason not to make the most of it while they could.

"Hell or plunder, dog-brothers." He straddled his dog

Fihdel and his feet found the stirrups as it rose. "Boots and saddles, gentlemen."

"Approximately one hundred seventy-seven thousand four hundred FedCreds. Gold," Muzzaf Kerpatik added. "That's allowing for the usual discounts on sales."

Raj grunted noncommittally, leaning one hand against the tentpole. It was a captured tent, from the baggage train Kaltin had overrun; they'd leave it behind in the morning. He looked out across the camp—not much of one, just the picket lines of staked-out dogs, the men cooking around their campfires. Odd to be in a camp where you heard more Namerique than Sponglish, but the central group was mostly MilGov troopers. *Fruits of conquest.* That was the true spoil of war; peace in the lands he'd retaken, and their fighting men here defending the Civil Government.

The MilGov soldiers, the ex-warriors of the Squadron and Brigade, were happy enough. An easy campaign so far, under leaders they trusted; they were warriors by birth and professional soldiers by the trade he'd given them, and indifferent to who they fought.

The sun was setting in the west, over toward the Drangosh thirty kilometers distant. It was hazed with burning, crops and buildings and towns; the raiding force had smashed a path of devastation a hundred kilometers southward. He could smell the smoke, faint under the cooking and dog odors of a war-camp.

"How much of that plunder is from Osterville's group?" Raj asked.

"Ah, unfortunately Colonel Osterville's battalions have had poor luck. Less than two thousand from them."

A chuckle ran around the table behind him. "I don't think," Raj said, "the men are going to find it amusing that Osterville's boys are holding out on them. Particularly given the recent service records, respectively."

"Raj, darling," Suzette said. "*Do* come and sit down. Or pace like a caged dog, but make up your mind."

He shrugged a little sheepishly and returned, sitting and taking up a drumstick. It was sauroid, but tasted pretty much like the chicken that was the alternative. As usual, Suzette had managed to find something better than you had any right to expect in the field; of course, the pickings were good. He stoked himself methodically.

"You don't like this, do you, darling?" Suzette said.

"No," Raj said. "I'm a thrifty man. The looting's good here because this area hasn't been fought over in a long time. It'll be generations recovering."

"Which will weaken the Colony," Gerrin Staenbridge pointed out.

He'd managed to shave and find a clean uniform, which was a minor miracle when they were all living out of saddlebags. *Every man pays the price he will for what he values*, Raj thought. Gerrin dressed for dinner the way he dressed line for a charge, with finicky care, as a mark of civilization.

"That's assuming the stalemate continues out here," Raj said. "The Civil Government of Holy Federation is the legitimate ruler of *all* humankind. The Colonials included."

Staenbridge raised an eyebrow: "Well, it hasn't had much luck enforcing that for millennia or so," he pointed out.

During which time the Colonials had besieged East Residence twice and the Civil Government had reached as far as Al Kebir once.

"I don't like it either," Barton Foley said.

They looked at him, and the younger man dropped his eyes to the cut-down shotgun on the table before him, his single hand slowly reassembling the clean, oil-gleaming parts. They went together with smooth clicks and snaps, and he slid it into the harness he usually wore over his back.

"It's not real soldiers' work, harrying peasants like this," he went on doggedly.

Gerrin and Raj nodded in chorus, and smiled at the coincidence. "Not good for morale, really," Raj said. "Not too much of it."

"Gets the men thinking like bandits," Staenbridge agreed.

Suzette shook her head. "Such perfect knights," she said with gentle mockery. Then: "Ah, Abdullah."

The Druze entered with two suspicious troopers at his heel, their bayonets hovering not far from his kidneys, and Antin M'lewis to one side. He bowed: "*Sayyid. Sayyida.*"

Raj leaned back in the captured folding chair, some *amir*'s hunting equipment. *I'll be damned. I didn't expect to see him alive again, I really didn't.* Suzette had an eye for picking reliable servants, though.

"That's all, men," he said to the troopers. They hesitated, and his tone grew dry. "I can handle one Arab, thank you." They saluted, threw Abdullah a warning glance, and wheeled smartly out.

Damn, this living legend shit can get wearing. The men wouldn't leave him alone for a moment, watching, listening, guarding. Damn their dear loyal souls. What was he, an invalid?

you are their talisman, Center said. **without you they would feel themselves lost.**

I'm only one man, Raj thought/protested. *And I've got competent officers.*

belief is its own reality.

Abdullah pulled documents from his ha'aik. He also accepted a goblet of watered wine; his particular brand of exceedingly eccentric shi'a Islam had some liberal notions.

"Lord," he began. "Ain el-Hilwa is swollen to bursting with refugees. Perhaps a hundred and seventy, a hundred and eighty thousand in all. They crowd the city and the suburbs outside the wall."

Raj nodded. That was no surprise. The spy's long brown fingers moved dishes to tack down the map and papers against the warm breeze of evening.

"The garrison includes ten thousand men of the Settler's regulars and the *ghazis* of the local *amirs*, but of these no more than two hundred are of single *tabors*." Banners, the Colonial equivalent of the Civil Government's battalions, although usually a little smaller. "The rest have been sent on detachment to the Settler's army across the Drangosh.

"Likewise, their officers quarrel. The provincial *wali*, Muhmed bin Tarish, is a court favorite; he hides among his women and sends messages commanding the men to stand fast within the walls. Haffez al'Husseini, the most senior of the military officers, is a veteran of the Zanj wars, but slowed by his wounds. He—"

The report flowed on, full and concise; units, strengths, weapons, dispositions, guns, the state of the fortifications and the water supply (which was good, since the city straddled the Ghor Canal). Center drew holographic projections over the map.

Abdullah's voice ceased. The others waited, in a silence filled by the flutter of canvas in the wind and the muted sounds of the camp; a dog howling, the brass of a trumpet calling, a challenge and response at an outlying vedette. Ten minutes later Raj blinked.

"Yes," he said, softly, to himself. "That should do." He looked up. "Excellent work, Abdullah. You won't regret it."

Abdullah bowed. "My life is to serve, *sayyid*."

Raj waved a hand. "If your son still wants that cavalry ensign's commission—and I'm still around and in command when he turns sixteen—it's his."

A very rare honor for one not of the Star Church;

although Abdullah's faith allowed its adherents to freely observe the ceremonies of other religions, where advisable. The Druze bowed again, more deeply.

"Gerrin," Raj went on. "We'll be concentrated by 0900 tomorrow?"

"All except for Osterville," Staenbridge said. "But he's—"

"—closer nor he said, ser," M'lewis put in. "Nobbut six klicks east."

Raj nodded. "Here's what we'll do. Barton, write this up. At dawn—"

CHAPTER EIGHT

"Allahu Akbar! Gur! Gur!"

The band of Colonials swept out of a side street in the maze of alleys. The morning sun burned bright on their scimitars and spiked helmets; beneath their djellabas they had wound tight linen strips, the winding-sheets of men determined to seek Paradise in battle with the unbelievers.

The main street was narrow and crooked as well; only one file of troopers was between Raj and the attack. Horace spun beneath him with a roaring growl, and his hand swept out saber and pistol. A grid of green lines clamped down over his vision, and the outlines of the Colonial troopers glowed. One strobed; the one with his carbine in his hands. Still a hundred paces away: a long pistol-shot but not impossible for a skilled man on dogback to make with a shoulder-weapon. And the Arab looked good. . . .

Raj moved his wrist. A red dot settled on the Colonial's midriff. His finger squeezed the trigger. *Crack*. The carbineer flipped over the cantle of his saddle. *Crack*. Another down. Place the dot and the bullet went where Center indicated it would. *Crack—crack—crack*. The revolver was empty, and the Colonials were through.

A clang of steel on steel as a scimitar met his saber. He flexed his wrist to let the sharply curved blade hiss by, then cut backhand across the Arab's face. A second was barreling in with his blade upraised. Horace lunged

137

with open mouth for the Bazenji's throat. Raj stabbed,
and the point of his weapon went in below the breastbone.
He ripped it free with desperate strength, wheeling.
Suzette's carbine clanged and nearly dropped from her
hands as she used it to deflect a cut. Raj rose in the
stirrups and chopped downward; there was a jar like
the blade hitting seasoned oak, and a splitting sound. It
nearly wrenched from his hand, sunk to brow-level in
the Colonial's skull, but the weight of the falling body
pulled the metal free.

There had been no time for fear. Something contracted
in a hard knot under his ribs when he saw his wife
clutching at her upper arm.

"It's nothing, light cut," she said.

He checked; in the background rifles barked as the
troopers put down the dogs of the dead Arabs where
they stood snarling over their masters' bodies. She was
right; she held a dressing over the superficial wound
while he tied it off.

"Damn, that was too close," he said. "Anyone else
wounded?"

His bannerman had gashed fingers where he'd used
the staff to block a cut. Suzette heeled Harbie closer
and went to work on that. The sergeant of the color-
party was looking at him wide-eyed.

"Spirit, ser," he blurted. "Five dead wit' five shots!"

Raj felt a flush of embarrassment. He wasn't actually
a first-rate pistol-shot; the sword was his personal weapon
of choice, and with that he was very good. With Center's
eerie trick, you didn't *have* to be good. He didn't much
like the experience. It was too much like being a weapon
yourself, in another's hand.

Whatever works, he thought.

precisely.

"Keep moving," he said sharply.

The suburbs of Ain el-Hilwa were burning already,

as the Civil Government troops shot and hacked their way through the crowds who ran screaming towards the gates. Shells went by overhead in long ripping-canvas arcs, to crash on the massive stone-faced walls behind the moat. It was a wet moat, full of canal water, right now dark with the heads of refugees swimming across; and getting no help from the garrison. The gates were jammed tight with a press of humanity.

"Forward!" he said again. "Dammit, bugler, sound *Advance at speed!*"

The brazen scream cut through the white noise of the crowds, the gathering roar of the flames. Sheer press of numbers was slowing the advance despite complete surprise. The people ahead *wanted* to get out of the way of the sharp blades and snarling meter-long jaws and rifle fire; they *couldn't.*

Should have stayed in their houses, he thought—or in the sprawling city of reed shanties and tents outside the suburbs. There was no wisdom in panic.

A field gun bounced up behind him. The crew pulled the trail free of the limber and spun it around, running it forward with the long pole held up and the nose of the gun down. They pushed it through the front line of Civil Government troopers and let the trail fall.

"Stand clear!" the gun commander said. He skipped aside himself and pulled the lanyard.

Pomph. The shock of discharge slapped at him, bouncing back and forth from the narrow walls.

So did the hundreds of lead shot in the canister charge. Men—and women and children—splashed away from the spreading scythe of it.

"Waymanos!" Raj shouted again. "Forward!"

The buildings dropped away on either side as they came out into the broad cleared area around the moat. Cannon and pompoms were firing from the walls, but most of the shots went overhead, into the belt of houses, helping with the work of destruction. In the gates, the garrison were firing down into their own people, dropping handbombs and pouring burning naphtha from the murder-holes over the arched entrances to clear the press. The gates swung shut, and the bridges over the moats gaped as hinged sections were pulled up.

"Damn," Raj said aloud. "Runner, to battalion commanders. Get the fires going and pull back."

A shell burst twenty yards ahead. Raj stood in his stirrups and brought out his field glasses, sweeping along the walls. Chaos, but active chaos—groups in the crimson djellabas of Colonial regular troops, infantry from the looks of them, and the white-and-colored patchwork of city militia. More and more of the fortress guns were getting into operation, too.

He turned Horace to the rear. "Come on, let's get out before the fires spread."

He was conscious of a few odd looks. Technically, this was a defeat—they hadn't been able to rush the gates, despite the shambolic panic of the Colonial garrison's response. Raj grinned a little wider.

A reputation for having something up your sleeve could be quite helpful. Even when you *did* have something up your sleeve.

Suzette was flexing her arm, wincing only a little, as they turned and trotted back through the smoke and noise. Shells whirred by overhead; ash and bits of debris fell into the dirt streets about them.

I'm almost glad that happened, Raj thought. Something sounded an interrogative at the back of his mind. *I was beginning to wonder whether I'd lost my capacity for strong emotion.*

i am not contagious.

The hell you're not, Raj thought. *For example, I wouldn't have dared to talk this way to an angel a few years ago.* He looked down at the city. *For another, I*

*wouldn't do what I'm going to do to Osterville a few
years ago. Even to Osterville.*

**ah. that is the effect known as "life," raj whitehall.
and it is contagious; not only that, but fatal. for
all of us.**

"Should be ready in about three hours, *mi heneral,*"
Dinnalsyn said.

The gunner and Raj stood together outside the
earthworks, five kilometers from Ain el-Hilwa. Two
thousand troopers and as many press-ganged Colonial
refugees dug steadily, hauling the dirt from the growing
ditch upslope in baskets, buckets, helmets, and cloth
slings improvised from coats. The sun was high, and the
men sweated as they worked; an hour on and an hour
off, with the off spent standing guard or watering and
feeding the dogs. The earthwork fort was two hundred
meters on a side, a standard marching camp with a ditch
as deep as a standing man, an earthwork rampart as high
inside with a palisade on top, and bastions at the corners
and gates with V-notches for the guns. The air was full
of the smell of sweat and freshly turned earth.

He walked over to the edge. "Found that buried cask
of beer yet, dog-brothers?" Raj called in Namerique.

The big fair men in the nearest section groaned
laughter. "Don't worry, lord," one yelled back. "By the
Spirit of Man of This Earth, we'll have a grave big enough
for all the enemy we kill if it takes us all day."

Raj waved as he turned away. *Not bad,* he thought.
Back home, these men scorned digging in the earth as
fit for peons and women; real men fought, hunted, and
drank. They'd learned something of soldiering, then—
granted he'd had to kill about a third of the adult males
in their nations to get their attention, but they were
learning.

Within the enclosure medics were setting up, and tents

being pitched in neat rows along the streets; everything
necessary for a mobile military city of five thousand men.
It could be made more elaborate the longer they stayed,
but by midafternoon the camp would be ready to defend.
It was said, not without truth, that watching a Civil
Government army encamp was more discouraging for
barbarians than fighting a battle with them. The Colonials
wouldn't be intimidated, but they'd know exactly how
hard it was to storm this sort of earthworks.

"Good, Grammeck," he said. "Keep pushing it. Gerrin,
once we've got the wall up, let all these Colonials go—
it won't hurt the troops to finish up by themselves. Kaltin,
you've got overwatch—"

"Ser," his color-sergeant said.

Raj looked around. A party of Civil Government officers
was riding up; not his own, Osterville's banner. Raj waited
in silence.

"General," Osterville said.

"Colonel," Raj replied. Formally: "Colonel Osterville,
I'm ordering you to bring your command within the walls
of this encampment."

Osterville sneered, a rather theatrical expression. "I'll
have to deprive you and Messa Whitehall of that pleasure.
As Commandant of the Military District of Sandoral,
our authority is concurrent. These commands remain
separate, and *I'm* not afraid of that lot of wogs over there."

He pointed; his own four battalions were setting up
camp on a hill no more than a kilometer from the walls.
Beyond that was a dense pall of smoke, as the ruins of
the suburbs beyond the wall smoldered. Not coincidentally,
there was an orchard and pleasant little country villa on
the hill.

"I warn you," Raj went on, stroking his chin, "that
the Colonials may try to sally. Your position is more
vulnerable than mine."

Osterville spat—toward the city, which made the

gesture ambiguous. "They're scum, with incompetent officers. Obviously, or they'd be over the river with Ali, wouldn't they?" His voice took on a faint hectoring, lecturing note. "Look at the way they reacted when we attacked this morning. As I said, *I'm* not afraid of them, and neither are my men. We're staying where we are."

"By all means, Colonel Osterville," Raj said mildly. "Perhaps it's advisable, all things considered."

From the ranks of officers around Raj a loud whisper continued the thought: "Considering what our men would do to those garrison pussies who've been shorting the take."

Osterville's head whipped around, finding a wall of bland politeness. He saluted and pulled his dog around, with a violence that brought a protesting whimper as the cheek-levers of the bridle gouged.

"Ser." A messenger this time, from the heliograph detachment who'd been setting up a relay back to the bridgehead. "Message from Colonel Menyez."

The silence grew tense. Raj read. "Ali's arrived," he said. "And tried the usual. So far—"

observe, Center said.

"Noisy beggars," Major Ferdihando Felasquez said.

The Colonial army was parading past the walls of Sandoral, fifty thousand strong. *Tabor* after *tabor* of mounted men in crimson djellabas and pantaloons, in a perfect order that rippled with the rise and fall of the trotting dogs. Between the blocks of men came guns, light pompoms and 70mm field pieces, with heavier siege weapons behind. Beyond that, on a hillock just out of medium artillery range, an enormous tent-pavilion in brilliant stripes was already going up. From the tallest pole flew the green crescent banner and the peacock of the Settlers.

And over it all came an inhuman pulse of drums, like

the beating heart of some great beast. Beneath that the clang of cymbals and the brazen scream of long curled trumpets.

Felasquez tapped his gauntlets against his thigh. "Should we send them a few love-notes?" he asked. "Some of the heavier pieces on the wall could reach that far."

"No," Jorg Menyez said, scanning down the line of units with the big tripod-mounted field glasses. "We're playing for time, so there's no sense in poking the sauroid through the bars. Ah, yes. Notice something?"

He stepped aside and Felasquez bent to the eyepieces. A forest of banners was going up before the Settler's pavilion. "Ali, Hussein the Wazir, the Grand Mufti of Sinnar, the Gederosian Dervishes . . . wait a minute."

Menyez nodded. "No Seal of Solomon. Tewfik's not here."

"Unless they want us to think that."

"No, that's not the way Colonials think."

Felasquez nodded. "I'd still feel easier if you weren't splitting up so much of the 24th Valencia," he went on.

"The garrison infantry need stiffening; we haven't had enough time to work them into first-class shape."

"You can't stiffen a bucket of spit with a handful of lead shot," Felasquez said.

Menyez clapped him on the shoulder. "It's not as bad as all that. They're trained men, sound at bottom; they've just been neglected recently. Standing behind a parapet and shooting is about the easiest type of combat for 'em. They just need some examples. How're the militia-gunner volunteers showing?"

"Pretty well; still have to see how they stand fire, of course. But the ones who stayed were the ones who *wanted* to fight. A lot of them were with us when we fought Jamal, five years ago."

Along the walls of Sandoral men stood to the parapet and looked out the merlons, but their numbers were sparse. Most of the garrison stood to in the cleared space within the walls, or waited in their billets. Apart from them the city was a ghostly place, where little moved but rats and cats almost as feral.

"It's all waiting now," Menyez went on, "and I want my supper. Runner; message to the *Heneralissimo*—"

This time the viewpoint shifted to a point on the rail line west. Raj recognized it: a long viaduct over a gully that was a torrent in the winter and spring. The burning remnants of the wooden trestle bridge lay scattered below.

A long file of Colonial dragoons rose from prayer and rolled up their issue rugs. Naiks and rissaldars screamed at them, and they returned to their work—hacking through the ties of the railway line. As each section of track came loose, they carried it at a run to one of the bonfires that blazed at intervals down the line and threw it on. The dry wood flared up like tinder, and in the heart of the furnace-heat he could see the thin strap iron turning cherry-red and then yellow, slumping and twisting into a mass of metallic spaghetti that would have to be carted to the forges and rolling-mills as scrap.

Raj nodded to himself, tight-lipped. No surprise; a railroad was the best military target there was. But it had taken generations to get the line from Sandoral to East Residence completed; until Barholm Clerett came to the throne and Raj reconquered the territories to the west, there always seemed to be a more urgent short-term priority.

The Colonials were doing a good professional job of the wrecking, and there were a lot of them.

Dust smoked up from the road. Sweat dripped off the twenty-hitch train of oxen as they strained at the trek-chain. The big tented wagon rolled forward, its axles groaning, man-high wheels turning at the steady, inexorable pace that would take it ten kilometers a day and neither more nor less. It was one of a line of two dozen, between them taking up several kilometers of road; all of them had the Crescent pyrographed on the wood of their sides, and the Peacock stenciled on their tilts.

The load was sacked grain, and bales of a repulsive-looking dried fish; even in the holographic vision he could imagine the mealy, oily smell of it. *Advocati*, the staple dog-fodder of the Drangosh valley, a sucker-mouthed parasitic bottom-feeder with no backbone. Dogs would eat it, just; even slaves would refuse it if they could. As he watched, the oxen halted as the drivers snapped their whips. Men with baskets of grain and dried alfalfa pellets went down the train, dumping loads by the draft cattle.

The escort sank down and unlimbered the goatskin water-bottles at their waists, stacking their light lever-action rifles. Infantry, with short curved falchions at their belts rather than the scimitars of the cavalry. Tewfik wouldn't be wasting his best men on duty like this, but here was about a platoon of them. The drovers were civilians, slight men in ragged clothes.

A voice called, and drovers and soldiers alike knelt in the dust, performing the ritual washing and unrolling their mats. A call, and they knelt to distant Sinnar, the holy city where the first humans on Bellevue had landed, bringing a fragment of the ka'ba from ruined Mecca.

A Colonial officer with gold-rimmed spectacles and a green-dyed beard stood beside a hole. It was outside the walls of Sandoral—he could see the city in the middle distance—but outside ordinary artillery range. There were several hundred Colonials working in the hole, mostly stripped to their loincloths, but they had the look of soldiers. Probably engineers; the Colony had whole units of them, rather than expecting line units to be able to double up at need, the way the Civil Government did. He'd never seen men work harder, or with more skill.

Picks were flying; plank ramps went down into the hole, and wheelbarrows came up at a trot, full of earth. The dirt was piled neatly in heaps not far away; other men were filling sandbags from the heaps. Still more shaped timber, raw beams from orchards around the city, or seasoned timber salvaged from houses. A knocked-down floor of planks waited to be assembled.

A bunker, Raj decided. *Cursed large one, too. Probably for Ali.*

Raj blinked, conscious of the eyes on him. They were all used to his . . . spells of inattention . . . by now.

He cleared his throat. "Ali's reached Sandoral and he's digging in around the city. So far he hasn't mounted an assault—bringing up his siege train, at a guess. He's got the full fifty thousand men with him; it must be straining his supply of wagons and fodder to keep them fed. Tewfik's banner isn't with the main army."

There was a stir at that. "What do we do, *mi heneral?*" Staenbridge asked.

"We dig, and we wait."

"Wait for what?"

"For the wogs" —he nodded toward Ain el-Hilwa— "to take the bait. In which case, we—"

The officers waited in silence, a few taking notes. "Is all that clear?" Raj finished.

"No reserve?" Staenbridge asked.

"Not this time; it's a calculated risk, but so's this whole expedition."

He turned and looked at the Arab city, surrounded by the smoldering wreck of its suburbs, crammed to the very wall with refugees.

"Either this will be easy, or it'll be impossible," he said.

**probability of action proceeding according to
current projections, 78%±7**, Center said helpfully.

"I'd put it at about three to one on easy," he went on.
"If not, we'll just have to react fast."

> *"When you go by the Camina Bellica*
> *As thousands have traveled before*
> *Remember the Luck of the Soldier*
> *Who never saw home anymore!*
> *Oh, dear was the lover who kissed him*
> *And dear was the mother that bore;*
> *But then they found his sword in the heather,*
> *And he never saw home anymore!"*

"Ser." Antin M'lewis was Officer of the Day; he slipped
into the circle around the fire. "Major Hwadeloupe t'see
yer."

Raj finished the mouthful of fig-bread and dusted his
hands, leaning back on the cushions—someone had
salvaged them from a nearby Colonial mansion, and they
were all resting on them and the Al Kebir carpets from
the same source. A roast sheep on rice had been
demolished, and they were punishing the sweetmeats
and pastries the Colonials were famous for. The wine
was too sweet, even diluted, but nobody was drinking
all that much of it anyway; they knew him better than
that. The firelight played on the faces around it, bringing
out scars on Kaltin Gruder's as he leaned forward to
light a twig and puff a cheroot alight.

"By all means, Antin, bring him along," Raj said.

Hwadeloupe commanded the 44th Camarina Dragoons,
one of Osterville's battalions.

"An' ser . . . he's got 'is men out there. Hunnerts of
'em, not too far."

"Keep an eye on them, Captain."

The strong male voices were roaring out the next verse,
the one that had gotten the song officially banned

centuries ago. It was a truth the Governors preferred
that the Army not be too conscious of:

> "When you go by the Camina Bellica
> From the City to Sandoral,
> Remember the Luck of the Soldier
> Who rose to be master of all!
> He carried the rifle and saber,
> He stood his watch and rode tall,
> Till the Army hailed him as Governor
> And he rose to be master of all!"

"Glad you could join us," Raj said as Hwadeloupe
strode up. "No, no, no salutes in the mess, Major. Have
some wine."

The soldier-servant handed him a mug of half-and-
half, watered wine. He gripped it distractedly, a middle-
aged man with the marks of long service on the southern
border on his leathery face.

"*Mi heneral*, if we could speak privately?"

"I have no secrets from my officers and Companions,
Major." Not *quite* true, but it was a polite way of telling
Hwadeloupe that he couldn't expect to hedge his bets.

"Ah . . . sir, I would like to transfer my battalion to
your command—to this encampment, that is."

The rest of the command group had fallen silent;
Suzette kept strumming her *gittar*, but softly. Without
the song, the minor noises of the camp came through:
dogs growling, a challenge from the walls, the iron clatter
of a field gun's breechblock being opened for some
reason.

"If I might ask why?" Raj went on implacably.

Hwadeloupe stood very straight. "Sir. Colonel Osterville
thinks there's no risk from the garrison of Ain el-Hilwa.
But I know you don't think so, and I see your men still
have their boots on, and your guns are limbered up.
Colonel Osterville may be right. On the whole, though,

when he and you disagree, I'll bet on you. With respect, sir."

Raj shoulder-rolled and came erect. "I can always use good men," he said. "And I don't think you'll regret that decision. Captain M'lewis will show your men to their bivouac area within the earthworks."

"Ah, sir. There's one other matter." Hwadeloupe kept his eyes fixed over Raj's shoulder. "We have, ah, a considerable quantity of booty with us. Just picked up, you understand. We'd like to turn it in now to the common fund, as per your standing orders."

Raj raised an eyebrow; one of Gerrin's expressions, and very useful in situations like this. "That's odd, Major. We've had several smaller parties in from Colonel Osterville's camp, and they've all had some late-arriving booty to turn in too." He extended his hand. "No hard feelings. M'lewis will settle your people in."

"I'll see to that myself, if it's all the same to you, *mi heneral*," Hwadeloupe said, taking the extended hand in his own. "And thank you, sir."

Raj returned to his cushion beside Suzette. "That's about two hundred in all," he said.

"Separating the sheep from the goats," Staenbridge replied. "Or those too stupid to live from the remainder."

Foley frowned. "Some of them are staying over there to follow orders," he pointed out.

"My dear," Gerrin said, "what's that saying—from the Old Namerique codexes—"

Foley was something of a scholar. " '*Against Fate even the gods do not fight*,' " he quoted.

"Exactly."

Raj nodded and leaned back, his head not quite in Suzette's lap. Both moons were out and very bright, bright enough to interrupt the frosted arch of stars. Her fingers wandered over the strings.

"It's twenty-five marches to Payso
It's forty-five more to Ayaire
And the end may be death in the heather
Or life on the Governor's Chair
But whether the Army obeys us,
Or we serve as some sauroid's fare
I'd rather be Lola's lover
Than sit on the Governor's Chair!"

Cut-nose Marhtinez lay in the dark and breathed quietly. He was ten meters from the walls of Ain el-Hilwa, outside the north gate. An overturned two-wheel cart hid him; the bodies of the two dogs who'd been drawing it until they met a cannonball were fairly ripe after a day in the hot sun, and so was the driver: black, swollen, the skin split and dripping in places, like a windfallen plum. He'd had about seven FedCreds in assorted silver in his pouch, though.

The night was fairly dark, only one moon in the sky and that near the horizon. The starlight was enough for him to see men moving on the walls—and they were moving without torches. He could even hear some wog curse when he ran into something and barked his chin. A whistling and dull thudding followed, about the sound you'd expect one of those nine-barbed whips the wog officers used to make. The yelp of pain that followed was strangled, and the next slash brought no sound at all.

Quiet's a whorehouse on payday, he thought scornfully. It was a good thing there weren't any Bedouin scouts with the Ain el-Hilwa garrison. Those sand-humpers were too good for comfort.

Cut-nose moved his head slightly. The star he was using was still a fingerbreadth above the horizon. An hour and a bit short of dawn, call it an hour and twenty minutes.

He moved backward out of the wrecked cart, keeping

it between him and the wall. Nothing on his body clinked or reflected light, and his hands and face were blacked; Mother Marhtinez might not have known exactly who his father was, but she hadn't raised any fools. Pause, move, pause, until he was behind a snag of ruined wall, still hot enough from the fire to feel on his skin. He picked up his rifle—nothing but a hindrance and a temptation in the blind where he'd spent the night— and eeled cautiously back to his dog.

Captain M'lewis was waiting there. Cut-nose grinned ingratiatingly. He didn't have much use for officers, and still less for a promoted ranker who might be a kinsman. He did have the liveliest respect for Antin M'lewis's wits, his wire garrote, and the skinning-knife he wore across the small of his back beneath the tails of his uniform jacket. All the Forty Thieves—the Scouts—had a standing invitation to go out behind the stables and settle things with knives if they felt they couldn't obey someone who wasn't Messer-born.

So far only one fool had taken M'lewis up on it; he was on the rolls as a deserter. Nobody had found the body. *Good riddance*, Cut-nose thought. The Scouts beat regular duty all to hell. Less boring, more plunder—a *lot* more in some cases—and no more dangerous. M'lewis wasn't the charge-the-barricade type.

"They're movin', ser. Gittin' ready, loike," he said in a soft whisper, directed at the ground—nothing to carry far.

M'lewis nodded. "Messer Raj was expectin' it, an' t'scouts at t'other gate says th' same," he observed. "Here, git this t'him fast."

"Sir."

Kaltin Gruder's voice. Raj rolled out of his blankets; Suzette was already reaching for her carbine. He fastened his weapons belt. His boots were already on; if the men had to sleep in them, so could he.

"Message from M'lewis just got in."

A Scout was behind the battalion commander. "Ser. Noise in t'wog town. I weren't more 'n ten meters off, an' heard it plain. North gates."

The ones nearest Colonel Osterville's camp. Raj took the message and read it. "Boots and saddles, please. Quietly. We'll deploy as arranged."

"Line of march?"

"Scout troop has pickets along it. They'll signal with shuttered lanterns."

Raj could hear the noise spreading; not very loud, no shouting, but a long-drawn out clatter as men rousted out of uneasy sleep and saw to their equipment. The Companions arrived, and the other battalion commanders. Shapes in the night, dimly lit by the embers of the fire, a feeling of controlled anxiety. He grinned into the dark. A night march. Difficult. An invitation to disaster, with any but very experienced troops. The handbooks were full of bungled night attacks, men firing on their comrades, whole battalions wandering off lost, irretrievable disaster.

"Barton," he said. "What's that toast again?"

" 'He fears his fate too much, and his deserts are small, who will not put it to the touch—to win or lose it all.' "

"Exactly. Messers, to your units. *Waymanos!*"

An orderly brought up Horace; he put a foot in the stirrup and swung into the saddle. The headquarters party fell in around him, bannermen and buglers and gallopers. Men blinked and dogs yawned cavernously; the wet *clomp-clomp* sound of jaws snapping closed rippled through the dark streets. Iron-shod wheels rattled on dirt as the 75's and splatguns moved. He cantered down the east-west notional laneway of the camp, the *wia erente*, keeping to the side. Men and dogs were moving the same way, the lead element of the 5th, followed by the 1st and 2nd Cruisers. The other gates were all open as well, flanked by lantern-bearing pathfinders. Thousands of heavy paws thumped the earth, an endless rumbling sound.

Flat terrain, mostly. Nothing between him and Osterville's camp but four kilometers of fields, with the occasional orchard or shallow ditch. The objective was on the same side of the Ghor Canal, thank the Spirit, even *Osterville* wasn't stupid enough to put an obstacle that needed bridging between him and the only supports available. *Keep in column,* he decided. In column they could move down the laneways, at a fast walk. Once deployed into line their speed would drop by four-fifths.

The night was still quiet, almost chilly in the last moments of predawn; overhead the arch of stars was a frosted road leading to infinity. The command group rode silently, no need for talk unless something went very wrong. The palms that lined the roadway were black silhouettes against the sky. He looked over his shoulder to the west and caught the faintest rim of peach-pink there.

He reined Horace sideways into the fields, a hunching scramble through the ditch, then stood in the stirrups to look. Nothing but a few watchfires from Osterville's camp. The north gates of the city were hidden by the western wall. Flags rippled behind him, his personal banner and the Star. Over his shoulder he could see the other gates of the camp, now; the spiked-log barricades were pulled aside, and a steady stream of men and dogs and guns was pouring out. Not a single jam-up, not a voice raised . . . *damn, but these are good troops.*

Three columns, each about half a kilometer apart, each a little over two thousand strong. And—

" *'The gates flew back, and the din of onset sounded,' "* Barton murmured.

"More Old Namerique?" Raj said.

"From the Fall Codexes," the young man replied.

When the Fall began, books had died with the machines that recorded them—the Church called it the Great Simplification. In the first generation the survivors wrote down as much as they could, most of it in Old Namerique, the official language of the Federation. Bits and pieces survived, even a thousand years later.

The gates of Ain el-Hilwa had certainly flown back with a vengeance.

"One hell of a din, too," Raj said; even at more than three kilometers, it was louder than the noise his own men were making.

Then light winked from the parapet of the low-set city wall, and a deep whirring sound crossed the sky. A dull booming echoed, and under it the sharper sound of the exploding shells. The winking lights, scores of meters apart, rippled from east to west across the north face of the city. Heavy rifles, aimed at Osterville's camp. The shells seemed to be contact-fused rather than airburst, but it would still be an unpleasant way to wake up, and there were a lot of those guns.

The white dust of the road stretched out ahead of him. The dawn was just touching the western horizon behind him, but there was a sudden flare of white light stabbing north toward Osterville's position, arc-searchlights from the city wall. *My, all the modern refinements*, Raj thought. Intended to light up the Civil Government position for the attackers and blind any defenders looking toward the city.

Dun and off-white, men were running up the long gentle slope toward the smaller Civil Government camp. On foot, mostly, with gun teams among them, pulling the light five-shot pom-poms the Colonials favored for close support. They were shouting, too, high wailing shrieks. Raj unclipped his binoculars and brought them to his eyes, body adapting to the swing of his dog's trot with the unconscious skill of a lifetime.

Only half a kilometer from the walls. And they didn't dig in at all. Osterville had been *very* careless.

A stutter of gunfire broke out from Osterville's camp, building rapidly. Raj could imagine the chaos, men rushing half-dressed from their blanket rolls, grabbing up the rifles stacked by their campfires. Red light winked from the hilltop, muzzle flashes like fireflies in the dark; the sun was just edging over the horizon.

The Colonials were making some effort to deploy, spreading out in an irregular mass—more a thick skirmish order than a real firing line. The pom-poms wheeled about and opened up, firing uphill. The *CRACK-CRACK-CRACK-CRACK-CRACK* of the clip-loaded weapons sounded through the dawn, and their little one-kilo shells burst upslope in petals of fire. The return fire was building fast, panicked, with no ordered crash of volleys. Smoke began to shroud the hilltop, from the defensive fire and the incoming Colonial shells, and—

"Bugging out already," he said. In the long-shadowed light of dawn he could see a trickle of mounted men heading north from Osterville's encampment. "Ludwig, how many of the Colonials would you say?"

"Seven or eight thousand at least, *mi heneral.*"

Raj nodded thoughtfully. The whole garrison of Ain el-Hilwa, or near enough. Attacking Osterville's position was actually not a bad idea—he would have tried it, in their position—but sending everyone haring out of the gates like this? *No more sense than a bull carnosauroid in breeding season*, he decided.

"Captain Foley, the signal."

Barton swung down out of the saddle and stuck the launching-stick of a small rocket in the dirt.

Fisssssth. The little rocket soared into the paling sky and burst with an undramatic *pop*. Red and blue sparks shot out in a perfect round puffball. Behind Raj trumpets sang in harsh antiphonal chorus. The long column dissolved as units spurred out left and right, like a huge fan snapping open. It was lighter now, light enough to tell a dark thread from a white, the traditional dividing line between night and day. Light enough for the men to move across the fields without much trouble, at least.

The other columns were following suit. Ten minutes, and there was a continuous two-deep line moving northeastwards with his banner at the center. Not parade-ground neat—the line twisted and curled a little around obstacles, with fifty meters or so of gap between each battalion. The guns pulled through, heading east and a little south, setting up by groups of batteries on prechosen hillocks. The Colonials were fully occupied, their front ranks within two hundred meters of Osterville's position and moving in fast. Close enough to use their carbines, and a huge snapping crackle went up from their front ranks; not *only* from their front ranks, either—they were losing men to friendly fire, if he was any judge.

"Sound *Prepare for Dismounted Action*," he said.

The bugles sang again, taken up and relayed down the line. Men pulled the rifles from the scabbards before their right knees, resting the butts on their thighs.

"Are they bloody *blind*?" Staenbridge asked in amazement, looking at the Colonials.

"No, just very preoccupied, and extremely badly led," Raj said.

There were probably individual men in the Colonial force who could see what was happening, but it was a scratch put-together and whoever had done the putting hadn't arranged for signals and gallopers. A penalty of taking all your best troops along in a single expeditionary force; what was left to defend against a counterstroke wasn't up to much.

Six hundred meters, Raj thought.

five hundred eight-eight and decreasing to nearest enemy element. five hundred eighty. five

seventy-six. Center provided a numbered scale on the whole Colonial formation; their right wing was just out of extreme rifle-shot.

More of Osterville's men were bugging out, but that wouldn't be visible to the wogs. A slamming close-range firefight ran in a C all around the front of the hill, as the larger Colonial force overlapped the Civil Government forces upslope. Most of the pom-pom shells were flying right over the hill, dangerous only to the deserters streaming northward—who deserved whatever they got. The Colonial rifle fire was uneven; their men were pumping out their seven-shell magazines and then pausing to reload. That had to be done by pushing one round at a time through the loading gate in the side of the weapon, which evened things out a little, but Osterville's fire was dropping off noticeably, as the Colonials beat down his men by sheer weight of numbers.

Five hundred meters. "Sound *Dismounted Advance.*"

The buglers sent the message down the lines: a four-note preparation, twice repeated, then a single sustained note taken up by the signalers in unit after unit. Six thousand dogs crouched. Not quite in unison, but nearly so within battalions. The men stepped free of the stirrups without pausing, and the dogs rose and walked behind, still in ranks as regular as the men's. A good cavalry battalion drilled six hours a day, six days a week for this moment, until the signals played directly on the nervous systems of men and mounts. Raj turned his binoculars to the far right of his line: Hwadeloupe's men were badly under strength, but they were carrying it off quite well.

A long clatter as the men loaded. Raj's head went back and forth; the troops were advancing at a steady walk, the splatguns trundling forward with the soldiers, two per battalion. They were light enough for the crews to manhandle them like that; they looked much like field guns, but each was actually thirty-five double-length rifle barrels clamped in a tube. He watched as one crew let the trail thump to the ground and loaded. One man swung the lever down, another inserted an iron plate with thirty-five rifle cartridges, the lever went back up with a thump. Waiting for the order—but they were artillerymen and very good at estimating ranges. He chopped out his palm. The buglers took it up. All up and down the line men checked a half-pace. And . . .

"Halto!"

Officers ducked ahead and spread arm and drawn saber to mark the firing line. Another bugle call and the front rank dropped to the ground and the men behind them went to one knee, right elbow resting on it. The platoon commanders and senior noncoms walked quickly between the two ranks for a moment, checking that the sights were adjusted for the range. The muzzles quivered as each trooper picked a target. The dogs crouched; only the mounted officers, Company-grade and above, marked the line. Company pennants and battalion banners too, of course; the men took their dressing from the flags.

Raj took a deep breath. It was a peculiar exultation, like handling a fine sword with perfect balance; the pleasure that came only from a difficult task performed exactly as it should be.

Some of the enemy were turning now, firing frantically. Far too late. The trumpets spoke again, preparing men for the order:

"Fwego!"

BAMMMbambambambabam . . . Six thousand rifles fired within a few seconds of each other. A discordant medley of battalion trumpeters sounded the *Fire by Platoon Volleys*. BAM. BAM. BAM. Rippling down the formation. Front line prone, second rank kneeling. Front rank fire-and-reload, second rank fire-and-reload, a steady pounding crackle. The dawn wind was from the east, blowing the new fogbank of powder smoke backward in tatters. The smell was overwhelming in the fresh morning air: a sharp unpleasant reek of burnt sulfur and stinging saltpeter. The smell of death.

The splatgun crew spun the crank at one side of the breechblock. *Brraaaap*. A long splat of sound as the thirty-five rounds snapped out. *K-chung* as the lever went back and the plate was lifted out by the loop on its top, a rattle as another was slapped home and the lever worked. *Brraaaap. Brraaaap.* Three hundred rounds a minute. An ancient design, ancient before the Fall, from man's first rise; primitive enough that men in these days could build it. The priests said that Man had been perfect, before the Fall. Raj had always been a believer; it was obscurely disturbing that part of that perfection was better and better mechanisms of slaughter.

He threw the thought aside, with a touch to the amulet blessed by Saint Wu; there was the work of the day to be done. Raj turned and cantered down the line. The Civil Government formation was at right angles to the Colonial formation, like the crossbar on a "T." The whole weight of its fire was crashing into the end of the Arab line. And most of the Civil Government cavalrymen could *hit* a man-sized target at three hundred meters, many of them at twice that range. Even if they missed, their 11mm bullets would run the entire length of the enemy line, with good odds of hitting *something*. The Colonials were melting away, men smashed to the ground by the heavy hollowpoint bullets with massive exit wounds that bled them out in seconds, or tore limbs from bodies.

He paused behind one of the ex-Brigadero units. A noncom was walking down the line, slapping men across the shoulders with the flat of his saber when they instinctively rose to fire standing. *Problem*, Raj though. They'd trained on muzzle-loading rifle muskets. You had to stand to reload those, tearing open the paper cartridge and pouring the powder down the barrel. They were excellent shots even by Descotter standards, but not used to getting under cover—and even at this range, some of the Colonial carbine-bullets would hit standing men. A few snapped by him.

Ludwig Bellamy rode up. "It's a slaughter, *heneralissimo*," he said enthusiastically. "Teodore—Major Welf—asks permission to remount his battalion and charge—"

"Denied," Raj said sharply.

Welf had been a very tricky opponent in the Western Territories, but he was still a Brigadero at heart and had a lingering fondness for cold steel. The Civil Government military style was economical of men where it could be, not having so many trained soldiers to expend.

"I'm not going to waste men on this lot." He raised the binoculars again. "Besides, about now—"

There was boiling confusion all down the front of the Arab army. A knot of mounted officers around a huge green banner was galloping toward the threatened flank, with more courage than sense. At their head was a portly gray-bearded man waving his ceremonial lash and shouting furiously, probably trying to pull units out of line and get them to face front left. Small chance of that, since Osterville's men were still firing from *their* front, besides which most of them probably hadn't realized what was happening, and facing about would put the morning sun directly in their eyes.

The enemy bannerman went down. Seconds later half a dozen of the officers around him did, and then the elderly man with the whip punched backward over the cantle of his saddle. His dog whipped about and sniffed him, then sank down on its haunches and howled.

"—they're going to bug out."

It started with the men in sight of the dead commander. They broke like a glass pitcher dropped on a stone floor, and fled back toward the city. Bullets kicked up dust around their feet like the first raindrops of a storm, and littered the ground with bodies. That unmasked the central part of the Colonial host, and for the first time they could see exactly what it was that had devoured the left wing of their army. And the steady, unhurried volleys punched out, from a Civil Government line marked by a growing tower of smoke that made their position clear even a kilometer away. The Arabs disintegrated like a rope unraveling from the left end, men throwing away their weapons to run screaming for the city gates. Droves piled up at ditches that a man could leap easily, as the first tripped and the men behind trampled on them.

"*Spirit*, sir—if we charge now—"

"Major Bellamy, all that charging now would do is give *them* an opportunity to hurt *us*." He looked around. "Messenger to Major Gruder: advance from the left in line, by battalions, pivoting on . . ." —he considered— "on the 3/591st." You had to start moving the outside of a line first, or the whiplash effect would leave the outermost man running.

"Are we going to let them back into the city, *mi heneral?*" Ludwig Bellamy asked, crestfallen.

Raj smiled unpleasantly. "By no means, Major. By no means."

"Range three thousand. Up three. And a bit. Contact fuse. Load."

Grammeck Dinnalsyn raised his eyes from the split-view rangefinder. Three batteries were deployed along the slight rise: twelve guns. Another three were a few hundred meters farther on, setting up amid the outer spray of the dead Colonials. Dismounted men were trotting by in waves as the left flank of the Civil Government force swung in to pin the retreating Colonials against the walls of Ain el-Hilwa, but that was no concern of the artillery today; they weren't tasked with supporting the dogboys. The riflemen were firing as they advanced, independent fire in a continuous crackle all up and down the line. The sun sparkled on the bright brass of the spent cartridge cases.

Breechblocks clattered as the big 75mm shells were passed from the limber and rammed home. The crew stood aside as the master gunner clipped his lanyard to the trigger and payed it out.

"Ranging gun, shoot," Dinnalsyn said.

Battery commander's work, really, but enjoyable, and he rarely got a chance to do it these days. The gunner jerked sharply.

POUMPH. A long jet of smoke shot out from Number One of A Battery. The gun threw itself backward in recoil, the trail gouging a trough in the clay. The crew jumped forward as soon as it came to rest, grabbing the trail and the tall wheels and running it back to the original position.

Dinnalsyn raised his binoculars. A tall plume of black dust sprouted from the roadway outside the northeast gate of the city, like an instant poplar that bent in the breeze and dispersed as the dirt scattered.

"Excellent," he said. "Batteries, range."

The thick tubes of the guns rose as the gunners spun the elevating screws under the breeches.

Excellent shooting on the first try, and it was excellent to serve under a commander who *understood* what artillery could and could not do.

The other two batteries were tasked with the northwestern gate, a bit farther—near maximum effective range. Their ranging gun fired seconds after his, and the gout of dirt flung skyward was a hundred meters short. Even that trial shot told, flinging parts of men and equipment skyward. Both roads into Ain el-Hilwa were black with running men, and more every second. They tried again, and the next round fell neatly before the open gates.

"Airburst, three-second fuse, shrapnel, load."

Blue-banded shells from the limbers, passed forward hand to hand three times; gun crews had redundant members to replace casualties in action. Not that there looked to be much counterfire this time. The master gunners pulled the ring-shaped blockers out of the noses of the shells, arming the fuses. Into the narrow hole went a two-pronged tool they carried chained to their wrists, to adjust the timers. A brass ring on the fuse turned, listing the time in seconds; within, drilled beechwood turned in a perforated brass tube, exposing a precisely calculated length of powder-train.

"Number one gun ready!"

"Number two gun ready!"

"Number three gun ready!"

"Number four gun ready!"

"Battery A ready!"

"Batteries will shoot, for effect. On the word of command."

He raised his free hand, the other holding his binoculars. *Use your judgment,* the general had said. Men were running through, but that was the first spray of them. He waited, gauntleted hand in the air. The gates were narrow, and so were the arched bridges that carried the roadways over the city moat. You *wanted* city gates to be a chokepoint, for defensive reasons, and Ain el-Hilwa had excellent fortifications. Routed, the Arab troops were not going to wait while they were marshaled through with maximum efficiency. Every man for himself meant a tie-up.

Sure enough, the roadways were black with men and great fans of them were spreading out along the edge of the moat. He chopped his hand downward.

"Now!"

POUMP. The first gun fired. A precise twenty seconds later the second followed. *POUMP. POUMP. POUMP.*

By the time the last gun fired, the first had been pushed back into battery and was ready to fire again. A steady two rounds a minute, to conserve barrels and break armies. No problem, with the men fresh. Pushing the ton weights of metal around was hard work, but they were trained to a hair and the day was young.

Four *crack* sounds downrange, as the shells burst. Ragged black smokeballs in the air over the crowd at the gates; below them panic, as the shells' loads of musketballs scythed forward in an oval pattern of destruction.

POUMP. POUMP. POUMP. POUMP. This time one of the rounds hammered into the dirt before exploding, a faulty time-fuse. No great problem this time; the crater made the pileup greater. He shifted his glasses to the other gate. The spread of shell was wider there, some far enough from the gate to kick up dust, but you expected that at extreme range.

The general cantered up with his staff and messengers. He paused for a moment, leaning on the pommel with both hands and studying the artillery. *Strange man*, Dinnalsyn thought. He saw too much, knew too much. Knew as much about guns as he did himself, and was better at judging distance and trajectories; a cannon-cocker's skills, not a talent you expected in a hill-squireen out of Descott. And he never *forgot* anything, never missed a detail—as if angels were whispering in his ear. There were those strange little trances, too. Grammeck was city-born to a merchant family, and prided himself on his modernity, but there might be something in the tales of Messer Raj being touched by the Spirit.

"I could do better execution with more tubes, *mi heneral*," he said.

They had fifty-five guns along, and they were all reconcentrated now that the raiding parties had joined forces.

Raj shook his head, his stone-hard face still turned to the gates where men screamed and died and the corpses tossed under the hammer of the shells.

"Not for this," he said. "We don't have the ammunition to expend."

True; they were limited to what they'd brought along. He made a mental note to shift things around to even out the reserve supplies between batteries before they broke camp. A glance at his watch told him it was still early, barely 0800.

"And speaking of which," the general went on, "give them another three rounds per gun and cease fire. Another few minutes and the guns on the walls will have you registered here."

As if to punctuate the thought, a heavy shell buried itself in the earth a hundred meters ahead of them and exploded, throwing clods of dirt as far as the second hillock.

"And then limber up and get out of range," Raj said. "*Si, mi heneral.*"

seventy-six rounds per gun, Center said.

Ah, Raj thought. About his own offhand estimate. Strange, that so much of Center's advice was a refinement of what he'd have done anyway.

of course. otherwise i would not have selected you.

Which was reassuring. There were times he doubted he was the same man who'd blundered into the centrum beneath the Gubernatorial Palace.

that youth would be gone forever by now in any case.

Raj shrugged and looked down at the field of battle with a mixture of distaste and the sensation a farmer had looking back over an expanse of grain cut and stooked in good time. The Colonials had finally gotten their gates shut and the cannon on the wall active; but that left most of their garrison trapped outside the wall and exposed to fire.

"Signal cease-fire. And get a truce flag ready."

"What terms?" Staenbridge said.

"The usual. Parole not to participate further in this campaign, and one gold FedCred per head."

One advantage of fighting the wogs was that they and the *Gubernio Civil* had been locked in combat so long they'd developed an elaborate code of military etiquette and generally observed it for sound reasons of mutual long-term advantage. One provision often used was releasing prisoners on parole, when the alternative was killing them for want of time and facilities. It put them out of action for the remainder of the war in question, and was about as profitable as selling them for slaves, which was the other choice. Granted that they could be used on some *other* frontier, which freed up troops to be used against you; on the other hand, both powers had an interest in keeping the barbarians at bay.

and the cause of civilization is served, as well.

Kaltin Gruder came up. Raj nodded. "Nice turning movement, Kaltin."

"Work of the day, *mi heneral*. Are we going to take their parole?"

Raj nodded. Kaltin's mouth tightened, but he nodded unwillingly.

"Ali might not keep it," he pointed out. Reluctantly: "Of course, it wouldn't *matter*, with these handless cows."

"There are no bad soldiers, Kaltin, only bad officers. But these have had their morale fairly thoroughly shattered, and they won't be any use to anyone for a good long while. See to it."

Another party rode up; this one included a number of bandaged and bleeding men. The most senior seemed to be a captain; Raj didn't recognize him, which probably meant he was from Osterville's command.

captain fillipo swarez, 51st mazatlan.

Thank you, Raj thought. Aloud: "Captain Swarez."

The man blinked at Raj through red-rimmed, exhausted eyes, holding his bandaged arm against his chest to limit the jarring of his dog's movement.

"General Whitehall. I am reporting as senior officer in . . . as senior officer of the other field force battalions."

Raj raised an eyebrow. "Major Gonsalvez?"

"Dead, sir."

"Colonel Osterville?"

observe:

A brief vision this time: Osterville's muddy sweating face, bent low over the neck of his dog and slashing behind with his riding crop. A string of remounts followed, and several servants, and pack dogs with small heavy crates strapped to their carrying saddles.

Swarez spat. "That for the *hijo da puta!* Nobody saw him after the shelling started, and his dogs and personal servants are missing."

One of the lieutenants behind him spoke. "*Heneralissimo,* let me send a patrol after him—let me *take* a patrol after him. I guarantee, he'll never trouble you again."

Growls of assent rose from the survivors; their mounts snarled in sympathy, scenting their masters' mood. *No zealot like a convert,* Raj thought.

He shook his head. "Messer Osterville" —he omitted the military rank— "suits me well enough where he is." He looked back at the captain.

"Captain Swarez, how many survivors?"

"Six hundred in all, sir. Two hundred wounded."

Half Osterville's original force, but that included several hundred who'd defected to Raj during the night, and the Spirit alone knew how many who'd bugged out this morning.

"How many of those in your 51st Mazatlan?"

"Two hundred twenty-six. Fit for duty, that is, sir."

Which meant they'd kept together fairly well. "All right. Tell the remainder that those who wish may transfer to your unit, or to any of my other battalions that'll take them—some of them are severely under strength. Have everyone ready to move shortly."

Swarez saluted, relief on his face. A soldier's battalion was his home and family, and his had just been spared from disbandment. The other survivors could count themselves lucky to have open slots waiting for them.

Raj watched the party with the white flag riding up to the gates of Ain el-Hilwa. He doubted the negotiations would take long; they'd be too hysterically thankful not to face a storm and sack, which they now lacked the men to stop. Say until noon to get the wounded sorted, police up and destroy the enemy weapons, collect the ransom . . .

Demand some fast sprung wagons as part of it, he decided. There were good roads all the way from here to the bridgehead opposite Sandoral. Then . . .

"Meeting of the command group at midday," he said. "Now let's get this wrapped, gentlemen."

He looked down at the field again before he reined about. A good workmanlike day's effort. Unpleasantly final for several thousand Colonials.

It wasn't going to stay this easy. This was a sideshow so far. Ali's main attention was focused on Sandoral.

CHAPTER NINE

"Fwego!"

Corporal Minatili opened his mouth and put his hands over his ears. His firing slit was close enough that the fortress gun would hurt his hearing if he didn't.

BOOOOMM.

"Reload, canister!"

The big soda-bottle-shaped fortress gun surged backward on its pivot-mounted carriage, muzzle wreathed in smoke. The wooden friction blocks squealed against their screw tighteners as they slowed the multitonne weight of cast iron and steel. It slowed to a stop at the end of the low ramped carriage, and the militia crew sprang into action. Two men leaped in with a bundle of soaked sponges on a long pole and rammed it down the barrel. There was a long *shhhhhhhhhh* as the water met hot metal and flashed into steam. They pulled the pole out and flipped it, presenting the wooden rammer head. Two more men were lifting the round in, a big dusty-looking linen bag of coarse gunpowder nailed to a wooden sabot, with a tin canister full of lead balls on the other end.

Minatili shuddered as he turned away. Canister from a light field gun was bad enough. Canister from a 150mm siege weapon . . .

The gun rumbled like thunder as the gunners released the blocks and it ran down the carriage to lift the iron shutter and poke its muzzle out the casement wall. Bronze wheels squealed as the four men at the rear threw themselves at the handspikes in response to the master gunner's hand signals. The gun carriage was mounted on a pivot in the center, with the front and rear running on wheels that rested on an iron ring set into the concrete floor.

"Bring her up two—they'll be trying again," the master gunner said. He accompanied it with hand signals, for the ones who had lumps of cotton waste stuffed in their ears. His crew spun the big elevating wheel at the breech two turns, and the massive pebbled surface of the gun elevated smoothly at the muzzle.

Keep to your trade, Minatili told himself, stepping up to the firing parapet. He usually didn't have much time for militia, but these gunnery boys knew their business. He peered through; the sunlight made him squint, after the shade of the wall platform with its overhead protection of timber and iron. The stone of the wall was cool against his cheek.

Outside, six hundred meters from the wall, the wog trench was still swarming. Men were dragging away the dead and wounded, the smashed gabions, wickerwork baskets with earth inside them. He could see flashes of heads and shoulders as picks and shovels swung. The trench was big, a Z-shaped zigzag running back to the main wog bastion twelve hundred meters out; that was a continuous earthwork fort all the way around the city now. Cannon flashed from it, and he could feel the massive stone-fronted walls tremble rhythmically under him as the heavy solid shot pounded selected spots. Dust puffed up, making him sneeze. He wiped his nose on his sleeve and spat.

There were hundreds of the assault trenches worming their way toward the walls, but this one was his section's particular tribulation.

The enemy guns boomed again. One bolt struck right

beneath him, and his rifle quivered against the stone it rested on with a harsh tooth-gritting vibration. It would be difficult for them to make a breach; Sandoral's walls were twenty meters thick counting the earth backing, and sunk well behind the moat so that only a lip showed . . . but it would happen in time.

Shells screeched by overhead, exploding behind him among the empty houses. The ragheads didn't seem to be worrying about ammunition supplies. He'd helped defend the walls of Old Residence against a hundred thousand Brigaderos, twice the number that the wogs had, but this felt worse. Back then they'd had Messer Raj, and the MilGov barbs had wandered around with their thumbs up their bums while the Civil Government force wore them down. The towel-heads weren't that kind of stupid.

He hopped down and walked along the space of wall his section held, and the platoon of garrison infantry they were supporting. One of those was stretched out on the walkway, most of the top of his head missing and brains spattered all over his firing niche.

"*Fuck* it!" Minatili screamed. "You—y'fuckhead—didn't y'*tell* him?"

The dead man's corporal looked up. "Couldn't make 'im listen."

The wogs had big bipod-mounted sniper rifles working from their forward lines, single-shot weapons as heavy as the sauroid-killers the Skinner nomads used. They had telescopic sights, too.

"Well, git t'body out of t'way," Minatili said angrily. Two of the man's squadmates dragged it away as it dribbled. Bad for morale to have corpses lying around if you didn't have to. It was a pity you couldn't remove the smell; it was hot and close here, and the blood began rotting almost at once.

Everyone else was keeping their head away from the

firing slit until told. Rifles were lying in the flat stone bottoms of the slits, with their levers open to keep the chambers as cool as could be. Each niche had a couple of wooden strips set into troughs in the stone, with rows of holes drilled in the wood. Each hole held a cartridge, base-up and ready to hand. Two thousand-round ammunition crates rested on ledges between firing positions, their tops loosened and the protective tinfoil curled back to show the ten-round bundles, one hundred bundles per box. Buckets of water and dippers hung from iron hooks; there was a wooden box of hand bombs by every man's firing position, round cast-iron balls the size of an orange, with a ring on top to arm the friction fuse. There were even some spare rifles in a rack, for the men disarmed by the jams that would be inevitable once firing got heavy and the weapons heated up.

The only thing missing was enough men to fill all the firing niches, plus the reserve that doctrine called for. What they had was one rifleman for every three slots, one man for nine meters of front. The Colonials had enough troops to attack anywhere along four kilometers of wall, without warning.

The lieutenant blew his whistle. Men tensed, thumbing rounds into their rifles and working the levers to shut the actions. Minatili sprang back into his niche and licked his thumb to wet the foresight. Enemy pom-poms raked the line of firing slits. The infantryman jerked his head down and squeezed his eyes shut as grit blasted through his, then blinked them open.

"Make 'em count, boys!" he shouted. "Thems *cavalry* you're shootin'."

Men were swarming out of the forward Colonial works, men in djellabas and spiked helmets. Their carbines were slung; most carried long ladders, and some lugged small mortars with folding grappling hooks and reels of cord attached. Others pushed wheeled bridging equipment to get them across the moat. Pairs carried little cohorn mortars, adapted to hurl grappling hooks at the end of a reel of iron cable.

Spirit, there's a lot of them. His narrow slit showed *thousands*, and more pouring out of the trenches like ants out of a kicked-over burrow.

White-painted iron stakes marked the ranges outside. The ramp sight on the rear of Minatili's rifle was set for four hundred meters. He steadied the forestock against the stone and curled his finger around the trigger, taking a deep breath. The first enemy crossed by the four-hundred-meter-mark, two files holding a ladder between them. He dropped the sight onto the front-right man, let it down to the man's knees, and stroked the trigger. A soft click sounded as the offset, the first slack, took up.

Gentle, like it was a tit, he told himself, and squeezed.

Bam. The wog stopped as if he'd run into a stone wall and dropped, the ladder sagging and swinging broadside onto the city defenses as his teammates staggered and tripped. *Last one I know for certain,* Minatili thought. Rifles barked in a stuttering crash all along the wall, smoke erupting from the slits. Men in the attacking force fell, and other men replaced them. Minatili worked the lever of his rifle and thumbed in rounds. Spent brass tinkled around his feet.

BOOOOMMM. The big cannon a few meters down took him by surprise this time; he'd been too involved in his personal war to notice the master gunner's orders. He did see the result, as the malignant wasp-whine of the canister round spewed out its hundreds of ten-gram lead balls. It caught the mouth of the assault trench with a fresh wave of ragheads just clambering over the gabions. They vanished, swept away in the storm of hundreds of marble-sized shot. Dust and fragments of wicker spurted up all over the face of the trench. When the dust cleared, the dirt was covered with a carpet of men pulped into an amorphous mass, a mass that still heaved and moaned in places.

"Reload, canister!"

Minatili himself reloaded, pausing to snap the ramp under his rear sight down to two hundred meters. The rifle was foul after more than two dozen shots, and the metal scorched his callused thumb as he shoved home the next round. The recoil was worse now too, and his shoulder would be sporting a fine bruise tomorrow, assuming he was here to feel it. Massed carbine fire pecked at the rock outside, some of it uncomfortably close. A round whined through the firing slit, the flattened lead going *whip-whip-whip* as the miniature metal pancake sliced air. It could slice him as easily. He bounced back up, picked a target, fired, ducked back down to reload.

Spirit. He was glad he was in here and not out there. There were as many wogs down as moving.

"Hold 'em, boys, or we're all hareem guards!" he called, and fired again.

Again. The cannon fired a third time, or was it the tenth? No way to tell. Smoke hung dense and choking, turning the ground outside the walls into a fog-shrouded mystery where crimson shapes dashed and bunched. The Colonials were nearly to the edge of the outer works, kicking their way through the caltrops—triangles of welded nails scattered through grass deliberately left to grow knee-high. Some distant part of Minatili was amazed that men would slow down in the face of rifle fire to avoid getting a nail in the foot, but many did.

Then the cannon from the projecting bastions cut loose. Each V-shaped protrusion took hundreds of meters of wall in enfilade, dozens of cannon sweeping the ground with loads of heavy canister. Most of them were carronades, short big-bore weapons like gigantic shotguns. Not much range, but they didn't need it.

Minatili paused to let his rifle cool a bit with the lever open, gulped water from a bucket down a throat as raw as if it had been reamed out with a steel brush. Drops fell on the metal of the breechblock and sizzled. When the smoke cleared enough for him to see again, he reloaded and aimed at one of a pair of Arabs dragging a wounded comrade back with them. He shot, reloaded . . .

"Cease fire! Cease fire!"

The bugles reached him where the shouted command did not. His finger froze on the trigger, and he worked the lever and caught the ejected shell. His fingers were black with powder residue, and it coated his lips, tasting of sulfur when he licked them. There were more dead wogs outside than he could count, coating the ground in sprays and swaths back toward the enemy works, bobbing in the moat below amid the wreckage of wooden bridging equipment and ladders. More up and down the foot of the wall. In places the carpet of bodies stirred and moaned; there were so many he could smell the blood-and-shit stink of ripped-open bodies all the way up here.

He took another drink of water and left his rifle lying on the stone firing slot, lever open. "Sound off!" he called. Then he trotted over to the platoon commander's station.

"Sor! Two dead, three wounded serious." That included the two sections of garrison infantry his eight men were overseeing. "Ev'ryone else ready for duty."

The lieutenant was a good enough sort, a bit young. He looked out through the slit next to him and returned his unused revolver to its holster. Perhaps because he *was* young, he spoke aloud:

"They thought they could rush us. No respect."

"Plenty now, sor."

The young officer nodded, unconsciously smoothing

down a wispy mustache. "Yes. Now they'll try starving us out."

Spirit, Minatili thought.

There hadn't been much but men, dogs, weapons, and ammunition in the trains that brought them east. Sandoral had been full of hungry refugees for a week before they got here, and the invasion had disrupted the harvest.

"Messers, to fallen comrades."

As youngest of the senior officers present, Barton Foley gave the toast in the three-quarters diluted wine. They all drank.

"Messers, the Governor." Raj gave that, and they tossed aside the clay cups.

As if to remind them of the fallen, a man screamed from the tent nearby where the wounded were being tended. Casualties had been light by every reasonable standard except that of the men whose own personal flesh had been torn and bones been shattered. Suzette was present, but her sleeves were rolled to the elbows and there was still blood spattered down the front of her jacket.

"I gather we won't be trying to take Ain el-Hilwa, *mi heneral*," Staenbridge said.

"Of course not; what would we do with it?" Raj said. He tapped the map on the table before them. "Messers, we'll split up into the same three raiding parties—Major Swarez, you'll accompany the center group with me" —Osterville's ex-follower nodded—"and Major Hwadeloupe, you'll be attached to Major Gruder's command.

"We'll head south by southeast along this axis." He traced it on the map. "Keeping west of the Ghor Canal."

"Our objective is the railway?" Staenbridge said, tracing it with one finger.

The scouts had given them a definite bearing; it came straight west from the main Colonial line along the Gederosian foothills.

observe, Center said.

A train screeched to a halt, sparks fountaining out from the tall driving wheel of the locomotive. It was a new machine, painted in black and silver, with Arabic calligraphy along the sides in gilt paint and up the tall slender smokestack. Behind it were a dozen cars, the last an armored box with a pom-pom mounted on a turntable behind a shield; thirty or so riflemen poked their weapons out of slits in the boilerplate that sheathed it. The other cars held sections of track, already spiked to cross-ties, piled up in stacks and secured by chains. Another train halted behind the first. This one had boxcars full of men and tools.

They boiled out, their officers waving the ceremonial lash and shouting; there was more noise than a comparable group of Civil Government soldiers would have made, but no more confusion. Teams jogged forward and undogged the chains holding the first train's cargo. They set up a light folding crane and lowered the sections of preformed track to the ground; other teams lifted them with iron hooks and trotted forward, keeping step with a wailing chant.

Ahead of the two trains was a section of wrecked track a quarter-kilometer long. Engineers gave the roadbed a quick check with levels and transit; gangs of workers shoved the burnt, twisted ties and rails to one side. The prefabricated sections were dropped in place and the hookmen went back for another load at the same steady trot. Another team slewed the tracks into alignment with long poles like gunners' handspikes and bolted them together.

❖   ❖   ❖

Raj shook his head. "There aren't enough of us, and we don't have enough time," he said. "The Colonial sappers can repair track faster than we can tear it up—until Tewfik can get back here. The major bridges will be heavily guarded. But we want him to *think* we're a threat to the railway line, and by all means tear up any stretch you reach."

"What news from Sandoral?" Staenbridge said.

"Ali put in a quick attack when he arrived in force, and when that didn't work he tried a full assault with engineering and artillery support. Total losses of four to five thousand, including wounded too badly hurt to return to duty soon. Our casualties were very light."

"My, my. I wouldn't like to be on Ali's staff right now,"

Visions crawled beneath the surface of Raj's vision; beheadings, impalements. Ali was quite mad.

"Gerrin," he said, "neither would I. He's still got forty thousand effectives, not counting his infantry garrisons." They had seven thousand cavalry, and three thousand infantry in all.

"More goblets than bottles at this banquet," Staenbridge agreed.

If there wasn't enough wine to fill all the glasses at table, beyond a certain point juggling the liquid from one glass to another wouldn't help.

"We might take their supply dump at the railhead," Dinnalsyn said thoughtfully. "That would embarrass them considerably."

"It's fortified, and there are ten thousand men in there," Raj said. "Not first-rate troops, but they're expecting trouble and they've got considerable artillery."

They all nodded. You might be able to take a position like that by a sudden unexpected *coup de main*, or if it was held by barbarians too dim to take the proper precautions. Not otherwise, not with a larger enemy field force free to operate against your rear.

"If that's all, gentlemen, we'd better see to business. Tewfik's banner hasn't been reported back at Sandoral either."

The main column trotted down a roadway through the early morning cool. It was twenty feet broad, well-graded dirt surfaced with gravel, winding down through terraced barley fields from a low ridge planted with a mix of olives and almond trees. Gullies running down toward the flat were full of reddish-green native scrub; a flock of sheep-sized bipedal grazing sauroids fled honking and gobbling into the bush as the troops passed. Dew still laid the dust on the rolling hillside. Beyond were flat fields, irrigated and intensively cultivated. The villages were deserted, ghostly, not a human or a domestic animal in sight. The peasantry had had warning enough to flee by now, driving their herds before them.

Raj finished a pear and tossed the core aside, squinting ahead. Then he stiffened and flung up one hand.

"*Halto*. Silence in the ranks."

The bugles snarled, and the column came to a dead stop in less than three strides. Silence fell, broken only by the occasional jingle of harness as a dog shifted.

There. A dull thudding sound, like a large door being slammed far away. It echoed, and was repeated. Again. Again.

"Artillery, by the Spirit," Staenbridge said softly.

Raj nodded, closing his eyes to concentrate.

civil government field guns, Center said. **two batteries, approximately 8.7 kilometers south-southeast of your present position.**

"Well, that's something serious," Barton Foley observed flatly.

Ain el-Hilwa had been the only action hot enough to need artillery support so far. The officers around Raj exchanged glances, and so did the men in the long ranks zigzagging back up the hill. The military picnic was over.

"Kaltin," Raj said. That was where Kaltin Gruder's *kampfgruppe* was operating.

He called up the maps of the area. A low ridge on either side, running east-west, more flat ground to the south.

"Sound *Reverse Front*," he said. "Then *Trot*."

The bugle screamed again, and the dogs turned in place. They waited the thirty seconds necessary to turn the gun-teams and broke into a rocking trot back up the slope.

"Messengers to the raiding parties, immediate concentration here," Raj began. "Colonel Staenbridge, establish your banner there" —he pointed to the notch where the road crossed the hill— "with a firing line on the reverse slope, ready to move up. Major Bellamy, that'll be your 1st and 2nd, and the 1/591st. Gerrin, anchor your left there" —he pointed to a reservoir— "and re-fuse your right with the raiding parties as they come in. Grammek, get your guns on the reverse crest too, but keep the teams close."

The artilleryman nodded. That was dangerous—risking immobilizing the weapons if the teams were injured— but gave essential seconds of extra time if you had to pull out fast.

"No fieldworks, but put up some quick sangars for the splatguns. Suzette, have those Church people ready to triage the wounded and move them back immediately; we won't be staying. Captains M'lewis, Foley, I'll be taking a company of the 5th and the Scouts forward with me. And one splatgun. Questions?"

Heads shook. "Good. To your positions, please. Gerrin." Staenbridge reined in. "I've got an unpleasant feeling we'll be coming back faster than we go. Be ready to stop them hard." Even veteran troops could turn unsteady if it looked like a rout.

Staenbridge nodded; they leaned toward each other and slapped fists, inside of the wrist and then back. "We'll be here, *mi heneral.*"

Raj met Suzette's eyes for a moment. No words were necessary.

"*Waymanos!*"

They trotted through a land silent and deserted, warming towards the crippling heat of a Drangosh Valley summer morning. Raj's little force rode in column, with a spray of pickets out ahead. The dogs kept up a steady canter-trot-walk-trot-canter, eating the kilometers. Their tongues lolled, but their ears were pricked forward, all but Horace's, which were a hound's floppy style. The guns sounded much closer now, thudding bangs. The terrain hereabouts was mixed, fingers of high *doab* running from the clay bluffs along the Drangosh into the lower, flatter country to the east that extended past the Ghor Canal to the foothills of the Gederosian Mountains. From the sound, the guns were firing on the next ridge south.

All the men had heard the sound before, and most of the dogs. The troopers rode with their rifles across their thighs.

Whistles came from up ahead. One of the Scouts came down the road at a quick lope.

"Courier comin', ser," he said.

The messenger's dog was panting. He pulled a sweat-dampened paper from a jacket marked with the shoulder-flashes of the 7th Descott Rangers. A smell of scorched hide came from the leather scabbard in front of his right knee, the smell a hard-used rifle made when it was slapped into the sheath still hot.

"Ser," he said, "Major Gruder reports we'ns ran inta a patrol. Thought't were a patrol, turned out t'be more wogs'n we could handle."

Raj read quickly; it was a request for reinforcements, with a quick sketch map of the action. He shook his head. Kaltin was a first-class tactician, but he had a tendency to over-narrow focus, to lock his teeth in a situation and try to beat it to death.

"My compliments to Major Gruder, and tell him I'll be there shortly. And to be ready to move position, quickly."

"Ser!"

"Barton, bring them up to a lope."

The messenger pulled his mount around and clapped heels into its flanks. The sound of the guns grew sharper as the ground rose. He could see powder-smoke rising above the higher terrain to the south. A trickle of wounded passed them, riding-wounded leading dogs with more badly injured men slung over them—it was all you could do, in a situation like this.

POUMPF. POUMPF. POUMPF. The guns were firing steadily; he could see them now, spaced out amid spindly native whipstick trees on the ridge. They were firing from the top crest, the crews pushing them back every time they recoiled. Raj pulled off the roadway, leaning forward in the saddle as Horace took the ditch with a bound and swung up the hill.

Kaltin Gruder met him. "Ran into a patrol," he said. "Company strength—one *tabor*. I jumped them, more of them came up, I called in my raiding parties, then even *more* showed up. There's a battle group of two thousand down there now, and they're not stopping for shit. These aren't line-of-communications troops. Regular cavalry, and good ones."

Raj grunted in reply, sweeping his binoculars over the slope below. It was sparsely wooded with whipsticks, tall spindly trees with branches that drooped up and away from the main stem on all sides, dangling fronds of featherlike leaves.

POUMPF. POUMPF.

The eight guns on the ridgeline kept up their steady shelling, the pressure-wave of the discharges slapping at faces and chests. At least twenty Colonial artillery were firing in reply from the lower ground to the front, half pom-poms and half 70mm's. They weren't attempting a counter-battery shoot, just searching the edge of the treeline to try and beat down the fire of the Civil Government riflemen. All across the open ground Colonial dragoons were moving forward on foot, line after line of them in extended skirmish order.

Gruder went on: "I've got the 7th in the center, with Poplanich's Own and the 1st Rogor to the right and left and the Maximilliano over there."

He pointed to the east, where smoke and the steady crackle of small arms indicated action. "Whoever the wog commander is, he knows his hand from a hacksaw— started trying to work around my flanks as soon as he got a feel for the depth of my firing line here. I moved the Maximilliano out to extend the line, but it thinned me here badly."

Raj nodded curtly. Gruder's three battalions—a thousand men or so, all under strength—were keeping up a steady crackle of independent fire. Down below figures in red djellabas were scattered on the ground or hobbling, limping, and crawling back toward the guns and the banners grouped around them. Advancing against veteran riflemen cost heavily. A splatgun gave its ripping *braaap* and a file of Colonials nearly a thousand meters away went down as the spread of rifle bullets hit them. Several of the enemy guns shifted aim; Raj could see the splatgun team trundling their light weapon to a new position just ahead of the pompom and field gun shells.

But more and more of the Colonials were making it to their own firing line close to the woods. Their repeaters were just as deadly as the heavier Civil Government weapons at ranges under a hundred meters, and they fired much faster. A haze of off-white powder smoke was drifting away from the thickening Colonial position. Even as he watched, several platoons rose and dashed forward for the woods. Many fell, but others went to ground in the scrub along the edge of the savannah. Once in among the trees, their repeaters would slaughter men equipped with single-shot rifles.

"We can crush them like a tangerine if you swing in with the main force, *mi heneral*," Gruder said.

Kaltin does tend to get too focused, Raj thought. His own mind was moving in cool precise arcs and tangents, like something scribed on a drawing-board by an engineer's compasses and protractors. Like a mental analogue of the way you felt when fencing; perhaps a little like the way Center felt all the time, if Center had subjective experience.

He felt more alive than anywhere else. It was a pity he could only feel this on the battlefield, that his art could only be practiced as men died. There were times when he lay awake at night, wondering what that said about him. But not now. Not now.

"No, Major, a full-scale meeting engagement isn't what I have in mind. If there's one Colonial battle group around, there's going to be others."

He considered for a few seconds. "This will have to be quick. We'll withdraw by leapfrogging battalions. Move Poplanich's Own back half a klick to that rise, and the guns. You'll take the 7th and the others back to join the main force. I'll hold the rearguard." Gruder didn't like retreating. "M'lewis, detach two men to each of the battalion commanders to guide them to the main-force position. Follow with the rest."

Gruder nodded briskly; he didn't like it, but that would make no difference to his obedience. Antin M'lewis turned and barked orders. Pairs of men galloped off.

"Trumpeter!" Raj went on. "Relay. Half-kilometer withdrawal. On the signal."

The complex call went out, was echoed. A single long note followed.

The battery on the rise fired one last *stonk* and let the guns roll downhill to their limbers. The teams snatched up the trails and slapped them on; retaining pins went home with an iron clank, the six dogs of each team rose, and the guns set off down the open slope at a trot. Three men rode the offhand dogs of the team; there were two seats on the gun axles and two on the limber, and the remainder had dogs of their own. Up from the savannah came the splatguns, hauled by four-dog teams; lighter, they overtook the field pieces despite the smaller draft.

The crackle of small-arms fire intensified. "Barton. We'll give the wogs a going-away present. Standing saddle-volley, use the crestline. Place the splatgun."

Company A of the 5th was nearest to full strength, eighty men, only forty down from regulation. They fanned out behind Raj, heeling their dogs a meter and a half downslope. The dogs turned and faced the crest, then crouched. The men crouched with them, squatting. It was an inelegant and uncomfortable posture—you couldn't let your full weight rest on the dog—but the men moved into a flawless double line with the ease of a housewife slapping dough for tortillas. Three-meter spacing between each, and the rows staggered so that the rear row matched the intervals in the front. He looked at their faces: stolid, immobile under the film of sweat, a few chewing tobacco and spitting. Every one of them knew what was about to happen.

Below, the Colonials hesitated a crucial handful of seconds when the fire from the Civil Government troops ceased. Just long enough to let them dash back to their waiting dogs. Center unreeled numbers as the depleted battalions trotted up the slope, rallied, and cantered northward. He winced slightly. Those units had been under strength before. A lot of them were still down there in the burning grass and shattered whipstick trees, and would never leave. Long curled trumpets sounded, shriller than his own. Half the Colonials turned and started to jog back towards their dogs. The others opened fire on the retreating raiders; not many went down, but some men and dogs fell out of line.

"Reacting fast," Raj murmured.

The Colonial commander was sending his mounted reserve forward, galloping up the hill. Two *tabor*, a little under three hundred men, with a pair of pom-poms galloping behind. Galloping guns was risky, especially on uneven ground like this. A few men, wounded or just extremely brave, had stayed behind among the dead. One rose to a knee and shot the off-lead dog of a pom-pom team. It collapsed, biting at its wounded leg. The gun slewed around, then tipped over and spun. The massive torque spun through the trail and the harness, turning the team into a thrashing pile of twisted metal and shredded meat that bounced downslope and scattered the dismounted Colonials who followed.

Raj watched the mounted Colonials approach. Numbers scrolled across his vision. The Arabs were keening as they charged. If they could prevent his men from breaking contact . . .

500 meters. 450. 400.

"Now!" he barked.

"Tenzione!" Barton Foley called, his clear tenor pitched a little higher to carry. The men rose from their squat to stand straddling their dogs. The long Armory rifles came up to their shoulders in smooth curves, the muzzles dead level except for the minute individual quivers as they picked their targets. The slope had

concealed them, and to the enemy it must have appeared as if the heads and shoulders popped up out of nowhere.

The Colonials reacted with veteran reflexes, crouching in the saddle and sloping their scimitars forward. Their dogs bounced into a full gallop, throwing themselves forward to get through the killing zone as fast as possible.

"*Fwego!*" Foley's sword chopped down in a bright arc.

BAM. Eighty rifles fired within a half-second of each other. *Braaaaaap*. The splatgun fired from its position in enfilade to one side.

The charging Colonials seemed to stagger. Dogs went down all across their front. It was only three-hundred-odd meters, and at that distance most of the 5th's long-service men could hit a running man, not to mention a thousand-pound dog. Men flew out of the saddle, and rear-rank dogs leaped and twisted desperately to avoid the thrashing heaps ahead of them.

"Rear rank, *fwego!*"

BAM.

"Reload!"

"Front rank, *fwego!*"

BAM.

"Reload!"

Braaaaap. Braaaaap.

"Rear rank, *fwego!*"

BAM.

Braaaaap. The crew worked the splatgun like loom-tenders in one of the new steam-driven factories. Its load struck like case-shot, but far faster and more accurate.

A Colonial trumpet brayed and drums sounded. The mounted Colonials withdrew, leaving their dead and wounded; the thick screen of dismounted men down in the woods ceased to wait for their comrades to bring up their dogs and started up the slope once more. Field gun shells went overhead with a ripping-canvas sound.

He's putting in an enveloping attack, Raj decided, feeling through the movements for the enemy commander's mind. *He's decided this is a sacrificial rearguard.* Half the enemy were mounted already; the dismounted thousand or so would swamp a small rearguard like this in moments, and then the Arab troopers could pour after the fleeing Civil Government soldiers. They were lighter men on fast desert-bred dogs, slender-limbed Bazenjis; they would catch what they chased, and with a two-to-one edge in numbers and more in guns the issue could not be in doubt.

"*Waymanos*," Raj said.

The dogs rose under the men and turned, and the splatgun crew hitched their weapon and leaped to the saddles and limber-seats. Ten seconds later Company A was moving downslope and north at a trot that turned into a rocking gallop.

They were two hundred meters away when the dismounted Colonials crested the hill. Carbine bullets cracked around their ears; the bannerman's staff jerked in his hand, and a man went out of the saddle with a coughing grunt.

"Don't mask their fire," Raj cautioned.

Foley flicked his saber to the left, and the block of men shifted course. Raj leaned forward against the rush of hot air, the banner snapping and crackling next to him. He looked back; the Colonials were re-forming on the hill, mounting up as their comrades led their dogs forward. North were flat open fields, marked with dust plumes where the retreating Civil Government battalions moved north toward his main force. A slight rise topped by a mosque and grove of cypress trees stood about a kilometer ahead.

Metal flashed there. Raj looked over his shoulder again. The Colonials were coming now, in solid blocks of mounted men; moving at a fast trot and deployed in double line abreast, for speed when they had to go into action. *Sensible*. They'd had a bloody nose twice this morning. He took a quick squint at the sun; 1100 hours. And about now . . .

There was a puff of smoke from the cypress grove ahead. A whir went by overhead, like heavy canvas being ripped in half. A malignant *crack* behind, and another puff of smoke, as the time-fused shell burst over the charging Colonials.

"Hope none of them fire short," Barton Foley shouted, grinning.

Raj felt himself showing teeth in response. "Take them home, Barton," he called.

He shifted the pressure of his knees and turned Horace directly for the left end of the formation ahead—Poplanich's Own, four hundred men strong. Plus two batteries of 75's, now firing as fast as the gunners could ram the shells home, reckless both of the barrels and the ammunition supply. Rounds whined by overhead and burst, in the air, or throwing up fountains of dirt if the time fuse failed. He crouched over the dog's neck and set his teeth as the battalion's splatguns opened up; no need to look behind. Closer, and he could see the two staggered rows of men in prone-and-kneeling formation. Then rifles came up and the steady BAM . . . BAM . . . of platoon volleys started. The smoke was thick enough to half-mask the troops as he pulled up in a spurt of gravel by the battalion commander's position.

The Colonials were closer than he expected, four hundred meters but wavering under the unexpected hail of fire. *Yes, about two thousand of them still,* Raj thought; and their artillery was coming over the hill, pompoms and field guns both.

As he watched, blocks of mounted Colonials veered to left and right, moving to flank the Civil Government blocking force. Without prompting, each battery ceased fire for an instant and heaved its guns around to deal with the new threat; the flanking forces moved farther out, but the Colonials in front seemed to disappear. Raj read their trumpet signals: *Dismount* and *At the Double*. The line shrank as the dogs crouched, then turned into a long double rank of men on foot coming forward at a uniform jog-trot.

"In a moment, Major Caztro,". Raj said.

The Major—he was a cousin on his mother's side of the late Ehwardo Poplanich—nodded.

"The gunners aren't happy about it," he said.

"Better grieving than dead," Raj said dryly, taking a drink from his canteen; the day was already very hot.

"And . . . *now!*" he said. The major relayed the order to his buglemen.

The gunners fired a last round from their weapons. He could hear one sergeant cursing as he wrenched the breechblock free and tossed it to one of his men. Then he jammed a shell backwards into the opening, stuck a length of slowmatch into the hole where the fuse would normally go, and lit it with the last of the stogie clamped between his lips.

"Fire in the hole!" the noncom shouted. It was echoed down the gun line. "Ten seconds!"

The troopers were already double-timing back to their dogs and swinging out the rear of the cypress grove around the mosque.

"Retreat by platoon columns, at the gallop!" Major Caztro shouted.

Raj looked to either side as he touched his heels to Horace's ribs. The flanking parties were still well back, and the main Colonial force were just remounting and kicking their beasts into a gallop—which must be rather frustrating for them.

The noon sun was blinding-bright. The white dust of the road reflected its heat, and sweat rolled down his forehead out of the sodden sponge-and-cork lining of his helmet. Horace was panting, his black coat splotched with dust. Raj uncorked his canteen and rubbed a little of the water into the dog's neck; if it went down with heat prostration, he was deeply out of luck. Another check behind: the Colonials were coming on fast, but they were staying in line and bringing up their guns with them.

Cautious, but smart, Raj decided.

Barreling in hell-for-leather might have caught him quicker, but he'd already given them the back of his hand twice. There was nothing to show that he didn't have the battalions who'd retreated from the meeting engagement waiting at intervals to mousetrap an unwary pursuit.

Which is our margin, he knew. The Colonials would have won a flat-out gallop.

"How far, *mi heneral?*" the major asked, swerving his dog over to Raj's side.

"Just under seven kilometers," he said. The nearest Colonials were half a klick back, now. "Twenty minutes at this rate."

Caztro looked back as well. "Just long enough for them to get convinced we're going to run all the way to Sandoral?"

"Exactly, Major."

If everyone hasn't bugged out when Kaltin's men came in hell-for-leather.

"*Halto!*"

Raj pulled Horace to a stop, then let him crouch to the ground. His wheezing pant sounded half-desperate, and he was a strong-winded dog. Some of the others were collapsing outright; men brought buckets of water and sloshed them across the moaning, gasping animals. Raj pulled off his sweat-damp neckerchief and turned to trot for the command group below the crest of the hill.

"They're right on my heels," he said.

And everything looks klim-bim, he thought, with a wave of relief so enormous that he felt slightly dizzy. The ground was good—he'd picked it himself—and Gerrin hadn't been wasting his time. The men were spread out along the ridge, well back from the crest and invisible from the other side. Officers lay prone at the top, with their flags furled and laid flat among the scattered olives; inconspicuous rock and earth sangars had been prepared for the guns and splatguns. Back north behind him there was an aid station waiting for field surgery, and relays of men were bringing up buckets of water from the irrigation canal. Kaltin's battalions had watered their dogs and moved up into the firing line, all but Poplanich's Own; two more were on the far right flank, waiting still mounted. Farther north, a small force trotted away dragging brush on the end of their lariats to simulate the dust of a much larger body retreating towards Sandoral.

"And they're coming on like there was no tomorrow," Staenbridge said.

Raj knelt beside him and looked south. The Colonials were advancing at a round trot, deployed for action in two double-file lines with their guns and command group between.

"Message to Colonel Dinnalsyn," Staenbridge went on. A runner bent near. "My compliments, and the first stonk should be directed at the enemy artillery, before it has a chance to deploy."

Raj looked up and down the long curving line. "Guns?" he said.

"Splatguns forward, and the bulk of the field guns to either side." Staenbridge pointed downslope, to a clump of greenery around a small manor house. "Masked battery there."

Raj's breathing slowed. "Good work keeping everything calm when Kaltin's men came galloping in," he said.

"He had them well in hand, and Suzette and her helpers were there with bandages and water," Staenbridge said judiciously. "I doubt anyone in this army would dare panic while she was looking."

Raj nodded. *Still good work, Gerrin.* He leveled his binoculars and took another swig from the canteen, remembering to follow it with a salt tablet; the last thing he needed was heat prostration.

leading elements at 2300 meters, Center said helpfully. **closing rapidly.** A set of numbers appeared in the upper right corner of his vision, scrolling down as the enemy trotted nearer.

"Wait until their scouts stumble over us?" Staenbridge said.

"Agreed."

Damned if I'm needed here at all, he thought ruefully. *I could go take a nap.*

you are the source of overall direction, Center reproved. **you have chosen and trained competent subordinates.**

I'm not the only one, Raj thought.

"Keep the initial reception low-key," he added aloud.

A screen of scouts preceded the Colonial main body. A dozen of them came loping up the roadway toward the crest, eyes restless. Raj saw their officer half-check as he neared, looking to right and left. *What spooked him—*

it is too quiet. no birds or pterosauroids except the scavengers.

Raj looked up. Huge wings circled at the limit of vision, supporting long-beaked heads and patient, hungry eyes. Slightly lower were the true birds men had brought with them from lost Earth, crows and naked-necked vultures.

Damn. "I wonder what they do when there's no war?" he said.

Staenbridge looked up too for an instant. "When isn't there war?"

The Colonial scouts came closer. Their leader spurred over the crest of the rise not a hundred meters from Raj, and froze in horrified shock, his bearded mouth dropping open into an O of surprise.

Braaaap. A splatgun fired point-blank, and the scouts went down into a tangle of kicking, howling dogs and wounded men. Troopers swarmed over them in a flurry of shots and bayonet thrusts. Several broke for the rear. Picked marksmen were stationed along the crest; they fired with slow care. One Colonial went down, another . . . and then the third, already crouched wounded over his saddle.

Raj turned his binoculars to the Colonial banner; it was his first glimpse of the enemy commander. A square middle-aged face beneath the spired helmet, dark and hawk-nosed, with a gray-shot forked beard. Not Tewfik, but a junior product of the same hard school. *Come on, be a good wog,* Raj thought urgently.

He'd done it by the book twice now, stopped and deployed when meeting a rearguard. Both times it had cost him time, time for the enemy force which had ravaged his country to escape with their plunder. And there were those dust plumes. If he did it again, the Civil Government troops might escape altogether. Overruning a small rearguard without putting in an attack on foot would force him to spend lives, but that was a cost of doing business.

Yes. The Colonial trumpets brayed and the enemy force rocked into a slow gallop, the front rank drawing scimitars and officers their pistols.

"He's going to try and roll right over us," Staenbridge said with a cruel smile. "But this pitcher will find himself catching, nonetheless."

Raj nodded tersely. He looked to the right. "You kept the . . ."

"1/591st as strike reserve—they're at full strength, their dogs are fresh, and they're fond of the sword," Staenbridge said. He turned back to the front. "Not long now."

750 meters. 700 meters. 650 meters.

Raj nodded. Staenbridge jerked a hand at the signalman, who bent to touch his cigarette to the blue paper of the rocket. It arched skyward and went *pop*.

The banners of eleven battalions rose over the crest of the ridge in a single rippling jerk. Four thousand men rose and took six paces forward, the front rank dropping to one knee and the rear standing. Gunners heaved at the tall wheels of their weapons until the muzzles showed over the ridge. Splatgun crews pulled the concealing bushes away from their dug-in weapons.

The Colonial formations halted as if they had run into a brick wall. They were all veteran troops, and they realized instantly and gut-deep what the sight before their eyes meant; it meant they had all just been sentenced to death.

The battalions opened fire independently, but within a few seconds of each other. All the enemy were on the long gentle upslope, which meant that even if a bullet was over head-height when it reached the enemy formation—high trajectories were inescapable with black-powder weapons—there would probably be someone in front of it before it struck the earth. The platoon volleys rippled up and down the Civil Government line in an instant fogbank of dirty-gray gunsmoke, an endless BAM*bambambambambam* of sound. Brass sparkled in the bright sunlight as the troopers worked their levers and ejected the spent rounds. A steady, metronomic round every six seconds; forty thousand rounds in a minute. The four splatguns per battalion added half as many again.

The masked battery down on the flat opened fire simultaneously with the riflemen above, since they didn't have to manhandle their guns into position. The range was nearly point-blank; eight shells fired at minimum elevation whistled down the corridor between the first and second waves of the Colonial force. Two burst early, slashing shrapnel into the backs of the men and dogs of the first wave. One arched over and burrowed into the soft alluvial soil, sending up a nearly harmless plume of black dirt that collapsed and drifted on the wind. Five airburst within a hundred meters of the enemy command group amidst the limbered-up guns. Five black puffballs, each with a momentary snap of red fire at its heart. The green banner went down, and there was a circle of wounded dogs snapping at their hurts around the place where it lay in the dust.

Ten seconds later, the forty-eight guns of the massed artillery reserve fired from either end of the ridge. Their fire wasn't nearly as accurate as the masked battery; the range was longer, and the gunners had less time to estimate the range and adjust their pieces. The shells were contact fused. Many gouged the earth short, or fell long; both did damage enough. The score or so that fell on target hammered into the Colonial artillery train, still tied to limbers and teams. Dogs died or were wounded into howling agony—and a half-tonne of berserk carnivore was much more hindrance than a dead beast. Ammunition limbers exploded in globes of red fire, flipping wheels and barrels and bits of men dozens of meters into the air. Even then the crews of the surviving guns tried to unhitch them and swing the muzzles around to bear on the enemy who were slaughtering them.

Futile. The crews were within easy small-arms range of the ridge; dozens went down in the few seconds he watched. More shells burst among them, and overhead as the Civil Government artillery switched to time-fused shells that flailed them with shrapnel from above. More ammunition limbers exploded. He saw Colonial artillerymen cut dogs loose from their surviving teams and spur to the rear; officers who tried to stop them were ridden down. The whole crimson-uniformed mass was in full flight, those who could still move. The men on the fastest dogs were first, with the dismounted running or limping or dragging themselves afterwards.

Smoke drifted across the Civil Government line, thick even though a stiff breeze was blowing. Crewmen crawled forward from the splatguns, staying low and calling targets and distances back to their fellows. Officers directed the troopers' volleys with their swords.

Gerrin Staenbridge raised an eyebrow at Raj, who nodded. Another signal rocket hissed skyward, and this time the starburst puff of smoke was blue. A trumpet snarled six notes out on the right flank of the Civil Government force, and the cry of *cease firing* ran down the battalions on that end of the line. The 1/591st trotted their dogs over the ridge and down the slope, speed building. The swords came out in a single ripple of sun-struck silver as the speed of the charge built. Slowly at first—those were big men on heavy dogs, huge-pawed Newfoundlands and Alsatians sixteen hands at the shoulder. They growled as they charged, a sound like massed millstones grinding away in a cave, and the men shouted:

"*UPYARZ! UPYARZ!*"

"Nicely done," Raj said. "Oh, *nicely* done."

The charge swept down the hill and crashed through the flank of the disintegrating Colonial formation. The ex-Brigaderos held their ranks with fluid precision, stabbing and hacking and shooting with the revolvers most of them wielded in their left hands; the dogs were well enough trained to need no guidance but knees and voice and their place in ranks. The lighter Arab cavalry would have had trouble meeting a charge like that mounted at the best of times. With half their men down and unit cohesion gone, they reacted the way a glass jar did dropped on a flagstone floor. Men spattered in every direction; the 1/591st rode through their line, rallied to the trumpet call, dressed ranks and charged through again in the opposite direction. Hundreds of dismounted Colonials were holding up reversed weapons or helmets, asking quarter.

The barbarians in Civil Government service were whooping like boys as they cantered up the slopes again, despite a few empty saddles; shaking bloodied swords in the air and chanting their guttural Namerique war cries.

"Damn, but that's frightening," Raj said, shaking his head and scanning the enemy.

"Frightening?"

"One mistake, and two thousand disciplined troops with an able commander get creamed."

"*Their* mistake, fortunately."

Raj nodded grimly. "*Un*fortunately, Tewfik has enough men that he can afford to make a mistake—and he won't make this one again. If we make one mistake like this, the campaign is lost and so is Sandoral and the war. We'd lose everything south of the Oxheads as far west as Komar."

Staenbridge blinked. "It must hurt, thinking ahead like that all the time," he said. "General pursuit, *mi heneral*? I think we can take the lot of them, here."

Raj nodded. "That would be best. I hate to see so many good soldiers wasted like this, though."

wait. listen.

"Wait," Raj said automatically. Then: "Sound *Cease Fire* and *Silence in the Ranks.*"

Staenbridge looked at him oddly, then signed to the trumpeters. The call rang out, and silence fell—silent enough so that the sounds of wounded men and dogs were the loudest things on the battlefield.

And off to the northeast, a muffled thudding sound, very faint.

"Guns," Staenbridge said. "You've got good ears, *mi heneral.*"

distance 18 kilometers.

An hour or two at forced-march speed. "All a matter of knowing what to listen for," Raj said. Center had to use its ears, but it could pay attention to *everything* they detected, however faintly. "We went looking for Tewfik, and we've bloody well found him, haven't we?"

"You think that's him?" Staenbridge said.

"It's another battle group of Colonial cavalry meeting one of the raiding parties I called in," Raj said. "And where there's two, there'll be more. Tewfik's here, and if he's got less than twenty thousand men with him, I'm a christo. He's probing to find out where we are, and once he knows he'll pile on."

He tapped one fist into the palm of the other hand. "Messenger, ride to the sound of the guns; that's probably Major Zahpata's group. Tell him to withdraw as quickly as possible and rejoin on the route north. Gerrin, let's get ready to move out of here, and do it *now*. Hostile-territory drill."

"We have to move anyway," Raj said, preparing to rein Horace around.

The doctor's shoulders slumped. Suzette moved over two steps and laid her blood-spattered hand on Raj's knee. The dog bent its head around and snuffled at her. She shoved it gently away as she looked up at her husband.

"We'll do what's necessary," she said. He nodded wordlessly and pulled on the reins with needless force.

Suzette moved back to the line of wounded. *Not this one*, the Renunciate's eyes said.

Suzette looked down at the soldier sweating on the litter. His olive face was gray with shock, his eyes squeezed tightly shut. There was a tourniquet around the upper thigh of his right leg, and a pressure bandage over a wound below the ribs. He *might* have survived the leg wound, although he'd have lost the limb—there were fragments of bone sticking out of the mass of red-and-gray flesh below the tight-wound cloth. There was a faint sewer smell from the stomach wound, though.

"Here, soldier," she said in Namerique—from his coloring the man was MilGov. "Take this, it'll help with the pain."

The blue eyes fluttered open, wandering, the pupils dilated. She lifted a shot-glass sized dose of liquid opium to his lips; enough to knock a war-dog out, and fatal for a man.

Better than leaving them for the Colonials, she thought. It was bleak comfort.

"Yes!" Major Hadolfo Zahpata said. "Pour it on, *compaydres*. Give those wogs hell!"

He walked down the firing line—more like a C with the wings bent back, now. *Fifteen hundred if it's a man*, he thought, squinting into the bright sunlight. *I have perhaps three hundred fifty. And we had to run into them facing the sun.*

Twigs fell on his uniform coat from the apricot trees of the little orchard, cut by the bullets of the Colonial dragoons to his front. More went overhead with flat cracking sounds; he looked down and saw the left sleeve of his jacket open to the elbow, sliced as neatly as by a tailor's shears. One millimeter closer, and . . .

They were advancing by squad rushes across the open grainfields; several hundred were behind the lip of an irrigation ditch about a hundred fifty meters to the front. That gave them cover, which was very bad. His guns were firing over open sights, trying to suppress them, which meant that they had to more or less ignore the steady flow of men *over* the embankment and into the open ground—although, thank the Spirit, they had knocked out the brace of pom-poms there. And the enemy were working around his flanks, both of which were now re-fused.

A body of the enemy stood to charge. A few meters down the line a splatgun crew slammed another iron plate of rounds into their weapon and spun its crank. *Braaaaap.* Two more of the rapid-fire weapons joined it. The Colonials staggered, the center punched out of their ranks. Company and platoon officers redirected the troopers' fire, and volleys slammed out. The Arabs sank back to the ground, opening fire once more. A splatgun crewman went *ooof* and folded over at the middle, dropped, his legs kicking in the death-spasm. Another stepped up from the limber to take his place. Bullets flicked off the slanting iron shield in front of the weapon with malignant sparks.

Thank the Spirit for the splatguns, and for Messer Raj who made them, Zahpata thought. He was a pious man—most who lived on the Border were—and Messer Raj was living proof that the Spirit of Man of the Stars watched over Holy Federation. *Despite our sins,* he added, touching his amulet.

A Colonial shell screeched overhead to explode behind him. There was a chorus of screams after it, men flayed by the shrapnel, and howls from wounded dogs. A revolver banged, putting down the crippled or dangerously hysterical among the animals. Beside him his aide ducked involuntarily at the shell's passage. Zahpata smiled and stroked his small pointed black chin-beard.

Spent brass lay thick around the troopers prone in the shade of the fruit trees; wasps and eight-legged native insects crawled over the shells, intent on the windfallen apricots scattered in the short dry grass. Their sickly sweet scent mingled with the burnt sulfur of powder smoke and the iron-and-shit smell of violent death.

"I'm glad to see you're not concerned, sir," the aide said as Zahpata lowered his binoculars and leaned on his sheathed saber.

Zahpata smiled thinly; the aide was his nephew, something not uncommon in the Civil Government's armies and very common in the 18th Komar Borderers. All of them were recruited from the same tangle of valleys in the southern Oxheads five hundred kilometers west of here, and half the battalion were relatives of one sort or another. The aide—his mother was Zaphata's older sister—was a promising youngster, but inexperienced at war. Except for the continual war of raid and skirmish and ambush with the Bedouin along the frontier, but all Borderers were born to that.

"I am not as concerned, *chico*, as I was before I saw that," he said, pointing. "The unbeliever commander must be so delighted at the prospect of our destruction he did not notice."

He pointed. The aide leveled his own binoculars, squinting against the sun. Zahpata knew what he was seeing; a line of slivers of silver light. Sun on sword-blades.

"Are they ours?"

"Would reinforcements for the sand-thieves advance with drawn blades?" Zahpata asked. By the length of front, that was two battalions—his City of Delrio and Novy Haifa Dragoons, reconcentrating as he'd ordered before this began. Doubtless they'd stepped up their pace to the sound of the guns. "In a moment—"

There was a frantic flurry of trumpet-calls from where the enemy commander's banner stood. Zahpata grinned like a war-dog scenting blood as the Colonial artillery ceased fire and began to limber up with panic speed.

"Sound *Fix Bayonets!*" he said.

The bugle's brassy snarl sounded. Surprised, men checked their fire for an instant; then there was the long rattle and snap as the blades came out and the men slid them home. The enemy had checked their advance; now they rose and turned to retreat. Fire slashed into their backs. Out in the fields beyond, the two Civil Government battalions glinted again as the sabers came down and the charge sounded.

"Sound *General Advance with Fire and Movement*," he said happily. A good many enemies of the Spirit were going to the Starless Dark today.

The troops rose and dressed their ranks by company and battalion standards; the men at either end of the line double-timed to turn their C into a bracket with the open end facing the enemy. *Hammer to the anvil*, he thought. The oncoming battalions spread wider, and their artillery wheeled about to unlimber and open fire.

Zahpata frowned. *Hope they're not overconfident.* Any shells that overshot would be coming straight at his men; and if he had many casualties from friendly fire, there would be floggings.

An orderly led up his dog; Zahpata put one hand on the saddlehorn and vaulted up. A whistle brought his head around.

The messenger was a Descotter, with the shoulder-flashes of the 5th. "Ser," he said, in the grating nasal accent of his home County. "T'*heneralissimo* sends his compliments, an' yer t'rejoin immediate—on t' road headin' north. Fast, loik, ser."

Zahpata's aide moved his dog closer as the major read the slip of paper the messenger pulled out of his glove.

"Messer Raj has been *defeated?*" he asked incredulously.

"Don't be more of a fool than your mother made you, Hezus," Zahpata snorted, reading. "Ah—a great victory. Another infidel group, defeated with small loss."

He wrote on the reverse of the first message. "My

compliments to the *heneralissimo*, and we expect to intersect the northern road at . . ." What was the heathen name? Ah, yes. ". . . at Mekrez al-Ghirba."

That should put him on an intercept course, or even get there ahead of time. The messenger saluted, pulled his dog's head around, and clapped his heels to its ribs.

"If we're not defeated, sir, why are we pulling back?"

Zahpata looked at the eager young face and sighed inwardly. The boy was here as a military apprentice, and you expected the young to be fools. *Although Messer Raj was only a few years older when he had his first independent command.*

"Messer Raj met and defeated one enemy column; perhaps two thousand men, twenty-five hundred. With twenty guns. We met and defeated another—fifteen hundred men, ten guns. What do you think will happen next?"

"Oh," the aide said.

Zahpata clouted him alongside the head, half-affectionately; his helmet *bonged.* "Live and learn, boy— or don't learn and die." He looked around. "Messenger, to battalion commanders. 18th Komar will lead; City of Delrio follows, Novy Haifa to rear. Scout-screens on all sides, maximum alertness. *Hadelande!*"

CHAPTER TEN

It was dark, with the sun down and only Miniluna in the sky. The earth gave back the day's heat, radiating from the bare clay of the badlands in the Drangosh bend; the darkness turned the ochers and umbers of the canyons to a uniform gray. Pterosauroids cheeped and mewed overhead, swooping after night-flying insects; Raj caught a gleam from the huge round eye of one, a vagrant trace of starlight. Earth-descended bats passed more silently. Off in the tangle of gullies and sinkholes something roared on a rising note, ending in a pierced-boiler screech; there was a rattle along the lines of dogs as the big animals raised their heads and cocked ears toward it. Some carnosauroid; they were hard to eliminate, in any area without a dense population, and the Civil Government force was into the belt of uncultivated land that extended from just west of Ain el-Hilwa along the river north to the border.

Raj sat, wrapping his officer's cloak around his shoulders and looking up at the stars that stretched in a thick frosted band across the sky. The Stars where man had once dwelt, before the Fall—and would again, if Center's plan succeeded.

The unFallen had the powers of gods, Raj thought. *Yet from what Center tells me, they were still men— not sinless, as the Church teaches. They had their wars and their intrigues, as we do; their tragedies and defeats, as we do.*

true, the voice in his mind said. **my analysis is that such are inherent in the nature of your species.**

Raj leaned back against the clay and lit a cheroot. *What's the point, then?* he asked. *If all I'm doing is letting people make mistakes on a bigger scale and a broader canvas?*

Center was silent for half a minute. **this is a difficult question, and one at the limits of my powers of analysis. i was not constructed so as to be capable of philosophical doubt.**

Another pause. **in your terms: the fall represented a limitation of human choice due to suboptimal decisions. the greater capacities of a unified and technologically advanced civilization free humans from the determinism of nature. both their triumphs and their failures become matters of choice.**

Ours aren't?

only to a very limited degree. the vast majority of humans on bellevue are peasants, because you lack the productive capacity to organize yourselves otherwise. this precludes forms of government and social organization less authoritarian, because the civilized regions depend too heavily on coercion to produce the surplus on which cities and a literate leisure class depend. if the fall continues, even agriculture-based societies will collapse and maximum entropy will be reached at a hunter-gatherer level. the survival of human life on this planet will then be in doubt.

As if to illustrate the point, the carnosauroid's retching scream sounded again through the night.

a new civilization may eventually emerge; but it will lack any continuity with the ancestral culture. and fifteen thousand years of savagery means hundreds of generations of human lives without the opportunity to exercise their capacities.

Raj nodded. Peasants were old at forty, and every day in their lives was pretty much the same, except when something went badly wrong. The Church said it was punishment for men's sins—which seemed to be literally true in Center's terms as well—but there was no reason for the punishment to go on forever.

He shivered slightly, despite the warmth of the earth at his back. *The fate of the human race for the next fifteen millennia rests on me, then. And our chances of pulling it off are no better than even.*

correct.

He stood and flicked the stub out into the darkness, a solitary ember that arced away and was lost in the night. He turned. Behind him the command group was gathering about the pool of light cast by a kerosene lantern, the undershadow putting the bones of their faces into hard relief. They were unfolding maps, munching on hardtack and pieces of jerked meat; their smiles and eyes looked as feral as so many war-dogs in the yellow light.

"Well, sooner started, sooner finished," Raj said. He strode into the light. "Right, gentlemen. Tewfik's main force is rather smaller than I'd expected—about sixteen thousand men, according to Captain M'lewis's report."

"Countin' banners, sir. Couldna' git closer. Them wogs is screened tighter 'n a cherry inna raghead's hareem."

Everyone nodded. Colonial units were less standardized in number than their Civil Government equivalents. One reason for that was a deliberate attempt to make it harder for observers to get a quick, accurate tally of a Colonial army's numbers by counting the unit standards.

"We'll take sixteen thousand as a ballpark figure— which worries me, Messers. We're here" —he put his finger on a spot west of Ain el-Hilwa— "and we have to cut the bend of the Drangosh to get back to our bridgehead opposite Sandoral. I hope you all realize that after leaving Ali's main army—"

He moved his finger to the west bank, and north almost to Sandoral, then south again to the Colonial pontoon bridge.

"—he could have dropped forces off to cross the river and take up blocking positions *north* of us."

By their expressions, the thought was an unpleasant surprise to a few of the battalion commanders—although not to his Companions.

"That depends on Tewfik's estimate of our numbers and intentions. We'll let the men rest another hour, then start out at Maxiluna rise." With both moons in the sky, there would be more than enough light for riding. "We'll make use of every hour of darkness we can; it'll be cooler, too.

"Colonel Staenbridge," he went on, "you take the three companies of the 5th and lead the way. Spread out but move fast. Captain M'lewis, you'll be the scout screen for the scout screen. Gerrin, if you run into anything you think you can handle, punch through. If not, go around if *that's* possible, screening our retreat. Major Zahpata, you and your 18th Komar will follow in column of march right behind. Exercise normal caution, but rely on Colonel Staenbridge for your intelligence. Gerrin, if you run into anything you *can't* handle, Major Zahpata is to move up immediately and support the 5th at your direction. Understood?"

Both men nodded. *At least I don't have to wonder who'll take orders from whom,* Raj thought thankfully. That sort of thing had nearly gotten him killed in the Southern Territories campaign, at the hands of the late unlamented Major Dalhousie. The problem was that the Civil Government didn't have permanent field armies or a structure above the battalion level—large concentrated field forces were too tempting to ambitious generals. By now, all these men had been on campaign with him long enough to work smoothly together, and he'd disposed of the purblind idiots, one way or another.

"The rest of you will be following in double column up these roads," he said, tracing the route northwest with two strokes of his finger. "They're never more than a kilometer apart, so you'll be close enough for mutual support. If Colonel Staenbridge runs into a major blockforce, you'll flank and go round—taking a lick at them from the rear in passing. Boot their arse, don't pee on them; we *cannot* afford to get tangled up in a meeting engagement."

"My oath no," Staenbridge said mildly, still studying the map. "Not with Tewfik and sixteen thousand wogs after our buttocks."

"Exactly."

"What's the source of our intelligence on these pathways through the badlands?" Zahpata asked.

Raj had drawn those in himself. "Personal sources, Major. You may rely on them." *Center can do more with my eyes than I can,* he added silently.

"Major Gruder, I have a special tasking for your command. Otherwise, the order of march will be as follows—"

When the other officers dispersed to their units, Raj lead Kaltin Gruder out into the mouth of the notch.

"Kaltin, I want you to execute a battalion ambush on Tewfik's lead elements here," he said.

Gruder squinted up at the eroded clay hills, comparing them with his memory of the same scene by daylight. "Good ground," he said. "And we've given them a couple of bloody noses—he'll be more cautious this time."

"Probably. Time is exactly what I want you to gain; but *not* at the price of your battalion. Understood?"

Gruder nodded. Raj went on: "Tewfik knows he has two ways to win this campaign. The quick way is to catch us and smash us up before we get back to Sandoral. He's got numerical superiority, but it'd still be expensive. On the other hand, a quick victory is always preferable;

the sooner you win, the less time the other side has to come up with something tricky. The slow way is to chase us back into Sandoral and starve us out. So he'll probably be willing to take a swipe at you to save time, but it won't be a reckless one."

Raj reached a space of flat sand, coarse outwash detritus from the bluffs above. He smoothed it further with his boot and drew his sword to sketch in it.

"This is your position. More or less of a very broad V, with the open end facing south. Have your men dig rifle pits at the foot of these hills; I'll detail the City of Delrio to help before they pull out. Scatter the dirt, and it'll be difficult for them to estimate your numbers before they get close. I suggest you place them by companies like this." He traced lines. "With your dogs reasonably close to hand, here and along here. I'll also have the Delrio leave you their splatguns—that'll give you eight total. Put them down here—here—here—here, in pairs."

His sword marked spots along the face of the V. Gruder frowned.

"Down on the flat?"

"They're not artillery, Kaltin—those are bullets they're shooting, not shells."

Gruder nodded thoughtfully; a bullet was dangerous all along its trajectory if it was fired at a formation with any depth. Fired from above, it either hit the target it was aimed at or plunked harmlessly into the dirt; fired on the level, it went much farther.

"That'll give you crossfire from both infantry and splatguns, like this." The tip of Raj's saber traced X marks across the sand.

"Now," he went on, moving the sword to left and right on either side of the notch, "this terrain is pretty well impassable to formed bodies of troops. Certainly to artillery. Put observers *here* and *here*. Tewfik may try to work dismounted troopers around your flanks in those areas.

If he does, block them with your reserve company—it ought to be easy, in that ground.

"Over here, about twenty klicks, is the only other path suitable for artillery and large formations of troops. That's where he'll go when he decides he can't just rush you out. Put a relay of men between here and there; when his flanking force gets there, pull out."

He raised his head and met the other man's eyes, his own flat and hard. "I give you *no discretion* concerning that. When his men reach there, you bug out. Understood?"

"*Si, mi heneral,*" Gruder said. He grinned. "I have learned something over the past five years."

"I certainly hope so, because I can't spare you *or* your battalion," Raj said.

"Hmmm. Artillery here?" Kaltin's saber pointed to the apex of the V.

"Yes, and start the guns out first. Also, walk all that ground tonight, and have your company commanders do it too. Ranging marks, all the bells and whistles."

"*Si.*" Kaltin studied the improvised sand-table. "I'll have them come and look at this, too. You have a good memory for terrain, *mi heneral.*"

Which was true, and even more so with Center's assistance. "*Waya con Ispirito del Homme,*" Raj said. They gripped forearms. "Get me an extra half-day."

"The Spirit with you also, General. Consider it done."

Tewfik ibn'Jamal, *Amir* of the Host of Peace, lowered his binoculars and cursed. Arabic was the finest of all languages for that, as for all else—as would be expected for the language God chose to dictate His word in—but the rolling, guttural obscenities did not relieve his feelings.

"And may the fleas of a thousand mangy feral dogs infest the scrotum of the *kaphar* general Whitehall," he concluded.

Ahead was a broad slope five thousand meters across at its mouth, narrowing down to barely a hundred where the roadway snaked into the badlands. The hills behind and to either side were not high, but they were steep as the sides of houses, crumbly adobe scored and riven by the rare cloudbursts of the Drangosh Valley winter. The roadway was graded dirt—a secondary road. The main highway—Allah torment in the flames of Eblis the souls of the engineers who laid it out—ran parallel to the Ghor Canal, through the populated districts farther east and towards Ain el-Hilwa. *That town of fools and dotards.*

Taking that would mean two days' delay, more than enough time for the invaders to scuttle back to the walls of Sandoral—and take any hope of concluding this accursed war quickly with them.

Another *tabor* of dismounted troopers trotted up into the V, angling for the enemy's foremost position on that side—if they could dislodge the outer rim, they could unravel it up the foot of the hills. A steady *braaaap . . . braaaap* sounded, and men fell. Figures in crimson djellabas dropped into the hot white dust of the valley floor, to lie still or twitching and moaning. He could see puffs of dust where the bullets struck, smoke pouring from the positions of the new rapid-fire weapons, a steady crackle and bang from the rifle-pits where the infidel troopers kept up a continuous hail of well-aimed fire. A pom-pom galloped up to support the soldiers.

The rapid-fire weapons from both sides of the V shifted to it. The dogs of its team went down in a tangle, and the gun's long slender barrel slewed around in futility. He watched a survivor drag a wounded comrade into its shelter. Bullets fell on it like a rain of hail to ricochet off in sparks and whining fragments.

In the gun-line directly before him crews heaved at the trails of 70mm field guns and pom-poms. More smoke billowed out as they fired, a ripple of red tongues of fire from left to right. Dirt fountained skyward along the enemy lines, and a spare team was galloped out to retrieve the pom-pom and the wounded.

"Can you not suppress those Shaitan-inspired weapons?" he asked.

His artillery chief shrugged unwillingly. "Insh'allah," he said. "*Amir*, whatever they are, they do not recoil as artillery pieces do—so they can be deeply dug in. All we see is the muzzle and the top of an iron shield. To make good practice we must draw close—and you saw the result of *that*. Also they have a battery of field guns above, with a two-hundred-meter advantage in height. If I push our gun line forward, they will come under artillery fire from the heights as they try to deploy, as well as from small arms."

"Move guns to the left, concentrate on the outer arm of the enemy defenses."

"As the *Amir* commands," the gunner said.

Tewfik turned back to the map table. Sweat dripped from the points of his beard onto the thick paper, reminding him of how thirsty he was. The goatskin *chaggal* at his side was half-empty; his men's would be worse, and there was no source of good water sufficient for fifteen thousand men within a half-day's ride.

"Muhammed," he said, and one of his officers bowed. "Sound the recall."

"Another push and we will be through, *Amir*," the man said stubbornly.

"Another push and we will lose another hundred men dead," Tewfik said. Just then a pair of stretcher bearers trotted by. Their burden moaned and tried to brush at the flies crawling on the ruin of his face. "Or like *that*. I do not continue with a plan that has failed."

"I obey."

"And start men moving here." He traced a line to the

eastward on the map. "The going's passable for men on foot. Put some of those Bedouin hunters to use; the sand-thieves do nothing but sit on their arses and eat better men's food. They should know the footpaths. Work around toward the rear of the enemy position.

"Anwar," he went on. "You will take the reserve brigade and go" —he moved the finger in a looping circle far to the west— "twenty kilometers. A tertiary road—passable for wheels, according to the reports. Push all the way through to open country on the other side of these badlands, secure the route, and I will follow. Mutasim, you will put a blocking force across the mouth of this deathtrap; I'll leave you thirty guns. When the *kaphar* pull out, pursue, slow them if you can; we'll see if whoever Whitehall left in charge has sense enough to flee quickly as we flank him."

Mutasim scowled. "So far we have accomplished little," he said, tugging at his beard.

"There is no God but God; all things are accomplished according to the will of God," Tewfik said. He fought the urge to grind his teeth. "We were sent to stop the enemy's ravaging of our land; this we have done. We will pursue him. If we catch him, we will destroy him; if not, we will besiege him in Sandoral, which has not the supplies to support his men for long. In a week, they must begin to eat their dogs—which destroys all hope of mobility. After that, it is merely a matter of time. This was a damaging raid, no more. Insh'allah."

"As God wills," the others echoed.

"Go. Move swiftly."

The officers departed, and trumpets began to sound. Only the aides, messengers, and the *Amir*'s personal mamluks were left, silently awaiting his will. Tewfik stood and stared up the valley again, unconsciously fingering his eyepatch. It had never stopped him seeing into the heart and mind of an enemy commander before.

Whitehall, Whitehall, what is your plan? What dream of victory do you cherish in your secret heart?

That was what bothered him. He remembered the El Djem campaign; he'd caught Whitehall there, beaten him—although the fighting retreat had been stubbornly effective, preventing him from finishing the young *kaphar* commander off without paying a price that seemed excessive. He'd bitterly regretted that decision a year later, when the Colony's forces met Whitehall's army.

May the Merciful, the Lovingkind, have pity on your soul, my father, he thought. Jamal had been a hard man and a good Settler, but no great general. *You ordered that we attack directly into the* kaphar *guns, and we paid for it,* Tewfik thought bitterly. Jamal had paid with his head, the House of Islam with thousands of its best troops and a legacy of civil war. All Whitehall's doing; it had been a good day's work for Shaitan when Whitehall had been born among the infidels of the House of War instead of a believer.

Since then Whitehall had made war in the West, while Tewfik repaired the Host of Peace and prepared for the next round of battle. This time there should be no doubt about the outcome. He had overwhelming numbers, and even Ali wasn't going to force him into the sort of error their father had made.

Yet the Faithful had good intelligence sources in the western realms. Tewfik had followed Whitehall's campaigns closely, and spoken with eyewitnesses. *Why this raid?* By bringing his force out from beyond Sandoral's walls, Whitehall had exposed them to the risk of defeat—without any countervailing chance of decisive victory. True, he had ravaged rich lands; true, he had inflicted stinging tactical reverses on the Muslims. *Our losses were greater than his. But we can absorb them without strategic consequence, and he knows this.* Nor were burnt-out villages in this one little corner of the Settler's domains any sort of strategic loss; yes, a tragedy for those who suffered, and enough to wake screams of rage from the nobles whose estates were ravaged, but nothing mortal. At least once in the past *kaphar* hosts had ravaged their way to the walls of Al Kebir itself, and the House of Islam still stood— there were vast and rich lands south and east of the capital to draw on. This was nothing by comparison.

Whitehall must have *something* in mind, something decisive. But *what*?

Tewfik plucked at his beard again. "He threw as many troops as he could into Sandoral before we reached the walls," he muttered to himself. "Yet it would have been better to send one-third as many, and use the other trains for supplies." Sending all the civilians out of the fortress city had been a shrewd move, but not enough. And why so many cavalry, when the issue would be settled by fighting from behind strong works?

"He has too many troops to hold the walls, and not enough food to feed the numbers he brought—yet not enough men to meet us in the field."

Three pounds of food per man per day, fifteen per dog; Whitehall knew the importance of logistics as well as any man. What was his plan?

There was something else here, something beyond a young *kaphar* chieftain with a genius for war. The infidels whispered that their false god rode at Whitehall's elbow.

He shrugged off the notion. There was no God but God. "Insh'allah," he said again, snapping his binoculars back into the case at his waist. "We waste no more time."

"Hadelande!"

Robbi M'Telgez pulled the rifle free from the scabbard and kicked his feet free of the stirrups. Dirt clouted the soles of his boots as Pochita crouched; he turned and ran up the crumbly slope, coughing in the dust Company

A kicked up in their scramble. He chopped the butt of his rifle into the dirt to help the traction, feeling the dirt sticking to the sweat on his face, blinking his eyes against the sting and thanking the Spirit for the chain-mail avental riveted to the back of his helmet. It might or might not turn a swordstroke, but the leather backing of the mail protected your neck from the sun pretty good.

Captain Foley reached the top and his bannerman planted the company pennant. The officer stood with arm—hook arm—and sword outstretched, to give the alignment. M'Telgez flopped down on his belly and crawled the last three paces to the ridgeline, because bullets were already cracking overhead. *Got guts, that one,* he thought.

Foley stayed erect until the unit was in place, then went to one knee only a little back from the crest. Some men in other units gave them a hard time for having the colonel's boyfriend as company commander. He didn't care weather Foley banged men, women, bitch-dogs or sheep—as long as he knew his business, which he did.

There were plenty of wogs making for the same crestline from the other side, hundreds of them. The slope was steeper there, though; he could see clumps of them falling back in miniature avalanches of rocks and clay, down to where their dogs milled about in the dry streambed below. Others were prone on the slope, firing at the Civil Government banners that had appeared on the ridge above. M'Telgez flipped up the ladder sight mounted just ahead of the block of his Armory rifle and clicked the aperture up to 800 meters.

"Pick your targets!" the ensign in command of his platoon shouted.

He did, a wog with fancywork on his robe walking around at the base of the hill and followed by signalers. A long shot, and tricky from up here, but he had the ground for a firm rest. He worked the rifle into the dirt, fingers light on the forestock, and took up the first tension on the trigger.

"*Fwego!*"

BAM. Eighty rifles fired. The butt punched his shoulder; a measurable fraction of a second later the wog in the fancy robe folded sideways under the hammering impact of the heavy 11mm bullet. He fell, kicking. *Not goin' t'git up, neither,* M'Telgez thought. Not with a hollowpoint round blowing a tunnel the size of a fist through his stomach and intestines. The Descotter whistled tunelessly through his teeth as he worked the lever and reloaded, the spent brass tinkling away down the slope to his rear. Most of the others had picked closer targets; bodies were sliding back down the steep slope. Live ones, too, as the more sensible wogs decided that toiling slowly up a forty-degree slope of crumbling dirt under fire wasn't the way to a long life.

BAM. He picked another hard target, a Colonial prone behind a slight ridge and firing back. The djellaba blended well with the clay, but he aimed up a little. The wog jerked up seconds later, clawing at his back. Lever, reload.

"Five rounds, independent fire, rapid, *fwego.*"

M'Telgez's hand went back to his pouch; he pulled four bullets out of the loops and stuck their tips between his lips like cigarettes. Another went into the chamber, and he snapped the ladder-sight back down to the ramp.

Damn. There were too many wogs who'd decided to chance it. *Bam.* One down. Out one of the rounds between his lips. *Bam.* A miss, but the target yelled and danced sideways. *Bam.* Head shot, and the spiked helmet went end-over-end downslope in a splash of blood and brains. *Bam.* Couldn't tell, smoke too thick. *Bam.*

The oncoming enemy wavered, then fell back; most of them turned over onto their backsides and tobogganed down the slope, controlling the slide with their feet. There were boulders and rocks enough at the bottom to take cover behind, if they were careful.

"Dig in!"

The order came down the line. M'Telgez cursed; like most cavalry troopers, he hated digging—back home in Descott, a *vakaro* resented any sort of work that couldn't be done from the saddle. Resignedly, he spoke to his squad:

"Even numbers! Odd numbers on overwatch. C'mon, lads, 'tain't yer dicks yer grabbin', put yer backs inta it."

He reached to the back of his webbing belt and undid the leather pouch that held the head of his entrenching tool. It was a mattock-and-pick if you put the head in the central hole, a shovel if you put it into the slot behind the broader section. He unhooked the wooden handle that hung from his belt by the bayonet on his left side and knocked it into the main hole. A few swift blows cut through the hard crust of the adobe; it came up in chunks, and he piled those and handy rocks ahead of him, working down the slope behind to make a cut that would let him lie comfortably and fire through a couple of notches.

The afternoon was savagely hot, and the sweat ran down his body in rivulets that he could feel collecting where his shirt and jacket met the webbing belt. The damp cotton drill cloth clung and chafed. A carbine bullet went by overhead now and then with a malignant wasp-whine, encouraging him. A man came by with extra ammunition slung in canvas bandoliers from the pack-dogs; M'Telgez snagged an extra fifty rounds and cut a notch to support them with a few quick strokes of the mattock.

"M'Telgez! Report to the captain!"

Shit. Jest whin I wuz gettin' comfortable, loik, the corporal thought resignedly. "Smeet, y'got it fer now. Don't fook up too bad, will yer?"

"We'll a' git kilt, but it'll na be *my* fault, corp," the older trooper said cheerfully.

M'Telgez wiped his hands on the swallowtails of his jacket and picked up his rifle, then stepped-slid downhill a pace or two; running crouched, his head was below the ridgeline. The crunch of entrenching tools in the dirt marked his passage, and the steady crackle of fire from the alternate numbers keeping up harassment against the wogs. He also passed a few dead men; head and neck wounds were generally quickly fatal.

"Ser," he said when he came to the company pennant.

Barton Foley braced his pad across his knee with the point of his hook and wrote. "You have the way back to battalion, Corporal?"

"Yesser," M'Telgez answered.

He had a good eye for that sort of thing; and it was an officer's job to remember what his men could do.

"Detail one man of your squad to accompany you, and take this to Colonel Staenbridge."

"No problemo, seyhor." He'd take M'tennin, the lad was young, eager and a good shot. Smeet could handle the squad—he was a good junior NCO, when there was no booze around. Drunk, he didn't know a sow from his sister or an officer from an asswipe.

"Verbally, add that we can handle it for the present but would appreciate reinforcements. Report back immediately with his reply—and watch out, there may be wogs in these ravines."

M'tennin screamed.

M'Telgez took one look over his shoulder and clapped his heels to Pochita's ribs. The thing already had the younger man's shoulders in its jaws and one clawed foot hooked into his dog's side, ripping downward in a shower of blood and fur and loops of pink-gray gut. Pochita needed no urging; she brought her hindpaws up between her front and leapt off in a bounding gallop, teeth bared, ears flat, and eyes rolled back, right down the narrow floor of the canyon. Her rider whipped his head around as something screeched behind him, a sound like a steam-whistle gone berserk.

He could *smell* its breath, like a freshly-opened tomb in hot weather. It was bipedal and longer than a war-dog, probably heavier, but it ran with a birdlike stride—lightly, on the toe-pads of its three-clawed feet, so lightly that the shotgun blast of dirt and stones spraying back from each impact was a surprise. The body was a dusty orange-yellow, striped irregularly with vivid black; the open mouth was mottled purple and crimson. Teeth the size of his fingers reached for him, and the clawed forefeet on either side. Behind it another much like it—hunter's reflex told him they were probably a mated pair—was tearing at the bodies of M'tennin and his mount with impartial gluttony. Its muzzle went skyward, the long narrow jaws dislocating as it swallowed a leg and hip.

"Hingada tho!" M'Telgez screamed. "Fuck ye!" The carnosauroid shrieked back at him, another carrion-scented blast.

His rifle was in the crook of his left arm. He snatched the pistol out of his boottop with his right and thrust it backward, not three meters from the thing's mouth. Even so half the rounds missed. Three did hit; none of them seemed to do much good. A blood-fleck appeared on the shiny black skin between the angry red of the nostrils, and one fang shattered into fragments of ivory. That got the beast's attention, at least; it spun sideways for an instant, snapping and rearing on one leg as the other slashed at whatever had struck it.

Then it realized *he* had hurt it. Some of the bigger carnosauroids were too dumb to do anything but kill and eat; the smaller agile ones like this could be a lot smarter. There was more than simple hunger in the cry it gave as it bounded after him once more, body horizontal and long slender tail snapping behind it at the tip like a bullwhip.

"Fuck *me*," M'Telgez muttered through a dry mouth, and hurled the revolver at the beast. *That* hadn't been such a good idea.

He leaned left and then right as Pochita took the curves of the narrow gully at dangerous speed. The carnosauroid didn't let little things like turns slow it down; it just ran right up the wall of the cut, letting momentum keep it upright with its head parallel to the ground for an instant. The man wound the sling of his rifle around his right forearm with desperate speed. He'd have only one chance, and that wasn't much with a single-shot rifle. Reloading at the gallop . . . he might as well try to fly like a pterosauroid by flapping his arms.

The sides of the gully opened out a little. The carnosauroid screamed again and speeded up, half-overtaking the fleeing human.

Right. Likes t'knock yer over afore it bites.

Normally holding the long Armory rifle out one-handed would have made M'Telgez's arm tremble. Now it was steady, everything diamond-clear to his sight. Even the sideways lunge of the predator seemed fairly slow, an arc drawn through the air to meet the questing muzzle of his weapon.

Bam. The shock of recoil was a complete surprise, hard pain in his arm. The weight of the carnosauroid slammed into Pochita's haunches, and the dog skittered in a three-sixty turn before resuming its gallop. The torque of the outflung rifle nearly dislocated M'Telgez's shoulder, but the pain was negligible next to the horrifying knowledge that he'd failed. Footfalls still ripped the earth behind him, only a little further back—and Pochita's tongue was hanging out in exhaustion.

He rounded another curve—

—and nearly ran into a screen of mounted men in blue jackets and round bowl-helmets. Their guns flicked up, but their eyes were behind him.

"Shoot, ye dickheads!" he screamed, as his dog braced its forelegs and sank down on its haunches to stop.

They didn't. Bent over his pommel, gasping and wheezing, M'Telgez looked behind to see why.

The carnosauroid lay prone not five meters behind him, its muzzle plowing a furrow in the dry gritty dirt. One leg was outstretched and the other to the rear, as if it had done the splits in mid-stride. Tail and head beat the ground in an arrhythmic death-tattoo, then slumped into stillness. A neat hole drilled in the yellow scales just behind and above one ear-opening showed why.

"Well, fuck me," M'Telgez mumbled again. It took three tries to return his rifle to the scabbard, and two to get his canteen open.

"There's one'll na try it, dog-brother," one of the troopers said admiringly. Two rifles cracked as the corpse of the sauroid went through another bout of twitching, the jaws clashing with an ugly wet metallic sound. Carnosauroids took a good deal of killing.

A jingling and thump of paws sounded in the draw; the battalion standard came up. M'Telgez pulled himself erect with an effort and saluted.

"Colonel, message from C-captain Foley," he said. "Ah, we're, ah—"

"Take it easy, lad," the Colonel said, not unkindly, looking at the dead predator and then at M'Telgez's dog. "You had a close shave, there, Corporal."

M'Telgez followed the lifted chin. Pochita's tail was half-missing, ending in a bloody stump; now that the dog wasn't running for its life it was trying to twist around and lick the injury. He dismounted and reached automatically into his saddlebags for ointment and bandages, a cavalry trooper's reflex, and a lifelong *vakaro*'s.

One bite closer . . . he thought. The image must have been clear on his face, because the Colonel leaned down and clapped him on the shoulder.

"Good shot," he said. "Anything with this?"

"Ah, t'Captain 'uld want some reinforcements, loik," M'Telgez said. In an effort to clear his mind: "We'nz goin' t'push through 'em, ser?"

In many line outfits that might have been insolence; Descotters had an easy, unservile way with their squires, though. And he was a long-service man with a good record.

"No, Messer Raj knows a way around," Colonel Staenbridge said. "We just have to block them while the main force gets through. I'll come myself. Lead the way, Corporal."

M'Telgez looked around at the bewildering tangle of blind canyons, sinkholes, and ragged hills. *The Spirit must be wit 'im,* he decided. Which was a comforting thought.

"Cheer up, lad," Staenbridge said, as the column formed up and passed the dead predator.

One of the troopers tossed him a fang as long as his hand, with a lump of bloody gum still on the base. M'Telgez dropped it into his haversack; it'd be something to show the girls, cleaned up and worn around his neck on a thong. Might as well get something out of that; that poor *fastardo* M'tennin wasn't going to, not even a burial. There wouldn't be anything left of him or much of his dog by the time they got there.

"Cheer up. Could have been worse—it could have been wogs."

M'Telgez looked down at the four-meter length of tiger-striped deadliness lying in the dirt. He nodded. That was true enough. The carnosauroid had only wanted to kill and eat him.

Wogs might have taken him alive.

✧   ✧   ✧

"Good," Raj said. "That was clever of Tewfik, but he had to split his covering force up into too many detachments—there are a lot of badlands out there."

Staenbridge nodded. "Only two or three hundred men on the route we actually took," he said. "Still, it might have gotten sticky if we couldn't go around—they had an excellent position. How *did* you know that section of earth was thin enough to cut through behind them?"

An angel told me, and it could tell the thickness of the gully walls by measuring how inaudible sounds passed through, Raj thought sardonically. He wondered what Staenbridge would make of the explanation. Raj didn't understand a word of it himself.

sound waves are—

Forget it. I know it works, I don't have to know how or why.

"Lucky guess, Gerrin." The tone ruled out any further questions. "We're about—"

two point six kilometers.

"—two and a half klicks from the bridgehead, now. This is going to be tricky."

"You expect Tewfik to catch us crossing?" Staenbridge said, raising a brow.

"No, but he's not the only competent commander in the Colonial army, and he'll be in heliograph contact with their main body. What I want you to do is—"

CHAPTER ELEVEN

"Come on lads, put your *backs* into it," Colonel Jorg Menyez shouted. "Messer Raj needs this finished and ready to go by full sunrise!"

Arc lights hissed and kerosene lanterns cast their softer light across the chaos on the riverbank quays of Sandoral. Miniluna and Maxiluna were both on the horizon, paling to translucence as the sun cast bands of yellow and purple up into the fading dusk of night.

At least it's a little cooler, the infantry officer thought. That should speed things up. He'd had the preparations going on all night, what could be done without attracting attention.

There was no more point in trying for silence now, not with two thousand men splashing and clattering as they moved the big boxlike pontoon barges into position. Most of the supports had been beached along Sandoral's long waterfront, just outside the river wall. Teams of men grunted and heaved, some pushing, others prying with beams and planks. One by one the square shapes surged out into the river, then jerked to a halt as the anchor-ropes caught them. Other ropes were payed out and men hauled in groaning unison to pull the barges to the growing eastern end of the bridge. North of it was a line of cable floating between barrels; each marked a line dropping down to an anchor on the riverbed. Naked boatmen swam out with more lines to secure the barges to the cable.

As each was tied off against the current, notched beams went into the cutouts in the bulwarks, and sections of planking were pegged down on top. Men scrambled forward to the next even while the mallets were still pounding on the one they ran on; water slopped over the upstream side as the weight of scores of infantrymen and their burdens of timber and cordage rested on the end barge alone. Down in the hulls others threw buckets of water overside and screamed abuse at the work teams above.

A long hollow *boooom* sounded from the southward, from where the nearest part of the Colonial siege line had anchored itself with an earthen fort on the riverbank. A long whirring crash followed, and men froze as a heavy roundshot hit the water and skipped like a thrown rock across the surface of the water by a playful boy. Once . . . twice . . . three times, and the final plume of water was shorter than the others. The Drangosh drank down the big cast-iron ball as easily as it would the boy's pebble. Menyez blew out the breath he had not been aware of holding.

Two kilometers. A little too far. There were ironic cheers from some of the men, and the hammering clatter of work resumed. He looked eastward. The bridge was nearly to the other shore, where a company of infantry was heaving at winches anchored in the dirt, hauling the last few barges. *Nice fast piece of work,* he thought. It helped that they'd done it before, of course.

Booooom. A little sharper this time, a rifled piece. The sound of the shell was higher as well. It came much closer, only a few hundred meters south, but struck the water only once. A tall fountain of spray reached skyward, high enough that its top was touched red by the light of the sun rising in the west.

"Close, but that only counts with handbombs," he said.

Far off and faint, trumpets spoke on the eastern bank.

A message began to flicker in from the heliograph station there, as the light strengthened enough for the tripod-mounted mirrors to catch it.

The problem was that there were other heliograph relays farther down the river—Colonial ones.

"Come on, *mi heneral*," Menyez said under his breath.

He looked back over his shoulder at Sandoral. The city was eerily quiet, hardly even a thread of smoke marking the hushed stillness of the morning. Not even a cock crowing; all the chickens had gone into the stewpots several days ago.

And nearly the whole garrison out here working on the bridge, he added to himself. Pretty soon that thought was going to occur to somebody else.

Ali ibn'Jamal lowered his telescope. "My so-brilliant brother has let them escape," he said bitterly. "Allah requite him for it. And their bridge of boats is nearly finished to receive the ravagers of the House of Peace."

Everyone else in the clump of nobles and commanders maintained a tight silence. A cool morning wind ruffled robes and beards and the peacock and egret plumes in turbans and helmets, but many of them were sweating nonetheless.

Cowards, Ali thought, and raised the telescope again. The *kaphar* were working like men possessed on their bridge, getting the surface laid before Whitehall appeared. Tewfik was going to let him ride back into Sandoral like a conquering hero!

"Commander of the Faithful."

It was one of the cavalry generals, a protégé of Tewfik's. *Who cannot be Settler. But who could rule from behind the Peacock Throne, with a puppet Settler.* It had happened before.

The man knelt and touched his forehead to the floor. "The deserters have told us the *kaphar* are on half-rations—they have been for a week. With another eight thousand men and eight thousand dogs within the walls, they will eat their stores bare in a few days. Then the city must fall."

Eight thousand. Tewfik hadn't killed more than a few hundred of them, after they spent more than a week ravaging his lands. *His* lands! *I do not want them to surrender. I want them to* die.

Of course, they could die after they surrendered . . . but if he allowed them terms, it would be unwise to break them. Not with Tewfik and his officers so close around him—not when they absurdly, blasphemously valued a word given to an unbeliever.

He raised the telescope again. It was incredible how quickly the infidels had gotten their bridge put back together. Cannon were firing from the walls of the earth fort around him, but doing no damage—the range was so great that only sheer luck or divine intervention would land a shell where it could accomplish anything.

They must have their whole garrison working on that, Ali thought. He could see them clearly now that the sun had risen.

Ali smiled suddenly. Those watching his face flinched and looked away, then forced themselves to turn their heads back; it was not safe to be unaware of the ruler's moods.

Ah, Tewfik my brother, you did not think of that. All his life he had been in Tewfik's shadow in matters of war; blundering and hacking his way through the complex problems of the battlefield in confusion, while Tewfik cut to victory with a lambent clarity. But this time, he was the one to see.

"You," he said to the kneeling officer. "Ubaydalla Said. I order an assault on the walls—an immediate assault. Rise, take command of the forward troops, and execute my commands."

"I hear and obey, Settler of Islam," the officer said. He paused thoughtfully. "That is an excellent suggestion. But the preparations—"

It was the expression on his face that moved the Settler; the surprise, that Ali could have come up with a workable plan. He plucked the ceremonial whip out of the man's belt and lashed him across the face with it. An upflung hand saved Said's eyes from the nine pieces of jagged steel on the ends of the thongs, but blood dripped heavily into his beard and from his gashed mouth.

"Are you a coward as well as a fool, pig? Are you *deaf*? I said immediately! If you have time to prepare, so will the enemy! And you are to lead the attack, personally."

"As God wills," the officer said quietly. He bowed again, blood dripping on the priceless carpets, and wheeled away sharply, calling for his subordinates.

A whistle blast jarred Corporal Minatili out of exhausted sleep. It was much like waking up after a payday in Old Residence. For a moment he lay blinking in puzzlement. It must be Star Day, why were they calling him to work at the quarry already?

The whistle went on and on, sharp repeated calls. A trumpet joined in, sounding: *Stand to, Stand to* over and over again. Then he knew exactly where he was: on the parapet of the wall at Sandoral, with hot white sunlight slashing through the firing slits. He erupted up out of his blanket roll and grabbed his rifle and webbing in either hand, running to his duty station. His muscles ached from a night of hard labor, and the two hours of sleep seemed to have dumped a skullful of hot sand behind his eyes. He was hungry too, mortally hungry with the aching need of a man who had been using twice as many calories as he took in. None of it mattered.

He buckled his belt and leaned back slightly from the wall to make sure that everyone in the squad was at their posts—seven men to hold a section of wall that had been undermanned with forty. Seven men and the six militiamen left of the dozen that usually operated the big gun to his left. Probably the rest of the walls were just as empty. Spirit!

"Oh, *scramento*," he said as he knuckled the crust out of his eyes and looked out the slit.

From left to right across his field of vision the Colonial earthworks were belching jets of smoke with lances of red fire at their hearts; the siege guns were cutting loose. Underneath their deep booms he could hear the sharper sounds of the field guns in the forward bastions, and the rapid *pom . . . pom . . . pom* of the quick-firers. Much of the ground between the Colonial outworks and the city moat and wall was still covered by bloating bodies, and the ripe oily stink was thick—the wog commanders had refused the usual truce to remove the dead. That didn't seem to be slowing down the men who boiled out of the forward ends of the assault trenches any.

In the days since the first attempt at an escalade, the Colonials had braved constant sniping to rig overhead covers for the last few hundred meters of the trenches—platforms of palm logs and sandbags that wouldn't stop a heavy shell but did quite well against rifle bullets and case shot. Now the last ten meters or so of that were jerked down, and the soldiers in crimson came out like red warrior ants. They didn't seem to be as well organized this time, but there were an awful lot of them.

"Ready for it," Minatili called, clearing his eyes with the thumb of one hand. The fabric of the fortifications quivered underneath him as the heavy solid shot rammed into the granite facing of the concrete-and-rubble wall. Dust quivered up from every crack and crevice. He took an instant to gulp water from a dipper, stale and welcome as a mother's love.

The wogs were running forward with their long ladders,

built to cross the moat and not break even at an acute angle to the ground. The walls of Sandoral were not very high; they could not be, and be thick enough to resist modern rifled cannon. Others carried grapnel-throwing mortars.

"Now!" he shouted, and fired. Shots were crackling out all along the walls, and the deeper roar of cannon.

Booom. The fortress gun fired. A swath of the enemy went down, but the scratch crew were cursing with the shrillness of panic as they struggled to reload and relay the huge piece; there just weren't enough of them. Minatili fired again and again, as fast as he could work the lever—worry about overheating and extraction jams later. Wogs fell, to lie among the bloated, swollen remnants of the previous attack, but they kept coming. Grapnels thumped out of the mortars and blurred up to the ramparts, trailing snakes of cable with knotted hand- and footholds. A shadow fell across his eyes as a ladder toppled toward the wall, slanting out to the ground beyond the moat. He dropped his rifle on the stone ledge for a moment and reached into a bin, pulling out a hand bomb and snagging the ring on top on a hook set into the wall. A quick jerk freed the ring, and the bomb began to hiss as the friction primer within burned.

Toss. A vicious *crack* over towards the base of the ladder. Men fell, and the heavy eucalyptus poles of the construct swayed. A dozen men cut loose with their repeaters at Minatili's gunslit. Thousands were kneeling all along the edge of the moat, bringing the fighting platform under direct aimed fire. A little way down from Minatili a lucky pom-pom shell blasted right into a gunslit and exploded; an instant later so did the hand bombs in the bin there, blowing chunks of stone and flesh out into the moat and back down into the cleared zone below the city walls. He ducked down and back as ricochets buzzed through the narrow space, then dashed to the next slit. A file of wogs was already running up the ladder—it was no steeper than some stairways—toward the roof of the fighting platform overhead. He fired again and again. Men fell tumbling off the ladder and down into the foul water of the moat; some of them bobbed limply, others swam for the shore.

Boom. The fortress gun cut loose again, and another swath of wogs went down back toward the assault trench—but there were far too many already near the wall. Almost at the same time an enemy shell struck right underneath the muzzle of the gun. The huge banded barrel jumped backwards; a trunnion cracked, and the weapon pivoted sideways with a squeal of ripped bronze and crackling timbers. A gunner's legs were caught in the way, and the man smeared against the pavement and the iron guide-ring like liver paste on bread.

More carbine rounds flicked at Minatili's firing slit. He ducked back again, fixed the bayonet on his rifle, then slung it across his back. He filled his hands with hand bombs, slipping his fingers through the rings to carry them—dangerous, but fuck *that* right now for a game of soldiers.

"Saynchez! Hold 'em!" he screamed, and ran back down the covered walkway to the dismounted gun.

The other five militia gunners were standing gaping, looking at their dead comrade.

"Get yor fukkin' *guns*," Minatili screamed. His hands were full, so he kicked one of the gunners in the arse to get his attention; the man whirled, gaped, then went for his personal weapon. The gunners were equipped with shortswords, revolvers, and double-barreled shotguns: just the thing for the sort of short-range scrimmage that was all too likely in a moment. He could hear boots on the roof overhead.

"The wogs is over the wall," Minatili shouted, and leaped for the top of the gun.

There was a circular hole above it, with an iron ladder and an octagonal observation-point of timber and boilerplate above, usually for the master gunner. Minatili scrambled up it, stuck his head out of the hatch, and began throwing hand bombs. There were wogs clambering up onto the roof of the fighting platform by the score—though many were cut down by the enfilade fire of the light swivel guns on the bastion towers to either side—and thank the *Spirit*, none of them looking at him!

The cast-iron bombs clattered on the stone flags; he ducked back down as they burst with rending *crang* sounds, and bits of casing peened off the outside of the observation point. He rose again and threw the last of them; wogs were shooting at him from the outer edge, pausing at the top of their scaling ladders.

He dropped back down. Case shot hammered the boilerplate outside as a swivel gun tried to sweep the ramparts clear.

"Hingada tho!" he cursed at the unseen gunner in the tower, and dropped back to the gun. He could feel the heat of it through the soles of his hobnailed boots.

"Follow me!" He jumped down to the decking with a clash and spark of nails on the concrete.

The militia gunners ran behind him as he dashed back. A wog with his carbine slung and a long curved knife between his teeth swung down from the lip of the overhead, hung by both hands and jacknifed himself in to land on the very edge of the platform, with a fifteen-meter drop behind him. Minatili shouted and lunged; he had just time enough to meet the Colonial's eyes, black and unafraid. The man was trying to draw the revolver tucked through his sash when the point of Minatili's bayonet thumped into his chest. The steel didn't penetrate the breastbone, but it was enough to send the man backward over the edge, snarling in frustration.

Another landed beside him. A militiaman fired his

shotgun from behind Minatili, powder scorching his side. The spreading buckshot caught the wog in the gut, blasting him over the edge with his limbs flailing like a jointed doll. Another was hanging from the lip of the roof—it was deliberately made with an overhang beyond the fighting platform below, to make this sort of thing difficult. Minatili lunged again, this time between the dangling legs. The wog let go with a scream and plunged downward. His drop revealed another kneeling above, aiming a carbine. Minatili fired from the hip; the Colonial threw himself backward out of the line of fire.

The infantryman pivoted. Two of the militiamen were down, and a pair of wogs he hadn't even noticed stood on the deck. Two more were fighting another; one blocked his scimitar with the barrel of his shotgun, then reeled away wailing over fingers hanging by threads of flesh. That gave his comrade time enough to draw a revolver and fire five times with the muzzle almost pressed against the Arab swordsman's back.

The body hit the ground with a thump. The survivors of Minatili's squad were at their firing slits, shooting and throwing hand bombs. No, one was stabbing outward with his bayonet. The corporal started towards that slit, hands reloading his rifle of their own volition. The last militiaman shouted from behind him, warning in the tone.

Minatili turned. Another wog was coming at him, carbine clubbed. He caught it on the bayonet, pivoted the rifle and buttstroked the wog in the face; turned with frantic speed and caught another through the throat with the point. The militiaman was at his side, but more and more wogs were dropping down to the firing platform, some coming through the observation hatch over the gun. His men turned from the firing slits. He shouted to them to rally.

Something flashed very brightly, and there was a soft floating sensation. A heavy pressure. Blackness.

❖   ❖   ❖

Raj drew up beside Menyez at the western end of the pontoon bridge. The infantry commander grabbed at his stirrup-iron. "Wogs over the wall," he said. "Everything's committed—no more reserve!"

"I'll handle it," Raj replied. "Organize this end and get the remainder and the artillery concentrated in the plaza. *Waymanos!*"

The lead cavalry were coming over the bridge at a round trot, the fastest safe pace.

"Bugler," Raj snapped. "Sound *Charge!*"

The man obeyed instantly, but his eyes went wide. The troops responded as if the call were playing directly on their nervous systems, clapping their heels to their dogs and plunging forward. The floating bridge rocked and shuddered under the sudden impact of thousands of half-tonne dogs accelerating to their running pace. Howls and shouts rose over the massive thudding and creaking; Raj ignored them, drew his sword and spurred Horace across the Maidan, the empty space by the riverside, to the main water gate. It was broad, thank the Spirit; more than broad enough for cavalry to take in four-abreast column, and there was a wide straight avenue from there to the *Plaza Real*.

He looked westward, squinting into the sun and straining to hear the sounds of combat from the city walls. Green arrowed vectors painted themselves over his vision.

major penetrations at these locations.

"There!" he yelled, pointing with his sword.

Gerrin Staenbridge went by with the banner of the 5th Descott; his reply was a flourish of his own saber, and the men followed his abrupt curve with fluid precision.

"There!" Raj directed the next battalion. "There! There!"

A fourth. "Follow me!"

❖   ❖   ❖

Not only over the wall, they're into the bloody city,
Staenbridge thought, as the column of the 5th Descott
burst out of the street into the harsh light of the open
ground just inside the city wall. Broad stairways angled
up from the roadway to the fighting platform; right now
they were swarming with Colonials, their crimson
djellabas a solid blotch of color in the dark shade, an
occasional helmet-spike or officer's plume glinting. More
were milling about on the ground at its foot, the survivors
of the first wave. They were disorganized—not many
in any unit would have made it this far—but that wouldn't
last. Men who'd made it through the killing ground
outside and over the wall in the first wave would be too
aggressive to sit around waiting for orders.

"Deploy in line of companies!" he roared. Buglers
relayed the order every man half-expected.

The column of mounted troopers pouring out of the
mouth of the street split on either side of him, fanning
out like the arms of an outstretched capital Y with his
banner as the dividing point. In thirty seconds they were
in a line facing the wall, and moving forward three
hundred strong.

"Dismount! Fix bayonets!"

The dogs crouched and the men stepped free, drawing
their rifles from the scabbards. Steel glinted as the long
blades snapped home.

"Advance with fire, volley fire by platoon ranks!"

BAM. The men moved forward at the double. Colonial
officers were hustling the wogs at the foot of the wall
into makeshift firing lines, moving them forward in turn.
Can't give them room to deploy. He'd be outnumbered
too badly if he did. Unless more troops arrived up from
the river, and he couldn't count on that.

BAM. BAM. BAM. The 5th could double forward and
volley-fire at the same time, something possible only

with endless practice. There weren't many Colonials at the foot of the wall . . . yet . . . and more of them were reloading than firing, pulling rounds out of the loops across their chests and thumbing them through the loading gates of their carbines. Men fell on both sides, stumbling out of his line, flopping backward when the heavy 11mm Armory rounds punched them in the Colonials ahead.

A sound of iron wheels on flagstones. A splatgun crew wheeled their weapon around and ran it forward. Staenbridge pulled his dog aside.

"The stairway!" he barked.

The master gunner nodded and spun the elevating screw down to maximum. The honeycombed muzzle of the weapon rose like the nose of a hunting dog sniffing the wind. Two more crewmen moved the trail to his direction as he crouched over the breech. He snarled satisfaction and spun the crank.

Braaaaap. Thirty-five rounds punched into the mass of Colonials on the stairway. A bubble of dead and dying sprang into existence in the thick crowd, instantly filled as more pressed down from above. *Braaaap.*

Staenbridge spurred back to his banner, dismounted. The rest of the command group followed. He drew his revolver, tossed it into his left hand, then drew his saber and filled his lungs. Barton was beside him, hook ready, his double-barreled coach gun in his good hand. Their eyes met for an instant.

"Charge!" he shouted, and broke into a run forward.

With a bellow, the 5th Descott threw themselves after their Colonel.

"Charge!" Raj barked.

The trumpeter sounded it; the brassy clamor echoed back from the silent walls of the houses on either side.

"UPYARZ! UPYARZ!" the men bellowed in reply.

Raj snarled silently and leaned forward, point outstretched beyond Horace's neck. The 1/591st filled the street from wall to wall; some of them were riding down the sidewalks, inside the line of plane trees and gaslights that separated the brick walkway from the granite paving blocks of the street. The heavy paws of the big Newfoundlands made a drumming muffled thunder, and the column filled the road for better than two hundred meters back. Even at a slow gallop it was insanely risky; he gritted his teeth against the memory of what men looked like after a hundred war-dogs trampled over them.

Just have to be careful.

Horace was a little ahead of the pack, beside Raj's personal bannerman; the battalion standard and Teodore Welf were to one side. Ahead was a thin scattering of Colonials, running down the road; except for the ones turning to run away when they saw that juggernaut of huge black dogs and white fangs, bared swords and shouting barbarian faces. One officer—a high-ranking one, from the spray of plumes at the front of his helmet— had managed to find a dog, in Civil Government–issue harness. It was highly restive under its new rider. Dogs were like that; you had to train with them a good long while before they accepted you, if they had any spirit. He was keeping the reins and the cheek-levers they controlled tight, and slapping at men's shoulders with the flat of his scimitar as he hustled them into a semblance of a firing line.

His eyes grew wide as he saw Raj's banner. He turned to meet the onrush, drawing an ornate silver-inlaid revolver with his other hand. He clapped spurred heels to the dog's flanks; it bounded forward and a little to one side, crabbing against the ruthless skill of the rider as he forced it forward.

"Whitehall!" he cried in Arabic. "Shaitan waits for thee, Whitehall—and God is great!"

Crack. The bullet scorched past Raj's face. *Going to have a coal miner's tattoo from that one,* a distant corner of his mind recorded. The Arab had bleeding wounds across his face in a nine-line pattern, but his eyes were utterly intent. One well-placed shot or slash, and the heart would be out of the Civil Government force.

All the rest of his attention was on the point of his saber. Luck as well as skill saved the Colonial; his restive dog jibed at the last instant, and the swords crossed in a unmelodious skirring of steel on steel. Nimble, the Colonial's dog pivoted in its own length and started back to avoid the trampling rush of the Brigaderos. The dismounted men ahead had no such option. They managed one volley, an eruption of smoke and red fire. The whole front of the attacking line seethed as men and dogs went down across the fifteen-meter front. Men arched through the air to smash with bone-shattering force against the hard stuccoed stone of the house walls or crumple on the pavement; one landed with gruesome accidental accuracy on the crossbar of a gaslight and hung impaled and twitching like a shrike's prey on a thorn.

But there was too much momentum behind the charge for a single volley to halt, and many of the wounded dogs kept their feet. The light 10mm bullets of the Colonial carbines were deadly to men, but it took a lucky hit to kill a twelve-hundred-pound dog with one shot. Riderless dogs were almost as dangerous as the ones with swordsmen on their backs; one seized a Colonial by the head in its half-meter mouth and flipped him over its tail with one flex of its massive neck. The rear files squeezed by the thrashing chaos of the front rank, and the thin Colonial line went down in a flurry of swordstrokes and two-inch fangs.

The Colonial officer was very much alive. He took aim again; Raj threw himself down on the right side of his dog, holding on to the pommel with one heel. A trick a Skinner nomad had taught him, and it paid off . . . the pistol bullet went snapping through the air where his body had been an instant before. He drew his pistol and shot underneath Horace's belly, into the stomach of the Colonial's dog. The animal hunched itself up in an astonishing leap that made the Arab release the gun and grab for the reins; then two 1/591st troopers were on him. The scimitar flashed against the heavy MilGov broadswords for one stroke, two, three; he slashed one trooper across the face even as the other slammed his heavy blade through the Arab's stomach.

Raj heaved himself upright. That had been *close*. For a moment there were no wogs in sight except the ones running away—and running away from a dog in a straight line was a losing proposition. Then they were out into the cleared zone just inside the wall. The main city gate— the one with the railway entrance—was just to his right; it was wreathed in smoke, but the Civil Government's banners were still flying above it, and the cannon mounted there were a constant rolling *booom* of thunder. Ahead of him a thin line of Civil Government troopers—the three companies of the 5th he'd left as the main reserve— were holding against a growing tide of wogs pouring down from their foothold on the wall. Just barely holding, and not for long; the Colonials had lost all unit cohesion coming over the wall, but they were forming up again like crystals accreting in a saturated solution, and more every minute.

The 5th's volleys rang out, crisp and unhurried, but as he watched, they were losing men like a sugar lump under a stream of hot tea.

Teodore Welf drew rein beside him as the 1/591st fanned out into line. "Dismount?" he asked.

Raj shook his head. "Not enough time. We've got to hit them before they get organized."

These MilGov knights liked cold steel, and this was the situation for it. The whole scene in front came in glimpses, flashing through gaps in the drifting clouds of sulfurous smoke. More every second, as cannon and rifle fire pumped it out. Bullets went by with an ugly *crack* sound. Five men down the line a trooper gave a grunt and toppled slowly out of the saddle.

A captain of the 5th dashed up, breathless. "Sir?"

"Get them out of the way, Fittorio, then re-form on my left and give me fire support. Welf, get those splatguns out to the right now we've got room for them. *Move!*"

The bugles sounded. The Descotters ahead gave one last volley and turned, moving back at the double. The ragged line of Colonials beyond them gave their yelping cheer and charged in turn, unaware of what awaited behind. Unaware until the bugle sang, and the dogs of the Brigaderos howled in unison. The screams of their riders were only slightly more human. There was just space enough to build up momentum, but plenty of room to deploy in the drill manual's double line. The cavalry came looming up out of the smoke, big men on big dogs, their swords bright. They crashed into the dismounted Colonials like a baulk of timber swinging at high speed; men went down, slashed and stabbed and bowled over by sheer momentum.

Now we see how well their training has sunk in, Raj thought. Aloud: *"Halto!* Dismount, fix bayonets, forward with fire and movement, independent fire!"

One or two of the troopers vanished into the throng ahead, eyes fixed and froth dripping from their mouths. The rest halted and stepped off their crouching dogs, sheathing swords and drawing their firearms—although some might not have, if the dogs hadn't stopped automatically. *Click,* and the long bayonets snapped onto the Armory rifles. The men walked forward in a steady line, not quite straight—more like a very shallow C—

taking their dressing from the battalion standard and Raj's beside it. The front of their formation showed level for an instant, then vomited smoke. The sheet of fire smashed into the Colonials clustered at the base of the stairway.

The detachment of the 5th moved into place on the left flank, swinging in like a hinged door. The splatguns wheeled by at a trot and unlimbered, pushing into place to cover the gap between the end of the line on his right and the bare ground around the gate, swept by fire from the bastion towers.

Raj took a step forward. "Charge!" he shouted.

The troopers leveled their bayonets and ran in pounding unison; he ran along with them. The Colonials wavered, and then fled. *The bayonet's a terror weapon,* Raj knew. It didn't really *kill* all that many people, not in this age of breech-loaders, but there were times when it could make men *run.* Or try to run; the stairway that slanted down along the wall was too jammed with men for the ones on the ground to make much headway. Figures in crimson djellabas began to fall from the stairs in ones and twos, caught and squeezed out when the pressure from above and below forced the thick torrent of men to buckle sideways.

"*Halto!* Volley fire!"

The order relayed down the chain of officers. One rank knelt, the other firing over their heads. The rifles came up, aiming upward into the press. BAM. BAM. BAM. Rippling down the line, rounds whanging and keening off the stone, punching through three and four men at a time.

"Platoon column," Raj roared. "Welf, feed them up after us—you men, follow me!"

"To hell with *that*," the young MilGov noble said, and relayed the command. A column of forty troopers formed, with the banners only a few ranks from the front.

"Hadelande!"
"Upyarz!"

Many of the first Colonials went down with the bayonets in their backs. The troopers to the rear of the column fired over their comrades' heads, up the broad stairway. From the foot of it, six hundred men did likewise, and the splatguns with their muzzles raised to maximum elevation. Trapped, the Colonials on the stair turned to fight.

Raj found himself shoulder to shoulder with Teodore Welf; bayonets bristled on either side of them, and the banners waved behind. *Up a step.* Raj caught a scimitar on the guard of his saber, shot under it into his opponent's body. It tumbled down underfoot, and he nearly went over himself, with no room for his feet. An Armory rifle shot next to his ear, leaving it ringing. He threw himself back into swordsman's stance, right foot forward, and lunged again. Again. Welf was fighting with a long dagger in his right hand, using the heavy single-edged broadsword in his left like a ribbon saber; blond hair flew about his shoulders as he howled some Namerique war chant with every other breath. Fire swept the stairs ahead of them; Raj's hair crawled on the back of his neck at the thought of what would happen if somebody aimed a little low.

Or if these wogs had the time to reload. One did. Center's green aiming-grid slapped down across Raj's vision, outlining the figure in strobing light. He moved the red dot onto the center of mass and pulled the trigger, and the man spun away with the carbine flying out of his hands. Another target designated; he turned slightly, the pistol outstretched, squeezed the trigger. It was a hand bomb beginning its arc downward towards him, an impossible target . . . impossible without Center. Left-handed, at that. The iron sphere exploded less than a meter from the thrower when the bullet struck it.

A lot of men had seen that, seen his arm like a pointer

and the result. It was close enough to a miracle as no matter, to anyone with practical experience of firearms. Welf shouted:

"Spirit with us! Spirit of Man for Messer Raj!"

The Brigaderos behind him took it up; and some of the stubborn fight went out of the Colonials ahead. More and more were running back up, trying for the grappling lines and ladders over the walls. Raj chanced a look over his shoulder; more banners in the open ground beneath the wall: the 18th Komar, the 7th Descott. The stone was slippery underfoot, slippery with red rivulets running down from above. Fire from the ground was raking the firing platform above, deliberately built with little rear cover.

Not often you actually see that, see ground running with blood. The last time had been in Port Murchison, when Conner Auburn's fleet had sailed into his ambush.

Suddenly he was staggering onto level ground, the fighting platform on the wall; fire from below ceased, and a huge cheer went up as the bannermen waved their flags back and forth. Bodies heaped the pavement. Men poured out of the bastion towers before and behind him, shooting and wielding bayonet and rifle butt, shotguns and clubbed ramrods for the gunners. Ladders toppled as men thrust with poles or the points of their bayonets, through the firing slits and from the roof above.

Silence fell—comparative silence: only the cannonade and the screams of the wounded that littered the platform and stairs and the ground on both sides of the wall. He stepped up to a gunslit and looked out. The Colonial artillery was firing again; shells whined by overhead and crashed into the city behind.

"Get—" he turned and croaked; then stopped, realizing that he didn't recognize the man holding his banner. There were always volunteers for that job, and a continuous need for them. One of the runners was still there, though, reloading his pistol with a hand that dripped blood. "Verbal order to the battalion commanders. Pull their men back into cover. Get me Menyez. And then get that seen to."

"Ser."

The staircase was emptying; men rushed up it to take positions at the firing slits. Others helped or carried the wounded back below; the enemy went over the side to fall like bundles of discarded clothing to the hard-packed earth below. Except that bundles didn't scream on the way down, sometimes . . . *Well, no time for niceties.*

A voice spoke in Namerique: "Otto, this whore's son is alive—shoot!"

Raj looked up sharply and said in the same language: "Check there isn't one of ours alive under there first, man."

The big trooper braced himself and then began dragging bodies away by their legs; two of his comrades waited to either side, bayonetted rifles poised, and an ensign joined them with his revolver drawn. Half a dozen of the bodies were Colonial regulars, the remainder Civil Government infantry—24th Valencia, by the shoulder-flashes.

24th's been taking it on the chin, Raj thought. *They died hard, though, by the Spirit.*

Suddenly he had time to notice his own panting exhaustion, and the way his harness seemed to squeeze at his ribs. He felt for the canteen at his belt and found it empty, the bottom half ripped open in a flower of jagged tinned iron. Somebody made a joke as he tossed it aside, and he felt his testicles trying to draw up. He wasn't afraid of death, much—it was more that he had so much to *do*—but there were some wounds that were much more terrifying. A trooper handed him another canteen and he rinsed out his mouth, spat, and drank; it was water cut with vinegar, cutting through the dust and phlegm in his throat.

"*Tenk,*" he said—the Namerique word for thanks—and handed it back.

He started to wipe his mouth on the back of his sleeve, then stopped when he realized it was still sodden with blood. There was a little less on his left arm, so he used that instead. Now he could feel the sting of a half-dozen minor wounds, mostly superficial cuts, and a couple of bone-bruises. He broke open the revolver, ejected the spent brass and reloaded, then cleaned his saber a little, enough to resheath it. A trooper swore from the pile of dead.

"This one *is* alive, and he's one of ours!"

Raj moved over. His brows rose; that looked like a minor miracle. The infantryman was even more covered with blood than Raj, although—just like the stuff all over Raj—most of it didn't seem to be his own. A huge bruise covered one side of his face; a rifle lay beside him, the butt shattered and bayonet bent. The rings of a half-dozen handbombs were still on his fingers.

Raj whistled silently, and a number of the cavalry troopers nodded. He went on one knee and extended his hand; someone put another canteen in it, and he used that and his neckcloth to wipe some of the crusted blood from the man's face. He was young, no more than his early twenties, and rather light-skinned.

corporal minatili, Center supplied. **enlisted in old residence two years ago. literate, watch-stander.** Details from the service record ran through his mind with the icy certainty of the ancient computer's data-transfer.

Damn, if he's as good as he looks, make that Ensign *Minatili,* Raj thought.

The noncom's eyes snapped open, and he started violently, hand reaching for the knife in his boot. Raj caught it with irresistible strength.

"Easy there, fellow soldier," he said.

Minatili controlled a dry retch. Raj checked his pupils; no noticeable difference in the dilation, so the concussion couldn't be too bad. A day's weakness and a bad headache. Lucky: any blow strong enough to knock you out was a real risk to life and limb.

"Sor," he said. The situation seemed to be sinking in. "Anyone else, sor?" he said hoarsely, with a clipped Spanjol accent under the Army dialect of Sponglish.

Definitely Ensign Minatili, Raj decided. He looked up at the 1/591st junior officer with a question in his face.

"One other, sir—we're giving him first aid now. Looks fairly bad but he might make it."

"Sorry, son," Raj said.

"Spirit," Minatili whispered. "Did our best, sor, but t'ere was just too many."

"You did fine, soldier. You held them long enough for us to get here."

He slapped the young man gently on the shoulder and rose. Teams of stretcher bearers were coming up the stairs at a run, now that they were a little clearer. A messenger preceded them.

"Ser. From Colonel Staenbridge—wogs back on their sida t'wall. Same frum Major Belagez."

That was a relief, though not unexpected. This had been the most dangerous penetration, the one nearest to the main gate.

"Raj!"

He looked around quickly; it was Suzette, with Fatima in tow and a Renunciate nun-doctor, who was bending over the wounded men being loaded onto the stretchers. Raj looked down at himself . . . well, it *was* a little alarming. She finished helping tie off a bandage and picked up her kit, walking over to him with a determined expression.

"It's not mine," he said, slightly defensive.

"Well, what about *this*?" she asked.

Raj looked down in genuine surprise. There was a long slash down his right arm, starting just above the wrist and running to his elbow. He worked the fingers. Not deep enough to really hurt, and it was with the grain of the muscle anyway. The soft scab broke and fresh blood oozed out along the path the scimitar had traced. *Must have been a good one,* he thought absently. They had some really fine swordsmiths in Al Kebir and Gedorosia, who made blades you could cut through a floating scarf of *torofib*-silk with; ones that would keep the edge when they hacked through bone.

"Take that jacket off right now."

Suzette's voice was determined. Raj obeyed automatically, and caught some of the soldiers concealing grins. *All part of the legend,* he thought resignedly. Even Horace had his place in it, and they all had to follow their roles willy-nilly. He swore mildly as she swabbed out the cut with iodine and washed down the arm before bringing out a roll of bandages.

"Is all that necessary?" he said.

"It *should* have some stitches," she said tartly. "Try not to use it too hard."

"I'll try," he promised. Then he smiled. "I couldn't let you be the only one to collect a scar from this campaign, now could I? Think of my reputation."

She gave an unwilling snort of laughter. "Your reputation will suffer even more if you get killed doing a lieutenant's work. Let the younger men have a chance."

"When you stay home and do embroidery, my dear, it's a deal."

He levered himself erect from his seat on a ledge and looked up. *0900,* he thought. Less than two hours past dawn.

Looking down from the fighting platform, he saw that the cleared ring inside the walls was mostly empty. Except for the enemy dead, of course. *Burial parties*. He'd look in on the wounded . . . *Get those fires under control*. The Colonial shelling had started more; luckily, Sandoral was mostly a city of adobe, brick, and stone with tiled roofs supported by arches—timber had always been expensive here, and he'd ripped out most of it for the bridge.

"Back to work," he said, and walked toward the staircase. Flies rose in a buzzing cloud from the stone, amid the faint sweetish smell of blood beginning to rot in the hot morning sun. A severed hand lay almost in his path; he started to kick it aside, then shook his head and walked down the stairs.

The flags crackled in the wind as his bannermen followed.

CHAPTER TWELVE

Suzette was pale. Fatima looked up in alarm; neither of them was a stranger to field-hospitals after all these years, so it couldn't be that. With a shudder, the Arab girl remembered her first time here, the first battle, four years ago. *Then* there had been huge wooden tubs set up at the feet of the operating tables, to hold the amputated limbs. And they had been full, all that endless day. Barton had lost his hand that day; she'd held his shoulders down while the surgeon worked.

This was mild, by comparison. Only a few dozen shattered limbs to come off, with plenty of time to dose the worst cases with opium. A few hundred others, and more than half would live. But Suzette *did* look ill as she walked among the cots set up in the main chamber of Sandoral's cathedron. The air smelled of old incense and wax, under the stink of disinfectant and blood.

She was still Messa Whitehall. She finished the conversation, turned on her heel, and walked without running to the door. Fatima followed, grabbing up a towel. Retching sounds came from the cubicle; it was a priest's vesting room, in normal times. Suzette knelt and vomited into a bucket. Fatima hurried up beside her and handed her the towel, then went back for water.

"I don't understand it," Suzette said, wiping her face and slumping back in the chair.

Fatima put a hand on her forehead. "You're not running a fever, Messa."

"No, I'm not. And I feel fine, most of the time; just these last couple of mornings I—" She stopped. "What *date* is it?"

"Second of *Huillio*. Why do you want to . . . oh!"

Suzette's eyes went round. She turned her head slowly and met Fatima's gaze. The younger woman's mouth dropped open; she squeaked before managing to get out a coherent word:

"I thought . . . I thought you couldn't, that is—" She stopped in embarrassment.

"No, there wasn't enough time," Suzette said dazedly. Then her face firmed. "This is *not* to go beyond these walls, understand?"

"Of course, Messa," Fatima said soothingly. "But wouldn't Messer Raj want to know?"

"Not while he's got so much to worry about," Suzette said.

The flat rooftop terrace of Sandoral's District Offices made an excellent observation post, being close to the river and higher than the tops of the maidan wall; it was also far enough in from the defenses that Colonial shells were unlikely to land in the vicinity. The noon sun pounded down, turning the blue tile of the floor pale, drawing knife edges of shadow around the topiaries and pergolas. City administrators had held their receptions here, amid the potted bougainvillea and sambuca jasmine that had already begun to wilt without care. The iron heel plates of the officers' boots sounded on the floors, harsh and metallic. A heliograph station occupied one corner, and a map table and working desk had been set up by the railing nearest the river.

"Well, he's not wasting any time," Raj said.

Through the tripod-mounted heavy binoculars the east bank showed plainly. Tewfik's seal-of-Solomon banner waved from the highest ground; around it several thousand men worked with pick and shovel.

Grammek Dinnalsyn was using a telescope, also mounted; he made a few precise adjustments to the screws and sketched on a pad.

"That's not intended for his whole force," he said. "About three, four hundred men, perhaps."

Raj nodded agreement and took another bite of his sandwich. *Which reminds me . . .*

"Jorg," he said. "You've had your men on half-rations while we were away?"

"*Si.* Mostly hardtack and jerky, some fish and dried fruit."

"The whole command is back on full rations as of now," he said. "Bait the dogs properly, too. Muzzaf, get me a complete inventory of supplies. And fuel."

"*Si,*" the little Komarite said. "*Seyhor,* I can tell you immediately—we have less than a week's supply at that rate of expenditure."

"Excellent," Raj said with a smile. The others looked at him oddly. "I presume Ali knows?"

"The outlines," Menyez said. "We've had a few deserters, mostly from the garrison units. Presumably they've 'taken the turban' and told him what they know."

Raj nodded thoughtfully. "Any the other way?"

"Three—two from their transport corps, claim to be Star Church believers conscripted for supplies. The other's a Zanj."

The Colony had conquered some of the outlying city-states there, but was fiercely resented. The Zanj were of different race than most of the Colonials, and followed a branch of Islam the conquerors thought heretical.

"They're probably spies, of course," Menyez concluded. "I've kept them in close confinement."

"I'll talk to them; I can usually get the truth out of a man," Raj said. He was conscious of sidelong glances;

another part of the myth, that it was impossible to lie to Messer Raj. *It is when Center's looking through my eyes*, he thought. "In any case, it doesn't matter what Ali knows. Or even what Tewfik knows."

Barton Foley pointed. "They're bringing men across."

Everyone raised their glasses. An overloaded fishing skiff labored across the current, on a trajectory that would land it just south of Sandoral's walls on the western bank. Heads and V-marks of ripples showed where dogs on lead-halters swam in the boat's wake. On the riverbank it had left, men were building an earth ramp down to the water's edge and putting together a raft from bits and pieces, date-palm logs and thin boards that looked as if they'd come from some sheep fence.

"It'll take him a while to get his men back to Ali," Gerrin Staenbridge said, examining his nails. The way the Civil Government forces had scavenged up every small boat and all available materials was handicapping their enemies badly. "You have something in mind, don't you, *mi heneral*?"

Raj grinned at him. "Possibly. Can you think what?"

Staenbridge shook his head. Raj nodded amiably.

"And that's an excellent thing too," he said. "Because you're an extremely perceptive officer, and you have *all* the information. If you can't figure it out, probably Tewfik can't either. Gentlemen, I want you to spend the rest of today and tomorrow reorganizing. Don't let your men settle in too tight—I want full readiness to move at a moment's notice. Those units that've been hit hard, do the necessary shifting around immediately. Weapons maintenance, ammunition issues, the lot—again, immediately, please. Understood?"

Nods. "Grammeck, this afternoon I want to go over some matters with you; bring the complete plans for the pontoon bridge, please. If there aren't any questions, Messers?"

There was obviously one burning one, but nobody was going to ask it. Jorg Menyez remained when the others had left the flat rooftop.

"Colonel?" Raj asked. It wasn't like Jorg to talk for reassurance sake. He was obviously a little embarrassed.

"*Heneralissimo*," he said. "Ah . . . I thought you'd want to know about Osterville."

"Osterville?" Raj asked. It was an effort to remember the man; he hadn't thought of him since Ain el-Hilwa. *And good riddance.* "It's enough that he isn't here, making trouble."

"No, he won't be doing that," Menyez said. "It was unpleasant, but as you said, it was necessary."

Raj looked at him. Menyez flushed. "All right, *mi heneral*. I destroyed the letter and your seal, and he went into the Drangosh with a sixty-kilo roundshot tied to his ankles . . . but I still don't like it."

Raj nodded. "Of course, Jorg." *Only Suzette has my seal.* "I understand."

He shivered slightly, despite the heat of the day.

A dot of red light arched over the wall, trailing fire through the darkness. *Thud.* It exploded among the vacant houses—hopefully vacant houses—and a column of fire rose into the night. Another spark. *Thud.*

"That makes six the past hour," Raj murmured to himself.

in the past fifty-five minutes thirty seconds, Center added. **harassing fire.**

"Ali's obviously decided to starve us out," Raj agreed.

An image drifted across his eyes: his own emaciated body, still living, naked and covered with weals and burns. Pairs of dogs were hitched to chains attached to each ankle and wrist. The drivers urged the dogs forward slowly, gradually taking up the slack. Ali ibn'Jamal sat watching, pounding his fist on the arm of his portable throne and laughing with pleasure, licking his full lips. Tewfik stood to one side, arms crossed and a look of faint disgust on his face, echoed by most of the noblemen and officers around him. Behind him a gallows stood skeletal against the sky, with the bodies of the Companions dangling from it—by meathooks through their ribs. Several of them were still writhing . . .

Raj made a grimace of distaste. "Even by the standards of Mihwel the Terrible, Ali is a prime case."

a subjective judgment, but accurate. child-rearing practices among the colonial royal family are conducive to severely dysfunctional personalities.

A step sounded on the tiles behind him. There had been no challenge and response from the sentries on the stair below, so it could be only one person.

Suzette leaned on the railing beside him, looking out over the city and the glistening water. "Full circle, my love," she said. "Sandoral, and a battle to come."

"And men dying unexpectedly," he said.

She turned her face towards him, drawn and pale beneath the moons. "Osterville couldn't lead and wouldn't follow and wouldn't get out of the way and let you work, either. Can you imagine the sort of havoc he'd have created back here, with everything depending on Jorg keeping things running smoothly? We'd have ended up *swimming* across, while Osterville tried to make everyone do things his way."

"Jorg—"

"Jorg is good man and a good officer, but he doesn't have your talent for facing men down—especially not men higher on the chain of command. You know that." A little anger crept into her voice: "How many better men have been killed on this campaign so far?"

Raj smiled ruefully and shook his head. "You always could out-argue me," he said. A shrug. "I just don't like having a fellow officer killed like that. It's the sort of thing Tzetzas does."

Suzette sighed. "I don't like it either," she said quietly. "But it had to be done."

Raj nodded. They watched another Colonial shell come over the walls.

"It's cold," Suzette said in a small voice.

Raj extended his arm and the long military cloak he wore. Suzette came under it and laid her cheek against his chest.

"We can't afford any mistakes this time, can we?" she said after a moment.

"No," Raj replied. He looked up at the moons. They'd be rising late, tomorrow evening. *Victory or death,* he thought. *All men die, but this has to be done.* "Let's turn in."

"Precisely this bearing," Raj said.

He drew a line in the dust with the stick. Behind him the artillerymen staked down their frame—two sets of rigid beams at right angles, with a slanted piece across the arms. They aligned it with the mark in the dust; once it was firmly in place, they pushed the gun up the slanted fronting of the frame and tied off the wheels at a chalk mark on the wood.

"Range is exactly 3,525 meters," Raj said. "Load contact, two-second delay."

"Sir," the gunner said, giving him a glance.

How could you know? Raj read in his face. And a trace of awe; men knew he didn't make empty boasts.

Raj walked on to the next gun's position as the iron clang of the breechblock sounded behind him. All fifty-eight surviving field guns were lined up just inside the north wall of Sandoral, all up on the frames; all aligned along the precise vector he'd drawn in the dirt for them. Every single one, as far as Center could judge, was now aiming at the exact midpoint of earth above Ali's command bunker, behind the Colonial outworks—where he invariably retired after the sunset prayer. All the fortress guns in the fixed positions on the wall were aligned as well, those of them that would bear on the target.

Irregularities—wear on the rifling of guns, slight differentials in shell loading and drag, whatever—would spread the projectiles. It ought to be an unpleasant surprise, nonetheless.

Dinnalsyn looked back at the long row of guns. "Think we'll get him, *mi heneral*?"

"No," Raj said. "That's a very secure bunker. The last thing I want to do is put Tewfik in full command. But it'll certainly get his attention, and Ali's got a short temper. If I know my man, he'll do something stupid."

The limbers stood in a row five meters behind the guns, the dog teams in traces and lying down.

"Are the rafts ready?" Raj said.

"Ready and waiting, sir," Dinnalsyn said. "The planking and decking from the pontoon bridge was exactly as much as we needed . . . I suppose that's no coincidence?"

"You might say that," Raj replied. He clapped him on the shoulder. "Stay ready for it."

The last of the cavalry battalions on special duty were sitting by the wall, finishing their evening meal: beans and pigmeat and onions, dished out from kettles over camp fires and scooped up with tortillas. It was the 5th Descott. They were professionals enough to concentrate on eating, but he could feel the tension crackling off them. He walked over and made a beckoning gesture. They crowded around him and crouched or sat at his hand signal; only about three hundred fifty left—and the battalion had been at double strength when he took it west to fight the Brigade.

"All right, dog-brothers," he said quietly. That forced them to listen carefully and lean closer; it also made each man feel as if he was talking to that one alone, as an individual. "You've guessed that something's up. Two hours after sundown—"

The sun was just touching the western horizon.

"—the guns are going to cut loose with a five-round stonk. The second the last gun fires—but not before—you give the wogs five rounds rapid. Then you come back down from the wall, ride your dogs to the docks, get on the rafts and off we go."

He paused a moment. "You're all fighting men and all Descotters," he went on. "My father and grandfather and great-grandfather fought the wogs, and so did yours."

Nods; Descotter *rancheros* held their land on military tenure, paying their tax in men rather than money. Fathers and sons and brothers followed each other into the same battalions time out of mind; comrades were neighbors at home, officers the squire's sons.

"There's a lot of Descotter blood and bone buried around here. Now we have a chance to end it." That caused a rustle, men coming forward in their crouch and leaning on their rifles. "If we win this one, we break them—not just push them back, but wreck them for all time. If we lose . . ." He grinned. "Well, we haven't done much losing while we've been together, you and I, have we?"

A low snarl of agreement. "Everything depends on the wogs thinking we're still here, at least for a while. You'll move back to the docks quickly and you'll do it quietly, and with no foul-ups. Understood?"

Gerrin Staenbridge stepped forward. "You can count on us, *mi heneral*," he said solemnly. Another growl from the ranks.

"Keep it quiet, keep it quiet," Ensign Minatili said.

There were only fifteen men left in his platoon, now—several of them lightly wounded—so it wasn't very

different from running his squad. The star on the front
of his helmet still felt like a weight of lead to his spirit,
though. They formed up outside their bivouac, in the
forecourt of what had been a nobleman's house. Minatili
walked down his platoon, giving everything a final check.
The men's haversacks were full, three days' rations—
smoked pork and hardtack, dried apricots and figs—
and extra ammunition in their blanket rolls.

"Company G, fall in."

The men found their places by instinct, in column of
twos back from the company pennant. It was *dark* outside:
the city gaslights were out, of course—nobody left to
shovel coal and tend the tank-farms—and all torches
and fires had been forbidden.

Just as well, he thought. It was frightening how few
of them were left; the main Colonial attack had come
right over their sector of the wall yesterday. Forty men
in the company, barely a full platoon.

The battalion colors came by, and Major Felasquez
carrying a shuttered bull's-eye light. His one eye gleamed
a little as he turned, stopped for a brief murmur with
Captain Pinya and stepped closer to the men.

"All right, lads," he said, a little louder.

Don't expect the wogs could hear even if we shouted,
Minatili thought. *On the other hand, it gets everyone*
thinking *quiet.*

"We've had enough from the towel-heads; now we're
going to give it back, the way the monkey gave it to the
miller's wife, by surprise and from the rear. Mind your
orders, do it right, and with the Spirit's help and Messer
Raj's plan, we'll whip them." He stepped back. "24th
Valencia Foot—*Waymanos!*"

The column moved forward jerkily; it was strange to
the point of being dizzying not to step off to the beat of
the drum, and the troops had been told not to march
in step. The uniform clash of hobnails on stone pavement

was like nothing else on earth, and it carried. Instead they walked, with an occasional quiet curse as somebody stepped on the heels of the man ahead. Guides stood at intersections, their lanterns the only light in the deserted city. Minatili kept his hand on the hilt of his new sword and ignored the eerie quietness.

Through the river gate the darkness lifted a little; a one-quarter Miniluna and the stars reflected off the rippled surface of the water. Gravel crunched, then planks boomed a little under their boots. The column halted.

"24th Valencia?" someone asked ahead, a dim figure against the water. "*This* way."

They waited; the men ahead melted away company by company. "Company G, this way."

The men scrambled through the knee-high water and into the barge; it was one of the boxlike constructs he'd helped to cobble together out of wood salvaged from wrecked houses. A long steering-oar marked the notional stern, and there were men standing to the sweeps on either side, six to a flank. They had only a single shuttered lantern to work with, but despite the darkness and the crowding only an occasional thump and oath marked someone tripping as they clambered down from the planking to the hold of the crude vessel.

"You'll be pulling the outermost raft," Captain Pinya said.

"That one, sir?" Minatili said, pointing.

"That's right, Ensign."

Ensign. Spirit. My folks will never believe it.

He shook himself back to the present. There were so many more ways to fuck *up* at a higher rank. Right now, that could get *everyone* killed.

He saluted and climbed down himself, a little awkward with no rifle on his shoulder and a sword and pistol at his belt. He turned around as soon as he was at the bow, making sure everyone's equipment was blacked as ordered. *Right. Nothing showing but eyeballs.*

"Cast off," he said quietly.

The ropes were undone and the barge began to drift. "That way," he said, pointing.

The rowers were from the Sandoral District garrison; they'd all had some experience moving these damned things around. They dug their clumsy oars into the water and heaved, grunting. One step forward, lower the oar, haul it one step back. Minatili thumped the boards beside him softly to keep the beat, peering ahead to his target. It was almost invisible until they were on top of it, two sections of the pontoon bridge decking with some timbers in between.

"*Halto,*" he said.

Hands and poles on the raft fended them off and turned the barge around. Ropes were made fast to both sides of the stern, and then the barge released to drift slowly downstream. It halted with a slight jerk, held by the cables that anchored the row of rafts. Minatili looked back along them, back to the shore and the black silhouette of the city wall. The sun had been down at least an hour and a half. More and more of the pontoon barges and every other type of boat available on the Sandoral docks—the ones that hadn't had a chance to get upstream when the news of the invasion got here— put out into the darkening water, anchoring or sculling up to the rafts. The docks were a moving carpet of men, helmets and furled banners and the muzzles of slung rifles.

Not long now.

"Rest easy, boys," he said. "Rest a bit."

"Gently, gently," Suzette whispered.

The infantrymen assigned as stretcher bearers were well-meaning but clumsy. There were enough of them to manhandle the stretchers into the bottom of the barge and fit them into the crude racks the carpenters had made, turning them into improvised bunk beds. The wounded were dosed heavily with opium to dull the pain of movement, but now and then a man would moan in his delirium. The Renunciates and priest-doctors moved quickly among them, checking pulses.

"Spirit have mercy, this one's dead," a nun said.

"Leave him be," Suzette replied. *Damn.*

The final load came from the carriages and handcarts they'd pressed into service as ambulances.

She looked west, towards the ramparts.

"Drop it in, don't throw it!" Jorg Menyez hissed.

An officer relayed the order. Endless files of infantrymen passed sacks of hardtack and crates of dried meat and fruit from hand to hand, out from the wagons to the end of the pier. Once there, they knelt and let their burdens drop into the water. The current caught them, the hardtack floating for a few minutes before waterlogging dragged it down with a scatter of bubbles, the pierced casks and boxes sinking faster.

A good thing this is fresh water. There would be downdraggers in a feeding-frenzy if they tried this in a harbor. Doubtless the plesiosauroids out in the deeper water would be feeding full tonight, as it was.

"Colonel. Major Tormidero sends 'is compliments, and is 'e to load tha wine?"

"No," Menyez said, biting off the *damned fool* with an effort. "Tell him Ali's men may drown their sorrows as they wish, if they don't fear Allah's wrath."

But not a scrap of food will they find in Sandoral, he thought with hard glee. He sneezed into his handkerchief, not too badly; there weren't any dogs in the immediate neighborhood. It was pitch black. He looked anxiously over the river to the Colonial fortlet planted where the pontoon bridge had been. Evidently *they* hadn't seen anything unusual, either. *It's a siege. They don't expect anything to happen.*

"Spirit, but this is a madman's gamble," he whispered to himself, lips barely moving. The only chance at victory . . . but what a chance.

"And what a story to tell the grandchildren, if we pull it off!"

If they didn't . . .

Ali ibn'Jamal took another handful of rice and grilled lamb, belching politely. It was surprisingly good, considering what the cooks had to work with; the army was on preserved rations wagoned up from the bridgehead. His own cook had priority on what little the foragers were bringing in, of course. The bunker had been made quite homelike: silk tapestries and silk-and-gold thread Al Kebir carpets, embroidered cushions about low tables of chiseled brass, incense in crescent-shaped burners on tripods about the walls. The lamplight had been turned down to a civilized level, and zebec and zither played melodiously from behind a screen in one corner. Ali ate, and held out his hands for the slave to wash with rosewater and towel dry.

"Your appetite should be better, Tewfik my brother," he said, and belched again. "Think of how the *kaphar* pigs within Sandoral's walls would drool and slaver at the sight of such a feast!"

Tewfik turned from a low-voiced conversation with his officers. "Indeed, Settler of the House of Peace," he said. "They are very short of supplies. That is why I fear some new trick of this Shaitan's-seed Whitehall."

Ali scowled for a moment, then gestured expansively. "Whitehall is trapped," he said. "He cannot sortie—our men outnumber his and are strongly entrenched; our rear, even, is protected by great works, even though no relieving force of any numbers can approach. He cannot build his bridge of boats again, with your fort and its guns covering the opposite bank. What can he do but starve?"

"Commander of the Faithful, I do not *know* what he can do. And that is what—"

"My lord." One of the duty officers of the Settler's guard came up to Tewfik and bowed. "You commanded that we notify you: the infidel have launched a signal rocket from the walls. One blue starburst."

A gun boomed in the distance. They all ignored it; the Colonial artillery was lobbing a steady round every twenty minutes into Sandoral, to keep the infidels from sleeping easily.

Another boom, and another; and the explosion of a shell, far too close. Another junior officer dashed down the stairs into the bunker.

"From the walls!" he shouted. "Lords, *all* the *kaphar* guns are firing from—"

"Fwego!"

Grammeck Dinnalsyn swept his saber downward. POUMPH. The first of the field guns vomited a long tongue of red flame into the night, backlighting the cloud of smoke that swirled away from the muzzle. Like a ripple, the line of explosions swept down the row of guns, repeated fifty-eight times. The noise was deafening, shock-waves echoing back from the high flat surface of the city wall like pillows of hot air smacking into face and chest. Already the stairways were showing running men, the militia gunners; one per gun on the walls, each to pull the lanyard on a weapon pre-laid on its target.

The first field gun had already fired its second round by the time the last piece discharged at the other end of the line. The crews moved with smooth, metronomic precision. The guns couldn't recoil, up on the elevating frames—although he hated to see the trails overstressed like this; it was asking for trouble later. Each piece had a stack of five extra shells next to it, with preset fuses. Swing the lever and wrench the breech aside; the brass shell clanged out, with a puff of sulfur-reeking smoke. Loader shoved the next round in, breechman pushed the interrupted-screw block home and slapped the lever down, master gunner clipped his lanyard to the toggle, and *fire*.

Six rounds, and silence except for the ringing of abused ears. The master gunners of the two central pieces slashed the ties holding the wheels to the elevating frames with their swords, and the pieces ran down the sloped timbers. The crews snatched up the trails before the pieces could slow, running them back to the limbers and slapping the locking-rings down. The pins went home with an iron clank, men leaped into the saddle or swung onto the axletree seats, and the guns rumbled off down toward the docks at a round trot. An instant later the sound changed to a hard rattle as the metal rims of the wheels rose onto the cobblestones. The maneuver was repeated again and again, each gun out from the first two cutting loose and limbering up to follow.

Dinnalsyn neck-reined his dog around. The guns were vanishing into the night, and small-arms fire crackled from the ramparts above. Alone but for his aides and messengers, he saluted the walls.

"Here's to you, *heneralissimo*," he said. "I don't know how the hell you manage it, but it's never dull. *Waymanos!*"

He clapped heels to his dog.

Corporal M'Telgez was acutely conscious of Messer Raj standing quietly behind him as the artillery bellowed. It was blacker than a meter up a sauroid's butt here on the wall's fighting platform; and it smelled of old death, rotting blood and bits of bodies. He willed himself to ignore the smell, and the feeling of confinement—he was a dog-and-saddle man, not a mole or a town-dweller—and the far more nerve-wracking presence of the *heneralissimo*. Not that he was one to interfere with a man doing his work, far from it. It was just a little disconcerting to have Messer Raj and the Colonel and the Captain all pick *your* spot to pause when the balloon went up. There was a gap in the gabions he'd picked earlier for his first aiming point. Invisible in the darkness now, but pretty soon—

"*Fwego!*"

The stubby mortars on the towers chugged. Starshells burst over the wog entrenchments, throwing a flickering blue-white magnesium light. He exhaled and squeezed the trigger. *Crack*. His rifle punched his shoulder. He worked the lever and reached for one of the rounds in the wooden holder beside his hand. *Crack*. A Colonial gun fired from the forward trenches. He adjusted his sights and aimed for it, with any luck a round might ricochet off the barrel and into one of the crew. *Crack*. *Crack*. *Crack*.

"Cease fire! Rearward, on the double!" he called out.

His squad was closest to the staircase. They double-timed down it, through the hot dark and the faint reflected light of the starshells, while the field guns blazed away to their right. Eyes and teeth glimmered from the dogs crouching in neat rows in the open space within the walls; they were too well trained to move when they'd been told to stay, but the noise made them eager and uneasy. They rose with a surge as their riders straddled them. M'Telgez's feet found the stirrups, and he slid his rifle into the scabbard, taking the reins in tightly with his left hand. More and more men poured down the stairways by the gates, until the whole battalion was mounted.

No trumpet calls, but the men fell in—every dog knew its place by smell, if nothing else. M'Telgez saw the shadowy length of the battalion standard go by, and an arm flash up. He tapped his heel to Pochita's flank, and the whole column broke into a fast walk that turned into a slow loping trot. They moved south of the last of the guns, under the arc of the last shells, then turned eastward toward the docks. The sky ripped above them. M'Telgez felt his shoulders hunch; his hindbrain knew what that meant, only too well.

CRUMP. A heavy shell sledged into the empty space behind him. Seconds later dirt pattered down out of the air. At least they weren't firing airburst; it must be too difficult with no observation of the fall of shot. *CRUMP. CRUMP. CRUMP.* The last one fell on a gun that was moving parallel to the column of the 5th Descott, and the limber went up too in a huge ball of red-orange flame. Men screamed and dogs wailed ahead of him. An officer rode out; his pistol cracked as the dogs were put down, and the men swung up behind comrades, no time for first aid now. *CRUMP. CRUMP. CRUMP.* More shells went by overhead and blasted into the upper stories of empty houses. Adobe brick and fragments of roof tiles and burning planks cataracted into the streets. He kept his head down and followed the man ahead of him, hoping that the officers knew where they were going. Shells were coming overhead in a continuous stream, but a whole city was a big target.

Mother, he thought. This was worse than a battle; then you could *do* something.

Horace knew he was being ridden toward another boat ride. He turned nose-to-tail and circled. Raj cursed, but he didn't bother yanking on the reins; you could pull until the levers gouged a hole right through his cheeks, and Horace wouldn't pay much attention. Instead he let the knotted reins fall on the pommel and leaned forward, thumping the hound's neck with the flat of his hand.

"Come *on*, you son of a bitch," he said firmly. "We've got places to go and things to do. Stop this nonsense."

Horace lowered his ears and head and turned, breaking into a shambling trot. Raj's banner snapped in the night air; the Colonial shells went by overhead with their mechanical wails, a continuous diminuendo punctuated by the crash of the bursting charges. He pressed with his heels as a barricade of brick and burning rubble closed the way. Horace took it in a single long leap, then checked a pace to let the others come through. Heat slapped at him as they passed over the flame; a dog yelped suddenly as it stepped on a hot ember.

Raj grinned into the darkness. *Well, we certainly got their attention,* he thought.

all colonial guns are firing at maximum speed, Center noted. **even with ample ammunition reserves, this will degrade performance and shorten the life of the barrels.**

Raj nodded. Wasteful. The hotter a gun got, the worse the wear on the lands of the rifling. After a while it had to be sent back to the foundry to have a new sleeve fitted into the barrel and rifled, and it was never quite as good after that. The third time it had to be scrapped.

"Want to do the honors, *mi heneral?*" Jorg Menyez said.

He waved to the lines of slowmatch that snaked away among the warehouses and boatyards of Sandoral's docks. The raw smell of kerosene and gunpowder was thick in the air.

"Dinnalsyn assures me that it will all go off at about the same time."

Raj looked around with grim satisfaction. When the warehouses and shipyards went up, it would also take all the remaining timber in Sandoral suitable for boats or rafts or bridging materials. Ali might get the city, but he was damned if there'd be anything immediately useful in it when he did. No food, no building materials.

"I wouldn't dream of denying you the pleasure, Jorg," Raj said.

Menyez ceremoniously puffed on his cigarillo and applied the end to the slowmatch. It lit with a sullen hiss and trail of blue smoke.

"And now we bid farewell to beauteous Sandoral: land of exotic giant cockroaches, intolerable sticky heat-rash, and picturesque, hairy wogs with razor-sharp gelding knives," the infantryman mock-quoted. East Residence had enough of a middle class to support a tourist trade, mostly steamboat excursions to the Bay Islands. Guidebooks were common, too. *"Hadios, mi heneral."*

It probably did the men good to see their commanders relaxed and confident. *It does me good. Jorg's usually a worrier. Morale's probably as high as it should be.* Possibly higher than it should be . . . *Now who's worrying?*

"Hadios, Jorg. See you downriver."

He turned Horace. Raft after raft was heading downstream, casting off behind its towing-barge. Sweeps tossed up small chuckling ripples of green water, a faint sheen under the crescent of Miniluna. As each loosed its ties to the anchor cables, another cluster of dogs and guns would trundle out across the linked rafts to the outermost. War-dogs whined as chain staples fastened their bridles to pins in the decking; the wheels of guns and limbers were lashed down, and another raft and barge combination was under way. Beyond the rafts boats speckled the water, sloops and ferries, and score after score of the pontoon barges.

Messengers trotted up, reported, left. *Damn. Amazing. Only one traffic jam.* And that caused by rubble blocking a street and the battalion assigned to it swerving into another's route. Paws and feet and wheels filled the night with a low rumble of purposeful noise, none of it as loud as the whistle and crash of two hundred Colonial guns bombarding the city. More starshells lightened the sky to the west, Colonial this time, put up so their artillery had better visibility.

"Shall I order a cease-fire?"

"No, Hussein," Tewfik replied, also in a whisper.

The central roof of the bunker had caved in, but the beams had not given way completely. They sagged to the floor, their jagged breaks splintered, like bone-white teeth. Dry dirt poured down still, pooling and spreading; soldiers dug bodies out of the pile, some wounded and some dead, and carried them up the stairs. Ripped down and stamped in a pile, the tapestries still smoldered from the burning kerosene that falling lamps had sprayed across them—sprayed across men, as well.

Although not, unfortunately, across my brother, Tewfik thought. It would be a disaster if Ali died just now. It might be salvation if he were struck down by an incapacitating injury; the longer, the better. *There is no God but God, and all things are accomplished according to the will of God.* But sometimes it was difficult to understand His tactics. He wrinkled his nose at the smell of burning carpets. More waste. The cost of them was enough to pay a brigade of cavalry for a year, and now they would be replaced. Transport would be commandeered to replace them, while the guns ate a month's reserve of ammunition.

"*Amir*, we will lose guns soon if we keep up this rate of fire," the officer warned. "The barrels are so hot we'll have cook-offs during reloading."

"Reduce the rate, but not so much that *he*" —he nodded to the other chamber of the bunker; Ali's sputtering curses could still be heard there, and occasionally a woman's scream— "will notice. Better to shoot the lands out of the barrels than have more executions."

The officer stroked his beard and leaned close. "*Amir*, it is time to consider if the House of Peace can stand, with this man at the head of it."

Tewfik stared into the other man's face for a moment; the brown eyes met his single one unflinching. *Good. I have no cowards on my staff.*

"He has no sons," he said quietly. "Nor do I."

"The Prophet Muhammed had no sons; but many rulers sprang from his daughters."

"And many wars sprang from the claims of his daughters' descendants and the orthodox caliphs, beginning with Kharballa," Tewfik pointed out. That had started a split that echoed down millennia, not even ending with the Last Jihad. "There are also too many nobles with enough of the Settler's blood to make a fair claim. Ali is no fool, he's killed the only ones with indisputable claims or great ability, or both. If we have civil war now, the *kaphar* and the Zanj and the northern savages will race each other to pick our bones. We must continue."

"For the present."

"For the present," Tewfik agreed. *Until Ali alive becomes more a menace to the House of Islam than Ali dead*, went unspoken between them. "Now go, and have the gunners reduce their rate of fire by one-third. On my authority."

I control the Host of Peace, but I cannot rule, he knew bitterly. Not in his own name. If only there were a male heir, a regency might be possible—but there was not. The mullahs would not issue the Friday prayer for one-eyed Tewfik; men would not obey, not without a soldier standing behind them. He would shatter what he most wished to preserve, if he tried that.

"Insh'allah."

The acrid gloom of the bunker was stifling. Left hand on the hilt of his yataghan, he strode up the stairs, past the protective curves and the intermediate guardroom. The blue-white sputtering light of starshells made him slit his eyes at the dark motionless bulk of Sandoral's low-slung walls. They mocked him from behind the moat, tantalized him. Men and dogs labored to bring the ammunition forward to the siege guns from the bombproofs set behind the main line, along pathways sunk into the ground with protective berms on either side. The gunners toiled, stripped to the waist, their faces and torsos black with powder smoke. Many had balls of cotton wool stuffed in their ears, but they courted deafness as well as death with every shot. It did not stop the smooth choreographed sequence of laying, swabbing, loading, ramming, firing.

A heavy shell bit a section out of the firing parapet in a clap of orange flame and rumble of sound. Water spurted up where the stone fell into the moat, leaving a ragged gap in the concrete core. No fire replied from the city.

"Was that your plan, Whitehall, to weaken our artillery? Did you know how my brother would respond to your taunt?"

The stonk on the command bunker had been wickedly well-placed. Whitehall was well served, good officers, brave and well-trained troops, well equipped. *Does he know us well enough to predict that my brother would waste ammunition and guns like this?* He nodded. Certainly.

"Yet it cannot affect the outcome of the war," he mused.

Could it be cover for another raid? Unlikely. With a pontoon bridge for rapid withdrawal and a secure fortified base, Whitehall had still been unable to do more than divert him temporarily. Now the land across the river was unfit to support moving troops. What could the infidel accomplish with the smaller number of men they could smuggle across the river now?

That was the problem. He did not know.

"Lord *Amir*. The Settler requires your presence."

Tewfik ground his teeth. *He has beaten enough women to feel brave again,* he thought. *Now he must play at commander. And waste my time!*

With an enemy like Whitehall, time was one thing you never had a surplus of. From all reports, Barholm Clerett was almost as difficult a master to serve as Ali ibn'Jamal—but at least he was far away.

The little galley Raj was using as his HQ had been some rich merchant's toy before war came to Sandoral, or perhaps belonged to a landowner with estates on the riverbank who wanted to be able to commute to his townhouse in the district capital. For a moment Raj wondered where he was, that little provincial oligarch. On the road west, grumbling in his carriage with a nagging wife and the nurse fussing with the children and a train of baggage carts behind? Perhaps already in East Residence, imposing on some distant relative or dickering with a lodging-keeper not at all impressed by anything from beyond the walls of *the* city. Or caught on his country property by Colonial raiders, and now tumbled bones in a ditch.

We must be making ten klicks per hour, he thought.

a range of 9.7 to 10.1, averaging 9.9 overall, Center said.

Tonight and tomorrow to reach their destination, traveling with the current. The men in the barges and boats were sculling, but more to keep station and direction than for propulsion. There were enough in each vessel to change off at frequent intervals, too.

"Over to Major Bellamy," Raj said, pointing.

The galley came about sharply, bringing a protesting

whine from Horace and Harbie on the foredeck. The
crew were all ex-boatmen and used to the shattering
labor at the oars; one side dug theirs in hard, the other
feathered, and the man at the tiller pushed it over. The
slender boat turned in almost its own length and stroked
eastward. Beside a raft crowded with troops and dogs
it halted; Raj leaned over the side, one hand on the rail.

"There's your destination, Major," he said, pointing
southward, downstream. "Remember the timing's
crucial."

Bellamy waved back wordlessly, his bowl-cut blond
hair bright in the darkness. His rowers bent to their work,
and several of the other barges followed. Raj's galley
curved back toward the main body of the straggling
armada, like a sheepdog with its flock.

More like a pack of carnosauroids, Raj thought,
watching the dull glint of moonlight on the barrels of
the field pieces on a raft.

Suzette came up beside him, a cigarette glowing in
its holder of carved sauroid ivory. "The waiting's the
hardest part," she said.

"No, just the longest," Raj said. "Having to send others
out, that's hardest."

She put an arm around his waist and leaned her head
on his shoulder.

CHAPTER THIRTEEN

"Stake the dogs," Ludwig Bellamy said.

His second-in-command blinked at him. "It's more than a kilometer to the objective," he said in surprise.

"*Ni, migo,*" Bellamy said in Namerique. "Walking that far won't kill us."

He shook his head as the man walked away to spread the order by whisper. Messer Raj had taught his Squadrone followers that fighting on foot was no disgrace, but they'd still rather ride ten kilometers than walk one.

He squinted at his map; an aide lit a match and held it over the paper. Messer Raj had penciled in the route with his own hands. *Yes. That's the gully.* There was a roadway of sorts along the river's edge, but it was entirely too visible from the other side, back around Sandoral. His scouts gathered around, holding the reins of their dogs.

"Lead the way," he said, tracing out the branchings of wash and ravine. "It's only a klick; but keep an eye out for wog pickets."

He looked up at the bulk of the unit; nearly everyone was ashore from the beached barges and rafts, although many were soaked to the waist. Water squelched in his own high boots. The last few came in sight, holding their rifles and bandoliers over their heads as they waded to the muddy riverbank.

"Fall them in," he said quietly.

The 1st Mounted Cruisers formed up in ranks four

deep, and the rabble of militia gunners behind them. They'd have no part in the immediate action, but they were important if everything worked right.

"*Migos*, Messer Raj trusts us to do this job right without holding our hands. Let's show him he's right. Keep it quiet and move quickly."

"Right face. At the double, forward *march*."

They swung off into the night, rifles at the trail. Bellamy trotted up along the line to the head, where the battalion banner was. His aide was leading his dog, back at the rear; the men would march with a better will if they saw the commander on foot too. Some of them grinned and shook their rifles in the air as he passed.

They're pumped, Bellamy decided. This had all the earmarks of one of Messer Raj's sauroid-out-of-the-helmet tricks. They trusted their leader's luck. And they hated being cooped up inside walls, no matter how strong.

He looked ahead. *You have to earn your luck.* It was much darker here, where most of the sky was blocked out by the clay walls of the badlands on either side. They panted up steep slopes, scrambled down others, slogged through sand and deep dust that sucked at their boots, splashed through a few wet spots where water from the spring floods still lay. Men panted, sweated, cursed in low voices. The ground rose toward the hills where the road from the east met the river, where Tewfik had planted his fortlet.

A scout came cantering back and pulled his dog up on its haunches. "As you thought, Lord," he said, leaning down. He was one of the old-fashioned ones, with his hair pulled up in a knot at the side of his head. "There is only a shallow ditch and berm on the landward side— my dog could jump it. And all the cannon point to the water."

Bellamy grunted with relief. Messer Raj had said that was the logical thing for Tewfik to do, but you couldn't count on an opponent having good sense.

He paced back along the column, personally giving the command to halt. The battalion came to a stop with a few lurches that ran one group of men onto another's heels, but nothing major. The company commanders gathered around him.

"Come," he said, leading them westward up a final line of ridge. Beyond was rolling open ground, sparsely bushed with thorny native scrub and some cacti. "There."

In the open, the moonlight was enough to make the Colonial works plain enough. He used his binoculars: not much of a ditch, and there were no obstacles—no timbers studded with old sword-blades, no thorn zariba. Doubtless those would have been added in time, but there had been no time. Across the water red specks crawled through the air and the endless flat thudding of the bombardment continued. There were enough fires in Sandoral now to cast a reddish glow across the great river, expanding and uniting into columns of flame without men to fight them.

"Spread your men out along this ridge, and order fixed bayonets," Bellamy said. "Every man may load his rifle, but no reloading once we're into the enemy camp."

Nods, enthusiastic from the *Squadrones*, less so from the Civil Government officers seconded to the battalion. Fighting at close quarters in the dark, friendly fire would be a greater threat than the enemy. Their repeaters gave them an advantage in a close-range firefight, anyway. Better to rely on impetus and cold steel.

"Nothing fancy," Bellamy said, repeating Messer Raj's words. "Just raise a shout and go in on my signal."

Across two hundred meters of open ground. But the Spirit was with them, and the initiative.

He lay on the ridgeline. "Uncase the colors," he said

to his bannermen; they pulled the leather tubes off the standards and gently shook the heavy silk free, taking care to keep both flags—the unit and the Civil Government blazon—below the ridgeline. To either side came rustling, crunching sounds as the men filed up company by company. Starlight glittered as they fixed their bayonets and then lay prone at the word of command. He could see one or two praying, among those closer; others were waiting, stolid or eager as their temperament took them.

And I don't think of glory, he realized. A few years ago that would have been his main concern in a situation like this; that men see him add honor to his name. *Now I'm just worried that nothing go wrong.* Messer Raj was right: civilization was contagious. It was more efficient than the old ways, but it took much of the color out of life. He swallowed water and vinegar from his canteen and loosened his sword in its scabbard, flipped open the cylinder of his revolver and checked the loads.

Marie will enjoy hearing about this. His Brigadero wife still thought war was glorious, and envied warriors. She'd probably have made a good soldier if she'd been born male—her cousin Teodore certainly did—provided she survived the seasoning. *I'd rather go through a battle than pregnancy, at that.* Strange to think of having children—legitimate children; byblows by peon girls didn't count. Stranger still to think of them growing up in East Residence; nobody had said he couldn't move back to the family estates in the Southern Territories, but he could take the hint.

He grinned. That would be terminally dull, anyway. At least Marie could sit out the war in a city with plenty of balls and theater and opera, or bullfights and baseball stadiums.

If we win this war, will there be wars for my sons to ride to? Possibly not; and was that a good thing, or the end of all honor?

Thud. Thud. Thud. There were explosions across the river, along the docks of Sandoral. Plumes of red fire rose into the night, spreading with startling suddenness. In less than thirty seconds the whole waterfront went up in a wall of flame, as the time-fused incendiaries caught among kerosene-soaked wood and spilled cooking oil. There was enough underlight to see the pillars of smoke, roiling and black and red-tinged by the fires.

He took a deep breath. *"Gittem!"* he roared, the old Squadron war shout. The trumpeters were playing *Charge*, over and over again, a raw brazen scream.

The flags went forward. The 1st Mounted Cruisers rose to their feet and threw themselves forward at a pounding run, their bayonets leveled. Ludwig Bellamy ran at their head, sword held forward like a pointer.

"GITTEM! GITTEM!" they bellowed.

Wogs all looking at the show, he thought with hammering glee. The wall stayed empty for long seconds. Then a few carbines began to crack, muzzle flashes like fireflies in the night. Men fell, but not many. He jumped down into the ditch, felt the jar as his boots landed in the muck at the bottom, scrambled in the chunky raw adobe of the berm. It was less than man-height; a Colonial appeared on the top, aiming a long-barreled revolver downward. It snapped a spike of fire, and the bannerman with the battalion standard went down. Somebody else grabbed it up, used the butt as a climbing-prop. Ludwig braced one hand on the berm and chopped with his saber, felt the edge slam into ankle-bone. The Colonial toppled and rolled down toward him, shrieking and trying to draw a dagger. Ludwig slammed the guard of his sword into the man's face and climbed over his body onto the top of the berm.

Cookfires lit the interior of the fortlet, and the glare of burning Sandoral across the river. Men in crimson djellabas streamed back from the gun line that faced the water, firing as they came. Ludwig gave a quick glance to either side; the berm's broad top was solid with his men. Company commanders were planting their pennants, platoon officers taking three steps forward and turning to face their men with outstretched arm and sword as a bar to give their commands the dressing.

"Sound *Kneel and Stand*," he snapped.

The front rank dropped to one knee and leveled their rifles. The men behind them stood and aimed. Here and there a trooper dropped as the Colonial fire began to thicken a little, falling forward to tumble loose-limbed to the foot of the berm. He waited an instant, until the target had time to thicken.

"*Fwego!*" Ludwig shouted. Then: "*Charge!*"

BAM. One long sound, like a single impossibly long shot. A bright comb of fire reached out towards the dim shapes of the Colonials, five hundred threads of it. On the heels of the volley the troopers ran forward through the thick curls of smoke, their steel glinting red in the reflected light. The Colonials wavered, then ran back the way they'd come, screaming their panic. A few stood and fought, emptying their carbines and drawing their scimitars, but they died quickly—spitted on dozens of points, beaten down with the butt, simply trampled.

Ludwig slashed at a man crawling out of a pup tent, hurdled another. Up the slope to the gunline that was this fortlet's main purpose, set here to command the river and prevent the rebuilding of the pontoon bridge. The guns had been dug in, set in revetments with V-shaped notches forward for their barrels. One group of Colonials, braver or better-led than the rest, was trying frantically to manhandle a pom-pom around to face the menace from the rear. He stopped, braced his legs and began to fire. *Crack. Crack. Crack. Crack. Crack.* Two men down in the confusion around the light gun, and then his troopers were past. Steel clashed on steel for a moment, replaced by the butcher's-cleaver sound of metal slamming into flesh.

Silence fell. 1st Cruiser troopers were standing on top of the fortlet's western wall, firing down—firing at the backs of the fleeing survivors of the post's garrison.

"Sound *Rally*," Ludwig said. "Benter," he went on to his younger brother. "To Captain Marthinez, and his Company A is to man the parapet. Get me a count of the casualties. Hederbert, find those militiamen and put them on the guns, right now. Mauric, see that those dead wogs are all really dead."

He walked as he spoke, over to the flagstaff before the Colonial commander's tent. The dead man lying by the flagstaff was probably the tent's owner, by the scrollwork on his djellaba; he'd been hit by three or four Armory 11mm rounds, and was very thoroughly dead. The smell of death was spreading on the cool night air, like raw sewage and a butcher's shop combined. Ludwig slashed the cord of the flagpole with his saber. The green banner of Islam fluttered to the ground; he used it to clean the sword before sliding it back into its scabbard.

His bannerman needed no prompting. Seconds later, the blue-and-silver Starburst of Holy Federation fluttered up the rough staff and streamed out, almost invisible in the darkness.

Let Ali take a look at that, when he gets tired of shelling an empty city, Ludwig thought, grinning.

The Cruisers cheered at the sight of the flag, man after man taking it up, shaking their rifles in the air or putting up their helmets on the points of their bayonets:

"Hail! Hail! *Hail! Hail! HAIL! HAIL!*"

Ludwig felt a rush of pride: less than six minutes from the moment he'd given the order to charge. Then he looked up at the flag. *The banner of the Gubernio Civil,* he thought. Four years ago most of these men had fought against the army that Messer Raj led under that banner.

There were perhaps half a dozen Sponglish-speaking natives of the Civil Government in the 1st Mounted Cruisers; the rest were MilGov and heretic to a man.

And here they were, crying the banner hail as if . . . *well, it is their own. Now.* Messer Raj had given them that.

Mustafa al-Kerouani jerked himself awake and checked his watch. Good, it was still a few minutes until the next status check. He bent to the eyepiece of the telescope and waited. Nothing from the relay to the north, the second from the siege lines around Sandoral. He frowned. They should give him three flashes from their carbide lantern; that was regular procedure. Allah might be merciful if they were all asleep, but neither their *tabor* commander nor Tewfik would. Besides, there was the honor of the engineering corps to consider. What were they, real soldiers or the *fellaheen* conscripts of infantry, who couldn't be trusted to remember to wipe their arses with their left hands unless an officer reminded them every time they shat?

He reached out and squeezed the handgrip of his own lantern. The slotted shutters over the front clacked open, revealing the brilliant chemical light amplified by the hemisphere of mirror behind it. Three long, two short— *acknowledge.*

Nothing. He swore again, looking around the little hilltop camp. A dozen men, eight of them sleeping, around a low-coal campfire with a brass *kave*-pot standing over it on an iron stand. Their riding- and pack-dogs, picketed out on a line. Two sentries, the telescope, heliograph, lanterns for night work, and their personal baggage. One of dozens strung between the bridgehead at Gurnyca and the Settler's headquarters outside the *kaphar* city. Paralyzingly boring duty; there weren't even any of the infidel *fellaheen* left around here, which meant no fresh provender except for some sauroid meat, and no women.

Three long, two short. Still no acknowledgment. *Ibrahim ibn'Habib is a lazy, wine-swilling son of a pig, but he isn't* that *negligent.* Best send someone over to take a look.

Mustafa blinked out into the darkness where the sentry paced. The bright light killed his night vision, but he could see the outline.

"Moshin?" he said. The other man was Qahtan ash-Shabaai, and much taller. "Moshin, take your dog and check those bastards on Post Three. They must be asleep, or dead."

"Dead," Moshin said—but it was not Moshin's voice, and the word was so thickly accented that he could barely understand it.

Mustafa al-Kerounai reached for his sidearm. He felt the bayonet that punched through his jaw, tongue and palate only as a white flash of cold. Then the point grated through brain and blood vessels within his skull, and the world ended in a blaze of light.

Antin M'lewis withdrew the blade with a jerk. Around him there was a flurry of movement; bayonets and rifle butts struck, and the pick end of an entrenching tool went into the back of a sleeping man's skull with the sound an axe made striking home in hard oak. Talker stamped on a neck with an unpleasant crunching sound, like a bundle of green branches snapping. Dogs wuffled and snarled, dragging at their picket chain as they smelled death. He ignored them and swiveled telescope and signal lantern around on their mountings. The alignment was marked in chalk on the fixed baseplate of the equipment, and he had the code for *acknowledge 0100 hours all is well* on his pad. He clacked it out carefully and waited for the return signal.

Good. There it was. They *still* didn't suspect anything.

He used one tail of his uniform jacket to shield his hand and picked up the pot of *kave*, pouring a cup into his messtin.

"Throw summat more wood on t'fire," he said. It might arouse suspicion if the sentinel fire went out during the night. He tossed aside the spiked Colonial helmet. " 'N git back ter yer dogs. We'ns'll see how many more of t' wogs is overconfident."

"Fwego!"

BAM. The single massive volley turned the supply convoy's night encampment into a mass of screaming men and howling dogs, with the oxen's frantic bawling as accompaniment. Major Peydro Belagez smiled, a cruel closed upturn of the lips. He could see the scene quite well, with the watchfires as background.

BAM. Men rose from their blankets and slapped backward instantly, punched down by the heavy Armory bullets. BAM. Maddened by pain and the smell of blood, an ox-team pulled over the wagon to which they'd been tethered and ran off into the night. The wagon's tilt fell across a fire and the dry canvas flared up brightly.

"Forward, *compaydres*," he said.

The two companies of the 1st Rogor Slashers moved forward in line, with a crackle of platoon volleys. Less than thirty Colonial troops had guarded the convoy, and they were infantry—support troops, hardly fighting men at all. The few who lived ran into the night, or knelt and raised their hands in surrender.

As Belagez watched, the platoon commanders called the cease-fire. Two surviving Colonials bolted when they saw the Civil Government troops more clearly; their dark complexions and the shoulder-flashes made it clear they were Borderers, men whose feud with the Colony was old and bitter. A bet was called, and two troopers stepped forward and knelt, adjusting the sights of their rifles.

The running Colonials jinked and swerved as they fled; the two Slashers fired carefully. On the third shot one of the Arabs flopped forward, shot through the base of the spine. His face plowed into the dirt, mercifully hiding the exit wound. The other went down and then rose again, hobbling and clutching his thigh as if to squeeze out the pain of his wounds.

"*Hingada thes Ihorantes!*" the first rifleman said. Death to the Infidel, the Slashers' unit motto. "You should do better than that, Huan!"

"*Malash*. The Spirit appoints our rising and our going down," the other man grunted. He breathed out and squeezed the trigger. *Crack*. Measurable fractions of a second later, dust spurted from the back of the Arab's djellaba. He went down and sprawled in the dirt.

Meanwhile the others had been rounded up. They sat, hands behind their heads, staring at their captors with the wide-eyed look of men who wanted very badly to wake from an evil dream and couldn't. The toppled wagon was burning fiercely now, with a thick flame that stank like overdone fish three days dead to begin with— *advocati*, no mistaking the stench. Sun-dried, they were oily enough to burn like naphtha.

Belagez pointed with his saber. "Get moving—push the other wagons over and tip them into the fire. Break open those crates, that'll be hardtack." The Colonial version came in thin sheets about the size of a man's hand; it would burn too, in a hot fire.

He switched to Arabic, accented but fluent enough. "You, you unbelieving sons of whores. Get to work."

The teamsters and surviving guards joined his men in heaving more of the supplies onto the growing blaze. Another wagon toppled onto it, and the smell of frying apricots joined the stink, enough to make his stomach knot a little. The blaze would be visible for kilometers, but there was nobody alive to witness it—not unless a survivor or two from the last convoy they'd hit had run very fast. The twenty-wagon parties had been spaced quite evenly at four-kilometer intervals along the road, commendable march-discipline and very convenient for the battalions the *heneralissimo* had landed on the west bank. He looked at his watch; it was bright as day now, and hot enough to make him step back.

0300. This would be their last, they'd have to ride hard to make the rendezvous with the river flotilla by dawn. He certainly didn't want to miss the end of this campaign. The fire grew swiftly; his men were in a hurry too, and the prisoners worked very hard.

Idly, he wondered if they knew they were building their own funeral pyres. Probably. Still, it was the Spirit's blessing that men were reluctant to abandon hope while they still breathed.

> *"Oh night that was my guide*
> *Oh night more loving than the rising sun*
> *Oh night that joined the lover*
> *To the beloved one,*
> *Transforming each of them into the other."*

Raj opened his eyes, then started awake. Suzette laid aside her *gittar* and smiled at him, handing over a cup of *kave*.

"This yacht has all the conveniences, my love," she said.

"What—"

"Absolutely nothing has happened except what you said would. Belagez and the other landing parties made rendezvous. The Colonials have no idea what's going on—we're moving faster than the news. It's noon."

"Ah."

He took the cup and sipped. He felt less jangled than usual on waking, less of the sense that something catastrophic had happened and had to be turned around immediately. *How long has it been since I slept without worry?* he thought.

Five years, one month seven days. defining "worry" as your subtextual intent rendered the term.

Thank you very much, he thought. Aloud: "Thank you, my sweet. You must have fended them off like a mother sauroid on a rookery."

Suzette smiled; not her usual slight enigmatic curve of the lips, but widely as if at some private joke. She shook her head.

"You've had five years to train them, Raj; and they're good men. They wanted you to rest while you could. They can carry out your orders, but we all want—need—you to be at your best when you're needed. Besides"—she dimpled slightly— "you look so young and vulnerable when you're asleep."

Raj laughed softly. *I'm committed,* he realized. *One turn of pitch and toss, winner take all.* It would either work or it wouldn't, and if it didn't he wouldn't be around to worry about it. There was nothing behind them but Ali and his fifty thousand men, barring the road to the border.

"What was that song?" he asked, finishing the coffee. Suzette poured him another and handed him breakfast—toasted hardtack, but she'd found some preserves for it, somehow.

"Very old. My tutor taught it me when I was a girl; Sister Maria, that was."

"Doesn't sound religious," Raj said.

the song is derived from the devotional poetry of st. john of the cross, Center said. **the musical arrangement was made approximately two thousand four hundred years ago on earth.**

"Ahem." A voice from behind the door of the little

stern cabin, out on deck. "I hate to interrupt this touching domestic scene, but . . ."

"Coming, Gerrin," Raj said ruefully.

He stamped into his boots and fastened on his equipment, then scooped up the map he'd been working on late into the night. The sun outside was blinding, the shadow of the awning above hard-edged and utter black by comparison. Raj blinked out over the sparkling green waters of the Drangosh. For a kilometer either way, out of sight behind bends in the high banks, it was covered with rafts and barges and boats. With men and guns and ammunition . . . *nine thousand men*. Nine thousand, to decide the fate of empires. *Nine thousand men relying on me to pull it off.* The thought was less crushing than usual. *If there was any force this size on Earth—*

bellevue.

—Bellevue, then, you pedant, this was it.

Raj smiled. Staenbridge and the other battalion commanders grinned back at him. Barton Foley chuckled.

Raj raised his brows. "Your thoughts, Captain?"

He spread the rolled paper on the deck; the officers and Companions crowded around it, kneeling, staking down the corners with daggers.

"*Mi heneral*, I was just thinking how much less pleasant this morning must be for our esteemed friend Tewfik, when he finds out we've left the party and stiffed him with the drink tab."

A snarling ripple of laughter went around the map. "True enough." Raj rested one hand on his knee and spread the fingers of the other over the map. It was his drawing, with Center supplying a holographic overlay for him to work with. "Gentlemen, this is our latest intelligence on the enemy's bridgehead camp and the pontoon bridge over the Drangosh. You'll note—"

❖   ❖   ❖

Bompf. The little mortar chugged, and a grapnel soared up through a puff of smoke.

Why? Tewfik thought. The fires had raged all through the night, as if the *kaphar* did not care that the city burned around their ears. No fire from the walls and towers, not all through the night and the bombardment. Now they were ignoring his herald under a flag of truce, for the whole hour since dawn. *Since I could finally free myself from my brother's whining and threats*.

The sun was bright in the east, eye-hurting. He shaded his eye with one hand, the other hooked through the back of his sword belt. The breeze blew from the river and fluttered his djellaba; it snapped out the blue-and-silver Starburst of the Federation from the gate towers of Sandoral, as well. The air was heavy with the sickly scent of things that should not burn—one of the constants of war. He had smelled the same in Gurnyca, and in burnt-out cities down on the Zanj coast. Worse, once, when they had shelled a warehouse full of holdouts in Lamoru and the dried copra inside had caught fire.

"Lord Amir, a lucky sniper from the wall—"

"I do not think this is a plot to assassinate me, Hussein," Tewfik said. *Allah alone knows what it* is, *but not that, I think*.

Men climbed up the cable the mortar had thrown. The first of them had a stick with a white rag attached to it thrust through the shoulder harness of his webbing gear; a flag of truce, by the one and only God. Let Whitehall respect it; he had a name for being scrupulous in such things.

The men climbed in through a narrow window high above the bridge that carried the railway over the moat and through the city wall. Tewfik waited with iron patience. A mirror flashed from the parapet.

Tower apparently empty, he read. He clawed at his forked beard, nostrils flaring instinctively as if to smell out a trap. More silent waiting, until there came the muffled *thud* of an explosion behind walls, and very faintly, a scream.

The officers around him tensed. A half-minute later, the mirror blinked again.

Boobytrap, six casualties. Tower deserted. Walls deserted. No enemy in sight.

A hubbub of oaths and excitement broke out around him; the word spread along the siege lines as the great gates swung open and revealed the dogleg passage beyond. A long slow roar like heavy surf welled up, as men climbed out of the entrenchments and onto the gabions, and others dashed from the tents and the cooking-fires behind.

"The city is ours!" someone shouted. "The *kaphar* have fled!"

Tewfik felt a great hand reach into his chest and squeeze. Azazrael's wings brushed darkness over his eyes. Almost, he prayed that the dark angel would come for him now; surely this would count as dying for the Faith, in the Holy War. Hussein and one of his mamluks cried out in shock and rushed to support him; he brushed them aside and staggered forward to the edge of the main works.

Fled? he thought. "Fled? Where? Northeast, to the valleys of the Borderers? To hide in their mud-built forts and make little raids, while we bottle them up with one-tenth of our strength and march to the gates of East Residence with the rest? Whitehall?"

"But . . ." The aide's face was fluid with shock. "If not north, then where?" He looked at his commander's face, and fear replaced the shock. "What is it, Lord *Amir*?"

"Kismet," Tewfik said. "Fate. If not north, then south . . ."

"But, Lord *Amir*, the message stations, the outposts along the road—we have heard nothing!"

"Exactly." He whirled. "Hussein. Twenty men, each with three led dogs. Kill the dogs with haste if they must, but make such speed as men may. To the commandant of the railhead camp; maintain maximum alertness, enemy in your vicinity."

Hussein gaped. Tewfik seized him by the shoulder-straps of his harness and shook him. "Fool born of fools, the entire raid across the Drangosh was a diversion—their bridge a disguise for boats and rafts to *float their force south.*"

"May the Lovingkind have mercy upon us!"

"Go!" He turned to the others. "Sound the alert. Mobilize the cavalry, *all* of it—"

"Lord *Amir,*" one officer said urgently. "The Settler . . ."

The Settler, who will delay for hours before he grasps the necessities. And with him every one of the great noble houses, and the orders of the Maribbatein and ghazis, all of whom will jealously insist on being consulted before a major move is made.

He raised his hands. "Allah! One day! That is all I ask of You, *one day.*"

Never had he prayed with such sincerity.

CHAPTER FOURTEEN

"Messers, the garrison is ten thousand men, not counting civilian laborers."

The Companions bent over the sand-map for the last briefing. Antin M'lewis hung back slightly, although his scouting this afternoon had provided the last-minute updates. Considerations of social rank aside, he didn't have a line command; his men would be split up and acting as trail guides for the actual units.

Raj went on, pointing with his sword. The wet sand allowed a surprising amount of detail; he'd spent about an hour getting it right, just possible with Center to overlay holograms and make each motion perfectly efficient. The long shadows of evening brought it out well.

"As you can see, it's a square earth fort; two-meter ditch, two-meter palisade and earth rampart, chevaux-de-frise in the ditch. Pentagonal bastions at each corner, gun lines along the fighting parapet, and four gates at each of the compass points. The railroad leads in from the east, and the pontoon bridge out from the west side. There are ten-meter watchtowers on either side of each gate; the gates are spiked timber barriers. Most of the artillery is concentrated in the bastions, which are as usual higher than the main berm; they bear along each wall."

"Ten thousand men," Jorg Menyez said thoughtfully. "*Heneralissimo*, that's a Starless Dark of a lot of firepower."

Raj nodded. "If we let them apply it, which we won't. They're line-of-communications troops, railroad labor battalions and engineers and supply specialists. Also they're not expecting us. We're not going to give them time to get ready, either; and there's one last little surprise to distract them.

"We're here." He moved his sword point north on the sand map, tapping a point on the east bank of the Drangosh. "Less than two klicks north of the objective as the pterosauroid flies. We'll move separately, by battalion columns, marching on foot, as follows."

He named the battalions, moving from left to right, east to west. "17th Kelden County Foot and the 24th Valencia on the extreme left—they'll have the farthest to go, but they're better foot-marchers. Cavalry battalions in the center, Sandoral infantry on the right, nearest the river. The 5th Descott and the 18th Komar will take the median and assault the camp's north gate. Colonel Menyez, you will have overall command of the left wing; Colonel Staenbridge, of the center; Major Gruder, of the right. I'll accompany the central command.

"Colonel Dinnalsyn, you'll split your guns into two Grand Batteries. One will accompany the 24th, one the Sandoral garrison battalions. Your objective will be to neutralize the enemy artillery in the corner bastions for the duration of the assault. One fast hard stonk, then shift fire to support, and when our banners are over the berm and palisade, cease fire and prepare to move up as directed. Understood?"

The artillery commander stroked his thin mustache with his thumb. "It can be done, *mi heneral*. But to be effective, I'll need time for ranging fire."

"I'll provide precise range data when we arrive," Raj said.

"That will be satisfactory, of course, *heneralissimo*," Dinnalsyn said carefully, the crisp East Residence vowels sounding a little strained. From the glances, everyone knew what it meant: *it's bloody eerie.* "You have an excellent eye for it."

Raj continued: "Messers, your approaches will be by the following paths." His sword sketched them out, through the maze of badland cliffs, naming the battalions. "I hope I don't need to emphasize the absolute necessity of caution as you approach the edge of the badland zone and the low country directly north of the enemy camp. There's a company of the Rogor Slashers in place, guided by members of the Scout Company. They'll take out the Colonial watchposts immediately before you debouche into the plain, and there'll be very little time after that— the attack, and the usual rocket, will be your signal. Come out of the hills in column; deploy as you move, and hit the wall running. By that time, the artillery will have the bastions under fire. Nothing fancy, gentlemen; we go in with the bayonet and one round up the spout, climb the wall and sweep" —his sword moved from north to south— "the wogs out of their camp. Then we stop for the night."

He drew his watch and opened the cover. "Synchronize, please. It's 1900 at . . . *mark.*" There was a subdued clicking as stems were pressed home. "Two and a half hours to full dark. Colonel Dinnalsyn, move your guns out now. All battalions will be on their way by 19:30. I expect the artillery preparation to begin at 20:15 and the troops to go in at 20:30. It's only a kilometer and the Scouts have the paths clearly marked, so despite the night march that's plenty of time. Questions?"

There were only one or two, technical matters. The plan was simple—startlingly simple. *It's the* strategy *on this one that's complicated,* he thought.

"Then it's all settled bar the fighting. May the Spirit of Man be with us, Messers."

"It is," someone said softly. "The Sword of the Spirit of Man."

Embarrassed, Raj cleared his throat and nodded curtly. The Companions slapped fists in a pyramid of arms and moved away. Junior officers moved in to study the sand table for a few moments, then returned to their units.

Raj walked down the shoreline; it was hard here, rocks lacing the clay of the bank. The barges and rafts were beached as high as human muscle and dogs dragging at the ends of lariats could move them. They weren't planning to go any farther on the water. Many of the men were preparing escalade ladders: simple balks from the rafts, with crosspieces nailed along them, a spike at the top to hold the pole against the sloping surface of an earth berm, and cross-braces at the bottom to keep it from turning. Not very heavy—they hadn't far to go. One standard part of Civil Government training was carrying logs cross-country, units competing against each other—it taught teamwork on a very practical level.

The rest of the men were waiting, some double-timing or stretching under the direction of their platoon officers, getting out the kinks and stiffness of the long crowded voyage. Raj stopped now and then, calling a man by name or slapping a shoulder.

"Ensign Minatili," he said to one very junior officer. The man's under-strength platoon was twisting their torsos with their rifles held over their heads.

"Sir," the young westerner said, bracing to attention. The men froze. He saluted with a snap.

"No names, no pack drill," Raj said easily. *Serious, but that's all to the good*, he thought appraisingly. Lower middle-class, not a social grouping you found many of in the Army and certainly not in the officer corps, but that was less of a disadvantage in the infantry.

"Ready for your first engagement at commissioned rank?" he said.

"Lot more to worry about, sir," the young man blurted. His sincerity was transparent.

Raj nodded. "The mental comfort level goes down as the rank goes up," he said. "If you take your work to heart. Carry on, son."

He walked on, to where detachments of the 5th were snapping the bridles of their dogs to a picket line. The cavalry troopers straightened, but they didn't come to attention; there was profound respect in their stance, but no formality.

"*Bwenya Dai*, dog-brothers," Raj said.

He smoothed a hand over the neck of one bitch-dog; it turned and snuffled at him, then licked its chops, satisfied at the scent of *Army* that marked ultimate pack-boundaries to a military dog.

"Nice beast," he said sincerely. Descotter farmbred, about a thousand pounds, lean and agile-looking but with powerful shoulders and chest. "Fifteen hands?"

"Ah, the best, that Pochita is, ser," the corporal said. "Frum m'own kin's *ranchero*. Fifteen one, seven years old."

"Robbi M'Telgez," Raj said. "Southern edge of Smythe Parish, yeoman-tenants to Squire Fidalgo? Near Seven Skull Spring?"

"Yesser." M'Telgez visibly expanded a little. " 'Tis true we're attackin' t' wog supply base, ser?"

Raj nodded. "A little stroll in the cool evening, and then we collect everything but Ali's underwear. The wogs may not like us helping ourselves, though."

The troopers grinned; catching the scent, the tethered dogs behind them showed their teeth in a distinctly similar expression.

"Carry on," he repeated.

Suzette was waiting beside Harbie and Horace. Seven thousand dogs would take up an intolerable amount of space in the strait confines of the badlands—that was why the operation was going in on foot—but he and his senior officers needed the extra mobility. Raj swung into the saddle and watched the last of the artillery moving out, teams disappearing into the canyon southward. Dust smoked up behind them, but not too much. Later in the summer it would have been a kilometer-high plume. Another reason to send the men in on foot and by widely separated paths.

"This is it, isn't it?" Suzette asked softly.

Raj nodded. "If it works, it's all over bar the shouting. If not . . ." He shrugged. "Well, we won't have to worry about that."

"And if it works, there's Barholm. Raj, he'll kill you the minute he doesn't need you any more."

Raj laughed, full and rich. "My sweet, at the moment that is the last thing on Bellevue I'm worrying about." *I'm not worrying about anything.* The operation was underway, and now all he had to do was deal with the unexpected; think on his feet and use his wits. He felt loose and easy, mind and body working together at maximum efficiency.

His face went blank. "Anyway, I'll have left some accomplishments behind, something that was worth doing."

Suzette touched his elbow; they'd reined a little aside from the bannermen and messengers. "Raj, speaking of things left behind . . . there's something you should know, just in case."

The boatman shivered. He was naked save for his loincloth and covered in soot mixed with tallow, the smell of the grease heavy about him. Ahead the little galley stroked its oars again, then came alongside. He could just see it in the growing dusk, the water lighter where the oars curled it into foam. Their careful stroke went *shush . . . shush . . .* through the night.

The Army officer lit the slowmatch and gave him a salute before vaulting over to the galley. It turned and stroked rapidly back upstream. He knelt on a burlap sack folded on the rough timbers of the raft and took the steering oar. It twisted in his hands, the familiar living buck of the Drangosh, the substance of all his days. He'd never steered a cargo like this before, though. The whole surface of the raft was covered with kegs of gunpowder, lumpy under the dark tarpaulin that covered them, outline broken by palm-fronds and branches. Iron hooks and spikes stood out all around the square vessel, anchored in the main balks.

The current was fast here in midstream, the banks just lines in the darkness to left and right. *Somebody* had to steer, though; otherwise the raft might swirl in towards the banks. He worked the oar carefully, never letting the end break free of the water. From a distance, in the dark, the raft would look like just another piece of river trash caught in the current. The fuse hissed.

There. Lights on the east bank, to his left. The wog camp. A scattering to his right: the ruins of Gurnyca. He bared his teeth. He'd had kin there, before the press-gang enlisted him in the Army. That was why he'd volunteered for this—though the thousand gold FedCreds and the land and the tax exemption for him and his family didn't hurt. But you had to live to enjoy those; revenge was a dish you could eat in advance.

And that Messer Raj. The priest is right. The Spirit *was* with him, you could see it in his eyes. For the Spirit, all men were the tools of Mankind.

A string of lights across the water: sentinel-lanterns along the wog pontoon bridge. Much bigger barges than the ones they'd used to build their own bridge up at Sandoral, with real prows and neat planking. The torches were oil-soaked bundles of rag on the ends of long sticks of ironwood, fastened to the railing of the roadway every fifteen meters or so. He crouched lower, tasting sour bile at the back of his mouth. There was a sheathed knife through the back of his loincloth, but that was for himself if he looked like being captured.

Closer, and he could see the spiked helmets and turbans of the soldiers pacing along the bridge. Cables swooped up out of the water to anchor the upstream prows of the pontoons, dark curves against dark water. Firelight glittered on patches of wave. He braced one foot against a timber, bare callused toes gripping, and threw the weight of back and shoulders against the tiller. The raft moved across the current, slowly, always slowly. His breath tried to sob out past tight-clenched teeth.

One of the wogs was singing, sounding like a man biting down on a cat's tail. It was hard dark outside the circles of firelight the torches cast, both moons down, only the arch of stars above. *Yes*. The raft was heading right between two pontoons. It might have gone right through without him aboard.

He waited until the shadow of the timbered deck above cut off the sky; there was reflected light enough from the torch on one of the pontoons. Then he raised a pole whose other end was set into the deck of the raft. The ironshod point sank deeply into the timber balk above as the weight of the raft and the force of the current drove it. Weight and current pushed the raft sideways, pivoting around the anchor driven deep into the hardwood above. The hooks along the side grated into the hull of the pontoon; he winced at the noise, but there was thick timber and three feet of earth on the roadway above. The raft heeled a little beneath him as they set fast and held against the long slow push of the water.

The boatman dove overside into the water and let the current take him out the south side of the pontoon bridge and a hundred meters downstream. Then he began to stroke in a fast overarm crawl, and the Starless Dark take secrecy. He had less than a minute to get out of killing range.

✧   ✧   ✧

"Change off," Ensign Minatili said.

The next platoon came up and took the escalade ladder off his men's shoulders. The shuttered bull's-eye lantern in his hand provided just enough light, although there were whispered curses and cries of pain in the tight confines of the dry wash.

"Let's get moving."

In a way it was fortunate that the wash was so narrow; there wasn't any way to get lost. He moved at a quick walk, stumbling occasionally over a clod or a rock. Men waited at junctions, directing the traffic along the proper path. A few minutes later he ran into the heels of the men ahead.

"*Halto!*" he hissed back.

Captain Pinya came down the line, identifying himself with a quick flick of his own lantern under his face. "We're there," he said. "Halt in place, prepare for action. Wait for the signal, then we go out in column, deploy into line on the move, and keep moving. There's a little more light out in the open."

I hope so.

He was starting to get some idea of how complicated it was to get hundreds of men moving in the same direction and have them arrive when you wanted them to. It was a lot more difficult than it looked when all you had to do was march when someone said, "By the left, forward."

All an ensign had to do in a field action was relay the orders, though. He was very glad of that.

"Fix bayonets. Load. Keep the muzzles *up*."

The last thing they needed was somebody getting stuck or shot because they fell over their feet. It was up to *him* to see that didn't happen.

Spirit.

✧   ✧   ✧

10:18. Raj shut his watch with a snap.

Can't wait much longer. With their outposts gone, the enemy camp would be waking up *soon*. A last iron clank came from the artillery position to his left, about twenty meters away; it was dark enough that he could only see vague traces of movement there. The gunners moved with exaggerated care, setting the fuses behind a screen of blankets that would conceal the brief flashes of light from the enemy. They'd be firing blind, essentially, except for the directions he'd given—Center had given— although the wogs were displaying a pleasant abundance of lamps and watchfires.

Another messenger trotted up.

"Major Gruder reports right wing in position, ser." He handed over a note.

Raj flicked a match between thumb and forefinger. *This herd of handless cows is ready to stampede,* he read. Kaltin was *not* happy at having five battalions of second-rate garrison infantry under his direction besides the 7th.

"Tsk."

Kaltin wouldn't expect to get the best out of a force of Descotter cavalry with that attitude; why did he think infantry would respond any better? A good tactician and very loyal, but there were some jobs you just wouldn't give him. Raj grinned mirthlessly. The chances were he wouldn't be giving anyone any jobs, after this.

He turned to look to the right, toward the river. The tiny dots of the torches along the pontoon bridge glittered like stars in the darkness. *I would have left it farther south,* he thought. Better roads here, and what was left of Gurnyca gave a secure anchorage for the western end, but putting a point-failure source closer to your enemy was a terrible risk. *Ali's doing. He tends to arrogance.* He began a gesture to the messenger beside him; there wasn't any more time.

Smaller torches were running along the center section

of the pontoon bridge. He pulled the binoculars from their case on Horace's saddlebow and focused them. Men leaned over the edge of the roadway, looking at the water below and pointing.

Raj turned his head aside. Even looking away, the flash of the explosion was bright; it lit the earthen walls of the Colonial fort the way a flash of lightning might, but for much longer. When he looked back a huge section of the pontoon bridge was *gone*, gone as if a vast mouth had bitten it away. There was a crater in the water, foaming as the river rushed back to fill the hole the blast had momentarily forced into it. Pieces of burning, shattered timber were describing parabolas through the night for thousands of meters all around. The sound hit like a giant rumbling thud, felt on the skin of the face and in the chest cavity as well as through the ears.

An alarm siren began to wail in the fort. More men were running out of it, heading through the west gate and onto the pontoon bridge, or what was left of it— large sections on either side of the gap had torn away their anchoring cables and were beginning to drift southward with the current. That threw more and more stress on the undamaged sections, cable and timber creaking and yielding as the two unconnected segments bent back. He could hear the gunshot cracks of materials yielding as they were pushed past their breaking strain. Parts of it were on fire, too; the sections above water would be tinder-dry, in this climate.

The officer in command of the base was probably an engineering specialist. His first thought would be to save the bridge. As if to confirm the thought, a fire engine pulled by six hitch of dogs thundered out onto the pontoon, dropped a hose overside and began spurting steam-driven water at the fires. Men dropped overside with ropes, swimming out for the anchor points. Others set up winches on the decking.

Raj chopped his hand downward. An aide put his cigarette to the touchpaper of a signal rocket and stepped back. The paper sizzled and the little rocket went skyward with a *woosh*, popping into a blue starburst high overhead.

POUMPF. POUMPF. POUMPF. POUMPF. Over and over again.

Tongues of fire shot into the blackness. Fifty-five guns, massed in two grand batteries of twenty-eight and twenty-seven pieces. Warm pillows of air slapped at his face from the nearby position. The night filled with the whirring ripple of shell fire, and seconds later the snapping *crack* of bursting charges and the red firefly wink over the bastions at each corner of the fortress walls. At three rounds a minute the shellbursts came at more than one per second over each target, an endless ripple of fire. The second stonk contained a proportion of contact-fused shells. The guns were firing at maximum elevation and nearly maximum range, their shells dropping down out of the sky at high angles. Dirt fountained up, and then a mammoth secondary explosion from the eastern bastion.

Somebody left his ready reserve ammunition exposed, he thought. He could imagine the scene in the redoubts, men running half-dressed from their bombproofs into the storm of razor-edged, high-velocity metal as they tried to crew their pieces.

"Dinnalsyn's on time and target," Raj said to himself, gathering the reins. *"Hadelande."*

He clapped heels to Horace's side and swung into a loping gallop down the slope. The flags crackled behind him, harness creaked, a bugle clanked rhythmically against the webbing buckles on a signaler's chest. Rock and dust spurted up under the dogs' paws, with a scent of bruised native scrub like bergamot. Trumpets sounded ahead of him—no point in keeping quiet after this—as the battalions poured over the ridgeline and down the last slope toward the flat fields. The routes he'd picked left them widely spaced, to minimize collisions in the dark, and the flaming chaos at each end of the north face of the Colonial base would help with the alignment.

The dense columns of men flowed forward onto the open ground, double-timing in battalion columns. Starlight glittered on a forest of bayonet points, sheened on the silver Starbursts at the top of the flagstaffs of their colors. He leaned back slightly, and Horace shifted to a swinging trot; they were coming up on the 5th Descott's position. The men gave a short roaring cheer as his flag went by to swing into position near the battalion commander's, a harsh male undertone to the crash and flicker of the guns.

He looked at his watch. 1040 hours. *Nearly on time. Amazing.* A memory prickled at him; nothing he'd ever experienced, but one of the holographic scenarios from Earth's long history of war that Center showed him. Not Hannibal this time, but someone else, and the battle had also been against Arabs . . .

lieutenant-general garnet wolseley, Center said. **tel el-kebir. twenty-five hundred years ago.** A pause. **the similarities are disquieting.**

Why? Raj thought. *This fellow Wolseley won, didn't he?* A night march and an attack on earthwork fortifications, as he remembered.

i was programmed to believe that a progressive improvement of human capacities is a priority, Center said. **the fact that two such similar engagements have occurred at this distance in time might support a cyclical rather than linear explanation of human history.**

Some things never change.

that, raj whitehall, is precisely the problem— and what we are attempting to change.

The 5th's buglers blew a six-note call and repeated it.

Raj turned in the saddle to watch; the fires on the pontoon bridge were out of control, and the easternmost Colonial bastion was a column of flame, giving enough light to turn the night to dusk. The solid column of troops suddenly opened, like a man's outstretched hand when he flared his fingers. Each of the four companies of the 5th turned at an angle to the axis of advance and double-timed outward, following the pennant of the company commander. Thirty seconds later the bugle sounded again, and the company columns spread likewise into platoons, and the platoons flared out like opening fans. In less than four minutes what had been a dense column of men was a double line, rippling as the veterans dressed their ranks on the move with unconscious skill.

This was what the endless parade-ground drill was for: the movements had to be unconscious. So instinctive that they could be done exhausted, or under killing fire— or here, in darkness so bad you could barely see another man at twice arm's length. A line of men couldn't advance at speed for long, not on anything but absolutely flat table-top terrain. A column could maneuver, but it was a hideously vulnerable target with no offensive capacity to speak of.

Gerrin Staenbridge reined in beside him. "After that march, I'm never going to make a joke about the blind leading the blind again, *mi heneral*. If it hadn't been impossible to get lost, we would have."

There was strain in his voice. The possibilities for confusion were enough to turn a man's hair gray . . . which reminded Raj of the silver dusting he saw in his own every time he shaved.

The splatguns had been bouncing along behind the infantry. Now they trotted forward, drawing ahead. One hundred meters, two, three, then the teams wheeled. The crews leapt down and spun the elevating screws to maximum.

"About now," Raj said.

The cannonade lifted for an instant, and starshells burst over the ramparts of the fort. Raj stood in the stirrups and looked right and left, halfway between dread and hope under the wavering blue-white light. *All honor and glory to the Spirit of Man of the Stars*, he thought sincerely. No major units seemed to be missing, as far as he could see—although the right flank was mostly hidden, and that was the one he was most worried about. A long, wavering double line of men stretched across the plain, with gaps of several hundred meters between battalions. Several of the battalions *were* severely out of alignment with their target, marching at angles that would have tangled them with their neighbors eventually. As he watched they started to correct.

"Signaler," he said. The man dropped out of the saddle and set two rockets. They hissed aloft and burst.

Staenbridge drew his sword. "Battalion—"

"Company—" Manifold, down the line.

"*Charge!*"

The trumpets sounded and kept up their shrilling, a long brass screaming in antiphonal chorus as all the signalers caught up the note. A long swelling shout rose from one end of the field to the other. Flags slanted forward as the whole formation broke into a steady uniform trot.

Braaaaap. The splatguns fired, shot arching down at extreme range to spray the parapet. They kept firing over helmets as the troopers swept by. A pom-pom opened up from the wall ahead, and the flicker of muzzle flashes showed there were *some* wogs on the parapet, at least. The little quick-firer's shells went overhead with a nasty *whack-whack-whack* as it emptied its clip, and burst on the soil behind. Raj drew his revolver, tossed it to his left hand and drew his sword, letting the reins fall to Horace's neck. The dog stepped up the pace to a

slow canter, keeping level with the men. The berm ahead
loomed up with shocking speed, and the skeletal shapes
of the watchtowers on either side. Company A of the
5th kept pace with them on either side, their boots
crunching on the gravel of the roadway that ran into
the gate.

A carbide searchlight flickered alight from one tower,
stabbing into his eyes with hurting brilliance. Seconds
later it disintegrated in a shower of fragments as five or
six splatguns turned their attention to it. The observation
platform at the top of the wooden tower came apart in
a shower of splinters and began to burn. The trumpets
shrilled on, and the men started to run.

They reached the edge of the ditch. Fire stabbed down
at them and some tumbled into it, to lie still or shrieking
on the spiked timbers there. More slid down into the
ditch on their backsides, clambered carefully through
the obstacles and the mud, and began climbing the steep
slope on the other side. They scrambled in the heavy
clay, chopping their rifle butts into the dirt. Others
brought up the escalade ladders, setting their triangle-
braced bases at the edge of the ditch and letting them
topple forward. The spikes at the upper end hammered
into the dirt and men ran up the crossbars, climbing
one-handed with their rifles in the other.

"Not much fire!" Raj said exultantly. *We caught them
with their pantaloons down, and now it's too late!* Surprise
was the best force multiplier there was, and it was working
in his favor.

Staenbridge nodded. He turned to Barton Foley and
laid a hand on his shoulder. "Now."

The younger man grinned and leaned out of the saddle,
extending his hook. One of his platoon commanders
dropped the loop of a leather satchel over it. Then he
lit a length of fuse-match that extended from under the
buckled cover.

"Ha!"

Foley clapped his heels into his dog's flanks, heading for the timber gate that barred the northern entrance to the Colonial fort. Men were fighting hand-to-hand on the wall to either side, shooting and stabbing and swinging clubbed rifles; there had to have been Colonials on duty at the gate, at least, if not all around the walls. Bodies tumbled down the steep slope of the berm, dead or wounded. Troopers in Civil Government uniform shot through the stubby planks of the palisade at the top, or joined to pull the wood aside, or boosted their comrades over the pointed tops. Probably the towers on either side of the gate had held swivel guns as well as searchlights, but they were both blazing torches now, burning hard enough to make the heat noticeable at a hundred meters.

Foley covered the distance to the gate in a few seconds. A mounted man drew attention, even in the melee above him. Bullets kicked the gravel roadbed around him; once he swayed in the saddle and Staenbridge stiffened beside Raj. The satchel arched through the air and thumped into the dirt at the base of the gate, its momentum wedging it under the palm-log timbers where they swung at ankle height above the roadway. At the same instant he pulled the dog's head around; the beast whirled so quickly that it reared almost upright on its hind legs, with Foley hanging on like a jockey. It landed facing the way it had come, and running. The rider's display of skill would have been worthy of attention in itself, in any other context.

"Damned good man," Raj said, easing back the hammer of his revolver with the thumb of his right hand. Horace tensed under him.

". . . Five, six," Staenbridge said. "Yes, he is, and I wish to the Starless Dark he'd stop *volunteering* for this sort of shit, the hand's enough. Seven, eight—"

Barton Foley had covered three-quarters of the distance back to their position when the satchel charge blew. There were twenty-five kilos of powder in it; the gates disappeared from sight, and chunks of wood flew past them. Foley's dog yelped and leaped forward so quickly that he had to slug the reins back with brutal force to stop it. A splinter a double handspan long stuck out of one haunch; the animal kept trying to turn and reach the wound with its tongue.

Two of Foley's troopers grabbed the bridle while he dismounted; one of them threw a neckerchief over the dog's eyes while the other pulled the splinter out with a single swift yank. The dog's howl of agony was loud even by comparison with the noises of battle.

"Go!" Staenbridge barked. "Go, go, *go*."

The dust billowed away from the gate, showing a shattered ruin that sagged back out of the way. Barton Foley was first through again, his riot gun in one hand; at his shouted direction a dozen men threw their shoulders against the splintered wreckage and walked it clear. Raj heeled Horace through a dozen paces, then drew him up with the pressure of his knees.

The interior of the camp was a checkerboard of stores in huge pyramids under tarpaulins, interspersed with tents. Some of the tents were on fire, and there was also light from iron baskets of burning greaseweed at the intersections. His head whipped left and right. To the left the Civil Government troops were already over the wall and down into the roadway that circled just inside it. The inner face of the berm was sloped dirt, or broad steps cut into the clay and faced with palm logs. Men poured down in, rallied around unit flags on the flat, moved off. There was a thick scattering of dead Arabs on the roadway, a few on the inner slope, more living ones running like blazes southward. To his right, toward the river, the fighting was still on the parapet itself. In a few places Civil Government banners waved from the parapet.

"All right," he said. *Just what I expected.* That section had had fewest of his veterans, and most of the Sandoral garrison troops. "Gerrin, let's collect some men and go help out. *Waymanos!*"

The issue of the day was no longer in doubt. Now he'd make sure the butcher's bill wasn't any higher than it had to be.

CHAPTER FIFTEEN

Breakfast was astonishing. *Well, we did just overrun a supply dump,* Raj thought, looking over the collection of delicacies.

He spooned up more potted shrimp. Peydro Belagez was eating them mixed with candied dates, which was something only a Borderer would do; Gerrin watched him with the horrified fascination of a gourmet, or a priest witnessing blasphemy. The commanders were seated at a long table in the huge pavilion tent that had been the base HQ. The Colonial engineers, left with time on their hands, had gone a little berserk. There were even *baths*, complete with kerosene-fired water heaters, enough for several hundred men at a time.

The morning air was fresh and hot, still a little smoky with the fires they'd spent half the night putting out. A bugle sounded outside, and a pair of mounted troopers trotted by with a long string of dogs on a leading rein: more of the force's mounts from the site where they'd landed. The barges and rafts were mostly here by now too, grounded on the riverbank or against the stub of the pontoon bridge that still extended halfway across. On the tall flagpole outside the HQ tent the Starburst banner snapped in the breeze.

The commander of the Rogor Slashers went on:

"And they still haven't stopped running, *heneralissimo*. They've split up into small parties and none of them show fight." Belagez's dark leathery face showed a combination of exhaustion and satisfaction. "Your instructions?"

"Ignore them," Raj said. "They weren't a problem in here, and they're not going to be one out there, either."

He swallowed another mouthful of excellent-quality *kave*—the Colony sat astride the trade-route from Azania and kept the best for itself—and looked at Suzette. She had peeled an orange and then set it aside untouched, looking a little pale. *Damnation. Think about that later.*

"Casualties?"

"Less than two hundred," Staenbridge said, sounding slightly surprised. "That's not counting walking wounded fit for duty. We only had twenty dead."

"Most of the live ones will pull through," Suzette added. "There are plenty of medical supplies here, and some excellent Colonial doctors, besides our own. Working under guard, of course."

"Prisoners?"

Kerpatik thumbed through his lists. "Over two thousand, *heneralissimo*. That is, two thousand military personnel. There were substantial numbers of camp followers here as well. The families of the soldiers have mostly fled. The, ah, commercial elements—" he rubbed thumb and the first two fingers of his hand together, "—they care little about the coinage as long as the metal is good."

Raj nodded. Where you had a military base, you got knocking-shops. He'd be willing to bet there was alcohol for sale too, Koranic prohibitions or not.

"Jorg, issue *Guardia* armbands to some of your footsoldiers and get that under tight control. We're still in the field, even if we've captured all the comforts of home. Let's not let the troops relax just yet."

"What about the prisoners?"

"Strip them down to their loincloths and let them go; tell them to start walking south. Now, we captured a good many documents here, including the daily logistics summaries."

Several men exclaimed in delight. That meant they would know the Colonial army's situation in detail, right down to the names of the units and their muster strength.

"Evidently they've been having problems getting the supplies from the railhead to the siege lines outside Sandoral—plenty here, but they're short of draft oxen and fodder over on the west bank."

Dinnalsyn nodded. "They were trying to use locomotive engines to rig up a couple of spare pontoons as steam tugboats, to pull raftloads up to Sandoral," he said. "I had a look; it would have worked, more or less. Whoever was in charge knew his business."

Raj nodded acknowledgment. "In any case, the Colonials have virtually nothing in the way of reserve with their field army. They were living from day to day on what their convoys brought in, once the countryside was laid waste. Now, Messers, here's what we'll do. Jorg, you're in charge here. How many dogs did we capture?"

Muzzaf Kerpatik looked up from a mass of papers. "Over twenty-five hundred, not counting gun teams, sir," he said.

"Good. Jorg, I'm leaving you all the infantry. Mount half of them—the best half—on the captured dogs. You'll also have, hmmm, Poplanich's Own and the 21st Novy Haifa for stiffening. And half the field guns. Move them north in parties of a couple of hundred; keep in continuous contact. Your objective is to prevent Tewfik from making any lodgment on the east bank. Shouldn't be difficult; there isn't much in the way of boats over there, and it would take weeks to put enough material together for another bridge. Which they couldn't build in the face of our artillery, anyway—but keep a sharp lookout; we don't want to get as overconfident as the previous tenants."

"Patrol the vicinity?"

"Vigorously. The infantry in good spirits?"

"Any better and they'd want to march on Al Kebir, *mi heneral*. Their tails are up."

"Deservedly so. Now, I'll take the rest of the cavalry, and the guns, over to the west bank. There are probably still intact supply trains on the road north, and I want to sweep those up immediately."

He rose, picking up his sword belt from the back of the chair. "I want to be on the move in no more than five hours. Tewfik is crazy like a ferenec, and Ali is just plain crazy; let's not give them time to think up any way out of their predicament. *Waymanos*."

"That will not work, Ali my brother," Tewfik said.

His voice was dangerously calm, and he left out the honorifics. Ali turned his head slowly, the great ruby that held the clasp of his turban winking in the stray beams of light that came through ventilation slits in the ceiling of the pavilion high above.

The nobles and officers sitting on cushions around the carpet looked at Tewfik as well, mostly with the same expression they might have used if a man kicked a carnosauroid in the snout.

"Dog will not eat dog," Tewfik went on. "This has been proven many times, as any fool of a soldier would know. Rather," he corrected himself, "most dogs will not. Nine in ten. So we will lose all our cavalry at once, and cannot preserve a portion of our mobility by sacrificing the rest."

Ali's face went a mottled color. It had been a very long time since anyone had dared to call him a fool to his face, even by implication. Even his brother.

"Go!" he said, pointing with a trembling hand. "You are dismissed from the *durbar*. Return when you learn manners!"

Tewfik rose and bowed deeply, hand going to brow

and lips and chest; the other clenched on the plain, brass-wired hilt of his scimitar.

His officers fell in about him. That brought another round of silent glances around the council carpet. It was also unheard-of for men to leave the Settler's presence without word. And Ali looked suddenly thoughtful, conscious of the gaps. The nobles remained, and the heads of the religious orders . . .

In the harsh sun outside, Tewfik halted, beyond earshot of the mamluks who stood like ebony statues around the Settler's tent.

"How long?" he said, to an elderly officer with a green-dyed beard.

"There is no reserve. None. The camp is on quarter-rations, but we have fifty thousand men, as many dogs, and twenty thousand camp followers here. There was no food to be had in Sandoral, none at all. I have set men to fashioning nets, and we may gain a little fish by trolling the river; but the *kaphar* hold the fort you planted on the eastern bank opposite the city, and the guns there command much of the water surface. There will be hunger by sundown, starvation by tomorrow's night. Our dogs will be too weak to carry men in three days, and dying in six. By then the men will be dying as well."

Tewfik's hand withdrew the scimitar a handspan, then rammed it home again. "If we lose this army, our people will perish," he said. "And we cannot maintain discipline, even, if we cannot feed the troops."

He looked around. "Ibrahim, put the camp on one-quarter rations—and the camp followers are to receive nothing. Confiscate *all* private supplies of food. Hussein, mount ten thousand men and be ready to ride within the hour."

"Glad to be out of the ruins," Staenbridge said, looking back at the walls of Gurnyca.

Raj nodded. The faint stink of the piles of heads still clung to the inside of his nose, an oily thing like overripe bananas. Almost as bad had been the rats and the scavenging sauroids, rabbit-sized scuttling things all spidery limbs and teeth. One had gone past him with a desiccated arm in its mouth, still wearing the lace-cuffed sleeve of a lady's day-dress.

"That sort of thing has to stop," he said quietly.

"I don't think the wogs will be invading us again in the near future," the other man said with a predatory smile.

Raj shook his head. "I mean it's got to *stop*. We did pretty much the same to the country around Ain el-Hilwa. Look at this!"

He gestured at the territory around them. A few weeks before it had been among the richest land in the Civil Government. Now the fields lay waste, empty except for the ragged scraps of sheep and cattle that the scavengers had left. Burnt stumps marked the remains of orchards, tall date palms and spreading citrus lying amid drifting ash. The adobe of the roofless peasant huts was already crumbling; the fired brick and stone of the burnt-out manors would last only a little longer. Weirs and sluice-gates and the windmills that watered the higher land were blackened wreckage as well. The long column of Civil Government troops rode through silence, amid a hot wind laden with sand. The sand would reclaim everything to the river's edge, in time.

"There are enough barbarians to fight, without wrecking civilization," Raj said. "*That's* why Ali has to be stopped. Barholm wants to unite the planet, even if it's only so he can rule it himself. Ali's a sicklefoot and he destroys for the love of it."

Staenbridge glanced around instinctively, with the gesture anyone in East Residence—or in the officer corps—learned to use when a too frank opinion of the

Governor was voiced. Raj nodded silently. Staenbridge had a family to protect.

Raj's lips tightened. Suzette should be in no danger even if Barholm killed her husband; her family was old and well-connected. A child, though . . .

"Well, this will simplify *our* logistics," Barton Foley said happily.

The wagons stood abandoned but not empty in the middle of the road, their trek-chains lying limp like dead snakes. From the sign, the teams had been driven on ahead with the dogs of the escort, but no attempt had been made to damage the cargoes.

"Which is fortunate," he murmured, taking off his helmet.

It was surprising; even now he had to remind himself not to scratch his head with his left . . . well, left hook. He juggled the bowl-shaped steel headpiece and ran a hand through sweat-damp black curls. His scalp felt cooler for an instant, then hot again as the noon sun struck it. He heeled his dog and rode slowly down the line of wagons. Half the loads were ammunition, loads for heavy siege guns. *Very* fortunate that the teamsters had been struck by blind panic. The other half was wheat biscuit and bundles of dried *advocati*.

"Ser."

A plume of dust was coming up the road from the south; the banner of the 5th and Messer Raj's personal flag at its head. He kneed his mount over to the side of the road, smiling to himself. Suzette wasn't along this time, and he suspected why. He knew the signs. Fatima had borne her first in Sandoral, during the winter Raj spent preparing to meet Jamal's invasion. The whole process was rather disturbing, like a good many things female, but the end product was delightful.

It was also pleasant not to be facing destruction at

the hands of an army that outnumbered them seven to one.

The command group pulled up, the battalion fanning out into the fields on either side. "Drag it all down to the river?" Gerrin said.

Foley shook his head. "It's about half ammunition. If we push everything together and set a fuse . . ."

Troopers came in by squads and pulled out bales of *advocati* to bait their dogs, filling their own haversacks with Colonial hard tack and strips of dried mutton. It was a little past noon and intensely hot, the land and sky turned white in the blaze of the sun.

"Ser." A much smaller plume of dust this time, approaching from the north.

The officers corked their canteens and waited with a stolid patience that ignored the discomfort. Their dogs twitched ears and tails against the omnipresent Drangosh Valley flies. Antin M'lewis pulled up at the head of ten of his Scouts.

"Ser," he said, with a casual wave that approximated a salute. " 'Bout a thousand wogs comin', all cavalry, six guns. Five klicks off an' closin' fast."

Raj nodded, wiping sweat and dust from his face with his neckerchief. "We'll give them a reception," he said. To a messenger: "My compliments to Majors Bellamy and Gruder, and would they close up quickly, please." He looked around at the terrain. "This should do; Gerrin, set up along this crestline."

"Guns to the left?" Staenbridge asked, pointing to the snags of a citrus orchard that ran down the gentle slope east of the road.

"By all means."

"I presume we don't intend to stay here long."

"No," Raj said. "The last thing we want is a general engagement; we'll just show them they have to stay bunched up and slow them down."

He turned to Foley. "Barton, how many wagon trains does this make?"

"Altogether? Including the ones wrecked when we were coming downstream?" At Raj's nod he continued: "Twenty-seven; four hundred twenty-two wagons of all sizes. Mostly these standard models," he concluded, waving a hand at the ones in the road.

"That means they shouldn't have recovered more than twenty or thirty tons of supplies altogether," he said. Softly: "Most excellent."

The messengers went out; on either side the 5th's troopers fanned out, sending their dogs back and unlimbering their entrenching tools for hasty heaped-earth *sangars* to their front. A few minutes later Ludwig Bellamy and Kaltin Gruder trotted up the roadway with their banners fluttering in the hot wind, the dust clouds of their commands behind them.

"*Mi heneral,*" Bellamy said, his beard-stubble golden against the brown tan of his face. "Dispatches from Colonel Menyez."

Raj took them and broke the seal; the wax was as soft as butter. "Ah. The Colonials are breaking camp outside Sandoral. I think friend Ali has just realized how badly his testicles are caught in the mangler."

The commanders grinned like a group of carnosauroids contemplating a dying sheep.

"This is their vanguard, then," Raj said, looking north. "All right. We'll punch them back, then move southward—they'll be substantially slower, but I don't want to take any chances with Tewfik. Messenger: to Colonel Menyez. I want enough barges to take us off held in constant readiness. We can always duck back across the river if they lunge."

"We'll have to keep a very close eye on them," Staenbridge said thoughtfully.

Raj tapped his chin with one thumb. "Constant patrols,"

he agreed. "I don't think they'll want to wear down their dogs with skirmishing, hungry as they are."

The carnivore grins widened. Gruder began to laugh; after a moment, the others joined in.

Center drew a graph across Raj's vision, of consumption balanced against maximum possible reserves. At the back of his consciousness there was a trace of feeling, a satisfaction colder and more complete than a human mind could feel.

"Hold your fire!" Raj snapped.

He blinked into the setting sun; four days in the saddle had left his eyes red-rimmed and sore, the Drangosh Valley was hell for dust. He wiped his sleeve across his face and brought up his binoculars. Around him on the hillock the platoon of the 5th lowered their rifles, and the crew of the splatgun looked up from their weapon. Horace stood under the shade of the carob tree and panted, washcloth-sized tongue hanging down, and drooping ears almost covering his eyes.

"Easy target, ser," the gunner said, hopefully.

Raj raised his binoculars. The main Colonial army was several kilometers away; this encampment was notably more ragged than the last. Hardly an encampment at all, with no baggage train; the animals had all been eaten, to judge from the cracked bones left in their campfires. Most of their cavalry were walking and leading their dogs behind them. Some were carrying the saddles as well.

It was the patrol riding towards his men on the hilltop that interested him now. There were two banners at its head, hanging limp in the hot still air. He waited patiently; a gust of breeze flapped them out. One was pure white; the other, black with a Seal of Solomon in red.

"Tewfik," Raj whispered. The sweat down his spine turned clammy.

"Ensign," he said. "We're staying for a moment; they're

coming under a truce flag. Get something white and wave it on a stick. Water the dogs, but keep a careful look-out. And have someone set out a blanket, with a piece of hard-tack and some salt."

They were out of extreme field gun range of the Colonial camp, but you never knew.

"Sir," the Ensign said, relaying the orders.

A detail trotted downslope to the well in the courtyard of a burned-out steading. A trooper unstrapped the rolled blanket from behind his saddle, spread it on the scraggly twistgrass beneath the carob tree, and set out a canteen, two cups and a piece of Colonial flat biscuit with a small twist of gray salt on it.

The men were looking at Raj curiously. "What does it mean, sir?" the young officer asked.

"I think," Raj said slowly, "it means the war is over. Escort our guest to me."

Raj saw Tewfik's eye widen in surprise as he recognized the Civil Government commander. The Colonial was much as Raj remembered him from the parley just before the first battle of Sandoral five years ago, perhaps a little grayer. Looking a little gaunt from five days on quarter-rations, but still stocky and strong. Like a scarred bull in a pasture, confronting a younger rival and twitching his horns. Raj knew that Tewfik would be seeing far greater changes in him.

"*Salaam aleikoum,*" the Arab said, bowing slightly.

"*Aleikoum es-salaam,*" Raj replied in accentless Arabic. Center had given him that, and practice made it come smoothly. "And upon you, peace, Tewfik ibn'Jamal."

"Shall it be peace, then?"

"If the Spirit wills. Come, let us talk."

Raj gestured, and the troopers retreated down the slope, out of immediate earshot and with their backs to the supreme commanders. The two men walked into the shade of the carob. Tewfik's eye caught the bread and salt; also the fact that they hadn't yet been offered to him. There was wary respect on his face as he turned to face his enemy and let the saddlebags he carried over one shoulder drop to the ground.

Carefully, carefully, Raj told himself. *Take no chances with this man.*

indeed, Center said. A brief vision flashed before Raj's eyes: the same meeting, but with the relative positions reversed. **if my physical centrum had been located in al kebir, rather than east residence . . .**

I'd be the one trying to salvage something from the wreck, Raj acknowledged.

"I will not waste words," Tewfik said abruptly, into the growing silence. "You have won this campaign. Without even fighting a major battle. My compliments, young *kaphar*; it is a feat for the manuals and the historians to chew over."

"More than the campaign," Raj said quietly. "The war. And I would betray my ruler and my State, if I did not use this advantage to ensure the Colony is no longer a threat to the Civil Government. We have fought you every generation for nearly a thousand years; it's irrelevant who was at fault in any given war. It must cease."

Tewfik nodded, his face still cat-calm. "Yet it is said that *Heneralissimo* Whitehall fights also for the cause of civilization on Bellevue," he said. "We of the House of Islam brought man to this world. We built its first cities. We preserved much of what learning survived the Fall, and we are the other half of civilized life on this world. Would you see our cities burn and the books with them, while the howling peoples camp in the ruins?"

Raj inclined his head. "You admit that the Colony is ruined if your army is destroyed?"

"That is as God wills; but too many of our high nobles are with us, our best commanders and the leadership needed to maintain the unity of our state. And our best troops; we left nothing but garrison forces on the frontiers. If they do not return, there will be civil war—fourscore separate civil wars; instead of one Settler, we will have a hundred *malik al'taifas*, petty kings ruling factions. They will not be able to maintain the irrigation canals, nor guard the frontiers against the Skinners and the Zanj."

"Or us," Raj pointed out.

Tewfik shook his head. "Conquering a hundred splinter realms would be impossible. You would have to garrison them heavily and there would be constant revolt; our people will not tolerate direct rule by unbelievers, not without such punishment as would destroy what you tried to govern."

"What do you propose?"

The Arab nobleman took a deep breath. "I cannot rule," he said, touching his eye. "And Ali . . . he is my brother, but he is a disaster for all Muslims. One way or another, sooner or later, he would have ruined the Colony. Already he has killed many of our best men— and anyone else who was there at the wrong time.

"What I propose is this: half our army to be disarmed and sent to East Residence. I suggest that you use them to garrison the Southern and Western Territories; there they will be hostages against the Colony's good behavior. I will take the other half back with me to Al Kebir, and there rule as Vice-Governor in Barholm Clerett's name. My daughter Chaba will go to East Residence and wed Governor Barholm."

He shrugged, and for the first time smiled slightly. "I have no sons, and I fear I have been too indulgent with her—even allowing her to be taught to read. Perhaps it will be better for her thus."

Well, Raj thought, slightly dazed. *That's emphatic enough.* Center's sensor-grid came down over Tewfik's face, tracing blood flow, temperature, pupil-dilation.

subject tewfik is sincere, the computer-angel said. **probability 82%±7.**

Raj was slightly startled. Usually the percentage was much higher, one way or another.

subject tewfik has an unusual degree of control over autonomic body functions. in your vernacular, a poker face.

"A moment," Raj said.

He turned and looked out over the dusty plain of the Drangosh. Then he turned back.

"That sounds acceptable, in outline," he said. "We'll have to settle a few details. Release of all Civil Government prisoners in the Colony, for instance; and an annual tribute sufficient to pay the twenty-five thousand men you'll be giving us. Customs, tariffs, that sort of thing the bureaucrats can settle."

Tewfik nodded, hesitated, then stroked his beard. "My offer, of course, would apply to any *other* Governor as well," he hinted. "From all reports, Governor Barholm is somewhat preferable to my brother Ali . . . but that is not a strong recommendation."

Meaning, take the Chair yourself and rule the world, Raj thought.

interpretation of subtext correct, probability 98%±1, Center clarified.

"How do I know this isn't a ploy to save Ali and half your army?" Raj said. "You could be planning to write the other half off. It'd still be a larger force than I have in the field, and campaigning down to the Drangosh delta would be a nightmare, particularly with this area too devastated to use as a base."

Tewfik smiled grimly and opened the saddlebag he'd brought. His curly-toed boot hooked it over to lie at Raj's feet. A head rolled out; fairly fresh, although the flies were already crawling around the hacked stump of the neck and the staring eyes. Raj did not need the ruby-clasped turban that rolled from the shaven skull to identify it.

"That for Ali," Tewfik said, and kicked the head to one side. "I should have done that years ago."

Raj raised his brows slightly. *I shouldn't be surprised if he's . . . decisive,* he decided. He gestured to the blanket. They sat down across from each other cross-legged, and shared the bread and salt. Raj laid the sword between them and Tewfik touched his hand to the hilt and blade.

"There shall be peace," Raj said. "I accept . . . in Governor Barholm's name."

"Wa sha' a-l-lah," Tewfik said, the formula full of a tired sincerity. He shrugged and spat on the head. "May God will it."

CHAPTER SIXTEEN

"All off!"

Raj swung down off the train. The East Residence station was crowded, full of the heat and smoke and steam of a busy summer's day. It felt humid after the Drangosh Valley; he rested his eyes on the hints of green higher up the hill and the fleecy clouds scattered across the sky. It was after 1900, near sunset, with Miniluna and Maxiluna both up, huge translucent globes hanging in a purpling sky.

"Move it, soldier!" the conductor said.

Raj smiled wryly and hopped down, ignoring the wooden steps the Central Rail slave was putting by the passenger car. He had a bandage over half his face, and he was dressed in common soldier's clothing—as a Descotter cavalry sergeant, which was probably what he'd have been if he hadn't been born to a noble family. The uniform brought a few cheers and careful claps on the back as he walked out through the station, a garrison bag slung over one shoulder.

That *was* unusual. Questions flew at him:

"Is it true *Heneralissimo* Whitehall cut off Ali's head with his own hand?"

"Are they going to march the prisoners through the streets?"

He smiled lopsidedly and pointed to his bandage; somebody thrust a goatskin of wine into his hand, and a free ticket to the bullfights. He dropped both of them off at the porticoed entrance to the train station—another of Barholm's construction projects—and plunged into the streets. They were thick with people, even though it was still normal working hours. Municipal flunkies were hanging ribbons and streamers from the standards of the gaslights, and a great cheer went up as an ox-wagon piled with huge wine casks halted at a corner.

The full treatment, he thought wryly. He nodded as the crowd began to chant his name when the wine cask was unloaded at the corner. *Barholm's not going to ignore that sort of thing.* It was bad enough that he'd been popular with the troops. Having the capital city mob on his side, no matter how he'd put down the Victory riots six years ago, would be the final nail in the Governor's coffin. *I wonder if they know they're condemning me to death?* he wondered.

Probably not. They'd been very frightened, and the euphoria of relief would be all the stronger for it.

Well, at least the troops won't have any problems getting a drink and a lay when they get in. They deserved that.

He was close enough to hear two of the men dipping their cups into the head of the broached wine cask. They wore the knee breeches, full-sleeved shirts, and leather aprons of prosperous artisans; their shoes had good pewter buckles.

"To Messer Raj and the damnation of all wogs," one said, drinking. "Ah, not bad."

"Looks like Barholm pulled it off again," the other replied. "This'll keep the Chair under his fundament until the day he dies."

"That might be thirty years."

"Thirty more years of Barholm. Spirit. Ah, his wine's good, anyway, and we deserve it—our taxes paid for it. To Messer Raj, Mihwel."

"To the Sword of the Spirit of Man—we won't see his like again, worse luck."

Raj ducked into the tiled entrance of a public bathhouse. *Where* . . .

Center strobed an indicator above one door. Not surprising that a bathhouse had a connection to the catacombs; all this section of the city was underlain by the Ancient tunnels.

"Raj!"

Thom Poplanich stirred to life in the mirrored sphere that was Center's physical being.

He gripped his friend's shoulders. "You did it!" His eyes noted the fresh creases, and the leathery tan of the Drangosh Valley's sun and sand-laden wind. "You did it!"

Raj returned the *embrahzo*.

"I did my duty," he said quietly. He shook his head, as if the magnitude of it was only now striking him. "I've reunited Earth—"

bellevue.

"—Bellevue under Holy Federation and the Spirit of Man of the Stars."

"The Fall is over," Thom whispered, awed. "After a thousand years, it's over."

the next cycle has begun, Center clarified. **this is only a beginning, but the direction of maximum probability has been reversed. there is no longer a strong drive to maximum entropy here on bellevue; and from bellevue, the human universe may be reclaimed in time. fifteen thousand years of barbarism have been reduced to a maximum of another five centuries. beyond that, stochastic analysis is no longer adequate. my projections indicate that human capacities will have increased beyond my ability to analyze.**

Raj laughed and ran a hand through his gray-shot curls. "I feel like a man who's been running down stairs and didn't notice that the staircase ended," he said. "The troops and the Colonials are on their way back; it'll take a while, but the first trains should arrive in hours. I came to say goodbye, before . . ."

Thom's smile died. "Before what?" he asked sharply.

Raj looked up in surprise at the tone of command in the other man's voice. "Before I report to the Governor," he said.

"Who no longer needs you. Who fears you," Thom said.

Raj shrugged. "I've done my duty to the Spirit of Man. I'm not going to flinch at the end. Barholm can't kill me deader than a Colonial bullet or a Brigadero's broadsword might have. It's not a safe profession, soldiering."

Thom turned, a terrible anger on his face. "There's no need for that! There's no need for that now—and even if there was, a ruler who treats a faithful servant that way doesn't deserve to rule, doesn't deserve to *exist*. Hasn't he done enough? More than any other man could have done?"

The shout rang in the strait confines of the sphere, then sank away as if the material had changed to absorb it.

raj whitehall has one further duty to the plan.

Raj put a comforting hand on Thom's shoulder. "I know. I said I was willing to die."

not that.

Both men started.

for six years, i have been training your friend here to rule as i trained you to fight. now it is time to put him on the throne of the reunited planet. you should find that easy, in comparison to the things you have already accomplished in my service.

The mirrored sphere flashed and vanished. They were

disembodied viewpoints watching a huge crowd surge through the gardens of the Gubernatorial Palace, crying out and eddying around the iron order of the troops who guarded it. Raj recognized the shoulder-flashes of the 5th Descott and the Rogor Slashers, of Cruisers and Brigaderos units . . . and Colonials, still in their crimson djellabas but carrying Armory rifles.

The great ebony doors with their hammered silver Starbursts swung open. Barholm Clerett came through; bandaged and bruised, his hands bound before him. Gerrin Staenbridge walked beside him with drawn pistol, Barton Foley on the other side, and a file of Descotters with fixed bayonets on either side. They hustled the blank-faced Barholm into a closed carriage at the foot of the marble stairs. Mounted troopers of the 1st Cruisers with drawn swords fell in around it, and the driver touched the white greyhounds of the team into action. The crowd parted reluctantly; a few rocks and lumps of dogshit flew at the carriage.

"To the frying post with the tyrant Barholm!"

"Death to Barholm the tax-eater!"

"Dig up Barholm's bones!"

The clamor might have turned to riot, but trumpeters blew a ceremonial fanfare from the balcony above. Tall windows swung open, and Raj Whitehall walked out and halted, his hands clasped behind his back.

Silence fell gradually, although the noise of the crowd was like distant surf or the rustling of leaves in dense forest.

Raj heard his own voice; the superb acoustics of the semicircular frontage of the Palace carried it out over the heads of the crowd.

"Citizens of Holy Federation! The tyrant Barholm is de-Chaired!"

Massed cheering broke over him like thunder, and cries hailing him governor. He raised his hand again.

"I am the Sword of the Spirit of Man, but not the Spirit's viceregent on Earth. Citizens, I give you your Governor. Governor Poplanich, grandson of Governor Poplanich, legitimate heir to the Chair."

In the slow, hieratic pace that the regalia imposed, Thom Poplanich paced out to stand beside his General. The sunlight blazed on metallized robes, on the Stylus and Keyboard in his hands.

"My people—" he began.

observe:

The sphere blinked. Raj saw himself standing under the great dome of the Cathedron that Barholm had built. A wedding was being held, a man and a woman standing in shimmering robes before the Patriarchal Arch-Sysup of East Residence, their hands entwined and bound with the sacred Cable. The man was Thom Poplanich; the woman was dark and round-faced, plain, with intelligent black eyes that sparkled with excitement. Raj saw himself step forward to give the groomsman's responses. It was obviously a great occasion of state; besides the nobles and clerics, his Companions were there, and Suzette . . .

Tewfik ibn'Jamal stood on the other side of the couple, in the place reserved for the father of the bride. His eye met the image-Raj's for an instant, and winked.

observe:

Chancellor Tzetzas stood and contemptuously turned his face to the pockmarked brick wall. Behind him the officer of the firing squad raised his sword. The rifles leveled and vomited smoke . . .

observe:

Raj stood in a testing room in the Armory, examining a rifle. He was older, his hair mostly gray. The weapon in his hands was one the younger self did not recognize; chunky and short, with a box-magazine protruding below the stock and a cocking-lever at the side. He raised it and fired at the target downrange. The rifle fired again

and again, spitting spent brass to the right, without any
motion but pulling the trigger. And there was no smoke
from the barrel . . .
   observe:
   A crowd of gaping peons stood at the edge of a
wheatfield—somewhere in the Central Provinces, from
the flat terrain and broad treeless horizons. Behind them
were the mud hovels they dwelt in; in front of them a
huge clanking machine snorted and backed, then surged
out into the ripe grain. It moved slowly, a whirring
contraption like a skeletal cylinder of boards bending
down the heads of the stalks. Beside it went an ox-wagon,
and threshed grain poured out of a spout into it as the
machine chewed its way into the wheat. As Raj watched,
it reaped as much land as a dozen peons could do in a
day; from the sun, scarcely an hour had passed.
   observe:
   Sullen, shaven-headed Skinner nomads surrendered
their huge sauroid-killing rifles to an officer in Civil
Government uniform. A huge engine on linked treads
of steel stood behind the officer, quivering with
mechanical life; the twin trails of its passage stretched
off into the distance, and weapons bristled from its
armored hull. Overhead a flying machine circled, with
stiff wings like a soaring pterosauroid and a buzzing
propeller at the rear.
   observe:
   An older Raj stood in the Cathedron once more.
Suzette was with him, older as well, but smiling. The
groom walked to his place beneath the dome; for a
moment Raj thought it was Thom, but then he saw the
differences, the darker complexion and the beak nose.
Thom's son, he realized.
   The image of a Raj twenty years older stepped forward,
the bride's fingers resting on his arm. The young woman's
green eyes glowed.

observe:

Barton Foley as an old man, in a nobleman's formal civil clothes. He stood in the presentation room of the Palace, and bowed his head as an official Raj didn't recognize placed a gold-chain medallion over his head. Beside him on the table rested a book. On the cover, embossed letters read: *Raj Whitehall and His Times.*

observe:

He was looking down from the roof of a great shed. The dust motes in the air shook with the force of the energies below. Incomprehensible machines crawled by on a conveyor-belt. Men and women in overalls swarmed about them, fastening on parts with tools that hummed and screeched and whirred and sent showers of sparks across the concrete floor.

A siren whooped. The noise ended as if cut off with a knife, and the workers downed tools and turned to troop out of the huge building.

observe:

A crowd gathered around a plinth in East Residence. They were just familiar enough to be disturbing, men with their hair in pigtails, women in skirts scandalously short, to their knees. A poster read: *Elections to the Consultative Senate to be held.* Beneath: *Vote Reform! The Anti-Peonage Act needs your support!*

observe:

A train streaked by. Raj *thought* it was a train. It floated above the tracks with no visible support, and the locomotive was shaped more like a rifle bullet or an artillery shell than anything he recognized. The hum of its passage lingered in the air long after it had passed the horizon.

observe:

An avenue in East Residence, with a view down to the harbor. Raj could recognize a few of the buildings: the Cathedron, the Palace. Most of the rest had changed, in styles totally foreign. Before him was a mausoleum. The viewpoint swooped closer. The walls around the base were sculpted in bas-relief, and they showed his troops. Marching, making camp, charging with leveled bayonets. The central column held high-relief bronzes; here he recognized faces, Gerrin, Barton, Kaltin—all his Companions, and Suzette. Their clasped hands ringed the broad pillar.

Atop it was a statue. A rider, on a great black hound. He was armed, but his outflung hand was empty, pointing to the sky. Below in gold letters was set:

RAJ WHITEHALL. THE CONQUEROR OF PEACE.

Beyond, from the bay where East Residence's harbor lay, something huge was lifting toward the heavens on pillars of pale fire.

Pigeons rose in a massed flutter of wings about the statue as the thunder of the starship's drive rolled across the plaza.

THE END

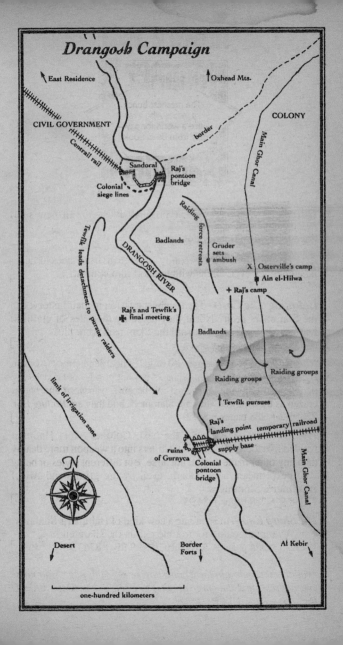

Drangosh Campaign

East Residence

Oxhead Mts.

COLONY

CIVIL GOVERNMENT

border

Centrail rail

Sandoral

Raj's pontoon bridge

Colonial siege lines

Main Ghor Canal

Raiding force retreats

Badlands

Gruder sets ambush

DRANGOSH RIVER

X Osterville's camp

Ain el-Hilwa

+ Raj's camp

Tewfik leads detachment to pursue raiders

Raj's and Tewfik's final meeting

Badlands

Raiding groups

Raiding groups

Raiding groups

Tewfik pursues

limit of irrigation zone

Raj's landing point

temporary railroad

ruins of Gurnyca

supply base

Colonial pontoon bridge

Main Ghor Canal

N

Desert

Border Forts

Al Kebir

one-hundred kilometers